MW00896195

SPARX
INCARNATION

FULL EDITION

SERİES İ

SPARX Incarnation—Full Edition:

Part I: Mark of the Green Dragon

Part II: Order of the Undying

SPARX
INCARNATION

FULL EDITION

K.B. SPRAGUE

SPARX Incarnation by K.B. Sprague

Cover designed by Damonza
Map by Josephe Vandel of MapForge

Published in Canada by GaleWind Books,
an imprint of Whisperwood Publishing, Ottawa.

Library and Archives Canada Cataloguing in Publication

Sprague, K. B., 1969-, author
SPARX incarnation / K.B. Sprague. — Full edition.
(SPARX ; 1)
Issued in print and electronic formats.
ISBN 978-1-988363-00-4 (paperback).—ISBN 978-1-988363-01-1
(epub).—
ISBN 978-1-988363-02-8 (mobi)
I. Title.
PS8637.P72S73 2016 jC813'.6 C2016-902815-1
C2016-902816-X

www.galewindbooks.com

This novel is dedicated to my loving wife
And our three little sparks

As a tree with the passage of time…

TO GLACE VALLEY

Western Tor

Dim Lake

HARROW

Dim River

Upper Malewin River

WHISPERWOOD

Harrow's Gate

DEEP WEALD

BEARDED HILLS

TO SCARSANDS

Proudfoot

Webfoot

The Mire

The Crossing

Stoutville

Blackmuk Creek

THE FLATS

Lower Malewin River

Akeda Ruins

ABANDON BAY

FORT ABANDON

Dory Crossing

Abindohn Ruins

GREEN ISLAND

Rapier Isle

BLACKTIP Mnt.

JAKKA HILLS

HIDDEN CITY
OF
GAN

DEEPWEALD

IRONEAGLE PEAK

Mining
Camp

Elkerin River

OUTLANDS

TO THE GREAT
EMBERS

PART I

Mark of the Green Dragon

With the vows of my former life fulfilled or pardoned by my untimely departure, I am now released of them, and make one and only one vow anew. By sun, wind, rain and earth I take this final oath, to protect the woodlands and the meadows, the lowlands and the marshes, the stands of tall pines and the fields of grass. I hereby declare my acceptance of the earthen form granted to me – Hurlorn of Deepweald – and accept all duties and responsibilities commensurate with that great honor.

- The Spirit Hurlorn Oath

CHAPTER 1

Heart root

The grove is as perfect a place to write as a lumbering beast might find. It is as bright as the day and sheltered from the wind. Though by the creak in my limbs, I daresay rain is coming, so I must make haste. And Hadamard is waiting.

It is an awkward thing, to tell a tale in this state, so huge and halting and overgrown. And a burl over one heavy eye has it sealed shut since early spring. The other is sure to follow. But I have my quill, at least, specially fixed to a long, deft claw by the ranger in these parts, whose father I knew very well, and I have my paper from my friend the birch. The monument in the centre of the clearing is wide and flat, and serves just fine as a tabletop. The ink-bottle is small and awkward though, and its contents may very well dry up before I ever get the lid back on. That cannot be helped.

This part of the story, this first record of events, I will tell as I saw unfold. It is the beginning of my story, the middle of others and, most importantly, the beginning of the end for some great thing. It is that which set things in motion.

Beware in the telling, as I have little patience to spare once stirred into action. I may skip a few years, or tens of years or maybe even a hundred years. Watch for shifts in the timeline. I am not always careful. And bear in mind that I may have to break off at times to accommodate the weather and such, and possibly lose my train of thought in the process. Oh, what I would do for a writing desk, a lamp, and a roof over my head! Such simple luxuries are now lost to me.

How did I become such a gnarled old thing anyway? Any who see me must wonder. The entire notion is ridiculous, I admit, but knowing that won't change bark to skin. Is there such a thing as magic? What else could it be? That will all become clear, soon enough, in the telling.

This tale begins before thick, heavy scales burdened my body. My legs were nothing like tree trunks and my shoulders did not bear the weight of a leafy crown. Don't get me wrong... I am not complaining. I can still get around. Slow? Well... mostly yes, but also quiet and well camouflaged if I stick to the tree lines, the copses, and the gardens – but not the bog. That which once sustained my former being is now poison to the heart root through which I drink. That quaggy water would be the end of me. The bog is doom, and I know of many who would agree, if only they could speak from their muddy graves...

And if I could speak as I once did, none of this would be necessary. This task would be trivial if I did not have to write it all down. But I am without choice in the matter – my spoken words are the baritone notes of a deep wind instrument, my sentences are melodies, this tale a song... all I have are these inked words and the Hurlorns' *whisper*. But who will hear if I do not get this out, in writing, to those who need to know? Who will know to listen for the rustling of leaves in the summer breeze for a message across, as the vow states, *the woodlands and the meadows, the lowlands and the marshes, the stands of tall pines and the fields of grass?* Who will hear the Hurlorns whisper my song?

Let us now begin, before the rain hits and spoils the pages...

The bog is a peaceful place. The blood shed there has long soaked into the black earth, and although a battle rages, it is unseen if you do not know where to look, and unheard by the untrained ear. Ever it looms though, dark and ominous and terrible and free, but silent and invisible to the simple folk that live among the rushes. They are the Pips, and they are happy.

- The Diviner

CHAPTER ii

Memories best forgotten

A bulging moon peered in through the reed-screened window. A single, flickering candle burned low and threatened darkness. On the verge of sputtering out, the flame renewed itself, steadied, and blazed on, unbroken. I sat cross-legged on my night sack, studying the deepwood box on my bedside table.

Paplov muttered to himself in the next room as he sorted through documents and drafted important papers for the lord mayor. "You should be paying more attention," he repeated all too often, amidst mutterings of "Ha ha… didn't see that coming – did ya?" and snarls that ended in "…you rat." The first was a criticism directed to me, I'm sure. The latter rumblings seemed to follow part of an ongoing negotiation that played out in his mind, complete with all its semantic thrusts, feigns and parries.

Clerical work did not interest me that evening. I had already clocked several hours during the day, and declined Paplov's invitation to help him with "a special task of great importance." Since becoming a full apprentice, every other task seemed to be "a special task of great importance." I figured it was just his way of spicing up the boring work that he wanted to offload. Most of the time, I let him get away with it, but not that night. That night, I hit the sack early, but with little intention of sleeping any time soon. In my own mind, thoughts were churning.

The casket lay quiet, motionless, as did I.

Over the years, I had heard many tales of terrible abominations lurking deep in the woods, and in the dark reaches of rivers, and in out-of-the-way corners of the bog. There were the boogalies more dead than alive with flip-flopping feet. They would come to eat you if you didn't finish your plate. And wolf men that waited in the woods for stray travelers to mount on a spit and roast alive. Then giants in the hills that stripped the flesh off their victims and ate it raw. But not even campfire tales alluded to anything quite like what I once saw in the forest, perched on a mossy boulder at the edge of a rocky grove.

The flame continued to waver as it pumped short, fluid bursts of liquid orange into the cool night air, darkness merely half a shadow away. And as the fire gasped for breath, the half-shadows grew fuller, longer. And when the light finally snuffed out, the subtlest of shades came out of hiding. The box became swathed in a faint net of threaded shadows, crisscrossing over diamonds of pale moonlight.

I might otherwise have been swinging on my hammock high enough to make the hanging posts creak. Or humming, whistling, singing, or even musing about secret findings or forthcoming adventures… were it not for that box. Fyorn's gift held my every thought within its confines, my every suspicion under its lid.

Still, as I lay deliberating, I heard no rattle from within and saw no drips of black ooze spewing from its seams. Nothing stirred whatsoever. In fact, the box, in-and-of-itself, was not intimidating or frightful to look upon in the slightest. It was elegant. Only the haunting memory it elicited gave me cause for concern. Thinking back to that afternoon long ago in Deepweald Forest, it all seemed so unreal; a vivid hallucination let loose from the over-active imagination of a curious young Pip on a maple sugar high.

I closed my eyes and thought back to a time out of memory. I thought back to when I could fly.

Like a bird, I soared over water, swaying reeds, mounds of grass and even treetops. The cool wind numbed my cheeks, flowed through my hair and dried out my eyes. And when a strong gust rose, I skipped along the turbulence with unparalleled elation. The air pushed at me so hard and blew past me so fast that it sucked the breath right out of my windpipe. I struggled against the forceful hand that drove me ever downwards to the mudflats, and fought against crosswinds aiming to rifle me into a rogue tree skeleton. *Oh no… Here it comes… I'm losing… I'm gonna hit… I'm gonna hit…*

I opened my eyes.

I was only dreaming then, but even long after in those early moments of morning slumber when the sensation of freefall returns, and when I feel my body rise and fall on a current of air, I still believe I can fly. Even when fully wakeful with my thoughts set adrift, I sometimes have to pause to remind myself that I never really flew in the world that I know to be real. It simply never happened, and could never really happen at all.

But what about that black orb with the central eye and legs like a spider? And that crooked old tree creature that attacked me? And that swarm of biting insects so early in spring? I was not dreaming then. It all happened. I know it happened. The permanent mark on my arm kept the memory grounded in reality – a reality I had kept secret all the years since.

Yes, it had been nearly four years since the incident in the woods. And over those four years, I had successfully avoided the journey back to my uncle's cabin. Paplov still went to see Uncle Fyorn regularly though. The woodsman shared important information with him that helped with his duties as councillor, plus Fyorn was the only one who knew where to find the rare deepwood Paplov needed for woodcarving. It was just a hobby to him, but he enjoyed it fiercely and often spoke of how one day, soon in the coming, he would pass his town duties over to me and dedicate his days to woodcraft.

Looking back, I believe that I just felt awkward about returning, and I wondered how Uncle Fyorn would react and what he might say. He had taught me how to snare rabbits and spearfish through the ice, not to mention the countless other survival skills I learned from just being in his presence. That kind of connection embodies a certain level of trust. Fyorn wasn't my real uncle, but Paplov always referred to him that way.

That day, Paplov set out alone to Fyorn's cabin in early morning, with plans to return by evening. My excuse for not accompanying him this time: "I have studies to catch up on and things to do at Webfoot Hall." Paplov accepted my reasons without pause, perhaps because they served him well. You see, for months now I had begun to act in some formal capacity as his aide in diplomatic affairs. Paplov was busier than ever lately, traveling from town to town on official business, in response to a sudden spike in the need for deal making.

Proudfoot was expanding into the southern mire and encroaching on Webfoot territory, while prospectors from the Bearded Hills were bidding for rights to bog iron in the western mire. Even Harrow, to the north, had commissioned boggers to scour the area in pursuit of some yet unknown interest, overturning every mossy boulder and exploring every dark crevice and ancient cave in the bog lands.

I went along with Paplov to the in-town meetings and attended important events, sometimes without him. I could even stamp or sign important documents on his behalf when he was not available. Still, the work I did never seemed to be quite enough. Paplov pushed me to accept more and more duties and responsibilities. It was getting in the way of everything.

After spending the better part of the morning getting my assigned tasks out of the way and the rest of the day at the riding range near the city gate, I returned home sore, with the sweet pain of hard work and hard play soaked into every muscle and every joint.

Paplov returned home that evening as planned, with an offering from Uncle Fyorn. He hung up his old grey-green traveling cloak on a peg near the front door of our hut, and then produced a wooden box from his side bag, straight from the gnarly old woodsman himself.

"Maple candy," he said, his hand shaking as he held the box out for me to take. "Uncle Fyorn sends his regrets that you missed out on your favorite treat again."

"I'm not a pipsqueak anymore," I said.

"What does that have to do with anything?"

I shrugged, and at the same time felt a tingle on my arm where the tree had left its mark.

"Well, he hasn't seen you in a mighty long time," Paplov continued. "He probably still remembers you as… just a sapling."

"We're all just 'saplings' to him," I quipped.

Paplov nodded. "I suppose you could say that," he acknowledged, then put his hand to his chin. My grandfather had been looking older lately – seventy if he was a day, with little more than wisps of white fluff to show on the top of his head. Somehow, his hair still managed to look messy though, especially on a windy day, which was just about every day. Even his eyebrows were messy, bushy and white with an inquisitive flick to them. But his beard was always in order, soft as down and stroked smooth to a point. His face was kind and his smile warm, but when he tried to push the box on me, I sprung back, fish-eyed. He laughed dismissively at my skittishness.

"Don't worry," he said. "It won't bite!"

It might.

It didn't take long for me to realize that the box was not *the box.*

A latch of dull black metal kept the lid firmly in place, fashioned in the likeness of a crow's head with a hooked beak for a clasp.

I should have told Uncle Fyorn what I had done straight away. Why would he give me something in a box like this, after all these years?

"Take it," said Paplov, "I can't stand here all day."

I took the box and shook it back and forth. Something inside knocked and rattled inanimately. I waited and listened. There was no "tap… tap… tap" like fingers on wood, the sound that had drawn me to the *other box* in the first place.

"Sound enough like candy?" said Paplov, with a smirk.

I just nodded casually, and then gave the lid a sniff. It did smell sort of "mapley."

I went to my room without so much as a "Thank you" to Paplov and placed the box on my night table, then debated as to whether or not I should open it.

I had to remind myself again that I was not that scrawny, naive little Pip that fled the woods that day. I was taller, springier and well-balanced. I was stronger and much more experienced. On Paplov's insistence, for nights on end I had studied the teachings of the old gods and the new ones, the elemental forces, the laws and customs of Webfoot and neighboring districts, on top of accounting, languages, navigation, and maps of lands and oceans both near and far. Still, despite all my training – a future diplomat's required curriculum – I had no real explanation for what happened so long ago, that spring day at the cabin. Really, who would believe me? *I could hardly believe me. Branches don't just lash out on their own like that. They just can't.*

I stood up, paced about my room and drew in a few deep breaths. I stretched my fingers apart as wide as they would go. Even in moonlight, I saw that the scars from the axe blade were still there. I clenched my hand into a fist; the tissue felt tight. Standing over the table, I pulled the box to the edge. It was more ornate than the one in Fyorn's attic had been, and professionally made. The lid bore a depiction of Gan, the Hidden City, inlaid with red-dyed horn. *The time is now.*

Finally, I lifted the latch and opened the box a crack. The sweet scent of maple flowed out, nothing more. I peeked in. There were no giant spiders inside, just the maple candy, as Paplov had promised.

I shrugged my shoulders and tried one; it wasn't as good as taffy, but it wasn't bad either – oversweet. I took my uncle's offering as a sign of goodwill. He wasn't mad at me, and if he had been, it was water under the bridge. *The next time Paplov visits, I am going too.*

That day came sooner than expected. Before long, I had a compelling reason to have serious words with Uncle Fyorn. Not because I wanted redemption, or maple taffy, but because I needed his advice. Uncle Fyorn knew the woods and the lowlands better than anyone did – like the back of his weather-beaten hands. And he seemed to know a great deal about abnormal things. In particular, he was the only one I could think of that might know something about a certain artifact that originated in the bog. Above all else though, he was the only Elderkin I knew personally.

CHAPTER iii

SPARX

I was not the only one to have discovered a corpse or two in the bog. My experience was the most bizarre of them all though. Besides me, there was this man and his son that found a bog body while digging for peat to burn as fuel. Then there was that lady's head with red hair that popped up the same way – digging for peat. She had a braided leather noose around her neck. Even "Pops" – a good friend's father – once stumbled upon a soup of pickled body parts while setting footings for a building in town. One might think bog people are everywhere. Well, as far as I know, they are not. But the stories accumulated over the years and decades into one long list of celebrity bog-body appearances. They became the sources of many a legend and the stuff of tall tales.

I was, however, the only one to have discovered a very ancient seed in the bog from the long-forgotten past; a kernel of admittance into a world I did not even know existed, a world not so far from any of us. I was the only one to have found a *SPARX stone*.

*

We never should have strayed so far from the creek that day. But the water was high and my usual path flooded. Despite the fact the morning had not gone as planned, Gariff seemed content enough.

It wasn't easy to tell though; he looked on the grumpy side normally. It's the way his heavy brow seems to scrunch his eyes into narrow slits.

The Stout took my hard-earned prize and held it up to the sun, one eye squinting. His broad head appeared to sit directly upon his solid shoulders. The first thing he did was shrug, as though it were no big deal. Perhaps the sunlight had made the stone's internal flicker barely noticeable, or perhaps he'd seen better quality stones similar in basic appearance. After having eyed the piece for a long minute, with a quick toss he sent it spinning up into the air, then caught it in his thick-fingered grip. He nodded his head in satisfaction, and plunked the bog stone back into my hands.

"Not a bad find," he said. "I wonder what it's good fer."

"Lots of things," I said, not having thought of even one, but knowing there must be many. "Something this rare has to be valuable."

Spearheads and rusty suits of armor were more Gariff's kind of treasure. "Useful things have value, like this here hat," he said, and went on to adjust his favorite "adventuring" headgear – faded red, floppy and wide-brimmed. The hat was a wayworn monstrosity, and he was the only one that didn't know it was ridiculous.

"Well, a rare stone like this can buy lots of useful things," I responded.

"Aye," Gariff nodded. There was no arguing with that.

Gariff Ram and I had known one another since before he could remember. The Stout's severe lack of free-spiritedness and imagination didn't stop us from being good friends though; it just got in the way at times. As part of what had become an annual tradition, his father and kinsmen worked in Webfoot and lodged at the Flipside Inn. Together, they labored through spring and the better part of the dry season. Gariff's apprenticeship afforded him just enough time for a day trip now and again, usually when work was slow or materials late in arrival.

The Stout had dropped by my place early morning on his way

to the Akedan ruins. We never made it though on account of our misadventure, after which we had decided to return to the creek and follow it back. Our heads had cleared noticeably after putting some distance between us and the sinkhole, and by the time we neared the Crossing we realized that, as unnerving as the ordeal had been, we had stumbled upon an opportunity, one that we had to protect.

"Gariff," I started, "we both have to promise not to tell anyone about the stone, especially Kabor."

"What about the sinkhole?" he said.

"The sinkhole's fair game," I replied, "but not until after we know more about staking claims."

"And the bog bodies?"

That one I had to ponder.

"We should keep the bog bodies under wraps too," I decided. "There might be more stones and we don't want to risk giving away the location. People will start digging around while the paperwork is going through, and who knows what they might turn up." As the last words were spoken, they struck a chord inside of me. I smothered it with a solid dose of denial.

"OK, I won't tell a soul," he said.

A voice cut in from across the creek. "Too late."

I flushed at the sound of those words. It was the mischief-maker himself. Impeccable timing, as usual. Gariff spun around to look, jaw gaping in surprise. Then he turned back to me with a chuckle.

"Kabor doesn't count," he said. "He has no soul."

Caught with the flashing stone still in hand, I deftly closed my fingers around it and slipped the piece back into my pocket. *It's bright outside*, I consoled myself, *and he probably didn't notice anything unusual from that far away, not with his poor eyesight.*

"Whatever," I said to Gariff. I closed my eyes and let out a heavy sigh before turning to acknowledge the Stout's sly cousin.

Kabor removed his spectacles and shoved them into his pocket. Then he moved to the edge of the Crossing – a convenient deposit of small boulders that served as stepping-stones across Blackmuk Creek. This time of year, the high ground on our side was far more navigable than the mud flats on the mire side, especially for the likes of Gariff and his heavy, mud-sucking boots.

From across the gurgling watercourse, Gariff's cousin turned his head sideways until I was well within his peripheral vision, which was his way of looking straight at me. He wore dark clothes better suited for a wake than a treasure hunt; always form fitting with him and never a hat, and he wore soft, black boots, unlike Gariff's which were painfully rigid. The cloak he held flapped violently in the wind, which had been gusting up since mid-morning.

The two cousins were both about my age and height, but the similarities ended there. Slight of build and a bit of a runt in comparison to his cousin, looks-wise Kabor was not your typical Stout – thin and wiry while most were wide and squat like Gariff. Also, Gariff liked simplicity. Everything was black and white to him. He was stocky, strong and completely inflexible. Kabor, on the other hand, was slippery as oil and to him everything was a shade of grey. I could never get a straight answer out of that one.

"So, what all did you find?" said Kabor. The uninvited cousin wore a mischievous, conniving grin that he alone owned. It bothered me to no end. Practiced or genuine, I could barely stand to look at it.

"Should we tell him?" said Gariff, anticipation in his voice.

I replied in a hushed tone. "Fine, tell him about the sinkhole. Leave the rest to me." Gariff erupted with excitement. The words nearly burst out of him. He called out to Kabor.

"We found bog bodies!"

"I heard," said his cousin. "You're not the first in these parts."

"But we're the latest," said Gariff.

"I suppose," said Kabor. "Jhinyari?"

"Doubt it," I said. "That would be a stretch."

Kabor acknowledged with a nod.

"Did you see any metal at all?" he continued. "There might be bits of it stuck to body parts or just lying around. Jhinyari would be wearing armor."

"Really?" said Gariff.

"No metal that I could see," I said. "I think these were just regular bog bodies."

"Well, maybe not," said Gariff, ever the optimist. "You never know." He started over the Crossing towards his cousin as he spoke, and nearly lost his balance on a wobbly stone while recounting his story about how a decapitated head "winked" at him as it rolled over, before sinking into the murky pit. The Stout went on to describe grizzly details about blackened appendages and rotting corpses. With all of his grand talking and holding onto his hat in the wind and wobbling about, he forded the creek with the grace of a pig on hind legs. I, on the other hand, bounded across effortlessly.

Gariff was prone to exaggeration at times when he became excited about something. Kabor should have known he was making up half of what he said. And I was not one to complain, nor would I spoil his fun. As long as Gariff didn't mention the stone, he could say whatever he wanted in order to astonish his cousin. Kabor soaked in his older cousin's words like they were whispers on the wind.

The three of us headed for the Mire Trail at that point. Kabor listened intently to our tale and probed for more details, especially about what remnants of clothing still clung to the bodies and if there were any other unusual items or signs of structures nearby. Gariff, by accident I am sure, spilled the beans about finding the bog stone, but I stopped him before he could say too much.

"So, where is this fancy stone, Nud?" said Kabor. "Is that what you slipped in your pocket back at the Crossing?"

Damn... how does he do that?

"Stone-*s-s-s*," I said to the cousins. "Clean out your ears."

Gariff gave me a look.

I fumbled through my pockets and pulled out some common quartz crystals I had picked up along the creek bank. There was nothing special about them, really. I knew that, but Kabor didn't know that I knew that. They created the perfect diversion.

"Three diamonds in the rough," I told the two cousins. "You can each pick one if you promise not to tell. I want to go back and get more. Kabor, you first, since you're the ugliest and I feel sorry for you."

I held them up for Kabor to see. He turned his head to the left and examined the three stones the way he always examined things, with a sideways stare and untelling eyes – dark and hollow looking. A long moment passed. He tilted his head and squinted. Finally, the cousin shrugged and contorted his face into a pained expression.

"They don't look like much," he said, shaking his head as he grimaced.

"Of course not, you can't see anything," I replied.

Gariff opened his mouth to speak, but I sent him a cold stare to quell his words. He fell in line, scrunching his forehead as he struggled to hold his tongue.

"I can see well enough to tell you those aren't diamonds, you simple-minded duck!" Kabor mocked. "But I like them anyway. I'll take this tiny nugget off your hands... *partner*."

Naturally, Kabor grabbed the biggest one. Then he turned to Gariff.

"Don't worry Cuz," he said, "I left the girly one for you."

I held out my hand to Gariff and raised my brow. He caught my look and graciously took the smaller of the two remaining – an elongated tablet shaped stone. I didn't actually care which one he took.

Kabor smirked. "That's the one," he quipped.

Gariff frowned. He had passed the first test and held his tongue about my true find. I put the last stone back into my pocket for safe keeping, next to the *real* one. My secret was still mostly a secret, but if Gariff's weasel of a cousin found out then everyone from Webfoot to the Bearded Hills would know too, soon enough. Kabor was a fast talker, a whisperer, and above all a shady deal-maker – all cause for alarm. All I could hope for was that he would quickly lose interest and that my find would be overshadowed by outlandish rumors of bog bodies and buried treasure.

"I bet artifacts are there too," said Kabor. "Good ones, well-preserved, not like the rusted out junk from Akeda."

"Hey!" said Gariff. "Akeda has the best stuff."

"No," said Kabor. "I mean ancient. Really ancient. You should have brought back an arm or a leg or something. Where exactly did you go? Did any still have hair?"

Gariff answered. "It's just off the creek where it starts to bulge out into little ponds. There's a section that's flooded – it's easy to spot."

Kabor slowed to a stop. "I'm going to check it out then," he said.

"I'm not going with you," I told him straight away. I needed to put more distance between me and that sinkhole. "Besides, you're not even dressed for it. That place is choked with flies like you wouldn't believe, and they love the color black."

"Best to go in drier conditions," Gariff argued. "The ground'll be more stable."

"Nonsense," said Kabor. "It's easier pickings after a heavy rain-fall. You both know that."

"A new sinkhole could open right up under yer feet," Gariff implored.

"Who are you, my mother?" he replied. "That has to be one in a million. I'll take my chances." Kabor started back towards the creek. After a few steps, he paused and then turned around to stare us down sideways.

"Well?" he said.

Neither Gariff nor I budged.

Kabor shrugged and continued on his way without us. He took one last look over his shoulder and sputtered: "Cowards!"

"So long," I said, content to let the little runt go rummaging through the boggy graveyard blindly and without us. *Maybe he'll fall in.* I shrugged my shoulders at Gariff and continued homeward, only to halt at the sound of his grumbling. He still hadn't moved.

"Ugh. What now?" I said.

Gariff scrunched his lips to one side. "C'mon Nud. Yer not still sore 'bout the flag incident, are ya?"

"What do *you* think?" I said. "I got slapped with three weeks of 'voluntary' service and, on top of that, a lashing. I could've done with just one week if only I had ratted out the rat. He deserved it."

Gariff's eyes shifted down to his feet, and then to his cousin in the distance. He knew Paplov could not have taken lightly to finding the Webfoot banner in my possession, whatever the reason, being on the council and all. Indeed, given the nature of the offence, Paplov had been unusually strict in his punishment. He seemed to think it was a black mark against my future in local politics. "They'll never forget," he had said. *They* being his esteemed peers, the other council members.

"What heat did *he* get for it?" I asked.

Gariff's silence said everything.

"That's what I thought. He has it coming, you know."

The Stout raised his head and looked over to me. His grumpy face turned apologetic and the two narrow slits beneath his brow widened into the darkest brown eyes.

"Kabor doesn't mean any harm'n it," he said. "He just does it in good fun."

"Fun for him you mean," I said, shaking my head. "I didn't

even want him to take the banner down. It's not like I was encouraging him. And I told him not to do it... I *told* him *not* to. You know the connections – Town Hall, the mayor... Paplov."

Over the years, Gariff had done more than his share of apologizing on behalf of his younger cousin. Granted, Kabor's parents *were* lost in a caravan raid when he was very young and so Gariff's family had taken him in. Plus, he couldn't see that well. The two combined had earned him more than his fair share of sympathy. I admit he had it rough, but I made it a point that he was not to receive any special treatment from me. Kabor wasn't the only one who had it rough. Still, I had to acknowledge that taking the town flag the way he did, when he did, was rather gutsy. And there was a certain thrill to it all...

"It's a wonder he didn't get caught climbing up that pole in broad daylight," I said, "right under their noses."

Gariff smirked and let out a reflective chuckle. "He never gets caught."

"Yeah, well, he will one day," I said.

There was a long, awkward pause between us. I knew what Gariff was about. Finally, he let it out.

"I gotta go after him, Nud," he said, shaking his head. Gariff slumped. He turned to follow his cousin, and started back towards the creek.

A couple of half-hearted complaints later, I followed.

*

Collapse. Sinkhole. Wet.
Mud like quicksand…
I never should have strayed from the creek.

What little voice that remained in me trembled. "Gariff…" I called to the back trail. I coughed and spat. My throat was raw. Still, no answer, and no wonder; I had left him well behind and I knew it. I was trapped. *This isn't happening.* I wanted to fly.

Seconds felt like minutes. I could almost see the mix rising as water from the creek flowed over the rim of the sinkhole and trickled down its side. I studied the mud wall and mapped out a probable escape path in my mind, but I needed a boost to get to the higher roots dangling over the edge.

Shoulder deep in a messy slop, I discovered a sturdy branch in the mud wall, pulled myself to it and held on. It was wet and grainy in my grasp. I started to climb. It snapped. *Another blackened, rotten stick... roots like curled fingers... like a fist – it is a fist!* Wrapped along its greater length were the twisted remnants of tendons and muscles. I whipped the severed forearm away. It stuck into the mud wall on the far side. I grasped for what appeared to be another branch. It was a leg with only half a foot attached. I lost my footing and slipped. Everything went black as pitch as I sank into the slop, mouth open, eyes stinging.

My arms felt heavy... stuck. Fully submerged, I kicked with my legs and pushed with my arms. For a moment, it felt as though I was sinking faster, despite my efforts. Somehow, by a twisting motion I can't quite describe, I propelled myself upwards and broke surface. I held there for a long moment, brushing muck away from my eyes. I spat to expunge the earthy grit from my mouth.

"DAMN IT GARIFF! WHERE ARE YOU?"

Finally, I heard crashing through the bushes.

"Hold on," roared Gariff. "I'm coming."

Gariff's colossal headgear eclipsed the sun as he peered into the hole. I breathed a giant's sigh of relief.

"Be quick. There are dead people down here!" I said.

Gariff immediately unshouldered his pack and began fussing with it.

The choking stench of the rotten earth made me want to vomit. The smell could have been week-old refuse, or a mixture of rot and mold. Water continued to pour into the sinkhole from above. Earth gave way at the rim... down rolled a blackened head to top off my experience. It settled on a sideways lean, floating on the slop.

Its eyes were narrow slits, its lips twisted and curled, and its mouth open and oozing red sand. The smell, the image before me, and the awful taste in my mouth overloaded my senses. I retched repeatedly, until my stomach had nothing more to offer. I couldn't help but to stare at the thing.

The expression on the bog person's face was not one I would have expected. It was not an expression of horror or surprise or betrayal. It was not even one of struggle or fight. Rather, it was more like normalcy, peace... acceptance, as though laying to rest in a bog were the natural thing to do.

Bile painted my tongue, and the grainy texture of the bog water lined my cheeks from the inside.

"Gariff!" I sputtered.

"Hold on," he said.

As I waited, the gnarled face began to roll towards me with the inflow current. I pushed it away with my foot. It lingered on the surface a while longer, spun twice, rolled over, and then slowly sank into the depths of the bog. When it was gone, I looked back to the rim and the sky and the circle of trees that surrounded the hole.

"Heads up!" said Gariff. He tossed me the rope.

"Not funny," I said, and grabbed it.

"What?... Oh, sorry."

I adjusted my grip, braced my feet against the slippery side, and signaled to Gariff. He began hauling me out. On my way up, several quick flashes in a row caught my eye. Where the earth had fallen away, a brilliant stone jutted out of the wall of mud. It sat cupped by outstretched roots like an egg in a crow's nest. I reached out with my right hand, swung my body over to the roots and pulled the stone free.

The Stout let out a heavy grunt. "Stop swingin' around," he complained.

As I crested the rim, I waved my prize at him. "Look what I found!" I said, and clambered onto solid ground.

Gariff wiped his brow with his shirtsleeve, leaving behind a dirty streak on one side of his neck. He let out a heavy sigh and brushed off his pants with his hands, but the burrs there remained. Sticky cobwebs coated his brown bush shirt from top to bottom, splattered with mud and peppered with bits of dry leaves and small sticks.

He leaned over the pit and looked inside. "Yuk!" he said. "Bog body soup by the looks of it."

And I was covered in it.

Water from the creek continued to pour over the rim of the sinkhole and trickle down its side. A pickled torso, black and shrunken, broke free. It slid down the wet wall and plopped onto the sloppy surface. Across from where we stood, a fist jutted out of the mud.

Holding the stone up to the sunlight, I rubbed some of the mud off with my thumb. It dazzled red and white. But there was more to its radiance than mere reflection. Inside, milky white bands twisted and curled, and every so often they flared a deep red and the stone would flash on and off like a firefly...

"Nud, snap out of it."

It was Gariff's voice, but he sounded far away, and he sounded like he was in a tunnel. But he was right beside me, but in a far-away tunnel...

"Nud... Nud!"

Who is shaking me?

"Nud," said Kabor.

Kabor? What is he...?

I snapped out of "recall."

I was lying down, staring up at Gariff's and Kabor's faces. They were staring back down at me.

"Nud," said Gariff.

I nodded.

Gariff turned to his cousin. "I never seen a Pip go into recall before," he said. "Is it always like this?"

"It's different for everyone," said Kabor. "Some remain standing with a far off look in their eyes, or even walk – like sleepwalking. Others collapse like Nud here just did."

"Some recalls are harder than others," I said, my voice scratchy. "And I didn't bring this on... it just happened when..."

I struggled to sit up, and then looked around. The sinkhole had completely filled in with mud, murky water, and a tree on a lean, leaving no signs of the gruesome scene. You wouldn't have known anything was different about the spot, just by looking at it. I checked my pocket. The stone was still there.

*

Once I fully recovered, the three of us spent the middle hours of the afternoon poking around the site as best we could manage without getting too wet or too muddy. Kabor attempted to fish unseen body parts out of deep spots with a stick, to no avail. Gariff dug for stones along the edge of the sinkhole, feeling through the wet earth and pulling up all kinds of rotting vegetation. I showed Kabor the tangled mess of tree roots, now submerged, where I had found my stone, careful not to mention the bursts of red light that drew my attention to it in the first place.

After much searching, nothing grand turned up. Near the end of our stay though, Kabor did happen to stumble upon a slim, orange post in the ground. An orange ribbon with writing on it was nailed to the top. Kabor took his spectacles out of his pocket and put them on. His eyes suddenly appeared three times bigger.

"HME-226," he read aloud.

Over the years, more and more of the posts seemed to be popping up throughout the Mire and surrounding territories. It meant that the location had been claimed already, probably for mineral rights. Kabor pulled the stake out of the ground.

"Stop," I said, immediately flushed with anger. He had no idea the administrative processes people had to go through just to stake a claim. Paplov had pawned his part of a recent overhaul of the process off on me, so I knew just how tedious it could be. Plus, I was fully aware of all the careful mapping and measurements required to put that post where it had been.

"Put it back," I went on. "We could all get in trouble for what you just did."

The sharpness in my voice drew Gariff's attention. He looked to me and then to Kabor, a worrisome expression written all over on his face.

"Oh ya?" said Kabor. His eyes narrowed. "Watch this."

"NO!" said Gariff, but he was too late to stop his troublemaking cousin. Without hesitation, Kabor tossed the wooden post high up into the air, towards the creek.

I closed my eyes in an attempt to contain my irritation. It was all I could take. *This again*, I thought, remembering the flag incident. Fuming on the inside, a distorted buzzing welled up in the back of my mind. It was weird. The sensation spread. I could not control it. It pushed at my skull from the inside. Pressure mounting, I put my head in my hands. It steadied for a moment.

Steady... steady... I couldn't hold the pressure back. Suddenly, it released.

SNAP! A noise sounded from the direction of the creek. I jolted back and opened my eyes, just in time to see the stake whiz past Kabor's head. It rifled into the bushes right behind him.

"What the heck?" I said. I was dizzy. I braced myself on a crooked alder.

"That was odd," said Gariff.

"Huh?" said Kabor, oblivious. He shot me a sideways glance as he squirreled his glasses away. Gariff gave him the run down.

"The stake flew into some branches overhanging the water there," he said, looking to his cousin, "and then she flung right back at you... What are the odds?"

Kabor rummaged through the bushes behind him, picked up the stake, and shrugged. "What are the odds of it happening twice?" he said.

"NO!" Gariff said again, reaching after it this time.

Kabor dodged Gariff's attempt to grab the stake. He whipped it back towards the water in a low arc. This time, it stayed clear of any trees and landed with a splash. The current caught the stake and whisked it away.

Gariff's eyes met mine and his shoulders slumped. He knew I was not impressed – I think he wanted me and his cousin to get along better. As annoying as Kabor was though, I was more concerned about the stake boomeranging back the way it did in the first place.

"How does that even happen?" I said, prompting Gariff.

The burly Stout shifted his weight back and forth with unease in his stance, eyes scanning the treetops. He had no explanation to offer. His cousin broke the silence.

"It's a bit gusty up there, that's all," said Kabor. "The wind bowed a branch and then the branch snapped back to hit the stake just right when it was flying by."

Scratching underneath his hat and with eyes still searching, Gariff shook his head. "It didn't look that way to me," he said, then paused for a long moment. "But what else could it be? I can't think of any other way."

I peered into the suspect branches overhanging the creek. The entire incident felt a little unnatural, amplified by the simple fact that freshly unearthed bog bodies lay nearby. The uneasy feeling sent a chill up my spine. My stomach felt tight.

"Time to move," I decided, "or we'll be crossing the Mire in the dark."

"You're worried about nothing," said Kabor, completely dismissive. He just waved me off. Nonchalantly, Kabor started off to the next pond by himself.

*

That left me and Gariff standing beside the sinkhole where the staking post used to be. We both agreed that a hasty departure was the best course of action, but our reasons were different. Gariff had grumbled on and off all afternoon that, with the time wasted, we could have made it to the Akedan ruins and back for some "real" treasure hunting. He made one final pitch for it.

"We can still get there," he said, "instead of poking around here in the mud. It'd be worth it. Kabor says there's secret stairs in d'em ruins somewhere, with a heavy stone door at the bottom openin' to an arm'ry. The finest blades ever 'smithed came out of Fortune Bay, they say." Gariff puffed out his chest. "Someday, they'll say the same about d'Hills."

I rolled my eyes.

"What are we going to do with a bunch of rusty old blades?" I said. He shrugged in a way to suggest he was about to name a long list of fantastic things, and then he listed a bunch of boring things. I wasn't convinced. Besides, trouble followed Kabor like his very own shadow, causing me to wonder what was in store for us if we actually did find those stairs. It suffices to say I wanted no part of his schemes.

"There's got to be something good there," Gariff went on. "Cuz seen it on a really old map, Nud."

"He can't even see his hand in front of his face," I retorted.

"Well... ya... but he can sort'a see his hand *beside* his face."

I had to give him that much. His cousin could read, after all.

"That map was in a box of notes n'letters n'such," he continued. "Property of the oldest, grizzliest Hill Stout you ever saw. The ole man was ready to pass on and he gave it up for nothing but three dirty jokes. And they had to be good ones."

If he had asked for clean jokes, Kabor would have been in trouble. No doubt, the old Stout was dead by the time Kabor passed on the story, making it impossible to confirm or deny.

"Well, where's the map?" I said. "Cough it up, let's take a look."

I had seen a good many maps and drawings of what Akeda used to look like. There were even maps portraying the old Abindohn settlement that preceded it. Akeda was once a first-rate staging ground for the defense of the bay, settled by Men on the north shore. Those who had once lived there abandoned it long before my time – Paplov's too – and moved further north along Dim River to establish Harrow on the shores of Dim Lake. According to legend, they destroyed their own city before leaving it behind and gave up seafaring altogether, although I have also heard that they continue to build magnificent watercrafts that grace the lake they now call home. As far as I could tell, no one really knew why they abandoned their city so readily and without a fight. Gariff did not have the map.

"Haven't actually... uh... seen'er yet Nud," he said. "I was sorta hope'n Kabor'd bring it along."

I just shook my head... typical Gariff.

"KABOR!" I yelled.

I jumped when he appeared out of nowhere. Apparently, he had been standing right beside us for quite some time. It made me wonder who was really blind – us or him.

"I thought you took off," I said.

"Changed my mind and doubled back," said Kabor.

Gariff looked to his cousin, expectation in his eyes. "Do ya have the map, Cuz?"

Kabor shook his head. "Nope," he said. "I keep it hidden back at the Flipside."

That sealed the decision to head for home. I didn't tell Kabor about the flickering stone that day, and by the time he found out, it didn't really matter much. I was right about one thing though. He would want it for himself.

CHAPTER IV

The Mire Trail

After my fourth "crossing" of the day, the three of us clambered up the creek slope and met the Mire Trail, heading home. Until mere weeks ago, light watercraft and mucky portages were the only way in or out of town. We had no worries though.

Two tall and full weeping willows marked the entrance to the trail. Their serpentine roots spread along the ground and curled in and out of the watery mud. The smell of algae and wood rot saturated the air.

The woods all but disappeared beyond the trailhead and into the bog. Poplar edging gave way to heavy border stones that had been set to define and contain the neck of the trail. That marked the beginnings of a section of corduroy road. Here and there along the water's edge, densely packed alders grew in clusters together with other mixed species of small trees and shrubs. The alders' slender and silvery trunks twisted up and around like corkscrews, as though avoiding unseen obstacles suspended in mid-air. Dainty triplets of thin yellow catkins dangled from the tips of lithe branches.

We plodded on, trudging past a lonely brotherhood of dull and rolling hillocks into a view plane that opened up to the outer reaches of the surrounding expanse. It was the largest single section of actual bog in the so-called "bog lands" – the unofficial but common name for the network of bogs, ponds, and all manner of wetlands encompassing Webfoot.

The terrain unfolded and flattened into a shallow waterscape, spotted with grassy tufts and old standing deadwood that crackled and knocked whenever the wind blew. Pools of still water mirrored the evening sunlight, splotching with orange a never-ending blanket of pale green moss that stretched out from the trailside to the horizon. Soon, a half-submerged sun would set the blanket ablaze with orange fire in the west.

"It's awfully late fer startin' the bog-pass, isn't it?" asked Gariff.

His voice wavered ever so slightly, betraying a hint of concern, and the words he chose were just another way of complaining that we had spent too long rummaging around the sinkhole. The Stout was far from the cradle of his beloved Bearded Hills and uncomfortably close to the fireside ghost stories of his youth. And although the bog was safe, as far as any of us knew, it just wasn't smart to be out and away from town late at night. Paplov would have never allowed it, had he known.

"We'll have daylight to spare on the other side," I replied, "unless you care to break for a swim?"

Gariff shook his head. "I don't think so," he said, "I don't have yer webbing, or love of leeches on my arse."

"No, you certainly don't have webbing," I said, stalling for time while spinning a respectable retort, "and as for the leeches… I'll have to take your word for it." I turned to size him up, probing for a sporting target to seize upon. Only one thing came to mind, and it fit his compacted expression so perfectly he could have worn it for a mask. After squatting in the bushes off the creek for the better part of half an hour, he had returned with only a grunt and a sour expression to show for his efforts.

"You're too backed up to stay afloat anyway – you'd sink right to the bottom. You need to let some loose," I said.

Kabor took one look at Gariff and broke out laughing. The sturdy Stout's scrunched face made the accusation hard to deny.

While Kabor chuckled on, I whirled around Gariff gracefully, leading a phantom partner by hand and waist: "Care to dance at the bottom of the bog... with the *Bog Queens?*"

"There's no such thing as bog queens," said Gariff. He turned to his cousin: "Right?"

Bog queens really were not something to joke about. I would have stopped there, we all should have stopped there, but Kabor picked up where I left off. His knack for digging up little bits of information and putting them together came in handy from time to time, and it just so happened that he knew the rest of the legend – even better than I did. What better time to enlighten his cousin than in the wake of a bog body discovery?

"Actually," Kabor began, in the voice of a noted poet, "on this very road and on an evening just like this, the Men of Fortune Bay and their families fled their homeland, on a heading north, to Dim Lake. A brutal Jhinyari warlord pursued them fiercely, and his minions even managed to cut off their retreat on the other side of the bog. The Men and their families were trapped. With their silvery blades, the Jhinyari slew Men where they stood defending their families. They cast the women into the bog and conspired to steal the children for slaves."

Kabor made sideways glances to his left and right as we strode, and then behind, as if to make sure no one else was within earshot. He cleared his throat and continued, in a whispered tone.

"Once the mothers understood what was happening, and saw that their plight was hopeless, each leapt into the bog willingly with their children in their arms, and swam under the moss to a watery death. They believed it an act of kindness."

"Is that true?" asked Gariff. He looked to me for confirmation. I shrugged.

"Oh, it's true all right," responded Kabor, "if *The Diviner* says so, then it's true. And he said so."

"So then what?"

"Well… then a great *Leviathan* was raised from the bog," Kabor spread his arms in a wide circular motion to emphasize the sheer size of the beast. "It appeared as a giant white whale. And the thing spoke to the last Men standing, weaving words of great knowledge and unsurpassed wisdom…"

The promise of the great beast's epic words hung in the air, but Kabor held his tongue. He glanced over to Gariff and took a deep breath. We plodded on, listening intently to nothing but our soft footsteps and the evening twitter of birdsong among the grasses. The storyteller's lips remained silent.

Gariff's brotherly impatience with his cousin erupted. He swung his arms to his side vehemently. "Well, what did it say?" he said, as riled up as ever I've seen him, "W-H-A-T did the white whale tell them?"

In stride, Kabor shook one finger at Gariff. "Now the Men swore an oath never to repeat the words spoken by the Leviathan that day. But I can tell you this much…"

Kabor halted sharply, dramatically, and with a strong grip took Gariff by the shoulder.

"As the Men fought on in desperation, the Leviathan made a deal with them, a deal that no one will speak of, even today, a deal that only desperate men would ever make. The beast, now satisfied, returned to the murky depths under the mosses. For a moment, the fighting stopped and there was nothing but an eerie silence, broken only by giant bubbles that rose to the water's surface and burst into the air."

Kabor added a pinch of rasp to his voice and raised his arms high over his head as he spoke the next words.

"Then, as the orange sun dipped below a luminous green horizon, out of the bog arose the dead mothers, in vengeful fury, and many other dead things dredged up from the bottom of the bog along with them. Together they entangled the Jhinyari, each with a grip like wet swamp grass, and dragged them down, one by one into the murky depths, until those few that remained finally fled in terror."

Kabor paused for effect before continuing with the tag line. He must have known that he had Gariff right where he wanted him, for he relished in the moment. Gariff said nothing as he glanced at the water-soaked mosses and tall tufts of grass that lined the trail, and then down to the muddy ground at his feet, kicking away small bits of dried mud with oversized boots.

The ending that Kabor devised had a dreadful spin to it. "It is said that the undying mothers still haunt these wetlands, and if they happen to discover children not in the company of adults on the Mire Trail at night, they grab them and pull them down under the moss for mercy's sake, lest the Jhinyari get hold of them."

As if on queue, a few fair-sized bubbles broke the surface of the bog waters right in front of us. Although commonplace to those accustomed to the bog, the unnatural timing of the event sent Gariff marching ahead at a quickened pace.

Kabor and I exchanged a few animated glances and smirks. We got him good… we got him good.

*

Well past supper we were still hiking. My legs were spent and I thought they might collapse under the weight of me if I had to walk much farther. When my stomach growled, it sounded like the noise came from a deep chasm. Gariff, encumbered by all our gear for the failed trip to the ruins, dragged his heals as much or more than I did. He just grunted whenever Kabor tried to make small talk.

The Bearded Hill's most notorious delinquent was getting

bored with us, so he reverted to a time-honored tactic that was more fun for him – unadulterated mockery. Gariff and I were too tired to counter.

Kabor made fun of our clothes, our hair, the way we walked and the way we talked. He told us exactly why we didn't have girlfriends, in less than kind words, and wondered openly why we smelled so bad.

For once though, his distinct blend of humor – that being pure, unconstrained ridicule – was not totally unwelcomed. Kabor's insults actually made us laugh as he shifted focus from one to the other, sometimes even killing two birds with one stone, so to speak, with a double slam.

Gariff seemed especially happy to be distracted from the "Mothers of the Bog" story, although I daresay he was hardest hit by the flurry of insults. In the end, Kabor lifted our spirits over the last leg of the journey just enough to bring us into town with a chuckle.

I was the first to spot the long wall that palisaded Webfoot. A passing memory brought me back to words that Paplov said so many times before, pointing with his walking stick and drawing my attention away from eyeballing the trailside for frogs and turtles, or interesting bugs. I repeated those words, in his voice.

"Behold the great wonder of the Mire," I exclaimed, "the Wet Wall of Webfoot."

"A great wonder it's still standing," retorted Gariff, "You Pips should've used stone to build your wall."

"Oh I don't know Gariff," Kabor grinned, "there's something charming about a twig fortress."

"Those *posts* are solid," I contested.

"What are they made of?" said Gariff.

"Oak," I replied.

"I think they're cedar," said Kabor.

"Whatever," I said. "Probably the sturdiest you'll ever see… in a place like this."

Gariff scoffed. "Parts of it are nearly leaning into the water," he countered.

The posts were, for the most part, set vertically and bound together with rope made from a common swamp grass, but spaced so as to keep the larger, dangerous sorts of wildlife out while allowing small fish and game to pass freely. As a further deterrent to anyone or anything that might try to climb over, a dense array of thin, sharp spikes jutted out at its base. One slip while attempting to scale its slime-covered surface could mean instant impalement and death. Gariff was right though. Some sections had seen better days. I decided to keep quiet about that comment.

As we passed under the arched gateway into town, Gariff's eyes scanned every post from bottom to top and followed every beam overhead. Every contact received a scrutinizing look.

"I don't care what you say, Nud," he remarked. "The whole thing is crude, makeshift and easily undone. Why even put effort into such a… *temporary* structure? Fire would undo her in the blink of an eye. It's easy to see that wind and the slow heave of winter ground have already taken their toll. You can't depend on a damn thing to stay still around here."

And then he summed it all up with an uncalled for comment. "Who even wants to be in a bog to begin with?"

Contrary to what outsiders might say, bog lands are not dull and dreary places. They are full of life, color and variety. It's all about the delicate balance in the bog, not stability and strength like life on a rock. I said the only thing I could think of.

"You Stouts can't use wood to build because there are no trees left in the Bearded Hills. You ripped them all out of the earth until you hit bare rock, and now you're ripping out the rock."

Kabor chuckled at that, despite himself.

"Your bricks and carved rocks would just sink to the bottom of the bog and decorate the halls of the bog queens," I continued.

Kabor liked that even more. He knew it would put his cousin on edge.

Gariff, however, dismissed my comments as unworthy of serious consideration. He stubbornly held his ground and stuck to his point. As we continued into town, he found more and more ways to criticize Pip architecture and construction than I ever could have imagined. Everywhere he looked, something laughable or on the verge of collapse was just waiting for him to point out. His eye for structural detail was like no other – a product of his bloodline, no doubt. For centuries, his kin proudly carved caverns out of rocky hills and built towns out of heavy, squared-off stone blocks. Hill Stouts were not to be argued with when it came to structures that would stand the test of time.

"You're totally inflexible," was all I could say in the end. "You're just not cut out for bog life. What would it take to change your mind or make you see past your own nose?"

"Some common sense, for starters," he said. Gariff's tone indicated that the conversation was over. Exhausted, I decided to just let it go.

Once in town we decided to sneak a few bites at the Flipside before calling it a day. We couldn't pay for the food, of course, but our little round friend, Bobbin Numbit, was sure to slip us something delectable.

CHAPTER V

Journey to the Flipside

E ver since passing the outer ponds, even Gariff, who had fallen behind after our brief tiff, seemed upbeat again as we made our way through the outskirts of town.

The sweet and pungent aroma of peat-fires was already strong by the time we caught sight of the first of the watergrass homes on the main road in. As evening gave way to twilight, a pale orange sky backlit the thatched dwellings and out came the glowflies. Fiery sparks sailed across a sea of mire rushes.

"Not long now," I proclaimed, needlessly.

The announcement was answered with a huff and a grunt, and I wondered if the lively pace taken up was less about high spirits and more about filling bellies. Perhaps the hint of home-cooked pippish stew blending into the night air had put them over the edge. Through open doors and windows, I overheard the merry high-pitched chatter of pipsqueaks at many a dinner table.

In the distance, a red reed door swung open violently. Two young Pips dashed out of the hut, the smaller one yelling fiendishly at a slightly larger, laughing version of himself. Their yard was little more than trampled reeds and a scraggly birch tree with a dangling swing rope; their cone-topped hut little more than yard materials standing erect – woven grass and mud over a stick frame, splashed with shutters dyed in bright red, blue and yellow. Apart from the openings, the little hut looked as though it had grown out of the small mound it sat upon. The modest dwelling was inviting, if not elaborate.

Off to either side of the road, watergrass homes sprung up haphazardly over the mudflats, occupying nearly every hummock big enough for three Pips to stand on. A convenient web of muddy trails connected each and every conceivable shortcut from one worthy location to another: hut to hut, hut to tree, tree to tree, everywhere to boulders, everywhere to main paths, and back again every different way. Stepping-stones dotted some of the main paths – a courtesy to out-of-towners who by-and-large don't fancy wet feet or mud on their boots. The neighborhood was mostly home to the more traditional Pip families who followed the old ways, and secondarily to young couples just starting out who could not afford a premium lot in town.

We hiked on past wild rice farms, stands of smoke weed, the salamander ranges, the glowfish farms and a row of covered longboat docks.

Crossing the intersection to Everdeep Pond – a rather affluent neighborhood – and then passing Ling's Boulder brought us to Wetwood. The Wetwood trail meandered west through a series of respectable neighborhoods before winding back north to the Everdeep cut-off. Further along and in the opposite direction was the high road to Drytown. We turned off the main thoroughfare at that junction and climbed the hill. Even before catching sight of the inn, the delectable smells of spit-roasted turtle and waterfowl filled the air, and as we approached the hilltop, twin trails of grey smoke from the inn's kitchen and hearth came into view, streaking across the faded sky.

At long last, by measure of our tired legs and empty stomachs, we crested the last hill. The Flipside was a fair sight to behold, a beacon of civilization in the backcountry. Fine aromas circulated in the air. It was a fair listen as well, with lively music and merriment spilling out onto the streets. I was already thinking ahead to the sweet drink, news, good food, and good company that awaited us. Surely, Paplov expected me home at a reasonable hour, but I only planned to stay out a short while.

CHAPTER VI

Interlude - Natural born story tellers

The wind is picking up and the treetops are whipping. The air grows soggy in the grove. Before the page I scribe begins to dampen as well, here is what to expect of the various folk lounging about the Flipside Inn – big and small, respectable and not, genuine and scheming. I'll start with Pips.

All you really need to know about Pips is that they pay acute attention to detail and have the sharpest of memories. This lumbering form of mine, for better or for worse, has retained that mental acuity, so you can consider everything I tell you as near record to the actual events. Keen memory, in part, is what makes us natural born storytellers – we actually Remember what happens, unlike some others (who will remain nameless). We do not *know* everything though, or necessarily make all the right *connections* that could be made, so the pristine pictures in our minds are not always as complete as they could be. Fortunately, we have a Creative streak too, unlike some others (who will also remain nameless). Don't let that worry you though – I will not feed you made-up fill-in-the-blanks fantasy. And I absolutely refuse to sour your tongue with speculative dribble.

I just realized I wrote "us" and "we" throughout my description. Habit, I suppose, and I still count myself among Pips, at times. But I was never quite as carefree as most, and there are times when I feel as far away as one could from such a soft-fleshed creature, fragile and naive in the world.

Stouts are very different. Hardworking and staunch, they are builders and planners by their very nature, with a stubborn streak now legendary. The younglings learn every practical matter there is to know about stone, metal, earth and hidden treasures. Adults, it seems, simply use that knowledge day to day, and slowly get better at everything. Stouts think their way through every task with clever resolve, but sometimes I wonder if they remember anything at all from along the way. Men, on the other hand, learn everything about everything and then forget most of it except what gives them power. As such, they rule nearly all of the lands and do as they will with reckless abandonment. Outlanders, at least those who are civilized, are equated to brutish Men by most, while those who are uncivilized are basically wild and wholly uneducated. Some of the more primitive types do not even learn to speak words as we know them – trust them as you would a predatory animal. Elderkin, the last to note, are not likely to be found at the Flipside. Seldom seen beyond Deepweald, they occupy themselves mostly about the ways of natural things, which might seem quite unnatural to the outsider.

Speaking of Elderkin, where is that ranger anyhow? It's getting dark and I am without light. I am not afraid of fire. Bring on the torches and the lanterns I say! When I find him, he is liable to get a piece of my mind. More is to come about Webfoot and the Flipside as soon as I am set up for the night's undertaking…

CHAPTER VII

A walk on the wild side

S tained in rich hues, the canvas canopy over the inn's veranda
depicted a green and yellow bullfrog lying flat on his back
under a table. Eyes closed, he wore a long and content grin
upon his face. The frog's hands rested over a well-rounded, tender white belly. On that majestic paunch was balanced an equally
majestic flagon, overflowing with golden suds.

"Built by Stouts, y'know," bragged Gariff Ram. As he nodded
his head vigorously, the Stout's tattered hat slipped down over his
eyes. That was only the beginning. "They dug deep and pumped
out ground water fer days before finally hitting something solid
under that hill o'muck – and that was just fer the footings."

The Stout wasn't far off the mark and I felt compelled to nod
back in agreement. Webfoot's Flipside Inn was one of the more
sturdy buildings in town: two full stories tall and not on a lean.
Mortared stone quarried out of the Bearded Hills formed the first
level, and the second was rough-hewn timber cut straight out of
the living heart of Deepweald, back in the days before logging
restrictions ended that enterprise. Red clay roofing tiles kept the
rain out, and a small stable with a thatched roof stood as a separate
building on the south side.

Apparently, Gariff wasn't done gloating. "That inn…" he went on, pointing with one hand and scratching his scruffy chin with the other. "Now there's something – unlike yer precious twig fence a ways back… y'know, the one that protects this town from tooth-less water-rats, wounded geese and fat-bellied pike – now *that* there inn's something that won't fall over when you lean against it, when the wind blows, or when there's a knock at the door."

Gariff kept talking, but I stopped listening to him and strained my ears to catch the melody being played inside. Kabor's eyes drifted to the rooftop dormer windows. He took out his spectacles and put them on.

"Kabor!" said Gariff. He crossed his arms. "Stop peeking at the red rooms, did y'even hear what I said?"

I couldn't help but to look as well. It was easy enough to catch fleeting glimpses of silhouettes casually passing by the second-story windows – the guest rooms. *Nothing yet*, I thought. But the night was still young and shaping up to be one of the wildest ever at the inn. Everyone seemed to be having fun. The Flipside was the hub of activity in an otherwise humdrum town.

"You can't tell me where to look," said Kabor.

"Why don't you make yourself useful and look for a table?" said Gariff. He pointed his cousin to the first floor picture window.

We made our way through the crowd on the veranda and peered into the great room beyond. Inside, as far as I could tell, every table was occupied. Near the stage, it was standing room only. Newly arrived seasonal workers reunited with seasonal friends and coworkers over hearty dinners next to a blazing hearth. A five-Pip troupe played fiddle and reeds over the buzz of patron chatter and the tinkling of eating implements. The band sang and clapped, thumped and stomped, all the while bobbing wildly about the staging area. Smoke rings wrought of the local weed billowed up over the heads of the gathered stage crowd, and hung there in a dense cloud. The sweet scent filtered out to the veranda through open windows.

"The Flipside" was a fitting name for the establishment. Loved by out-of-towners and despised by half the town's permanent residents, the local watering hole did not cater to the typical, upstanding and sensible folk of Webfoot. Rather, it tended to attract the atypical sorts, who more than occasionally consort with suspicious company. Trappers, prospectors, rangers, boggers, runners, builders and all shades of merchant folk could be found at the inn's tables or sitting at the bar. If a bog queen happened to drag her twisted body out of the murky depths one day and slither in through the front door, few in attendance would so much as raise an eyebrow at her fashionably grim entrance, unless she promptly announced that drinks were on her.

The inn also had a reputation among high appreciators of the culinary arts. The Flipside was known throughout the land for the fine fare served, especially for such an out-of-the-way place, but in fact, because of it. More than a few rare and unique delicacies graced the menu.

Clearly, the great room was too crowded. Even the veranda we stood on was full to capacity.

I felt my stomach gurgle in the aroma-saturated air.

"I'm starved, let's eat."

"I'm with you," said Gariff.

Just as we were about to go, I caught sight of a serving girl who stepped into the great room from the back hallway, carrying an overfull tray of food and drink.

"Who's she?" I said.

Kabor scanned the room until he found her.

"Oh her," he said. "She's my new girlfriend."

"How can you even tell from here?" I said, doubtful.

"By the way she sways when she walks," said Kabor. "And the

way she holds her head up high. I have my glasses on, by the way. I met her a few days ago and we really hit it off."

It was the first I'd ever seen of Holly Hopkins, as I would later know her name to be. Long, flowing auburn hair and slim as a reed, even her eyes smiled at the patrons as she glided through the crowded room. She looked to be around my age…

"Wait a minute… she told me she was my girlfriend!" said Gariff, sounding irked.

Kabor clued him in. "She just said that so you wouldn't feel like a dork – it's called pity. Plus she knows it makes me jealous – what a tease."

"She's too beautiful for the likes of either of you." I said.

"Beautiful?…yeah I guess she's not bad," said Kabor.

"Not bad? C'mon. Compared to Stout women she's gorgeous."

"What're ya talking 'bout? Stout girls are pretty," said Gariff.

"They basically look like Kabor – except *he* has less hair on his face."

"Bhaa," Gariff waved his hand dismissively. "You can't be afraid of a little scruff now…"

They both nodded. Kabor let out a mild chuckle and added, "I don't know Nud, some of them look down right handsome with braided chin hairs. Keeps their hubs warm on long winter nights."

Of course, not all Stout women grow beards, but the majority do have some facial hair – mostly just wisps of it. A minority proudly sport full-fledged, braided beards, beaded and dyed in bright colors. In the Hills, the most popular establishment for visitors is the "Friendly Muttonchops," owned and operated by a proud – and friendly – bearded lady.

"If you two know her then what's her name?" I said.

Gariff and Kabor spoke over one another in response. "Elena," said Kabor. "Chariot," said Gariff.

Kabor looked to Gariff, shaking his head. "Chariot? What kind of name is Chariot? Did you mean to say Charlotte?"

Gariff only shrugged. "Maybe she likes horses."

The two cousins continued to quibble. As they faced one another, I saw that they shared precisely the same family nose – prominent, protruding and high-bridged. Soon, my attention shifted back to the girl.

I watched as she wove her way through a sorry collection of Pips, Stouts, Men, and even Outlanders, politely smiling and excusing herself as she went. Besides seasonal workers, which formed the majority of the inn's patrons, a great number of merchants were also in from Fort Abandon that night. The merchants dressed in the fashion of city folks and they all looked like they belonged to the same club, sporting seasonal light coats with shiny pewter buttons and loose fitting trousers tucked into tall black boots. In full view, a table of disheveled Stouts outfitted for ranging blew off steam and drank away their hard-earned pay, garbed in bush leathers and weather-stained cloaks. The serving girl ended up at the Outlander's table.

Gariff tapped me on the shoulder, with eyes on her patrons. "Those ones look a little rough around the edges, don't ya think?" he said.

I nodded. I didn't like the looks of them. Maybe there were still too many stories about the Outland Wars in circulation and too many problems with the border regions to give them a fair shake.

"I recognize that one," said Kabor, pointing to the far end of the table. A particularly slick looking Outlander sat there. He stood out among them as able to blend his fiendish looks with some air of sophistication and refinement.

"Are you sure?" I said. Even with his glasses on, the Stout's vision wasn't that great beyond twenty or thirty feet.

Kabor nodded. "I've seen him in the Hills. He deals in… *rare herbs*," he continued.

We all knew what that meant.

"Cuz's right," said Gariff, squinting. "I've seen him too."

The roaring hearth added a fiery glow to the girl's hair as she served the beast-men barkwood ale (marked by the distinctive, bark-wrapped serving cups used), glowfish bowls (marked by the distinctive way they are served – alive and flipping in a colored glass bowl), and rice or herb side dishes.

The blood of beasts runs through them, I reminded myself. It was something Uncle Fyorn would say in the midst of wine-soaked retellings of stories from his glory days, long faded. He warred against the Outlands in his youth as a Kith ranger. My uncle and Paplov talked long into the night at times about his adventures far and wide, beyond the bog and the gentle shade of Deepweald; beyond the Trilands, Gan and the long reach of Harrow. Those wars were long over now, but they left their mark.

I happened to catch the Outlander's dark, beady little eyes sizing up the serving girl's shapely form while she looked away momentarily to gather finished plates and cups, and balance the serving platter.

I turned to Kabor, "What's his name?"

"Dunno," he said. "But I can find out if you're looking for—"

"NO!" I said, annoyed at the presumption. Kabor snickered.

The Outlander habitually stroked his well-groomed, chin-strip beard, smiling thinly at the girl's small words when served his ale. I could not help but think there was something sinister behind his shallow courtesy and cool, collected mannerisms. *He's one to watch out for.*

The party of Stouts on the adjacent table, on the other hand, were exceedingly unsophisticated, boisterous and fully out of control. Judging by the many flagons on their table, they had their fill and then some. The serving girl pelted one to the floor when he tried to grope her as she passed. She continued on as if nothing had happened. When the Stout stumbled to his feet, his companions jeered him. A shower of suds sprayed out of nostrils and mouths with all the crowing and snorting.

"She doesn't belong here," I said.

"She looks like she can handle herself to me," said Gariff.

"She's my kind of girl," said Kabor.

"What? Breathing?" said Gariff. Kabor gave him a shove. Gariff didn't budge.

Another group entered the great room as we stood there – all Men and Outlanders.

"Come on," said Kabor. "Let's steal around back and find Bobbin. It's busy and you beggars are too ragged to show your faces in there."

"Who cares? Half of them are drunk as skunks anyway," said Gariff. "They wouldn't so much as turn their heads if we walked in wearing grass skirts." He pointed to the rowdy Stouts. "And look at that crew. They look like they just rolled out of a mud puddle."

"I'm with Kabor," I said. Had we made our move a moment sooner, I would have avoided an embarrassment. The serving girl caught me at the tail end of my making eyes at her. I cracked an awkward smile. She looked away.

Kabor saw the whole thing. "Keep it up, dream-boy," he said to me. "The smoke is getting to your head."

"Wait… I changed my mind," I said. "Let's go inside. It's boring out back, and besides, we're not kids anymore."

The back area was mainly used for overflow seating when even the veranda was full, and by patrons or servers on break seeking private conversation or a quiet smoke. Otherwise, it did not see much activity.

"We'll never get a table in there," complained Gariff.

Kabor seemed up to the challenge though. "We'll see," he said as he led the way in. Gariff huffed and followed behind. But Kabor stopped abruptly when he got to the door. Gariff and I halted with him. He turned to face us.

"What is it?" said the burly Stout.

"Did you forget something?" I said.

Kabor spoke with earnest. "Did anyone else notice that?"

"What, Cuz?" said Gariff.

"We all just flipped sides," said Kabor.

Gariff scrinched his face into a confused look. "Huh? What'dya mean?"

"At first, you wanted to go inside. Me and dream-boy here wanted to go out back."

"So," said Gariff.

I punched Kabor in the arm for calling me dream-boy again.

"Ouch," he said, rubbing it. Then he continued. "Now, it's me and *dream-boy* that want to go inside, and you want to go out back."

Gariff blinked.

I waited.

Kabor shrugged, eyes wide. By wide, I mean more than three times magnified when you include his specs. "This really *is* the Flipside," he added with a smirk.

I groaned. "That sounds like something Bobbin would say."

"Must be something in the air around here," said Kabor. He put away his specs.

The three of us impaled ourselves on all the smoke, music and chatter of an energetic night on the town. Pale yellow lanterns cast a dim glow in the room. Many eyes fell upon us on entry – Pips, Stouts, Outlanders, and Men alike. One giant of a man with a long, drooping face took an especially long look. He was the only one in the room that sat alone. I nodded a "hello" to him and he returned the courtesy with a half-smile before sinking his eyes back into his giant-sized tankard.

I could barely hear Gariff's relentless pessimism over the blaring music. "See. No tables anywhere," he said. "Let's go out back. The – ... anyway."

"Hold on," I told him. "Just give it a chance. People come and go all the time."

As we waited and watched, acrobats bounded into the great room from the back entranceway. All heads turned to watch their antics. Checkered black and white from head to toe and wearing the sort of floppy-horned hoods a jester might cherish, they began to tumble. Some cartwheeled, some flipped and others simply bounced their way to the stage, and then bounded from one musician to the next when they got there. The band played on. The acrobats, unsatisfied that they were not able to disrupt the band, set their sights on the crowd. They flipped onto tables and cartwheeled through the startled onlookers. After a minute or so of spilling beer and knocking around plates as they bounded, a great clang arose out from the stage and the music halted. The acrobats – exclusively Pips – all stopped at once and stared at one another. They nodded their heads and smiled as the crowd clapped and cheered them on. "More!" some shouted, "Show us more!" After a long pause, the musicians started up again, but this time the band instruments rang with dissonance and the words they sang made no sense at all.

The checkered troupe gathered at centre stage to form a pyramid, one on top of the other. Stacked as they were, the acrobats wobbled as the crowd "whoa'd!" and the fiddles screeched, all the while feigning to topple at any moment. At one point, their sideways lean was so steep it seemed they would crush the percussionist. But they whipped back, vibrating into place like a lively spring. As soon as one of the onlookers in the crowd stood up to get a better view, everyone did. All eyes fell upon the tumbling Pips… all eyes save two that could barely see anything at all.

A gut feeling had me wondering what Kabor was up to. Sure enough, by the glint in his eyes I could tell he was scheming. Gariff's cousin had spied a vulnerable long table. With the former occupants standing forward of it to get a better view of the action, their backs were to us. Kabor snatched my arm and Gariff's. He dragged us to the table, and with a nod and a look, he coaxed his reluctant cousin to grab an end while he grabbed the other. My role was to move the chairs, despite a feeble protest on my part not to be involved.

You see, the clever Stout had also found an open space created by a large group having put two tables together. To complete the devious and covert operation, Kabor pilfered us each a near-empy tankard (for show, not for drinking from) and some near empty plates, replacing those he took with items from our table. If anyone noticed, they didn't seem to care.

Kabor, now settled and in his glory, stood on his chair like so many others and cheered with the crowd. He hollered at a particularly daring acrobat, who began head spinning at the top of the Pip pyramid, all to the tune of *Mighty Maelstrom* played at a progressively fast tempo.

"Don't look now," Gariff whispered to me. He and I were both sitting and gripping our stolen tankards.

And there they were, the rightful owners of the table, shrugging their shoulders and exchanging annoyed glances. One looked our way and met my gaze. I couldn't hide my guilt. I looked away, but it was too late. He knew, instantly.

"I think we've been spotted," I said to Gariff.

Sure enough, the four Men made their way over. Two were stocky, with soiled clothes and rough looks, probably construction workers in from Abandon Bay. Another was thin as a rake, wiry, and well tanned for the season, with a black cap over long straight hair. He could've been part Scarsander or from the Jakka. The first to speak was the rounder of them, with a fat face and sweaty hair that stuck to his head in tight curls. His voice was loud and full of spit, his breath as sour as the house garlic sauce.

"Get lost, Frog-face," he said directly to me, clearly irritated.

Kabor looked back over his shoulder and drew his attention. "What?" he asked.

"You heard me. You stole our table, now get lost before I put you on the menu," he said.

"Menu? No thanks. I'll have another barkwood though," said Kabor, "and bring some frog legs too." Kabor turned his attention back to the show.

The man, who looked to be middle-aged, picked Kabor up off his chair by the shoulders. One of the stocky brutes grabbed Gariff the same way, but couldn't manage to lift him.

That was when the giant stepped in, having totally misinterpreted the situation in our favor.

"No hurting littler Pipses, little Mens," he boomed, stumbling and waving his tankard at them.

I dove under the table before anyone could get a hand on me and rolled to the far side. And as I rolled, so did something else. My ears honed in on the sound – the unnerving clatter of some small object skipping along with me. Shuffling feet sent it skidding off in another direction.

Yes, it was the bog stone, sparking wildly as it zigzagged along the floor, lit up like some kind of half-crazed glow bug. I scrambled between the legs of onlookers to retrieve it. The floor was sloppy, full of grunge, and sticky in places. Heads turned, I was stepped on, and one curious person made a grab for my stone when it flashed. Every time I got near to it, someone kicked it away. Finally, a ricochet sent it spinning against a wall. Just as I closed in, one of the stocky men we had stolen the table from grabbed me by the scruff of the neck and hauled me up. The bog stone flashed and was kicked away again.

This time I didn't hear the giant's voice, but I did notice a giant tankard strike my captor over the head. Ale sprayed everywhere. His grip let loose. Scrambling again, I searched for the light of the stone. It was gone.

I scanned the crowd frantically. The room was in chaos. The confrontation over our table had erupted into an all out brawl. The giant shouted as he spun in circles with some brute and the skinny man clinging to his back. The trio knocked over patrons, dishes, cups, and chairs. Gariff got free when someone broke a clay flagon over his captor's head. The Stout then swung a chair at the round man with curly hair holding his cousin. He clipped him squarely in the knee. The curly man fell back onto a chair, which collapsed under his heavy weight. Kabor squirmed free and bolted.

Fueling the fray, Pip band members switched to pipes and played a spirited tune. That much was comical. They must have conspired with the acrobats, who took the opportunity to add to the mayhem by bounding on and off furniture and brawlers alike, teasing patrons with pokes, pulled hair, covered eyes, slaps in the face, stolen food and pinches before leaping away. One acrobat received a square punch to the nose for his antics. He responded by pulling the offender's pants down and kicking him in the rear. The man stumbled onto the lap of a well-rounded Stout woman gnawing on a chicken leg, her wispy scruff soused in grease.

Then I spied my hard-earned prize. *Of all the luck.* That blasted Outlander with the thin beard had my stone. He stared at it in a pondering way as the light flickered in his hand, painting his face in its pulsing red glow. He looked the part of a slick devil.

"That's my stone!" I cried. Heart pumping, I charged through the crowd at him. He was about to slip it into his vest pocket.

I slapped at his hand and the stone went flying. Flying and sparking in a high arc. I ran and dove and caught my prize before it smashed to the ground. Stone in hand, I scuttled along the floor and underneath the ruckus, making my way to the nearest exit. I slipped out of the room and backed up against the foyer wall, hidden from sight. Gariff and Kabor met me there in short order. The bar fight raged on without us.

"That was close," I said, wiping the sweat from my forehead. The Stouts agreed. Out we snuck.

Kabor was the first to start chuckling. A second later, we were all laughing our way onto the veranda. Behind us, the fight continued to build. Outside, patrons viewed the skirmish, some with amusement, others with disapproving looks on their faces. One woman commented "What a bunch of idiots" and shook her head. A grizzled-looking Pip with unusually large forearms said, "I'm getting a piece of this!" and hobbled off towards the door. Others spoke with hushed voices.

"Can we go around back now?" said Gariff, "before we get into real trouble?"

"I think we're done here," I said.

Kabor, holding his chest to catch his breath, nodded in agreement. At last, we stole around back as originally suggested. The path was cobbled and unlit, lined with tall pines that blocked out any and all light. The fresh scent of resin spiced the air, and fallen needles softened our steps underfoot. Gariff and I stumbled along, while Kabor passed like a ghost from one end to the other, unseen and unheard.

"Looks like we have the place to ourselves," said Kabor when we caught up to him. It was open and airy out back, spilling with ambient light from a covered passage that connected the inn proper with the kitchen house. A dozen empty tables occupied the cobblestone patio. Gariff strode over to one, let his pack slide off one shoulder, then the other, and thudded down on the bench.

"Kabor, light us a lantern," Gariff commanded. "Nud, you get moving and find Bobbin, and make it snappy – get back here with some food before I eat my hat! I'll hold the table."

I rolled my eyes.

"Nevermind that. It was yer blinking rock that got us here this late in the first place," he stated bluntly, carelessly, "a little flash here, a flicker there, next thing I know yer mystified." Gariff wiggled his fingers at me in true magician form. "So the least you can do is put a rush order on our grub, thank-you-very-much!"

"What do you mean by blinking? Mine doesn't blink," Kabor jutted in. He turned to look at me as he reached for the lantern. "What's this about blinking?"

"It just sparks easy," I replied. "And he meant 'blinking' like 'Where's my blinking hat?'" So much for secrets.

"Flint?" said Kabor. "Quartz?"

I said nothing, contemplating how I might answer. A liar knows a lie when he hears it. Gariff's blank look did nothing to help my cause.

An unexpected voice cut through the awkward silence. The voice – a rough, older voice and distinctly country – called out from the shadows. "Blinking rock aye? Now that's something I'd sure like to see. How 'bout we have a looksie?"

CHAPTER VIII

Deepwood arrows

The arrows Paplov made were deadly accurate. Proper grain and weight of wood made them fly true, even when fowl hunting in dense bush. But there is more to the craft than that. The arrow and the bow have to complement one another.

Paplov kept an exact duplicate of Fyorn's bow in his workshop. It was the original model, bought at an estate sale in Proudfoot. Precisely how the old farmer had come across such a fine piece of equipment in the first place is still a mystery.

After a trip to Fyorn's cabin, Paplov would set aside the best pieces of collected wood for the footed shafts. Each arrow was carefully constructed by blending a softwood shaft with a heavier deepwood footing to create a perfect balance between strength of impact, weight and flexibility. Paplov worked the wood until every shaft was flawless before attaching the pointed heads and fletching to complete the arrows. He made scores of them for each trip to Deepweald. My uncle spent many arrows and fashioned his fair share as well; Paplov's were just to supplement his own stocks. Once he even admitted preferring Paplov's to his own. It might have been the wine talking though.

It was mid-morning when I finally crawled out of bed, still

wearing the previous day's clothes. My head ached. Paplov was out fletching in his workshop again, as he had been on and off over the last several days. I had arrived home in the early hours of the morning and had stumbled into bed, tired and sore and in need of a visit to the bathhouse. I felt my pockets right away. The stone was still there. I pulled it out to verify. After one streak of quick flashes, I put it back.

I made my way to the study and sat in Paplov's favorite chair. I spotted my grandfather working behind the open shutters of the workshop. I watched as he notched a new arrow and tested the draw. He picked up another one and eyed the two closely, peering down the shafts and examining the ends with a magnifying lens. He balanced them on a scale – dead even, I suspect.

Consistency is important.

An arrow flies in an arc, not a straight line, and if one arrow is a different weight and length from the next, the shooter will have to adjust the vertical cant of the bow in order to compensate for the arrow's drop as gravity draws it downward and air resistance slows its flight. Arrows have different designs as well, especially if they are made by different fletchers or for targeting different sizes of game. Arrows meant for a specific purpose need to be of consistent quality. Paplov fashioned a single kind of arrow for Uncle Fyorn, the kind that will take down a deer at one hundred feet. The woodsman had used the same kind in the Outlands, back in the day.

I tried to remember all that had happened the previous night, but it was all a blur. For the first time, my memory failed me. I remembered meeting one Mer Andulus, a grizzled old prospector in search of the "mother load," and I remembered how Bobbin waddled onto the back patio of the Flipside like a contented duck, wearing a fancy, white doublet with frills and loose trousers under a food-stained apron. He saw me right away, and flashed me his "what a pleasant surprise" smile. He wasn't alone. The portly Pip, and innkeeper's only son, was escorting a striking young serving girl, the very girl we had been ogling from the veranda. She had beautiful eyes, an inviting smile, and a carefree laugh. She wore a necklace that reminded me of one my mother used to wear. Had I not been caught eyeing her earlier, maybe our greeting would have been less awkward. Bobbin helped break the ice for me. "Holly Hopkins, from Proudfoot," he had said. Later came great food and fantastic barkwood ale. I don't remember a lot else after that – as non-Pippish as that might seem. Even Pip memory has its limitations, and alcohol is one of them.

Paplov spied me watching him. "It's almost noon," he said, with more than a hint of sharpness in his voice. "I could use a hand out here."

I sat up too fast and the sudden motion made my head hurt. I waited out the vertigo, then hurried as best I could out back, groggy and without breakfast. Not having any breakfast wasn't a big deal – my stomach was still unpleasantly full and queasy from the night's feasting.

As keen as I normally was to help Paplov with fletching, on that day I simply couldn't focus. I felt light headed all the while Paplov explained what needed to be done. All I could think about was the stone.

Once alone in the workshop, I sat down on the most uncomfortable wooden chair ever made, and nearly dozed off. I let the silence of the day soak in, with gentle interruptions from the twitter of birdsong, the gentle drone of buzzing insects in the garden, and the twang and thump of target practice from the range out back. It smelled like sawdust.

Slowly, images from the night before began to form in my mind. Mer – the old prospector who overheard us talking about the 'blinking rock' – spoke with a bone pipe clenched in his teeth, smoke pulsing out of his nose and mouth. The pipe was shaped like a whale. Rocks of various sorts from his pack had been strewn about his table the moment we showed interest in them, and he gave us a spiel about each unique piece. Then he pointed to where they had come from on the many maps also laying about, describing the intricacies of the local geology as he did so. He kept saying something about the "mother load." I got the feeling he could talk for hours about his precious rocks, maps and the weird combination of witchcraft and geology that he preached. Maybe he did. One thing I remember distinctly is what Mer Andulus had said about my stone. He said it was not a proper stone at all. The closest he could come up with was some kind of amber – prehistoric tree gum. But it definitely was not amber.

I got up off my chair, closed the workshop shutters and unveiled my precious find once again. I raised it high above my head in the darkness. The spark ignited instantly. It was bright, strong and burning red – a rising sun in my outstretched hand, shining of its own eternal radiance. *What have I found? Should I ask Paplov? – No, he might think it's dangerous and take it away…*

Paplov called from outside, snapping me out of my trance. "Quite the batch this round," he said, admiring his own handiwork. He was on his way over.

My heart raced. *I can't let him see it, not yet.* Hurriedly, I went to put the stone away, but fumbled it in my hands. I felt a blood rush, dizzying, my head suddenly spinning in a frenzy. Paplov shouldered the door to the workshop and it creaked open.

"Good grain," he said, unsuspecting.

As sudden as it came on, the sensation collapsed. I felt a rush of air out of the room. It sucked the breath right out of me. The door slammed shut, nearly knocking Paplov over.

"Wha?" said Paplov.

The feeling passed quickly and I squirreled the stone away.

Paplov tried the door again, and this time stepped in slow and steady, peeking in as he did so.

"Why did you do that?" he said, a little ticked.

"I didn—" he interrupted.

"It's not funny. You could have seriously hurt me. I was holding one of the new arrows at about eye level." He demonstrated, squinting as he looked down the shaft.

"I didn't," I said.

Paplov looked about the room and sized up the situation. I had been quite far from the door.

"Must have been the wind, then," he said. "Apologies for accusing you."

"I felt the air get sucked right out of the room," I said.

"I'll have to look out for that. A good lesson anyway – don't walk around looking down an arrow shaft." He shook his head, probably counting his blessings.

"Did you hit the bullseye?" I said.

"And why is it so dark in here?" he complained, glancing about. "You can't possibly work like this." Paplov put the arrows down on the table and opened the shutters.

"Bullseye, of course!" he replied at last.

I picked an arrow up and examined the fletching. Paplov never allowed me to practice with the arrows he made for Fyorn.

"Maybe you have a few extras to spare… for target practice?" I said.

"Regular arrows are best for that." Paplov said, "They'll keep your aim honest."

"But I can shoot from a lot farther now than ever before. If I adjust my sighting for regular arrows, your arrows fly high when I shoot them." Something about staring down the shaft of a deepwood arrow imparts a focus that literally blurs out the world around – blurs out everything but the target. Distracting at first, after some practice I came to rely on it. I could hardly miss the bullseye at ten paces. At fifteen paces, I was still on target more often than not. There was definitely something weird about Paplov's arrows.

"How do you know that?" he said.

Stupid. I was not so clever that morning at all. I knew it was wrong to sneak his true-strike arrows onto the range, but sometimes I did just that, making sure to return each and every one of them before he discovered they were missing. I didn't even try to forge an answer.

"You're adjusting your aim for distance? Hmm... Well, just try aiming at the target as if you were half as far away," he replied. With one sharp nod, he declared it the final solution.

"Easier said than done," I said. His recommendation solved nothing. "I don't know exactly how far away I am when I shoot. I just make my best guess based on... I don't know, what feels right."

Paplov took a long minute to think things through, as he often did before coming to even a minor decision. "Well, now that you're of age, maybe Fyorn will see fit to take you hunting with him. He can let you in on a few secrets."

"Really? With seekers?"

"Of course with seekers! What else? He taught me a thing or two about hunting when I was your age, that's for sure."

His words caught me off guard for a moment, until I remembered Uncle Fyorn's lineage. Paplov looks so much older than my uncle does.

"It's time we made you enough deepwood arrows to get you through a good, long deer hunt."

"Uncle Fyorn really knows a lot about hunting... and nature," I said. "Doesn't he?"

"Fyorn knows a great many things about a great many things." Paplov smiled.

"And little about little," I added.

"He is one of the Elderkin, after all," said Paplov.

"Trees especially, right?" I said.

"I suppose."

"Ancient trees?"

"What? Well… I don't know. I guess."

Uncle Fyorn was also the most well-traveled person I knew; always talking about his adventures in far away lands. He was the only one I could think of that might know more about my mystery stone than Mer, other than the Diviner. He was also trustworthy, and he trusted us with his secrets – like deepwood, for instance. He would definitely keep my secret, and he would know what to do. But Paplov wasn't due back to the woodsman's cabin for several months.

"Are you planning an extra trip to Fyorn's?" I said, innocently.

Paplov stopped his whittling for a moment and nodded in the direction of the woodshed. "I already have more deepwood than I know what to do with. Last visit was right after a wicked wind storm and I had to charter a pack lizard at the Handlers' Post just to get it all into town, without you there to help out."

I ignored the jab.

"But… uh… do you have enough for the both of us?" I asked.

He stared with his mouth half-open, head tilted down, and spectacles half-way down his nose. His eyes begged for an explanation.

"What I mean is, I was thinking about maybe taking up wood-craft like you. I'd like to learn more about the arrows, especially… and the carvings too. Have you ever made a lantern?"

Now that was just about the lowest trick in the book, but guaranteed to work against someone as sentimental as he was. Anyone who knew Paplov well enough also knew his passion for the hammer and chisel. And he always brought up passing on his skills to me. He had many hobbies, but working the deepwood was the only one he ever made time for. He might not have been the most skilled fletcher in Webfoot, or the fastest, but he was the only one who worked with deepwood.

"Oh?" Paplov smiled at that. He put the knife down and gave his smooth beard a tug. "Hmm," he said, with a thoughtful nod of the head. "I don't know much about lanterns out of wood. They're usually made of metal and glass."

Not for bog stones, I thought.

"But," he continued, "you could certainly get started with woodcraft easily enough. You already know more than you realize."

I carefully studied the arrow that I held, running the shaft between my thumb and finger. Paplov started work on a new one.

"Does that mean yes?" I said. And to seal the deal, the next words that rolled off my tongue hit the air with such sincerity that no grandparent could ever refuse them. "I just want to carve as expertly as you some day, that's all, and maybe advance enough to trade with Fyorn like you do... some day."

Hearing my own words, as noble and utterly convincing as they were, I nearly believed them myself. I had no shame.

Paplov stared down at the pile of arrow shafts and slowly bobbed his head a couple of times. He looked older than usual, as if he'd had an "age spurt" the way young children have growth spurts.

"Tomorrow I'm to have morning tea with the new lord mayor to discuss some political matters," he said.

Paplov put his hand on my shoulder.

"Then in two days I'm off to Proudfoot," he continued, "and I'll need you to come along with me and help out with the documents."

"Oh," was all I could say. I let out an exaggerated sigh.

"I'll need you to learn those documents and cite relevant passages as they come up in conversation."

Easy. I nodded.

"Not just memorizing either – I need you to know what it all means."

Not so easy. "OK," I said.

A warm smile crept across Paplov's face and he added: "If I can finish up early, with your help, we can drop in on Fyorn a day or two after that... if you like. He's been asking about you."

"Great!" I could barely contain my energy.

"Then it's settled," he said. "We'll leave for Fyorn's cabin after Proudfoot, but only if you help me finish off enough arrows. That ole woodsprite was hoping to get them early anyway. Asked for bright orange feathers on them. Must be going blind."

Paplov laughed and passed me a handful of shafts, with a smile on his face that stretched a mile wide.

CHAPTER IX

The lizard handler

Two days later, on behalf of the council, we commissioned a blue-tail and handler to carry us south to the Outland Trail. The trip to the Stout town of Proudfoot would be easier on Paplov that way. He could be stubborn about getting his hiking in, but it had been raining straight for two days. Given Webfooters' sorry record for maintaining the Mire Trail, that time of year blue-tails were the preferred mode of transportation into and out of town for anyone sensible, especially during wet spells. Year by year, the corduroy portions of the beaten track slowly unfurled, but still more than half lay undeveloped.

While packing arrows in the shed with Paplov, I caught sight of one Mer Andulus strolling up the road to our hut. He wore the same tans, leathers and floppy hat as that night at the Flipside. Both hands gripped the worn, leather straps of his backpack as if they were suspenders. The old prospector chewed his whalebone pipe as he walked, and sent a thin stream of smoke trailing over one shoulder and up into the fresh morning air.

"Just a sec," I said to Paplov, and ran out to meet Mer at the twig gate to our yard. A light drizzle feathered my face, coating it with a warm, thin film. The prospector looked a little damp himself.

"Gidday-gidday," he said as one long word, out of the corner of his mouth. "Glad to see yer up and about." He pulled the pipe out. "On my way to your bog to stake our interests. Any chance you can get yerself together? We can swing by and pluck yer partners out'a bed at the Flipside." Mer's voice was fully animate – nothing like the tired old coot I had him pegged for when he first emerged from his shadowy seat on the Flipside patio. His weary eyes with the bags underneath were a testimony to hard living, and his weathered cheeks to an outdoor lifestyle.

"Is that all you're bringing?" I said, motioning to his pack.

"Pick, hammer and shovel," he said. "The rest is already out there." He laughed to himself. I could not help but smile back.

"Sorry, but I'm off to Proudfoot today on a diplomatic errand," I said.

Now that sounded important. With a squint of one eye and a slight rise of the chin, Mer gave me an examining look.

"Horses won't be seen for another two weeks, give or take. Are ya taking a lizard or flip-flopping?"

"Blue-tail," I said.

"Yep. What else," he said. It was not a question.

"I'll be back tomorrow. But then shortly after I'm off to visit… an Elderkin associate."

An Elderkin associate? "Yes," I should have added. *I am so important that I regularly meet with Elderkin nobles, and they always ask about when I can come back to honor them with my presence. I might mention your name to them…*

Mer raised his eyebrows at the mention of Elderkin and then just shrugged his shoulders at the change in plans.

"What are you going to do out there, in the bog?" I said.

"Well, everything we discussed I s'pose."

I waited for a long moment while the prospector took his time to give me that evaluating look of his again, all the while stroking his tangly beard. His eyes measured my worth.

"You don't remember, do ya?"

"Well…"

"I worked six summers with a frog-faced old-timer by the name 'a Clop. Remembered everything to the N'th degree, 'cept all the stupid things he did after a few barkwoods."

"Oh."

"Oh is right. Let me remind ya's. I'm off to check on that spot where the ole glowing tree spit turned up – lookin' fer staking posts to see what's claimed by HME and what's not."

"Who's HME?"

"Harrow Mining and Exploration – they're just about everywhere in the bog lands these days, according to the town clerk, Old Remy."

"I know him," I said. Paplov relied on Remy a lot for anything to do with maps.

"Problem is though," said Mer, "half the claims data's in his thick head, so's I have to go find the stake posts myself. Remy only seems to know where they're s'pose to be, but where they're pounded into the ground is what counts. Interest'n he says this one's the first claim south of the trailhead."

"Humph," I said.

"By the way," Mer went on, "we're going equal splits on the financial side, 'cept you and Gariff get double weight, 'case you don't remember that either."

"OK."

"OK is right. And don't forget you promised everyone a treasure hunt day."

"Who's everyone?"

"Well, myself fer starters, but I might not make it. The two Stouts, the well rounded Pip, as you might say, and the girl you were making googly eyes at. That's everyone."

"Oh… OK." My knees shook a little at the fact that none of this sounded familiar. I must have looked stunned to the prospector.

"Nud, you ready?" called Paplov from the hut.

"Well, alrighty," said Mer Andulus. "Hope ya have a good one, and catch ya at the Flipside. We'll keep it fast and loose 'till then." He turned to go.

"Wait," I said.

The prospector halted and looked back over his shoulder.

"Nud?" called Paplov.

"In a minute," I called back to Paplov.

I turned to Mer. "Can you swing by the Flipside on your way out anyway?" I said, "...to pass some news to Bobbin – the round one." Mer gave me a slow nod. "Tell him to be ready to hit the trail in a few days, right after the Elderkin... meeting. Bobbin can tell Holly and the cousins."

"Gotcha covered," he said. "And while I'm out and about in loon goop, I'll keep an eye on the trail and an ear on the Handlers' Post then."

Mer took a step back and raised a hand in salute. "Go easy," he added with a nod.

"Go easy," I replied with half a wave. The words felt strange, borrowed. I could never own them the way he did.

Proudfoot lay cradled between two rivers, a full day's march away. Any delay would see Paplov and me on the trail at dusk, which is never a good idea in the open wetlands or along the forest edge. I convinced Paplov to have us dropped off midway.

When the handler finally arrived, only half-dressed it seemed, Paplov took the seat up front with him and I sat in the rear with the baggage. The handler wore naught but tattered shorts, a wide-brimmed hat, and a belt with a long knife in its sheath. He was so thin and wiry that the bones in his elbows and shoulders looked as though they might punch through his leathery skin. He didn't seem to care about the drizzle. I doubt he would have blinked if it rained newts. Wyatt was a real bogger.

"How do you keep the flies off," I said to him. "The midges must eat you alive out of town."

Wyatt glanced back and flashed me a one-tooth smile. "Bugs don't bug me anymore," he said, "only snot-nosed little boys do."

Snot-nosed? I'm almost sixteen!

Paplov laughed at the look on my face, and louder still when I wiped my nose with my shirtsleeve. He leaned over to whisper something.

"Don't mind him," he said. The whisper was loud and the bogger could not help but to hear it. "Old Wyatt's just sore."

"Damn right I'm sore," he said. "Eleven years as a prisoner in Harrow is enough to make anybody sore."

"Prisoner? How did you get out?" I said.

"Well, they let me go when I finally gave them what they wanted – a secret I swore I would never give up."

"What?" I asked.

"Are ya sure ya want t'know?" he said.

I nodded.

"The one I swore it too 'disappeared' – poor bastard. They told me I was next. I never gave them any more than the half of it anyway."

"Is that true?" I said.

"'Course it's true," said Wyatt. He shook his head in frustration. "Look at that, a snot-nosed kid calling me liar. Are you calling me a liar?"

I shook my head.

"They'll come looking for the other half once they figure it out," said Paplov.

Wyatt didn't answer. He just kept his eyes to the trail and handled the mount. It was common knowledge that the youngest of the riding lizards – the so-called "blue-tails" – were paired to the oldest, grumpiest handlers. That was certainly the case with Wyatt. That isn't to say that young riders make better handlers. Young blue-tails can be difficult to control and tend to go off on their own or flip over, whereas older redheads are so worked in, even a novice can handle them.

Although the topic had grown stale, a question still burned inside of me. Asking Wyatt another question felt like pulling out his last tooth, but I did it anyway.

"When you were in Harrow, did you see any other prisoners? I mean anyone you knew, like another Pip… or someone?"

Wyatt looked to Paplov. They stared at one another without either saying a word. I didn't know what it meant, but it meant something.

"Nope," he said. "Not a one from the Trilands."

Wyatt loosened up a bit by the time we reached the watergrass homes. The first bit of gossip out of his mouth concerned a crazy story about a glass trinket with a firefly trapped in it, waved around by some party-boy at the Flipside a few nights back. "I was there," he said, "And with my own two eyes I saw him holding it over the pretty girls' heads, begging for kisses. Then I heard he got a slap instead from some girl. Half the town is talking about it!" I shrunk down between the traveling bags and felt my face, wondering if it stung a little. *Maybe.*

It seemed as though I had managed to contain my secret for little more than half a day, and the count for those in the know was substantial: two friends from the Hills, one Webfooter who worked at the busiest establishment in town, a pretty Proudfooter I had never seen before who also worked in the busiest establishment in town, a traveling prospector who had been just about everywhere and that I had never seen before, and a tavern full of patrons from lands far and near.

Soon, the conversation migrated to politics – it always did with Paplov. As the blue-tail strode along, I could see that the handler kept himself in tune to the lizard's every sway and step. The subtle calls, the slight taps on the sides of the lizard's neck, the pushing and pulling of the reins – it all blended together in complex ways to form one simple command: "GO STRAIGHT." At times, the handler would grunt and squeeze his bony ankles into the lizard's sides. And every so often he'd follow with a string of frustrated remarks, pull a fish out of the side bag, and pitch it well ahead. Our mount dashed at the offering, scooping it up in his bridled jaws, mid-stride. As we rode on, I noted that whenever the lizard began heading off-course or became a little testy, the handler would squeeze. Whenever that wasn't enough to set her straight, he'd toss her another fish. They didn't teach that at the riding school – all reins and whip.

By the time we met the misty bog, the morning air felt heavy, still and silent.

The ride along the Mire Trail was mostly uneventful. We were alone on the trail that morning. The slow rhythm of the lizard's stride and gentle lurching after bait had me nodding off before long.

I had fallen asleep, probably for only a few minutes, but sleeping nonetheless, when a sudden jostling and the handler's angry shouts brought me out of slumber. Without known cause, the lizard darted off the trail and into the bog. The handler's fish went flying as he grasped the reins, pulling back with both hands. We all bounced and shook violently on the lizard's back as she zig-zagged from hummock to hummock. The girl's pretty blue tail detached in the commotion. It twisted and writhed on a patch of thick moss.

It took some coaxing, a few long tipsy moments, and more swear words than I ever heard strung together before Wyatt was able to rear the tailless blue-tail and get her back on track.

"No worries," he said when the lizard was nearing calm again. He spoke partly to Paplov and me, but mostly to his mount. His tone was reassuring. "She'll get us to the Outland no problem, just you wait and see, with time to spare, I'll wager." He stroked her neck and looked back to where the tail used to be.

"Everyone all right?" he said. "Lose anything."

Paplov gave me a quick once-over and inspected his gear. "All good," he said.

"Well," Wyatt admitted, "something's got the ole girl spooked. I've run this route many a year and none of my lizards have ever been so skittish. It might be a good idea to make arrangements now for safe passage on the way back."

Paplov nodded. I couldn't help but wonder if it was all just a show to drum up more business. Either way, the handler eventually brought us as far as the Outland Trail, as promised. It was as far as Paplov would allow. Riding lizards were outlawed in Proudfoot ever since one young Stout had gotten himself eaten and another trampled, all in a span of two spring months. On top of that, the full journey would be costly – more than the town was willing to pay out, so any farther would have to come out of Paplov's pocket.

Before Wyatt turned back, Paplov arranged for the old bogger to meet us for the return trip.

We journeyed the rest of the way on foot, as Pips normally travel. Paplov and I had not said much to one another along the way. With about an hour left to go before meeting the Dim River, he finally started in on the diplomatic particulars of the visit.

"We have important work to do today, you and I," he said. "This evening, at Lord Mayor Otis' manor, I am to debate Proudfoot's proposal to extend their agricultural region by draining a sizable portion of our wetlands. In return, they are suggesting a minimal lease fee and reduced prices for some crops. But they want the option to increase rates due to the heightened mineral exploration activity in the area as well, claiming that if a mine springs up on their property, the cropland will be devalued and they won't realize projected future gains. I'm not giving in to that one – if a mine springs up the property value will increase substantially."

I had reviewed the documents in detail the night prior, and

was well acquainted with the particulars of the mission. But in usual form, Paplov saw fit to highlight the main points en route.

"Look! Is that a white raven? Over there. On top of that old dead tree." I said, pointing to the treetop.

Paplov looked up and nodded in acknowledgement. "Humph, lucky. I've seen that one around these parts before. Anyway, as I was saying: Lord Mayor Undle and the Webfoot council are mostly in favor, but they feel the lease fee is too low and it was pointed out that the reductions—"

"Can ravens really talk as good as Gariff says they can? He says they can sound just like a person," I said.

"Yes, yes," replied Paplov dismissively, "Gariff is right. Some are fantastic talkers."

Paplov halted for a second, and tapped his left hand to his forehead.

"Where was I… Oh yes, it was pointed out that reductions in crop prices were not at all quantified; it wasn't clear if the reduced prices meant that you had to buy through the town's common market – which is always more expensive – or if they applied when buying directly from the farmer, the way most sensible folks go about business. At any rate, it's our job to ensure that Webfoot gets—"

"Are there really white ravens at Dim Lake too?" I said.

"Maybe," he replied, again dismissively, "not that I've seen… As I was saying, we have to ensure that Webfoot gets good—"

"Gets a good deal," I finished. "Can we get a raven like Uncle Fyorn's, except white?"

Paplov raised his voice. "NO!" he said. "We're NOT getting a raven." He fixed his eyes straight ahead and pursed his lips. "And NO about getting a good deal. Well yes, I mean…" Paplov seemed a little flustered.

"Nud, you're almost sixteen now, and you can already sign documents in my place as aide and successor. Like so many others in this business, you seem to have more authority than the smarts to use it."

I didn't know how to respond to that. I blinked.

"It's time to WAKE UP," he impressed, "PAY ATTENTION, and GET INVOLVED in what's going on around you. You're too young to… you're too young to go out all night like that. And even when you're not too young, you still shouldn't. I don't plan to do this forever. I should have been done years ago… I thought I was done years ago, until…"

Paplov's head was shaking as he spoke; no, it was quivering. His hands were quivering too, and he continued to quiver for a long minute after his words trailed off, after he stopped short of saying *It*.

He bowed his head slightly and held it that way, looking very old again. *Yes, he is aging in spurts,* I thought. When next he spoke, Paplov's voice was low and it wavered a little.

"You're the one who's going to inherit these responsibilities," he said. Paplov found his stern voice again. "You're the one who needs to learn how to take care of the future. It's *your* future, not mine. My legacy maybe, but you have to live with it, day in and day out. Sooner or later, I'm free of it. And Harrow…"

Paplov shook his head and let time pass before calling again upon his diplomatic voice. He started over. "Back to the task at hand," he said. "We have to ensure that Webfoot gets good REP-RE-SENT-A-TION in the deal-making process. It isn't just about getting the best deal, or even a good deal. A deal that is too good for Webfoot is likely poor for Proudfoot, and that fact will carry forward into the next negotiation – it has its own… memory, and that can have undesirable consequences. It all needs to balance out. In the long run, it's about building good relationships, acting honorably, and having faith in the good folks you're dealing with – in this case the Proudfoot Stouts. Honor and faith are the pillars of trust and trust is the foundation of good relations."

"What if you're not dealing with good folks?" I said.

"Then you tread ever so carefully," said Paplov, like it should have been obvious.

He was right. The agreement with Proudfoot was meant to be long standing, and it influenced my future more than his – he wasn't getting any younger.

"Can't someone else just handle it?" I said.

A heavy, disappointing silence lingered between us for the rest of the journey.

All things tangled from the outside in,
All things joined in purpose.
All things bent to the One True Will,
Until the Next Insurgence.

- The Diviner

CHAPTER X

Diplomacy in Proudfoot

Before long, the wooded wetlands fell out of sight behind us and we came upon lush fields of young wheat on gentle, rolling hills, fresh with the passing of new rain. The dirt road cut through bright green pastures dotted with grazing cattle. Ahead it rolled alongside cornfields, sprouting vegetable gardens, many a farmhouse, and many a barn. Stretches of the Dim River gleamed in the distance. Diamond-bright flashes marked the division between a nest of craggy hills on this side of the river and the ghost pines of Whisperwood on the other side. An hour later, we passed into the Flats and sighted the ferry dock to Proudfoot and the curtain wall that rose above the opposing shore. The pang in my stomach reminded me dinner would be late.

The Stout town lay nestled at the merger of the Upper Malevuin River running southeast out of the Western Tor and the Dim River running due south from Harrow. The "Dim Crossing," as it is commonly called, is more of a back door to the town and the least traveled of Proudfoot's two river crossings. The wide, flat ferry had just landed on our side of the Dim as we approached. Two Pips and a Stout manned her, and two horses – one per side and facing opposite directions – powered the waterwheels. When the horses were calmed and the off ramp set, local farmers spilled out of the boat and onto the pier. With heavy feet, they led their horse-drawn carts and carried their sacks of leftover wares after a long day at the marketplace. In the midst of the crowd, a handful of bearded prospectors bearing sturdy packs chatted one another up, minds surely bent on the promise of gold or other earth-borne treasures of the Outlands. Those few who return with the bounty sought go on to become local heroes and inspire other adventurous spirits. The rest are mostly lost.

The return trip began with the horses' directions reversed and the waterwheels spinning the other way. I watched the beasts as they clopped along, every step propelling us across the slow, strong current of the river. Soon my eyes turned to the water. I peered into the river depths, trying to make out the shadowy shapes on its bottom: deadwood and rocks mostly, and the broken skeleton of a sunken dory resembling those seen in Abandon Bay.

The Stout ferryman minded the horses while one of the Pips steered. The remaining Pip did nothing, mostly, until we reached the other side, at which time he opened the rail gate, jumped out and roped the ferry in. Since there were no carts, he couldn't be bothered to set the ramp.

The next stop was the gatehouse. Paplov provided his name to a guard and handed over his letter of intent, complete with the official wax seal of Proudfoot pressed into the upper left corner. He also produced his diplomatic colors. That granted us access without a fuss or even the usual toll. Paplov told the guards I was his assistant – no papers required. He left a gratuity anyway.

"Why did you do that?" I asked.

"The ferry only runs until twilight," he replied. "If I'm ever stuck and need to get across, it doesn't hurt to have a good rapport with the guards – they can call the ferrymen to make another crossing."

The town layout was an inviting one, emphasizing greenery

and openness in a park-like setting. Proudfoot Lane, the main cobblestone throughway, ran from the east gate to the west gate and cut through the entire town. Lined with pink and white crabapple trees at measured intervals, it was wide enough for a horse drawn carriage to make a complete turn. Each tree had a small walled garden around it, and the sweet bouquet of apple blossoms scented the air. A series of cascading gardens also lined the road, putting on display all manner of shrubbery and seasonal flowers.

Sleek passenger boats with Pip rowers glided along the boatway parallel to the road, passing under numerous bridges that connected the common part of town to a neighborhood of stately homes owned by the more affluent Stout families. The network of narrow canals linked "anyplace to everyplace" throughout, with the flow of water regulated by floodgates and locks at the river junctions. The main east-west line fed into a southbound canal that eventually opened into the turbulent Lower Malevuin – a tricky run to navigate even for those familiar with the waters.

Stouts, Pips, Men and the occasional Outlander came and went as we made our way along the sparsely populated main street. I was reminded that Proudfoot Stouts are generally taller, slimmer and fairer than their Bearded Hills cousins, but no less resilient or of the earth. Their particular blend of affinity for the land has them taking more to farming than tunneling and mining though. Men often called them the "fair folk" and it is easy enough to see why.

To the west, the far end of town looked busier, with modest activity still underway in the market area. We soon came to a grand and decorative bridge about mid-town that arced over the southbound waterway. I slowed my pace and took a moment to look around and take in the sights. It was so much different from the bog.

"I really like how the Proudfooters built their town," I said as we passed over the south canal. "Gariff would like it too. It looks sturdy, but not so barren as the Hills… and the water's all… organized. This place has a nice feel to it."

Paplov stopped to gape at me in disbelief. "No, no," he started, head shaking. "Mind your history, Nud." He inhaled a deep breath, and exhaled a lesson. "Proudfooters had little to do with the actual construction of this town, they just live here. They don't even know how it runs, really. They did not build the wall, they just man it. They did not build the gardens, they simply tend them. Who do you think crafted that ferry we were just on? I don't know who, but one thing's for sure… it was not a Proudfooter."

Paplov paused, and seemed to engage in a moment of reflection. His words softened.

"I'm not being completely fair: they dug the canal," he said. "I'll give them that much, and the selection of all manner of greenery is to their credit." But his soft voice was short lived and his words were soon firm again. They became as rigid as the stubbornness of old age. "But you should know that the skilled hands of Bearded Hills folk built this town and everything in it, back in a day when common foods were traded for gold. Many worked themselves to near death just trying to feed their families back home, while perfectly good food spoiled in the cellars of hoarders. How 'nice' is that?" He ended with a scoff.

I had learned about the famine years and the long winters that accompanied them in my lessons with the Diviner. Everywhere in the Land, life had dwindled, was dying: crops, animals, and people alike. Even the bounty of the sea could not be counted on for sustenance. Everywhere, that is, except lush Proudfoot and the ever-fertile Stoutville Flats. Deepweald remained somewhat impervious, as the story goes, but during that period, the Wild Elderkins would let none pass into their realm. It was even worse than the desolation that hit the Scarsands, or so I am told. Hearing Paplov's words that way, I finally understood his caution in dealing with what appeared to be simple, hardworking folk. When it comes right down to the very essence of getting ahead in life, all bets are off with regard to decency.

"What are Pips best known for?" I said.

Without pause, Paplov responded. "The culinary arts, woodcraft, diving and river boating... those sorts of things."

"How did *we* survive the famine?"

"You mean Pips? That was long before even I was born. The first item on your list, I suppose. We Pips always had to be creative about how we foraged and what we ate. The Pip diet is a varied one."

"But food is just about everywhere, any time of year."

Paplov laughed. "You only know that because it has been hammered into your head since you were just a newt. Few Stouts, if any, see the natural world the way we do. Food comes on a plate to most, complete with knife and fork; or from the market; or is hauled up out of cold storage."

I shrugged. "I guess so," was all I said.

Paplov and I kept up a brisk pace through to the west side, but each time we passed by a water fountain I wished I could kick off my shoes, cannonball in and wade through the ruffled water. Three grand fountains graced the main throughway as we neared the marketplace, each three levels high. On top of the first, a bird spouted water from a long, curved beak; the second showed a whale, spraying water from its blowhole; and the third – the largest and most spectacular of the three – dominated the market square. Even from a distance, I could clearly make out its cascading assortment of spinning waterwheels.

Seeing the fountains triggered something – a memory. No, not quite, but something. The Mark on my arm began to tingle. A sudden blackness overcame me. A picture began to take shape in my mind: *Stouts... Bearded Hill Stouts.... thin... drawn... serious words of war... weapons clanging... attack... attack!... chains.* The image swirled and shifted like a cloud of dark smoke: *gardens...*

torn up… fountains… toppled… statues erected… massive statues… sea creatures… leviathans! All at once, the image dissipated. I found that I was still walking alongside Paplov. He was talking. I interrupted him.

"The Bearded Hills was planning an attack."

"What?" said Paplov. He sounded confused.

"During the famine. They were plotting to take over and force Proudfooters to work for them, as *slaves*."

"I've never heard that," he said. Paplov stroked his white beard. "That might explain a few things in the historical record, perhaps."

"And the fountains… they were going to be destroyed."

"Destroyed? Where did you get this information?"

"I… I don't know, exactly."

"You don't know? Then you are pulling my leg."

"No."

"Well, it's that or a 'false recall,' and I only ever heard of one case of false recall happening back… I don't even know when. I would have to check Webfoot Hall."

"I'm not lying."

"But Nud," he said, sudden concern in his voice, "the fountains were built *long after* the famine."

"Oh," was all I said.

We walked in silence. My behavior clearly disturbed Paplov and I tried to sort out in my mind what had just happened.

Before long, the faint but distinctive dirty smell of coal-smoke carried on the air as we made our way through the market square towards the Helmfast Inn. Paplov politely declined many a merchant as we strode past, while they peddled everything from tools to furs to spices to tapestries, to name a few. The Helmfast boasted the most respectable accommodations in town. Visiting dignitaries routinely opted for it, known for its hosting courtesies and hearty cuisine.

When we arrived there, Paplov again showed his letter, this

time to the Stout attendant, who happened to be the innkeeper. He was a round-faced and pleasant looking man, seemingly content to be in the thick of midlife. He stood behind a high desk.

"Lord Mayor Otis' aide dropped by this morning to reserve our best room," he said. "It has a balcony overlooking the market square. There will be dancing and entertainment later tonight. We have a performing troupe in from Dennington – theatre and songs."

"Very nice," said Paplov, pretending to be thrilled.

The innkeeper's hands soon were busy gathering paperwork and a quill as he chatted on. Motioning to an inkwell on the desk, he handed Paplov the quill and then the paper. "Please make your mark at the bottom so I can validate your attendance with the mayor, Councillor Lenokin."

"Thank you kindly," Paplov replied. He carefully studied what he was signing, and only then returned the paper with his mark.

"Streets are a little quiet this evening," said Paplov.

"Yessum. Been quiet for days. As soon as it starts getting dark, most everyone packs up – ever since the incident on the Outland Trail. Not tonight though!"

Paplov raised an eyebrow. "Incident?"

"Haven't you heard?" said the innkeeper. "The whole town's talking about it. One of many lately – a bad batch of low-life bandits from the Outlands, I say. And that's not all. Merchants and other travelers raided just outside of town, and traders raided *inside* town walls just the day before last, right out there under my nose, at dusk." He pointed to a window overlooking the square. "Unbelievable." He shook his head.

The innkeeper leaned forward on the desk, rested his chin on his hands, and stared out of the window. He looked as though he were about to speak, but no words came out.

"And the incident?" said Paplov.

The innkeeper look confused for a moment, then straightened up and slapped his forehead.

"Oh yes, pardon me," he said. "I got sidetracked. There hasn't been a lot of outsider traffic since a few days ago. Three, no four, or two. Two days. Mostly just locals about town. It's making for a slow start to the season."

"I see," said Paplov as he took the keys handed to him.

"One for each of you," said the innkeeper.

For a moment, the two just stared at one another.

"And…" prompted Paplov.

"And…" echoed the innkeeper, eyes wide and inviting, palms open to suggestion.

"The incident," said Paplov.

"Oh yes, the incident, pardon me. It was a most foul murder and theft – and good upstanding Proudfooters they were, falling victim that is – up your way near the split, so I hear. The whole town's talking. Outlanders, I say."

Paplov tilted his head at me. His eyebrows raised in all serious-ness: "We best keep our heads up and our ears pricked." He turned back to the innkeeper. "Thanks for the tip," he said, and flipped the man a coin.

Despite the lizard incident, we had kept good time and so could afford a short rest in our chamber before changing into more formal evening attire. Our itinerary began with dinner at the lord mayor's house at dusk, over which Paplov would no doubt engage in the usual polite conversation. Meanwhile, I could focus on enjoying a much-needed meal after such a long day of travel, politely nodding when prompted, and sipping last year's sweet summer wine from the local vineyards.

*

The evening began well, and my culinary visions seemed not far off the mark. We crossed the canal to Proudfoot Manor – the may-or's house, which was warm and aromatic on the inside from an afternoon of cooking. Immediately, we were greeted by the gracious mayoress and a gracious staff that led us to a hot meal as grand as anything I could have hoped for. Dimly lit lanterns and scented candles on ornate chandeliers set the ambience. I had already helped myself to a fair portion at the mayor's table before being called upon to take part in the evening's dialog. I did not even notice the tension building in the air.

Now, Lord Mayor Otis Dagger was known to be a cantankerous and irritable sort, but Paplov was quite masterful in the art of diplomacy. As a councillor, Paplov was adept at building up a trusting relationship in short order, able to break the ice quickly and establish common ground. The way I heard him talk with people, I sometimes made the mistake of thinking he was catching up with an old friend when, in reality, he had just met the person.

As I heaped a second helping of greens onto my plate to "fill in the corners," the mistress of the household leaned forward from across the table, smiled at me and near whispered: "You carry the same look in your eyes as your mother did." The woman had the gentlest voice.

"You knew my mother?" I was caught off-guard by the mention of her. Most people avoided the topic altogether.

"Briefly," she said, "though I would have liked to have known her better." The mayoress looked at me with an intense gaze as she continued. "Your mother had a warm heart and bright eyes filled with wonder and excitement." One of her daughters smiled shyly at me from across the table. She had a simple, friendly look to her.

"Yes, she did," I said. "Thank you." I recalled the warmth most of all.

The mayoress straightened back into her seat and shot her burly husband a loving smile before sipping more red wine. That was when I noticed the mayor's stern demeanor, and that his wife's smile had been wasted on him; to reciprocate might have broken his face.

"Harrow wants the Malevuin Bridge dismantled for larger vessels to pass," the lord mayor told Paplov. "Stoutville too." He shook his head. His tone was harsh. "They already have us floating across on the Dim side."

"Oh?"

The Upper Malevuin Bridge was a landmark in the region that stood as a testimony to the town's pride and sense of accomplishment. Intricate and overdone in every detail, the bridge received enterprising parties from Fort Abandon and the Bearded Hills, plus business-minded travelers from as far west as Dennington, and in days past, the Star Sands. The Stoutville bridge, on the other hand, was simply practical, especially for farmers and ranchers with land on both sides of the river.

"Naturally, the whole town is up in arms," Otis went on. "And who will they blame? It could cost me the next election."

"Most certainly."

Mayor Otis scowled at Paplov's response.

My body tensed as I looked to the mayor. His anger was palpable. And as his irritation grew, my outward disdain for Harrow grew along with it. How Paplov could remain so calm was beyond me, especially considering his suspicions. Although he had been careful to keep any such mention of Harrow to a minimum over the years since my parents' disappearance, the topic managed to creep up every so often. For the most part, we had moved on with our lives, or at least we convinced ourselves that we did.

"Do you know what it costs to run a ferry?!" Mayor Otis raged. "And who wants to wait?! Let Dim Lake pay, I say!" Fists clenched, the toe of his shoe tapped loudly against the floorboards. "And the ferry that we do have is treacherous in the winter… treacherous." He shook his head, and as he did so, his shoulders dropped. He rubbed his forehead.

"What can I do?" he continued, deflated.

Paplov sighed. "Harrow takes what Harrow wants."

Otis nodded, but the common saying only added fuel to his fury. He grimaced when he spoke. "I was trying to say 'there is just no negotiating with Harrow'... before you interrupted!" The mayor's face became beet red and the tie around his neck looked so tight it seemed his head might pop off. It wasn't an interruption though. Otis had clearly paused long enough for Paplov to inject a comment.

"I apologize, lord mayor," said Paplov.

What? Paplov's not going to buckle under, is he? My head started to throb.

The mayor waved a finger at him. "And you're next, you know," he added. "Harrow has spies all over your bog looking for some damned ancient battleground. They'll do anything to find it. And what do you think will happen once they do?"

What? I had heard similar talk before, but this time it really hit me. A new anger arose within, and the implications of the mayor's heavy words bred like wildfire in my mind. Negative thoughts ignited and multiplied. Consequences pressed against my inner skull, and nearly split through it. The lanterns and candles all flickered.

"Is there a draft in here?" wondered the mayoress. She rubbed her shoulders to ward off the phantom chill.

Mayor Otis' words still hung in the air. As worked up as ever I've seen him, he lifted his right hand a few inches from the table and let out a controlled, yet powerful slam to the hardwood top. I didn't think his face could turn redder, but I was wrong. He became so angry he started to shake.

Paplov remained calm despite the seriousness of the matter, and looked about curiously at the lamps and the candles. His eyes fell back to the mayor and he looked the man in the eye. "How do you know this?" he said.

"A friend in Harrow, about our size," he explained. "He works in the entertainment and culinary industries – organizing events, catering and such. He hears things."

I could not hold my composure any longer. I thought of the vision: the torn up gardens, the fountains toppling…

"We can't just sit here and take it!" I said. "Why doesn't someone stand up to Harrow?" The words just spewed out – there was no way to contain them. But really I didn't want to contain them, and unfortunately for Paplov I didn't try to hide the disgust I felt in my expression either. He was about to roll over to Mayor Otis the way he rolled over to Harrow years ago.

"Nud! Mind your place," he said. In the midst of his interjection, the room went dark.

The women all gasped, followed by a long hush.

In good time, Mayor Otis rose from his chair. "A moment," he said. In near darkness, he fumbled for a match, lit a lantern, and adjusted its dial for intensity.

"Ah, good," said Paplov. In the new light, he shot me a stern look then turned to the mayor, who was in the midst of igniting the next lantern. "Please excuse my grandson; he is a bit off today. Clearly he is out of line."

"No, you are," I said. "Why doesn't anyone else see it? Harrow—" Paplov cut me off.

"That's enough out of you!" he said. "Mind your tongue or… or I'll… you'll… regret it."

I felt my jaw tighten. We glared at one another. I opened my mouth to speak, about to say something I would probably regret.

That is when the mistress of the household reached up and gently squeezed her husband's arm. Her head tilted slightly towards the mayor and when he turned and locked eyes with her, an unspoken kindness transpired between them. I swallowed the words on my tongue. Mayor Otis lowered his head and let out a loud sigh. He sat down beside her. The redness in his face began to dissipate.

"The boy is passionate, I'll give him that!" he exclaimed, "and with enough hot air to blow out all the lights. He'll make a fine politician some day." Everyone laughed. Everyone, that is, except for me.

Turning to Paplov, he went on: "But such words are easier said than done – something experience has taught us both."

Paplov nodded his head, "Indeed."

"I suppose they are one in the same with Harrow – want and take," the mayor said. "We were told to 'take it down your way or we'll take it down for you.' That was the negotiation."

Biting his upper lip, Paplov shook his head. "Harrow takes what Harrow wants," he repeated, "always has, always will. There is little anyone can do about it. Proudfooters will know that it isn't your fault."

Great, another excuse to do nothing.

The mayor nodded as he met Paplov's gaze. "Indeed," he said. Otis sighed and seemed to relax a little. He shook his head quickly – almost a shiver – several times.

Then Otis smashed the table again. His voice boomed. "Give up the swampland, Paplov, or we'll…"

"Give it up for you?" said Paplov. They both laughed. The comment made more sense when served with wine.

Mayor Otis raised his glass to Paplov, "Our negotiations will take a more civilized route, no doubt," he said.

"Certainly," said Paplov, raising his own glass to the mayor's.

And with that, all the tension between the two fizzled. But it would take more than a toast to drown my emotions on the matter. I reached across the table and helped myself to a pint of ale. Paplov chose to ignore my indulgences and I returned the favor by containing any further outbursts.

"I take it you have full authority in the matter before us?" said Otis.

"Of course," said Paplov. "I have been fully briefed and

empowered by our own lord mayor and council, and I have all the necessary paperwork to prove it."

"Very good." Otis motioned to one of his daughters. Paplov looked to me. I fumbled through his carrying bag, eventually producing the relevant documents. The mayor's daughter came over and I handed them to her.

Now I hadn't expected official business to be conducted over dinner, but with those words, the dealing began. Paplov and Otis filled and refilled their cups as they spoke of economy and risk, of present and future value, of obligations, balance, taxes, who had devoted what forces to the security of the Triland area, the upkeep of the trail, and the dibbing up of the many concomitant roles and responsibilities that went along with the simple leasing of a parcel of land.

I kept an ear to the conversation, but also made small talk with the misses and her three chatty daughters. The youngest acted very strangely. Giggling, saying weird things and making weird faces. The middle one wasn't much different. Both were pretty, but I tried to avoid topics that led to input from those two, which mostly resulted in some kind of teasing. Instead, I focused on sensible conversation with the eldest and the misses.

Eventually, the spirit of a deal was hammered out and the two diplomats stood up, wobbled, and shook hands. Otis steadied himself with his other hand on the back of Paplov's chair.

After a half-pint of ale and a generous serving of desert, I retreated to the mayor's study with Paplov and Otis where they worked out the finer details of the deal. I was responsible for recording and witnessing the agreed upon arrangements. The mayor's assistant performed the same duty. She happened to be his eldest daughter, several years my senior, and was the one who had sat across from me at dinner. All I had to do was listen, write, retrieve forms from Paplov's carrying bag, and quickly draft up any understandings settled upon, organizing their wine-soaked notions into coherent and well meaning sentences.

As negotiations drew to a close and we took to packing away our things, Otis' daughter – the assistant – made her way over to me, smiling pleasantly.

"Will you be joining us later tonight in the market square for the dancing and entertainment?"

That was unexpected. Apparently, not everyone was afraid to be out at night.

I wondered how I might avoid stepping on her delicate toes.

Oda was friendly, and she was not bearded.

CHAPTER XI

Good company

The journey home was cold, wet, and tiresome. I had been up all night feasting and dancing with Oda and her sisters. Paplov, too stubborn to call for a wagon, would never have made it all the way to the Handlers' Post without falling over. I carried everything.

Otis had warmed up to Paplov considerably after dinner, behaving like his new best friend before the night was through. They shared stories about all the deal making and underhandedness on the political scene lately, then raided the wine cellar and sang songs until daybreak.

Wyatt looked like a drowned rat by the time he dropped us off at home, past nightfall. Paplov and I were equally drenched. The lizard handler had met us nearly halfway to Proudfoot after we didn't show up at the post on time. He'd heard the same rumors that the innkeeper had passed on to us, and was worried we might present a tempting target for would-be thieves. Paplov tipped him generously and thanked him profusely.

I slept dead to the world that night and Paplov left me undisturbed. Mid-morning, when I began to wake, my feet and legs ached from the long hike and the soaked-in chill of the rain. When

I tried to move, my neck felt cramped from the way I had slept, my head pounded, and my shoulders were terribly sore and chaffed from all the backpacking. I wasted an hour or more just debating whether or not it was worth getting up to eat. Finally, I could no longer ignore the rumbling in my stomach. I rolled out of my night sack and lumbered to the study.

Paplov rested in his favorite chair sipping tea, slowly digesting a book and a biscuit. The tea was a special blend, steeped from young five-finger leaves picked just outside of Proudfoot before we left. Paplov claimed the remedy soothed his throat and eased his aches. He was still in his night robe. A heavy wool blanket lay folded over his lap. I slumped into the chair opposite him.

A few nibbles of biscuit and the occasional handful of wild berries were all he could keep down. We were due to hit the trail soon, so preparations had to start right away.

Paplov knew it too, and he sighed when he looked at me with those tired eyes. He stared for a long minute, as though weighing something within. Then relief washed over him, and without cause for concern, he bade me to gather the arrows made, my wits, and some good company. I was to get myself together, stop at Town Hall to file the land lease records, and take my leave come morning the next day. He insisted I make the journey to my uncle's cabin with friends this time, saying he wanted me out of the hut until his ailment ran its course.

"Fyorn's eyes'll light up like fireflies when he sees some fresh young faces for a change," he said. "I gather he's getting plenty tired of that ole coot he sees in the mirror every day, with only one other old coot's company to look forward too." Paplov began to laugh, but his laugh became a cough. He had choppy words of advice for me, and a request: "Give him my best <cough>; keep <cough> one eye <cough> on the water and the other on the treeline; and no <cough> laggards."

Paplov shut his mouth tight, filled his cheeks with air, and did his best to muffle an oncoming flurry of coughs. I took the opportunity to blurt out something that should have been said years ago.

"Last time I went… there was something not right about the forest," I said.

"Not right?"

"I thought it was a tree at first, but…" I trailed off. I didn't know how to say it.

"But what?" he said.

"It moved."

"Pardon?" he wheezed, trying to suppress the inevitable.

"It moved," I replied, "and not just a little. It came at me. It was gnarled and crooked, with jaws and teeth and…"

Red-faced, Paplov raised his hand, shook his head, and then began to cough-roar at the notion. The act cleared his throat, at least. His voice was scratchy.

"Oh really?" he said, swallowing. "Boogalies too? And did you hear the flip-flap-flopping of their floppy wet feet? Maybe they were in the trees."

"It wasn't like that," I said.

He cough-roared again, then took a long moment to regain his composure.

"Maybe you *are* having false recalls," he said. "One thing's for sure, Uncle Fyorn doesn't miss a beat, especially in his own woods. And he never, ever mentioned anything to me about talking trees."

"They chased me. I didn't say they could ta—"

"I meant *walking* trees… whatever <cough>. You just have a vivid imagination."

I didn't say anything, but the glance I made at my branded wrist tipped him off.

"That has nothing to do with anything," said Paplov. "Looks like a rash. Better get it checked out – the Diviner probably has an ointment or some other remedy that'll take care of it. Did you scratch yourself against something up in that attic?"

My eyes went wide.

"Yes – I know you were there," he continued. "Rashes can be stubborn. They can persist for years. Does it come and go?"

I shook my head. He took a closer look, and muffled another cough.

"That mark has been there just about as long as I can remember, so no worries. You know, I'd say it was smaller years back <cough>, but you've grown since. Your stubborn little friend probably just grew right along with you."

His explanations were ludicrous, but to pursue the matter further would be pointless – my grandfather had no real answers to offer, only mockery and half-disguised criticisms.

*

The rest of the day I spent at Webfoot Hall and that evening, I packed what I needed. At the hall, I met up with Old Remy and filed the lease records Paplov and Mayor Otis had agreed upon. He sat by himself in a cluttered corner of the administrative wing, stacks of paper and rolled maps strewn everywhere. He was the only one in Webfoot who understood the filing system, if you could call it that. The grizzled old Pip's head was unusually small and shriveled, with only a few tufts of white hair that sprung forth from the scalp. Frog-like, his bloodshot eyes bulged out of their sockets. He reminded me that Council would still have to sign off on the final documents before they would become valid. While I was there, I got to talking about mineral claims. Old Remy provided me with a claims map and the forms that I would need to stake a claim. He said I could have them free of charge, but I paid the normal fee anyway. He also said I would have to make my own claim posts.

Back at home while packing, I pondered the coming excursion. Going to Deepweald without Paplov just didn't seem right at first, but as night drew nearer the idea grew on me. It could be fun. I would combine my two trips into one. What could be better after visiting Fyorn than a treasure hunt? And maybe – just maybe – we could get a start on a mining claim.

I debated which cloak to bring and whether or not to bother with boots. I chose the heavier of my two cloaks, despite the fact that the weather was warming up. It would keep the bugs from biting through the material in the evening on our way home, and it would also show better to Holly. And oh yes, Holly definitely would be invited. I could only hope that Mer remembered to make that point clear when he passed on my message to Bobbin at the Flipside – Stout memories are so unreliable.

Boots… I hated wearing them. The return trip could be problematic though, with bugs nipping at my toes near sundown. I decided to carry a light pair in my pack. I hooked my bow in as well, unstrung, in case my uncle had time for target practice. I expected a lighter load on the return trip, since Paplov already had a full stock of deepwood. As for the stone that Mer had referred to as some form of light-emitting, ancient tree gum, I wrapped it in leather to hide the flashing and stuffed it into my pocket.

*

The next morning, I skipped breakfast to save time. Fully burdened, I made my way to Paplov's night chamber to bid him farewell. It was empty. I stumbled in the dark to the study, and found him asleep in his favorite wicker chair again.

Now Paplov would have never let me go to Fyorn's without him if he was not sick, and adding time for treasure hunting afterwards would have been a tough sell. Lately, there had only been time for work, one kind of training or another, and chores. It was suffocating. Not to mention the recent dangers to travelers that everyone was talking about. *This trip is freedom*, I decided, as I watched him in his sleep.

Paplov jerked when I touched his shoulder ever so lightly. In the dim light, the spittle that ran down from the corner of his mouth was barely noticeable. I spoke quietly.

"I'm off to Uncle Fyorn's now, OK?" I said. "And then some treasure hunting."

Eyelids pumping, Paplov turned his head towards me and murmured something unintelligible.

I took that as a "Yes," whispered a soft goodbye, and left him sleeping as I set out to town. And that is how, without so much as breakfast, I was out the door and down the road in no time flat. Making up the lost meal would be easy enough: plenty of wild forage could be found on the way, even that time of year – sour moss berries that had wintered well and bitter catkins, for starters.

I picked up Gariff along the way, already hard at work with his kin – it was a family business. His "Pops" liked to get out early and accomplish as much as possible "before the bugs woke up" as he would say. With both hands grasping the sturdy wooden handle of his shovel and leaning all his weight on it, Gariff's father spoke with a gravelly voice.

"Come to steal away my best worker?"

"I'm not go'in anywhere," said a cousin.

Gariff was in the midst of lifting more than he should. He couldn't even see over the blocks he was carrying. The stumble in his step didn't deter him. When he unloaded, he looked up at his father like a hound waiting to fetch. All he got was a lecture.

"Why didn't ya tell me earlier?" said Pops to his son.

"Never plan yer day around a Pip," said an uncle. "Don't ye know that?"

Gariff shrugged his shoulders. Pops rubbed the beard on his chin, thick and grey-speckled, then sighed. "There's no arguing that point. Ahh, go on," he said. "It's nigh summer. Just be back in town before dark. Got it?"

"Got it!" said Gariff.

"And bring Kabor wit'ya this time!" he said. I detected a hint of annoyance in his voice.

Gariff brushed the dirt off his shirt and pants, took his hat off to give it a shake, and then placed it firmly on his head. According to him, Kabor hadn't left the Flipside, so we headed there next to round up the other three.

When we arrived at the inn, we met round Bobbin first, who just happened to be tidying up the foyer. As Pips go, he was a bit of a novelty. In the right light, the splotches of color along Bobbin's neck matched the pattern of a devil's paintbrush, replacing the usual muted green or brown markings that appear on most Pips with a slash of red. Although a few years younger than the lot of us, he made up for that deficiency through sheer entertainment value and, being the only child of the more than generous Numbits, by virtue of the palatable benefits that extended to his friends. He habitually raided the kitchen on our behalf.

"Hello Nud! Hello Gariff!" he said as we entered. "Mer told Holly who told me all about the treasure hunt and the claim staking. Are we leaving already?"

"Right away," I said. "I have to stop at my uncle's first though."

"What?" said Gariff.

"Is he the important Elderkin you were supposed to meet?" said Bobbin.

"That's him," I said.

Gariff mumbled something under his breath.

"Where's Holly," I asked Bobbin.

"We don't serve holly here," Bobbin tootled. "The berries are toxic."

Gariff shook his head. "Here we go."

"Don't worry, *Loverboy*," Bobbin said to me. "I'll find her. She's excited about going. Give me two shakes to get some food together too. We have to eat, you know."

Loverboy? My face felt hot, flush. *What does he mean by that?* Gariff chuckled and Bobbin wore a goofy look from ear to ear.

"Shut up!" I told the Stout, and gave him a shove. It was like trying to move a tree stump. He turned to Bobbin.

"Have you seen my busy cousin?" he said.

"I didn't know you had one," replied Bobbin.

"Too busy for work, that is," said Gariff.

Bobbin stopped. "Oh, *that* kind of busy. I haven't seen him at all this morning. He's probably still sleeping."

The young Numbit ran out back to the cookhouse to pack as much food as he possibly could carry and also to find Holly, who was not in her room.

Gariff went to fetch Kabor, leaving me alone in the foyer.

It was too early for the breakfast crowd. The greeter's desk was vacant, the hearth gloomy and lifeless. Stepping into the great room, I immediately felt a sense of loss, as though I had just missed my own birthday party. The place didn't look quite right so empty, so calm. It was too quiet, and too tidy.

The floor had been swept and the tables wiped clean, and extra chairs stacked up to one side of the stage. Windows were open, but the fresh morning breeze could not hide the layering of smoke, ale-soaked wood, and scented hints of old clothes left too long in a pile.

My stomach began to churn. I couldn't stop thinking about Holly. I wanted to remember everything about that night, but only if it was good. *And what if it wasn't?*

Just then, Holly entered the great room, alone and carrying a book. She wore a loose shirt and a form-fitting skirt. Her lean athleticism struck me.

"Hello, Holly," I said. "You look good."

"Thank you, Nud," she replied. "And good morning, what brings you here so early?"

"Plans have changed," I told her, "We're visiting my uncle *and* going treasure hunting, all in one day."

Holly bounced with excitement as though her perfect wish had just come true. "We get to do both!" she exclaimed. "That's even better than what Mer told me." She went on to very specifically confirm that, indeed, we were to visit a real, bonafide Elderkin.

"What's his name?" she asked, ears pricked. Her olive eyes shone and her slender jaw hung slightly open with anticipation.

"Fyorn," I said.

"Fyorn," she repeated, "that's a nice name." She said it again musically, teasing out the syllables with inflection. "*Fy*-orn." Dreamy-eyed, she raised a hand to her chest and ran her fingers along the beaded necklace that she wore. It was the same one she had worn that night when I first saw her.

Holly granted me a mischievous smirk and a gentle shoulder nudge. Her voice was playful. "You tried to kiss me," she said outright.

"I… err… sorry. I don't even remember the part about kissing girls—" She cut me off right there.

"Girl-*ss*," she said, emphasizing the 's.'"

"I mean…"

Disaster.

"Great. How nice for you," she said. I don't think she really meant it.

"Humph. I have to put my book away." She turned to go.

"What book is it?" I asked, my attempt at damage control. She paused and turned her head, nose slightly in the air.

"Elderkin legends," she replied. "Your friend Kabor helped me to track it down. He is quite resourceful *and* good company. Does he ever mention me?"

That was *not* what I wanted to hear. "No," I said.

Holly shrugged and left me standing there alone again. I shook off my carelessness as best I could, and then took out the claims map to study more carefully than I had at the hall.

*

Gariff returned first, fully laden. His adventuring gear had already been packed and ready. Kabor followed soon after and then Holly, minus the book.

Gariff addressed me about the map. "What do we have here?" he said, peering over my shoulder. Kabor and Holly came over to have a look as well. As we went over it, I explained to them everything that Old Remy had told me.

"I can make the claim posts on the fly, no problem," said Gariff. "I just need to know what to put on them."

"Do you know *where* to put them?" I said.

Gariff scratched his scruff. "I have an idea. I can bang them in the ground where I think they should go, but Mer should be the one to verify that they're placed right."

"Do we really need him?" said Holly.

"Sure do," said Gariff. "Like I said, I know enough to get us started and I can make a few pretty good guesses... maybe, but a professional has to look it over. There's lots to know when it comes to prospecting, if you want to do it right."

Bobbin was taking his sweet time.

"NUMBIT!" Gariff's voice boomed, and then echoed back.

From the cookhouse, our well-rounded friend squeaked back politely. "Coming," he said. Moments later, he repeated his assurance: "I'm coming... just a minute..."

Bobbin's jolly red face eventually bobbed into the great room, arms fully laden with everything he would need – food. His pack was already so stuffed he could not close it properly. Holly approached him and began fussing with it. She quickly became frustrated with his lack of organization.

"Don't worry," said Bobbin. "It'll be a lot less full on the way back."

"Not if you fill it with Fyorn's maple candy," I said. His eyes lit up. Holly grunted as she pulled hard on the straps, sealing the pack tight.

"The last thing he needs is more candy," she said, her voice stern. Bobbin's face went sour.

Despite all the antics and minor setbacks, all were eager for an adventure that morning. We set out for Deepweald together.

It promised to be a fine day for travel – cool and foggy so early in the morning, but it wouldn't be long before the sun burned through the mist and a good breeze blew up. That would keep the bugs down and spirits up.

CHAPTER XII

Interlude - Some great thing

O nce, I was much like a typical flesh-bearer, awake at dawn and asleep after nightfall. But now that I am scaled and bark-skinned, sleep is more of a seasonal thing. So I have no qualms about carrying on after sunset and into the dawn, and all the next day again and the day after that too, if need be. The real night for me is long and cold and goes by the name of "Old Man Winter." Not to say that you will never see a Green Dragon about in the winter months – it just doesn't happen very often.

No worries then, plenty of time, everything will be recorded before its too late… if I hurry. All must be scribed before that ranger's perfect storm arrives. The winds are howling tonight; it's the fury from the east he's been waiting for so patiently, all through the fall. So many colorful leaves will be blown to oblivion if this keeps up.

You might recall that early on, one of the first comments I made was that this tale is "the beginning of the end for some great thing." I suppose all beginnings are the beginning of an end of sorts. What begins and never ends? – sounds like a child's riddle. Maybe that all eternal Time is not a bad answer, but even Time is so constrained. Then so must everything be… well, almost everything…

It is coming. I can feel the surge through my heartwood. In all the days I was my former self – my flesh-and-blood self – I believed this saga began with the coming journey, the outing from the Flipside that I am about to tell tale of. But now that I am tapped into the Hurlorn consciousness, and as I near the very end alluded to, I know better. This part I speak of next is more of a tipping point than the beginning of an end.

My involvement was inevitable, really, and integral to the progression of a cycle that I had no idea even existed. I had become an important cog in a great wheel without even knowing it. It's the little things that the Hurlorns seem to pick up on, the subtle ways that can make all the difference when you sum them all up. I am sure that the stubbornness of the Leatherleaf family played a crucial role, as did an engrained independence streak and an overwhelming sense of civic duty. The ability to negotiate a deal factored in as well. Contacts also had to be an indispensible part of the grand scheme. But more importantly, it was the interplay of these factors on the great undertakings of my time, hanging in the balance, that made all the difference, together with the right combination of means to adapt to whatever came of them.

As so often seems to happen in life, the chains of events loop in on themselves. In a sense, the beginning and the end are ever entangled. Recognizing such things for what they are is important to a Hurlorn.

CHAPTER XiiI

Friendly passage

Gariff obsessed over the prospect of buried treasure. He kept our wandering minds fixed on the "real purpose of the trip" as we made our way out of town. "Nevermind Fyorn," he told us straight away, and "Don't waste yer time on Elderkin fancy," whatever that meant. My personal favorite: "Save yer energy for diggin'." He spoke over anyone that tried to get a word in edgewise, which was unusual for Gariff. Not even Holly chose to take issue with him, which was unusual for one so contrary. Excitement bubbled into every word, every breath, and that was all before we even reached the gate out of town. Once beyond the tall, oaken arch, the Stout seemed satisfied to have said his piece. For a long stretch, I took simple pleasure in the sounds of our footsteps and the fading voices of wall guards as they chatted endlessly about town gossip and the weather. But Gariff wasn't quite done talking yet.

"Do you think we'll find the 'mother load' that old coot was talkin' about?" he started.

Kabor took him on. "Mer's a bit delusional," he said. A wolfish grin began to form. "Do you really think a bunch of frogs are sitting on a gold mine? I mean really, it's a *bog*."

"Not gold," Gariff countered. "A *ruby* mine. And why not?"

Holly set them both straight. "Put it together dimwits – it was blue sapphires. Don't you two remember?" She lowered her voice and roughed it up a little. "It's the sto-wo-wo-wo-wone of dest-tiny."

Mer doesn't sound anything like that, I thought, with a slight shake of my head.

"Whatever," said Gariff. He gave Holly a dismissive wave.

"It's not whatever," said Holly. "It's *blue frikken sapphires… blue sapphires… blue sapphires…* get it?" She flicked Kabor in the ear.

"Ouch!" said Kabor. "Why'd you hit *me?*"

"That's what you get," she said playfully, and giggled. Then she turned to Gariff. "Boggers and whatnot have been scouting the place forever. I see them all the time at the inn. Don't you think they would have found everything there is to find by now?"

"No," answered Kabor, on behalf of his cousin. "Take Nud's little mud hut, for example. He could be sitting on a stack of gems half a league high and he'd never know it."

"Wait a minute," I contested. "Which side are you on, Kabor? You can't be on *both* sides of an argument." I was convinced that he said that just to annoy me. "And I don't live in a mud hut. It's sticks and, well, *fired* clay."

"Cuz is right," said Gariff, "ya gots to know the grounds. Mer knows the ground better than most Stouts, and most Stouts know the ground better than any Pip, even if they've been rollin' on it fer fifty years."

Kabor chuckled. "And even if the Stout *is* a little delusional," he added.

Holly frowned, as if something not quite satisfying was on her mind. "I don't see why we should split equal shares with Mer," she said.

Bobbin, strangely silent since we left, suddenly spoke. His voice sounded muffled.

"We shoul'ge just share wi'sh everyone," he said. Bobbin was already snacking on a bun, thick with butter. No one minded his naive comment.

I turned to Holly. "It's more complicated than you might think," I said.

"Sure is," said Gariff, nodding in agreement.

"Mer knows the process and he knows the competition," I went on, "and he can help us secure the rights so there are no mistakes, no oversights, and so we don't get scooped. I'm sure Paplov could help us too. All we have to do is convince him."

"Would we be rich?" she said, eyes sparkling.

"If we get the claim staked right and the paperwork in on time, then maybe," I said.

"Look," said Bobbin, pointing up, "a sailboat."

We all looked up. Slowly, we came to understand Bobbin's interpretation of the soft boundaries of a sail and the puffy outline of a boat's hull, set against the true blue backdrop of the surrounding sky. No one mentioned anything for a long minute. We just stared up into the sky where the lonely cloud sailed on a chance current of air. My mind drifted right along with it, dreaming of untold riches. *I could finally get some answers*, I decided. *I could finally find out what happened to my parents.* I could hire an investigator. I could pay informants. I could go to Harrow and find the underlying cause of what happened to them. And if they were being held captive, like Wyatt had been for so long, I could have them rescued or campaign to pressure the Iron Tower into releasing them – shame Harrow in front of the whole world.

Holly broke my trance. "How long can we stay at Fyorn's?"

"Pffaaa!" protested Gariff. "Half an hour, tops. We have a claim to stake."

"Let's start by getting there early – well before noon," I said. "It's still a bit of a hike. That'll give us maybe three hours to visit and the same for treasure hunting and claim staking. We need to get back before dark."

"What?" said Gariff. "You're not pulling that one on me again."

"We'll see," I said.

Without warning, Holly darted ahead. "I have to run," she called back to us. The sudden need to burn off energy came as no surprise. A spontaneous run is something Pips tend to do from time to time, without rhyme or reason to it. A Pip in the middle of just about anything will just up and run, then walk for a time, then run again, and then walk some more.

"I can't run with you, I'm eating," said Bobbin, apologetically. He had just taken the last bite of bread and was already probing his pack for more.

"Hold up," I said, and started after Holly myself. She kept a tight stride and it took a minute to catch her, after which we jogged together. The waddling Pip and the two cousins in our wake continued along at a walking pace.

As Holly and I passed the first stand of old tree snags, she began to make small talk about life at the inn, huffing in between short sentences. The two of us eventually slowed down to a fast walk to better accommodate our conversation.

She had started off talking about the regulars she encountered on a weekly basis at the Flipside, and then turned her focus to our coastal neighbors to the South.

"And a good number of the merchants from Abandon Bay are very well-to-do," she said, "and some of the wildest partiers – they could go all night."

She paused. It was my turn to say something.

"Really," I said, trying to sound interested. Claims and riches still occupied my thoughts and I had missed most of what she had been talking about. I was at a loss for words. Then something struck me.

"Your necklace!" I said.

"Oh," said Holly. She placed her hand on her chest, feeling the necklace under her fingertips and looking down at it. "Do you like it?"

"Yes, I do," I replied, "very much." It looked a little too familiar. "Can I take a closer look?"

We both halted. Holly turned to face me directly. She parted her hair casually and leaned in so that I could see the necklace more clearly. But I felt awkward. The necklace – it hung quite low on her, and her shirt could be revealing when she took on a certain stance... that stance. *Quite revealing*, I told myself.

Holly, on the other hand, appeared to be completely free of any inhibitions whatsoever. So in the end, I just went with it. I stooped for a better look.

"Ahem... Ahh... Hmm," was all that came out as I studied the necklace – and her to a shameful extent – ever so carefully.

At first glance, the necklace appeared much like a string of pearls with a red and green leaf pendant. On closer examination though, it was as I had thought. Each bead was actually bell-shaped, which I recognized as the tiny flower and winter leaf of the leatherleaf plant. The dangling leaves on the pendant, of course, were the leather leaves themselves.

"Yep, that's it," I said.

"What is it?" said Holly.

"My mother had one just like it. Those beads look like they come from the leatherleaf plant."

"Yes, I know," said Holly. "They're quite unique."

"Paplov talks about her necklace sometimes," I continued. "He says my father gave it to her – 'Leatherleaf' being the family name and all. It was supposed to be a family heirloom. I also recall a set of matching earrings – crystal and sort of bell-shaped."

"I have never seen the earrings," said Holly, "but they sound nice."

"I'll buy you some if I ever see any," I said. I stood up straight and looked into her eyes. "Wherever did you find it?"

Holly adjusted her shirt and let her hair fall over her shoulders. "Well," she began, "I get to talking to lots of people at the Flipside. Do you know Councillor Mrello?"

Harrow's man, I recalled. I was not fond of Mrello. Years back, he held a grudge against my mother because she won the council position he had petitioned for, which was Liaison to Harrow, even though Mrello had managed to produce a written recommendation from the Iron Tower supporting his application.

"I know of him," I replied. "The braggart that's always spreading his money around?"

"He's the one," said Holly. "Some nights, he buys rounds of drinks for everyone in the Flipside."

"I bet he does," I said, a hint of disdain in my voice. *But with who's money?* I grit my teeth, and felt my face flush hot with resentment. *And why did he have a necklace just like my mother's?* I didn't like the possible answers. My family's past dealings with Mrello and Harrow all came back in a flood of memories.

When Paplov came out of retirement and returned to politics, intent on resuming the role he had once passed to his daughter, he made all kinds of accusations against the Iron Tower over her disappearance. After all that had happened, the Council ruled it a conflict of interest to keep him as liaison, and so assigned the position to Mrello instead. But Mrello was crooked and Paplov complained to the Council that the man lives well beyond his means and that the authorities should investigate his spending habits and dealings with the Iron Tower. That investigation never happened.

My blood boiled in frustration. My head began to pound like a beating heart. *No*, I told myself, remembering the strange things that had happened when I felt that same rush earlier: the stake flinging through the air at Kabor while we searched the bog body site, the door slamming on Paplov in the shed when he was holding an arrow up to his eye, and the lights going out at the mayor's house. *Something is happening; something is not quite right.* The sensation continued to build. *Not again.* I fought against the surge of emotions. I fought it and cleared my mind. *I don't want Holly to get hurt.*

I heard her voice. It sounded small and distant. She repeated herself.

"Is something wrong?" she said.

I snapped out of it. "No," I said, blinking. "I'm OK."

"It looked like you went into recall for a minute."

"No... not quite... not really," I lied. "Where were we... oh ya. How did Mrello get the necklace?"

"Are you sure you're all right? You look a bit pale."

"I'm fine," I said.

"Well then," she continued, "Mrello said he bought it in Harrow."

Could it be? I wondered. My mind reeled with the implications. It was almost a confirmation. I pressed my hands to my temples. I couldn't stay still. I started to walk. Quickly.

"Wait," said Holly. She jogged to catch up. "Nud, what is it with you?"

"Nothing. I'm fine," I said. "Why did he give it to you?"

"Well," she started, as if the explanation could go on all day, "he didn't really give it to me. He just *loaned* it to me. At first, I said 'no' of course – I didn't want to lead him on or anything, but he insisted there'd be no strings attached and I gave in because it's *so* pretty. He was hoping I'd just try him on for awhile." Holly covered her mouth. "Oops," she giggled, "I meant to say try *it* on – Mrello made the same mistake. And then—" I interrupted.

"What?" I said.

"Oh," she replied. "When he gave it to me he said, 'If you like it you can try *me* on for awhile,' and then he pardoned himself."

"I see." *Well that figures*, I thought.

I began to wonder about Holly and the company she keeps. Maybe I had been missing something about her all along that everyone else knew. I thought back to something else along the same lines that I had been mulling over; something I had heard about the Flipside that nagged at me. But it was more than just something I heard. It was something I knew tended to happen there.

Before I could speak my mind, Holly had more information to offer about Mrello.

"He's *very* nice," she said. "I always get the best tips from him and Fort Abandoners, and he has lots of fun stories to tell." Holly giggled again. "I'm not sure if he's married or spoken for, but by the way he carries on, I suspect not." Her comment opened the door to my doubts, and the way she said what she said just fed the unsubstantiated notions rolling around in my stupid head.

"Holly," I said.

Anticipation ripened her voice. "Yes, Nud. Do you want to look at the necklace again?"

I shook my head.

Words popped into my mind and spewed out of my mouth before I had time to think about how dumb they were.

"You don't work… *upstairs* ever, do you?"

Her eyes narrowed instantly. "Do you mean the dormer rooms?" she said. "With the *red windows?*"

"Ahhh…"

"What's that supposed to mean, Nud?"

"Ah… I mean—"

"I *clean* up there, sometimes."

"Ahhh…"

The Flipside serving girl had only one word to say about that. She made it good though. She made it sound like the last word she would ever say to me.

"JACKASS!"

Holly stormed ahead, leaving me to wallow in a sea of loneliness and idiocy.

I looked over my shoulder to see if the others had heard. *Of course they did*, I thought. Sure enough, all three had stopped dead in their tracks to gawk at us… me.

Why did I ask such a stupid question? My pace slowed as I pondered that very thought, until the others caught up. Holly eventually fell back to walk with the group as well, but from that point onward, there was always someone between us, and if not someone, an invisible wall of indifference. She made small talk with Bobbin and Kabor and all the while would not even look my way.

To break my isolation, I caved in and mentioned a few desperate words to Gariff, playing up our prospects. Relief poured over me as he got all revved up again. Gariff did all the talking for a second long stretch of trail. I didn't process a word of it.

*

In due course, we arrived at the last strip of corduroy road that would bring us to the trailhead. Bulging hillocks welled up alongside the trail, matted in grass. After rounding a scraggly patch of alders that grew out of one of them, we caught our first glimpse of the upgraded Handlers' Post. As we closed in, it became apparent that the compound was unfinished. I let out a deep sigh and couldn't help but shake my head.

"What?" said Gariff.

I rubbed my forehead and looked again. It was dreadful. *I will never hear the end of this,* I told myself.

"Oh," said Gariff looking to the outpost. A satisfying grin crossed his face.

The Handlers' Post appeared rickety and the newly raised walls were already leaning, truly a pathetic sight. The main "building" didn't even have a proper roof to speak of. On top of that, the doorway lacked a door and the windows were shutter-less – that much at least could be accounted for by the fact it was still under construction.

Holly smiled at a young guard as we passed. He was hard at work erecting a post. The guard was shirtless, wore no boots and his leggings only went down to his knees. A second guard sat on a log nearby and someone else banged away with a hammer inside the main structure, unseen. The young guard waved in return, sporting a friendly smile. He couldn't have been more than two or three years older than I was, with a fresh complexion, bright green eyes and short-cropped, sandy hair. Tall for a Pip, he seemed an easy-going sort. Near where he worked, a long spear, more for reach than for throwing by the looks of it, stood leaning against a wall that was itself leaning.

He called out to us. "Greetings," he said, addressing the lot of us. He sounded my age too. And very polite. "Are you good folks coming back this way later today?"

We all stopped, and Bobbin jumped in to answer.

"Yep," he said, but it was Gariff who took it upon himself to speak on our behalf.

"Yes, sir," he replied, "Back by evening."

"Will you be here all day?" said Holly.

"Sure will," replied the guard. "Where are you folks off to today?"

"Err… we're off to do some hiking in Deepweald," said Gariff. "And then we're off to Blackmuk Creek to… ahh…"

Kabor finished the sentence for his cousin. "What he means is… uhh… we're going to Blackmuk to catch some fish."

"Really sparkly fish too, yep, if you catch my meaning," said Bobbin. He winked at the guard, who then flashed him a confused look.

"Fish, eh?" said the guard, sounding suspicious. "Where's your fishin' gear?" he inquired. He rubbed his close-shaven chin and gave us all suspicious looks. Not *real* suspicious looks though – they were only for show... for jest.

"Something's a little fishy all right," he added.

"We use our hands," Bobbin interjected.

"A Pip might, but not a Stout," replied the guard, eyeing Gariff.

"He's so ugly, he scares them our way," said Bobbin, "...not much good for anything else."

Gariff raised one arm, backhanded, and shot the Pip a stern look of warning. The guard laughed outright.

"I'm the spotter," said Kabor.

"But your half blind!" said Bobbin.

"So let me get this straight," began the guard. "A blind Stout spots the fish, an ugly Stout scares it towards three Pips who corner the fish with their hands and try to catch it. Do I have it right?"

"Yep, that's about right," said Bobbin.

"You're missing one part," he said to all. Then he winked at Holly and flashed her a smile. The next part he said only to her. "You must charm the fish with your beauty to draw them in."

Holly returned a confident smile. "It's true," she said, and shrugged. "They like me, poor things. Sometimes I even feel sorry for them."

I didn't appreciate where the small talk was heading and I didn't understand why we were making up an elaborate story to explain ourselves to the guard of a muddy trail. It was none of his business.

"We're rock-hounding mainly," I told him straight out, "and a rock-hound doesn't just give away his best turf."

"I hear you," he returned, satisfied. "Now here's something *you* need to hear, so listen up. Word is there's been some trouble on the Outland Trail that we don't need here." He looked to Holly, concerned. "So, if you happen to be going that way, be careful."

Holly smiled shyly and then turned her eyes slightly downward.

The guard addressed the group. "And if you come back this way late, you *will* be given a mandatory escort. You may even have to wait for one to arrive. This is by order of the lord mayor and, well, he is covering our fee, so it won't even cost none to ya… but gratuities are more than welcome, of course!" He grinned as though he was joking, but anyone could see the obvious pitch in it for a little extra take.

I caught Holly feeling outside her pocket for a coin.

"Thank you sir," I told him, "but I don't think we'll be needing an escort. We'll get along just fine."

"It's *mandatory*," he repeated.

Holly smiled at the guard, nodded, and then turned to me. "Ya Nud, it's *mandatory*… do you know what that means?"

I tried to ignore the jab and addressed the guard directly. "We both know that such orders are never strictly enforced. Besides, no one that I know of has ever needed an escort before. That sort of thing is reserved for important diplomats or wary merchants, and is mostly just for posterity."

"Yep, that may well be true… but those are my orders and I plan on carrying them out," replied the guard, with a coy smile and a wink to the Flipside girl.

Bobbin, acting like a complete fool, started dancing about and singing.

"Let's go catch some sparkly fish,
Shiny, sparkly glowy fish.
We'll serve them in a crystal dish,
Snuff the spark and make a wish!"

That earned him a big shove from Holly that sent him flying. The guard broke out laughing.

"I think your big sister has heard enough," he said to Bobbin. The Pip looked confused for a moment, but chose not to correct him.

On that note, we bade farewell to the guard and veered off the main trail east to Deepweald, leaving behind the mire and the "Stick'n Twine Outpost," as Gariff aptly named it. Few travelers ventured that way, ever since a freezing over of relations with Fort Abandon – Gan's main ally and trading partner. The Elderkin, of late, mostly kept to themselves, and did not take kindly to uninvited visitors. I don't know exactly how Paplov and Fyorn became such good friends under such circumstances, but the old Pip seemed to be the exception to the rule, being a diplomat and all.

After a good hour-long hike, the wind rose up with a cruel bite to it. We quickened our pace and soon crossed into the cool shade of Deepweald, welcoming us with its sheltering trees. I kept to the middle of the trail, steering clear of suspicious looking branches and tree hollows – a habit I had gotten into. Trodding deeper into the forest, the woodland trail seemed more confining than ever, overgrown and in dire need of clearing. Drooping branches loomed above our heads and many trees leaned heavily into the trail or had fallen across it over the years. Twisting roots curled out of the ground and threatened to trip us up, but at least they remained still.

By mid-morning, we climbed a long, rocky hill that brought us into the woodsman's territory. An unseen crow sawed out a warning and announced our arrival.

CHAPTER XIV

A long overdue visit

Uncle Fyorn had hands as rough as pine bark and a grip like roots that could crush bare rock into rubble. He always extended that gnarly right hand of his to me first when I visited with Paplov, and my hand always hurt when he shook it.

I caught a whiff of smoke on the wind from his potbelly stove as me and my friends rounded the final bend of the woodland trail to his log cabin, secluded in the wild. With crossed arms and a stoic stance, tough old Uncle Fyorn was ready and waiting, as usual, garbed in his bushiest bush clothes. At first glance, he appeared exactly the way I remembered him – the unshaven lumberjack. But there was something different about my uncle that day. He was still long and spindly, with knurled limbs and a slim, solid trunk. Yet, as we marched over, he did not seem to tower over me quite as much as he used to. And his wild dark hair had grown lighter and longer over the years; now tied back and fully tamed, away from his face. And his face, inquisitive and kind, was the same as always, except maybe thinner, more tanned, and showing a bit of weather. Fyorn's eyes shone the same hazel-grey that always seemed to blend in so well with Deepweald, a gentle shade of the sentient forest. But one question lurked behind those all-knowing eyes. At last, I would have to own up to what I had taken so many years ago, and give him his long awaited answer. Well, a partial answer anyway.

As we neared, the woodsman acknowledged me with a quick nod, then addressed the group with a smile and a general "welcome" before greeting each of us individually. His thick, outstretched hands reached for Holly first. He held her hands in his with the grace of a duke and spared her the iron grip. Next was Kabor. A quizzical look came across the woodsman's face as he tried to make sense of the Stout's sideways glances, but he said nothing of it. He gripped Kabor's hand with unbridled enthusiasm until he saw the Stout's knees begin to buckle. Next was Gariff.

"Brothers?" Fyorn asked, looking back to Kabor and then to Gariff again.

"Practically," I said.

"Cousins," corrected Gariff. The burly Stout held his own against the woodsman's crushing grasp.

When it came to Bobbin's turn, the young Pip did not want to give up his hand.

"Hmm." The woodsman exchanged glances with Holly and Bobbin, rubbing his square chin. "Brother and sister?" he said.

"Practically," said Kabor, still massaging his hands.

"No!" said Holly. But she could not ignore the wanting expression that spread across Bobbin's little round face. "Well… all right. Sort of."

Bobbin chimed in. "It's complicated."

Fyorn extended his hand to Bobbin. "Put'er there," he said. "I promise I'll go easy on you."

Reluctantly, Bobbin obliged. Fyorn grinned widely as he gave him just a bit of a squeeze.

I was the last. Fyorn addressed me in his usual way. "Glad to see you, Sir Nud."

"Glad to see you too, Uncle Fyorn." I was no sir and he was no uncle, so I guess that made us even. I extended my right hand and braced myself.

"Sorry about… you know," I said.

He engulfed my hand in his and, while I winced and prepared for the worst, he simply shook it… on the firm side but otherwise normal, just like he would Paplov's. But when the handshake should have been over, Fyorn did not let go. A serious look came over him, and he raised his eyebrows at me.

"I… uh… got your message," I said.

"Then you must have something for me," he replied.

"I have your arrows."

"Is that everything?"

"You mean…"

"You know what I mean."

Holly was standing next to me. She whispered into my ear. "Nud, what does he mean?"

I shook my head. "Nothing," I replied, and waved her off.

"No," I said to Fyorn. "I don't know where it went after… it got away… I couldn't get it back."

Fyorn nodded his head slowly in understanding, then breathed in deep and exhaled with a giant sigh. "A most unpredictable thing, it is. Impetuous. Deft," he said, and left the matter at that. Satisfied, he released his grip on my hand.

That wasn't so bad, I thought.

"Paplov's under the weather," I told him, "so he mentioned to bring some company along for the trip… and I did. He said you wouldn't mind…"

"I don't mind one bit," he said to everyone. "The more the merrier." He turned his attention back to me. "I really hope your grandfather is back on his feet soon – all this rain lately is to blame, no doubt." My uncle shook his head and then made one of his many unique gestures. He pressed his top teeth to his bottom lip and made a sound somewhere in between a whistle and a loud whisper.

"Fvit-fwit," he said, gesturing towards the cabin with a double backwards flick of his thumb. "I was just finishing up an early lunch. Come on in and take a load off – the table is set. Cider's chillin' in the cellar and I just smoked a batch of specs this morning. That'll set you straight." Uncle Fyorn winked at me. "And there's maple candy, of course."

The woodsman stepped back and beckoned us to follow. Holly wedged in her first question. "How did you know we were coming?" she asked.

My uncle was quick to reply. "Well, that's easy," he said, walking beside her. "It was the wind that told me, and the birds that cry out and take flight, and the insects that scatter, and the chipmunks that run up the tree trunks. These woods are like old friends that take in everything that happens, and I happen to know these old friends very well."

Bobbin fanned the air in front of his face. "I know the sensation," he said. "The wind tells all when Gariff is coming too…"

The offended Stout shot the young Pip a scornful look.

"Just keep your own wind outdoors," said Kabor. "It's a small cabin." He looked to Fyorn, "No offense."

Fyorn acknowledged the comment with a humbled smile.

Gariff chuckled. "One who is constantly eating is constantly—"

Holly interrupted in her strict, motherly voice. "Boys!" she said, then shook her head. I could not tell if she was embarrassed or simply put-off by their behavior. She shrugged Fyorn an apology on their behalf.

The moment my uncle opened the cabin door a warm waft of dry air invited us in. We stepped inside. The space felt a bit more closed in than I remembered, and no less hot with its sturdy wood-stove on a low burn.

We had entered the kitchen, which was also the bedroom, the

dining room, and the living room all in one. Behind the door, we hung our cloaks on wooden pegs, next to an assortment of gear and outerwear also hanging there. Gariff and I set our packs down on the floor, next to my uncle's masterwork longbow tucked away in the corner. Bobbin shrugged off his own backpack as well. It already looked considerably less stuffed than when we departed from the Flipside.

"Nice place ya gots here, sir," said Gariff, sizing up the structure. "Simple, but practical… and solid built." He walked over to the kitchen table and gave it a knock. "And this here table, well, it will just about last forever." The slab of wood was heavily marred with stains and nicks. Five covered plates and five goblets were set on the table, along with utensils, one dirty plate, and one goblet half-filled with cider – all made of wood.

Kabor headed straight for the table while I scooped water from the woodstove's reservoir and poured it into the washbasin. All three Pips used it to clean up. Over the washbasin, a small window overlooked the path to the cabin. The late morning sun shone through the dusty glass, diffuse and skittery.

"Sit where you will," said Fyorn. "They're all the same."

Holly sat across from Fyorn's abandoned spot and I squeezed in beside her. We enjoyed fish with cider and maple candy. The specs melted in my mouth and the candy was sweet and fresh. Time and again, Fyorn made his rounds as we ate, walking the length of the table with a jug and topping up our cups with cider as we chewed.

Holly only picked at her food while the boys kept busy on their forks. As soon as my uncle sat down, she had a question for him. "Hope you don't mind me asking, but how old are you?" she said with a coy smile, as if charm could excuse such an off-the-cuff question.

Fyorn popped his last piece of fish into his mouth as he contemplated his reply. When he was done chewing, he asked her something: "How old are you?" he said, "if you don't mind *me* asking?"

"Seventeen," she answered.

"Sishteen," said Bobbin. A piece of fish slid out of his mouth and stuck to the bottom of his lip.

"Well, I'm *almost* seventeen," she said.

"Can I have some more fish, please, Uncle Fyorn?" said Bobbin. "This stuff is great! Tastes like meaty candy. We could serve it at the Flipside. Can I have the recipe too?" He looked to Holly. "Sixteen."

"You can have more fish," said Fyorn. "As for the recipe… it's a bit of an experiment every time."

Holly, slightly annoyed by the interruption, waited for Fyorn to continue – to get to her question. She studied him patiently, nibbling at the remnants on her plate. When it seemed as though my uncle might skip the topic altogether, she made sure to keep it alive.

"I hear that the Elderkin never die," she said.

"You are relentless, aren't you?" replied Fyorn, wearing a kind grin on his face.

She nodded, gazing up at him with sparkling eyes, her hair tousled from the wind. It fell onto her shoulders in waves of rich, reddish-brown.

"Mr. Numbit says I'm *really* good at finding people out," she boasted. "He says I make them feel comfortable, like someone they know, and for that they open up to me… and maybe leave a fair gratuity," she said.

"Well, Holly," said Fyorn, "I think your talent works quite well out here too – I feel quite comfortable and at ease." He snickered momentarily. "And you certainly are getting the scoop on things, with that attitude."

Holly smiled at the compliment. Fully captivated by the Elderkin's presence and the attention he gave her, even her eyes seemed to grin. She arched her back and leaned forward against the table, resting her elbows on it and cupping her chin within her palms. Her shirt rode up her back a little, revealing a lean torso splotched with dabs of muted green.

"As for your question," he continued, "unfortunately, we are all trapped in these decaying bodies. The Elderkin do not live forever. In fact, I've seen them lose their lives by the hundreds in the Outland Wars."

Fyorn lifted his goblet, took a swig of cider, and set it down again with a knock. "I'm afraid, Holly, that Elderkin are just like everyone else," he said, "except they found a way to rejuvenate – to renew their lives again and again, and live long."

Kabor interrupted. His knowledge of history impressed even me. "The Elderkin weren't the only ones to make such a discovery," he said. "The very same Men of Fortune Bay who banished the Elderkin for dabbling in such arts ended up doing exactly the same thing, didn't they?"

"Almost true," said Fyorn. "Sorry, what was your name again?"

"Kabor," said the Stout.

The woodsman sighed and rubbed his day-old stubbles. His look was ever rugged and wild, but when he spoke, his voice took on an air of sophistication.

"To give you a sense," he began again, "after the *Grey Revolt*, those who were exiled from Fortune Bay entered Deepweald and founded the Hidden City. With only simple, natural means at their disposal, they continued their outlawed studies and invented a way to pass longevity to their unborn children, although they themselves went to their graves just as their fathers did before them. As Kabor mentioned, others also learned how to cheat death to some degree, but it was for themselves and not their offspring, and at great cost. That, however, is another story."

Uncle Fyorn glanced to the small window above the washbasin before continuing. A narrow beam of sunlight slipped between the curtains to catch his eyes. In that brief moment, a bright amber ring burned around his pupils. He turned his attention to the Flipside serving girl sitting across from him.

"I hate to disappoint you, Holly," he said, "but rejuvenation does not apply to me. You see, I am only half-Elderkin. The full-blooded Elderkin, the *High* Elderkin who live in Gan, call my ilk *Wild* Elderkin. Most of us live in Deepweald. I am afraid that I am nearly as old as I look."

"You basically look like someone from Abandon Bay, in his middle years," said Holly.

"Interesting you should say that," replied Fyorn. "My father was from the bay area."

Holly seemed to be in danger of finding out more about my uncle and the Elderkin in one day than I had learned over the last ten years. It's not that I wasn't interested, or attentive... I just never thought to ask such things. Paplov usually did all the talking.

The woodsman leaned forward, placing his own elbows on the table and folding his hands together. Streaks of earthy brown and dark green stained the sleeves of his shirt. Heavy leather patches covered his elbows. He whispered to Holly, but we could all hear his words.

"One-hundred and two," he said, then pulled away with an apologetic grin. With gaping mouths, we all looked my uncle up and down, trying to see the age in him. He didn't look much older than Gariff's dad to me who, strong as he was, always seemed tired and overworked, with big black bags under his eyes. And he looked far younger than Paplov ever did – rougher maybe and certainly more weathered, especially now, but definitely not older.

"You really are an old coot then, aren't you?" I said, "just like Paplov says." We all laughed and shook our heads in disbelief. Fyorn offered a humble nod.

Bobbin and the cousins finished off the last bits of maple candy and slurped up the final drops of backwash remaining in their cups. I slipped some maple candy into my pocket for the trail home and then requested a few minutes alone with my uncle to discuss the business of the day. The boys were eager to do some exploring. Bobbin walked over to where Fyorn sat and thanked him for his courtesies. Kabor and Gariff thanked him as well on their way out the door. Holly lingered behind.

"Fyorn and I have some private matters to discuss," I told Holly, "town business."

"I won't tell anyone," she said.

"I know that," I replied, "but those are the rules. You don't want to get us in trouble, do you?"

"No," she said, shaking her head. She paused, let out a sigh, then turned to Fyorn.

"Thank you for the lovely meal," she said.

"It was my pleasure," replied Fyorn. "Now mind the woods and keep an eye on those boys. Make sure they don't stray too far."

Holly nodded, and then out she went, carrying with her the responsibility of "the older sister." I witnessed my friends racing to the creek before she closed the door behind her. My uncle and I sat alone at the table.

"Your friend Kabor," he started, "does he have *shadow vision?*"

"Something like that," I replied. "He has trouble seeing straight on. Don't let him fool you though – he sees more than he lets on."

Fyorn stood up and closed the window shutters, eclipsing the daylight.

"That or he makes up for what he can't see some other way," he countered.

"I suppose," I said.

After he sparked up a lantern, Fyorn looked to my backpack on the floor, and then to me. "How many arrows for me today?" he said.

"Oh yes, quite a few," I announced with pride. "And some fine ones at that. Two full score of arrows, plus another two."

"Scores or arrows?"

"Arrows." I shrugged and couldn't help but laugh over my next words. "I don't know why you need so many... you must miss a lot."

Fyorn brushed off the slight with a roll of his eyes and another rub of his stubbly chin. "That's something Paplov would say."

A long silence passed between us. "So, how was Proudfoot?" he said.

Uncle Fyorn listened intently as I spoke about our trip, the land-lease deal, and Harrow's meddling. He shook his head angrily when I mentioned Harrow's demands regarding the Dim River crossing.

"Unbelievable," he said, disdain in his voice. "Taeglin is a buffoon. He never listens to anyone."

I didn't know exactly what he meant by his comment, but I had heard similar rumblings before. "Yet the Council and all the neighboring territories just give in to his every whim," I said. "It's pathetic. No one is willing to take action."

"Action comes at a very high price. Unfortunately, Taeglin is a very powerful buffoon."

We both smirked.

"Have you heard about the raids in and around Proudfoot?" I asked. "There was a horrible murder along the Outland Trail. The entire town was buzzing about it."

My uncle nodded his head in acknowledgement, and then offered his own observations.

"Let Paplov know that Wulvers are not to blame. One of my Kith brothers stopped by on his way back from Whisperwood – the packs there are too busy fighting amongst themselves. But one of the nomadic Outlander tribes has set up camp on a tributary of the Elderkin River, northeast of Old Akeda. They're a nasty bunch – thieves, slavers, and worse... you name it. Apparently, Gorbag the Torturer runs the show – if you can believe that. I think he's been killed about ten times now. A new one just springs up out of their ranks to take his place, every time. They're the ones likely messed up in your raids. One more note: the Council might catch wind of a small band of Scarsanders that slipped past the border guards, last seen skirting the northern edge of the Bearded Hills. Tell him they don't pose a threat – just a few desperate runners, that's all. I doubt they even have the scar."

"What about in the bog lands?" I said.

"Nothing I've heard. Why?"

"No reason… just our blue-tail acted up on the way to Proudfoot."

"They can be skittish," was all he offered.

I reached into my pocket and felt for the bog stone, bundled in leather. Slowly, I unraveled its cover. A muted flicker of light spilled out of my pocket for an instant and lit up the space under the table. Fyorn didn't seem to notice. He had taken that moment to stand up. He drummed his fingers along the old wooden slab, as though impatient.

"Well then," he said, "now that that's settled, how 'bout you take those arrows out back, Sir Nud? I'll look'em over in a jiffy. I just need to tidy up a bit first, before the syrup hardens."

Before I could say another word, Fyorn got busy collecting dishes from our mid-day feast. *Later*, I decided, and then rewrapped the stone. I grabbed my pack and went out the door. *I wonder what I'll find out there this time,* I thought, as I made my way to the workshop. I took a deep breath and shook off the feeling.

Fyorn's shed was nearly as big as his cabin and just a few steps away. Paplov helped him to build it, many years ago. When I stepped inside, it was cool as the day and smelled of freshly stained wood. After setting the pack down, I casually glanced around the room. It was exactly how I remembered it: a workbench cluttered with tools and hardware, planks of wood neatly organized by size, big cabinets, and at the back, hanging animal pelts stretched onto boards together with paddles for his narrow river-crafts. Bins sat here and there, full of bits and pieces of just about everything, and an axe leaned against the wall behind the door. It was a very familiar looking axe… *the axe*, in fact. The nicks I made had not quite disappeared in all the sharpenings since; abuses to the blade were many.

I stood under the attic door in the ceiling and stared up. It, too, looked smaller than before – no more than a square manhole covered by a board with no practical way to get up into it.

I never should have ventured up there, I told myself.

The real world began to fade away…

CHAPTER XV

The attic

Tap… tap… tap.

I remember exactly the noise from the attic: crisp and regular, like fingernails on wood.

Tap… tap… tap.

With the back of one hand, I rubbed my itchy eyes. Winds howled over the rooftop as my vision slowly adjusted. The first thing I saw clearly was a lone sliver of light. It shone in from the outside through a vent in the wall. I tracked its course. Over distance, the light spread out into a luminescent sheet, igniting dust motes like silvery sparks as it sliced through the darkness.

The attic itself was a huge, stuffy mess. Dusty junk spewed from every corner: broken furniture and countless old boxes, cords and ropes all jumbled and knotted, boots with holes in them, a cracked wooden shield with a tree sigil, and as many odds and ends as possibly imagined.

Tap… tap… tap.

Where is it coming from? I waited, and listened, and waited some more.

Tap… tap… tap.

There it is again. The sound originated at the far end of the loft.

Tap... tap... tap.

Scratch... scratch.

I crept along joists and wriggled between rafters to get to the source. Along the way, I gripped the severed leg of an old wooden table and used it to clear abandoned cobwebs in my path. *A thousand spiders to make those webs*, I thought.

Tap... tap... tap.

Scratch... scratch.

I reached the far side. An old metal coffer occupied the space, illuminated by light from the vent. There were handprints on its dusty lid. The coffer had a caved in side-panel and a broken latch, black and pitted. The latch, it appeared, was just about the only thing in the attic not completely covered in dust. I took it in my hand with a firm grasp, and hesitated. It was cool to the touch. The sounds had completely ceased. *Does the thing know I am near?* Before opening it, with the table leg I tapped on the box.

Tap... tap... tap.

The attic remained silent. Then I scratched it with the edge.

Scratch... scratch.

I waited. All that came after was a dull and unsatisfying silence, like waking up too early in a strange house.

I raised the table leg high above my head, like a club. With the other hand, I undid the latch. Slowly and gently, I lifted the lid – just a crack – and waited. *Nothing.* I could hear my heartbeat from the inside. I could feel the tension pull every muscle taught. I stopped breathing, and lifted the lid a little higher... higher... higher still. My heart began to pound. *Still nothing...*

TAP... TAP... TAP.

"Aaah!" I yelped, and released the lid. I swung the table leg hard and pounded the lid shut, then scrambled back into a pile of broken old junk. My heart pumped wildly as I struggled to regain my footing.

But I did not retreat. Instead, I sat there on the pile of junk, waiting and watching with both eyes fixed on the coffer. I heard the wind gust up again outside, and then fall off into a hush-hush. Slowly, I regained my nerve and crawled back to the coffer. I took a deep breath, and flipped the lid fully open.

This time, a puff of terrible smell rose up, oily like old fish, but with an exotic tang to it. I held my breath and leaned over the coffer to peer inside. Forgotten things, broken and useless, were scattered about its bottom, and a sticky residue covered everything. A thousand dead insects were stuck in there too, and a precious few barely alive ones still tugging on their immobile parts. The tapping started up again.

Tap… tap… tap.

And the scratching.

Scratch… scratch.

Many and more unusual objects filled that coffer as well. These things I could not identify or even begin to imagine the purpose of. Some looked to be tools after some fashion. Others had fleshy surfaces with oily threads sticking out everywhere – bits and pieces of broken creations not wholly natural. And amidst the clutter and sticky mess of tar was a shoebox-sized container made of dark wood. It did not belong with the rest.

Tap… tap… tap.

Scratch.

Tap… tap… tap.

Scratch.

Tap… tap… tap.

Scratch… scratch.

It came from the dark wood box. The sounds were more urgent now.

It did not occur to me that I should just leave the box right where it lay. And it did not occur to me that history might one day paint a fairer picture of the past if only I did just that. The tapping intensified.

TAP... TAP... TAP.

The dark wood box was plain in its design and nailed firmly shut. Scorched onto the lid was a crude representation of the Hidden City of Gan – tall trees and high towers fronting a waterfall, and mist billowing up from its base. I yanked the box free from all the goo and stickiness underneath.

The box had a fair weight to it. My hands shook as I held it. I felt along the edges and found the lid to be tight fitting. Some kind of resin sealed it shut.

TAP... TAP...TAP.

I fumbled. The box dropped back into the coffer.

A long pause followed, and then the pattern changed.

tap... tap... tap.

scritch... scratch.

Submissive. Wanting.

tap... tap... tap.

scritch... scratch.

Like a cry for help?

I waited a long minute and took deep breaths to gather up my nerves again. *It can't hurt you,* I told myself. *Whatever it is, it's stuck in the box.* Hands still shaking, I pulled the box back out.

tap... tap... tap.

I did not let it go.

Box in hand, I made my way back through the attic clutter to the trapdoor, then with a loud thump I dropped down onto the workbench. A bucket went flying and my ankle twisted, but I held on to that box as though the fate of the world depended on it.

The tapping had stopped completely. I gave the box a slight shake. It felt like dead weight inside.

Then I heard a voice – Paplov, on his way over from the cabin. He sounded hoarse, his voice on the verge of loss.

"Nud?" he rasped, and then cleared his throat. He mumbled

something to Uncle Fyorn. I didn't hear all of it, but it started with "He better not be…"

Their footsteps drew closer.

"Nud, are you in there?" said Paplov. "We heard something crash. What are you up to?"

I tucked the box under one arm and slid under the workbench. Then I dragged Fyorn's big ranging pack in front of me. I heard a click as the door handle turned. Someone stepped in.

"We're going out to fetch some dead wood," said Uncle Fyorn. "Wanna come?"

I ignored his call, held my breath and kept hidden under the table. Whatever was in the box stayed quiet as well.

"I guess he's not in here after all," said Fyorn.

After they left, I snuck out of Fyorn's workshop. On my way out, I grabbed the hatchet beside the door. I'm not exactly sure why I took it. I guess I thought a hatchet might come in handy. It did… and it nearly got me killed.

CHAPTER XVI

An Elderkin perspective

"Nud?" called a small voice, like a whisper inside itself. The faint sound twisted its way through a paradox and fell like hissing rain, only to drain away.

I did not respond. I could not respond. How can anyone respond to something like that?

The door to the workshop creaked open.

"NUD?" This time the voice slammed my ears and knocked me out of recall. There was a moment of blurriness, vertigo. Solid hands clamped my shoulders tight. The spin of the world began to slow; the image began to clarify. A part of a face came into view. Borrowed from the here and now, my uncle's hawk-eyed stare met my own blank gaze. He was expecting an answer.

The arrows.

"I'm back," I said. "I'm here."

Fyorn knew all about Pip recall, so I didn't have to explain myself to him. Carefully, he let go. Once assured that I could stand on my own, he looked up to the attic door, then back to me.

I felt ashamed, too ashamed to bear his penetrating stare. I felt as though the incident had just happened, as though Fyorn had just discovered me cowering beneath the very workbench I now stood at. Not that such displacement is unusual after recall; it just caught me out of sorts.

I turned away and took a few casual steps as nonchalantly as a guilty person can, and made my way towards the backpack. My knees were shaking. Still half in a daze, I stooped over, picked up the pack and brought it back to the workbench. I undid the cord, without looking up. Lightheaded but determined, I hauled out the deepwood arrows and set them in front of my uncle.

Fyorn picked up one arrow and brought it to eye level. He peered down its shaft and gave it a quick bend. Next, he tugged at the feather fletching and wiggled the arrowhead. Then he rested the arrow on one finger and found its point of balance. Finally, he wrapped his hand around the balance point and gave the arrow a gentle shake, as if to gauge the weight of it. He made a satisfied "humph" sound followed by a satisfied nod. A subtle, impressed smile formed on his lips.

"Not bad," he said and proceeded to inspect a handful more the same way, with the same results. "Not bad at all. Straight, solid and well-balanced… that's what I need. I like the blending."

Still examining the workmanship, he hit me with an unexpected comment: "I see now why you have not returned in so many years."

"Pardon?" I said.

The woodsman's eyes shifted from the arrow to my arm.

"The Mark," he said. "When did you receive it?"

"The Mark?"

Fyorn tapped my wrist twice with an arrow, put it down, and then picked up another.

"Your wrist," he added.

"Oh *that* mark," I said. "It's nothing, really. Paplov says it's a stubborn rash."

"How long have you had it?"

"Since about… the last time I came here."

"I see."

Fyorn fingered through a few more arrows and lightly scrutinized each one with little more than a passing glance. He put what would be the last arrow to inspect down with the rest.

"Let me have a look at that," he said.

I raised my arm and exposed my inner wrist. The woodsman grabbed my forearm and held it steady, then applied that same examining look.

"How?" he asked.

"A tree's whipping branch hit me when I was running," I said.

"So you were running through the woods and you swung your arm into a branch? Is that what happened?"

"Not exactly."

"I didn't think so."

He released my arm. "It's not a rash, Nud." Fyorn pulled up his left shirtsleeve, but only for a split second. I could hardly believe my eyes. He too bore the Mark, and like mine, the symmetry of the pattern was so fine and intricate it could have passed as something inked in.

"Such strange ways," he said to himself, with a slight shake of his head, as though rejecting a bad idea. A moment later, he was back to his usual self.

"Nud, thank you for bringing me the seekers," he said. "The craftsmanship… masterful, as always. And thank Paplov too for me, would you?"

"Sure," I said. "And you're very welcome, as always. You do so much for us, to keep us informed."

"Did you make any for yourself?" he said.

"Not many," I responded.

My uncle scooped up half a dozen arrows in his rugged hands.

"Keep these for target practice. Next time you visit, I'll teach you a few tricks about archery. Deepwood has a special… quality to it. I'd do it now, but I don't like the idea of your friends running about with arrows flying through the trees."

"You're not *that* bad a shot," I quipped.

He frowned and handed the arrows over to me.

"I have something else for you to bring back as well," he said. And without a moment's delay, my uncle was off to the far end of the workshop where he kept his best stock. I tucked the arrows away while he rummaged through a large, wooden bin. A minute later, he was back with an armful of deepwood, neatly tied, which I stuffed into my pack until it bulged. I pulled the drawstring tight around those pieces sticking out over the top, and tested the weight. Although it was not overly heavy, with all the long pieces sticking out it would be awkward to carry. I felt my chaffed shoulders. *Still sore*, I noted. Pips hate burden, and I was no exception.

"I threw in two exceptional pieces of deepwood," said Fyorn. "Paplov will know which ones. The thick one with the big burl on one end is destined for woodcarving, and the other one… well… I am not sure exactly what it is good for, but surely he will find some use for it. I would throw in more, but your pack is a little on the small side."

I acknowledged with a nod and slung the pack over one shoulder. It dug into the tender skin there. Having finished in the workshop, we made for the cabin.

As I stepped out of the door, voices of child-like commotion filtered through the trees. And as I made my way along the covered walkway, Holly screamed.

Immediately, I tensed, but the soft echoes of laughter that followed soon put me back at ease.

Once back in the cabin, Uncle Fyorn and I got to talking again. Many small things he revealed to me as we put away the dishes that he had set to dry. Pleasantries aside though, I had a purpose to fulfill, and I'd spent half a day already just dancing around it.

The others could be back any minute. *To heck with the dishes*, I told myself. The time had come.

"You need to see this," was all I said. I walked over to the table. At last, I pulled out my bog stone, unraveled the leather, and placed my curious find square in the middle of the slab. My uncle's eyes lit up with the first flash of light, as wide as an owl's. He gaped in wonder at the trail of sparks that followed after.

"How... wherever did you obtain such a thing?" he said.

"Well," I started, "I was with Gariff on Blackmuk Creek and... well... I heard the wind blow up and a crow caw and... well... it made me look and then, well... I fell into a sinkhole full of bog bodies and... when I got out, this stone was just sitting there, caught up in some gnarly old tree roots, then –" Fyorn interrupted.

"Sinkhole? Bog bodies? Tree roots? What sort of tree roots? What did they look like?"

Remembering is one thing, describing, quite another. Fyorn seemed to get that.

"I was hoping *you* could tell *me* what it is," I said. And when I tried to answer his questions and describe the event more fully, I fumbled every word. The woodsman put up his hand to interject, his voice calming.

"Enough," he said. "Clearly, it was not chance alone that brought this fanciful stone to you. Nud, I can tell by the way it happened that there are *Wilder* forces at work here, and that it was meant to be... the Mark, the stone... everything – gift or bane, the *Hurlorns* have chosen," he said.

"Meant to be? Hurlorns? What are Hurlorns?"

The translucent gem flashed a trail of red sparks, on and off like a firefly. Fyorn fixed his eyes on it. His voice was telling.

"I do not mean to say that it was meant to be in the sense of the greater cosmos or the grand scheme of things, heavens no. How could I even speculate on such a thing? I mean it in the sense of what might be the next best thing though... a higher consciousness in our midst, but it is just out of reach for most. We do not tap into it… not usually, but it is no less there because we are naive."

His mystifying words might have confused even the Diviner. Fyorn read my puzzled expression like an open book. He let out a heavy sigh.

"I think it is time you learned something of Hurlorns," he said, "since they seem to have included you in their plans."

"Plans?"

"Yes, Nud, plans. Maybe 'designs' is a better word. Have a seat."

I took the middle seat against the wall and Fyorn took his directly across from me, the stone between us. He rested his elbows on the table and sat forward, hands folded together, his thick fingers marred by fresh nicks and old scars.

"Hurlorns are far more than just trees," he began. "That much is obvious. The sages of Gan have studied the most common sorts extensively: 'Sleepers' they are called. A holdover from the days when behemoths walked these lands and hunted them for food, it is generally believed that early Hurlorns were more like giant bugs than trees, slow moving terrestrial invertebrates that fed on swarms of insects and vegetation. They had no hope of outrunning or outsmarting the crafty predators that pursued them. However, over time, the early Hurlorns adapted. And they developed some interesting defenses nonetheless."

The light continued to flicker on and off intermittently as he spoke, with five or ten seconds of dormancy between every flash-stream, usually. It was becoming part of the background, part of what was normal.

"First off," he continued, "Hurlorns evolved ways to blend in with the forest by mimicking features of the vegetation they consumed – green and brown coloration and the ability to remain absolutely still, for instance. As time went on, they also developed ways to pass messages over distances and to warn one another of a predator's destructive path. The messaging became more complex over time, and the distances greater. Having become observant and thoughtful, Hurlorns began to record the knowledge they gained and share it amongst themselves so that any one of them could access the whole – the beginnings of the consciousness I speak of. It took millennia upon millennia to evolve the capability into what it is today."

"At some point, there was a kind of divergence. As the behemoths got better at searching, some Hurlorns became better at hiding, even taking on the physical traits of trees – exoskeletons like bark, appendages like roots and branches, long narrow bodies and even leaves of a sort. A portion gave up movement altogether – content to live out sedentary lives. Those ones are the Sleepers."

"Others, well, they continued to become smarter. It seemed to happen all at once, actually, according to the sages who look into the past through the natural record."

The stone flared up super-bright with Fyorn's last words, and then stopped just as abruptly. A long pause in activity followed, during which I processed what he was telling me. *The tree creature I saw was real,* I thought to myself. I had known it all along. No words passed between us until, finally, I broke the silence.

"How would the sages know all of that?" I asked, skeptical.

"Oh, they have their ways," said Fyorn. "Fossil records, for one. Perhaps brain cavity measurements, movement patterns – I do not know. I have to confess I cannot say how they disentangle the past to such detail, but I will say this: if given the luxury to study a problem for a hundred years, I imagine you might have a pretty good handle on it."

He certainly had a point. Another bright flare-up occurred... Fyorn waited for the flickering to teeter off, before continuing.

"When prodded, Hurlorns tell a different story of their coming, more myth than fact if you ask me, but if looked at the right way it pretty much matches up with what the sages are saying, although with a little more drama."

"Behemoths," I said. "What happened to the behemoths?"

"No one really knows," said Fyorn. "Perhaps their food outsmarted them."

I chuckled. "Why doesn't everyone know about them – the Hurlorn trees?" I said.

"Remember Nud," said Fyorn, "it is in their nature to remain hidden and to whisper secretly amongst themselves. You will never breed that out of them."

"Then why did a Hurlorn tree reveal itself to me?"

"You do not say 'Hurlorn tree,' Sir Nud… it's just 'Hurlorn,'" corrected Fyorn. "You can say 'tree' as well, if you like; that will not offend. They feel a close kinship with trees."

"Okay," I replied.

"Unless you're talking about *Spirit Hurlorns*, that is," he added. "They are totally separate… much more sophisticated… and 'trees' simply won't do for them."

"All right then," I said. "Are there any other kinds to worry about?"

"Only one," said Fyorn. "But there hasn't been one of those for… well… since I was about your age."

"What happened to it?" said Nud.

"The forest has many secrets," he explained. "Sometimes, the secrets are best kept that way."

He knows, I decided, *but for some reason he can't tell me, or won't tell me.*

Fyorn took a moment to confirm that none of my friends had returned. Following that, he stood up and casually strode over to the lantern to dim the light. When back at the table, the woodsman furrowed his brow as he watched the bog stone flicker on. Arms crossed again, he just stood there and drew in a deep breath, as though to speak. When the words came out, something in his voice had changed. He sounded different, more serious. For many and most, such gravity in tone would not be a strange thing. But for Uncle Fyorn it made all the difference. He had never been so completely earnest with me as he was in that moment.

"Nud," he said, "the Mark of the Hurlorn is something most often reserved for bearers of precious knowledge that the Hurlorns value, knowledge that must be preserved at all costs. It is received from time to time by great heroes and sages, and those that have performed some great service and proven their worth."

"I am no hero or sage," I replied, "and I am not sure who I have proven my worth to. I'm only fifteen and the aide to a diplomat of the smallest community anywhere."

"Fifteen," repeated my uncle, and then he raised one eyebrow. "Humph."

"You have a mark too," I said. "What *precious* knowledge do you possess that must be preserved?"

"Well Nud," he said, amused at the brashness of my query, "first you must understand that Hurlorns are known to mark their own as they see fit, and for the most part without any discernable rhyme or reason to it. Being obvious is not their way – that much I can vouch for personally. There are times though when, in retrospect, I can say that they saw something coming, and in their own way planned for it by selecting the talents needed to deal with the situation well in advance. I do not know why a Hurlorn chose to mark you, Nud. You are a most peculiar and unprecedented choice. I am sure the Hidden King would not approve, but something tells me he was not consulted. As for myself, the Kith are the exception. We receive the Mark as a matter of course to bind us to the Hurlorns and to our brothers who came before us. It is not so much for our knowledge of great things as for our services rendered. Our community is one in the same with the Hurlorns. We are joined."

The woodsman picked up the rough, amber-like gemstone. He wore a weighing expression as he observed it emit another series of flashes. I had seen that look on his face before when he spoke with

Paplov, discussing delicate political situations and wondering what to do without setting someone off. He seemed to be deliberating. Raising the stone to eye level, he rolled it repeatedly in his hand, the hand on the same arm that bore the Mark, and he examined each facet one by one. Then something changed.

Fyorn suddenly tensed. His eyes widened, like fear. His head jerked up, the vessels in his neck bulged, and he drew in a frantic breath. The lantern snuffed out completely as wood all around the cabin began to twist and creak – the floorboards, the walls, everything. I stood up. The light itself brightened, almost burning. The heavy table slid. And his arm… his wrist… the Mark there began to bleed. Blood trickled down his arm. He let the stone drop.

And it fell.

The next instant, a deeper darkness flooded the room with a chill like death in winter. I heard the stone clatter on the table. My bones turned to ice.

A long minute passed, and then everything went back to normal. Dim, yellow light spilled forth from the lantern, and daylight filtered through cracks around the shutters on the kitchen window. The warmth of the woodstove returned. And the mysterious stone from the bog resumed its usual pattern of flicker.

Fyorn held his wrist, blood dripping through his fingers and onto the floor. His breaths were heavy and quick. I ran and got him a washcloth. With a concerned look, he rolled up his shirtsleeve, took the cloth and wrapped it around his arm. I tied it for him, tight, then pushed the table back into place.

"Are you all right?" I said. I had never seen him so much as flinch before in all my life.

He nodded. "Everything is fine," he assured me. Fyorn took a deep breath and exhaled.

"What happened?" I said.

"I don't know really, Nud," he replied. "I don't know for sure.

It was like… it was like a ringing; a ringing that became stronger and stronger until I was ready to burst."

Carefully, slowly, he took his seat. I sat back down across from him, grabbed the stone and put it back in my pocket.

"I know what you mean," I said. "I felt something like that too – before. Like a buzzing in my head. Weird things happened."

"They will not stop happening," he said.

"Someone could get hurt. Should I destroy it then? Put it back in the bog? Give it to you?"

"It is not meant for me," he replied. "That much is clear."

"What, then?"

For a long while, he just breathed, without answering.

"Can I get you some water?" I said.

Fyorn waved off the gesture. Finally, he spoke.

"This is your dilemma to solve, Nud," he said. "There is no second-guessing the Hurlorns, so just do what you need to do." He rubbed his chin.

"Your friends," he continued, "they seem like a good bunch. Can you trust them to keep a secret?"

I wasn't sure how to answer that. I certainly did not want him to discover how careless I had been at the Flipside. I just nodded.

"Good friends are important in the world," he added. "May I see your stone again? Don't worry; I won't touch it this time."

I took it out and held it for him. He gazed at it – into it, more like, all the while applying pressure to his wrist.

"A natural beauty in the rough," he said as the next flurry of flashes lit up the cabin. "I have never seen anything like this."

"I will have to find out more in Gan," he went on. "Best to keep your stone under wraps for the time being. As I alluded to, I suspect there is a deeper meaning to all of this. On the off chance you happen to find any others, please do bring them here, to me, for safekeeping."

"Really?" I said, unable to conceal the disappointment in my voice. After all, we were planning a treasure hunt.

"If you are wondering about value," he said, "I am fully certain the sages of Gan will offer more than a fair price for such rare wonders, after determining exactly what it is you have found."

That works, I thought. *Gariff will like that – a guaranteed buyer already.*

"They might even cut and polish something like this to adorn the king's crown."

"I have it on good authority that it's some kind of ancient tree gum," I said.

Fyorn raised an eyebrow at that. "Ahh," he said, nodding in acknowledgement. "I am not completely surprised to hear that."

The woodsman grabbed my hand and closed my fingers around the stone.

"I do not know what more to tell you about this," he said, "except to say that what you have found is something unknown to Men. I can tell you something more about the Mark though. Of that, I have done my own collecting for my own reasons, as you have seen."

Uncle Fyorn laid his left arm flat on the table, slowly undid the cloth, and showed me his wrist. The bleeding had stopped. His mark seemed to spread out radially from mid wrist. On the dark edges that defined the boundary, green tendrils curled up and out, then dove sharply into his skin, as though the image had been stitched on. He wiped the area as clean as he could, then nodded at my arm.

I also laid my left arm on the table, the Mark fully exposed. Mine appeared faint compared to his. From a central axis instead of a point, pale dots with fractured geometry branched out in elaborate looping patterns that curled in on themselves, smaller and tighter until they disappeared. There were no tendrils.

"According to the archives in Gan," he explained, "the Mark

will grant you a choice at a time when choices do not exist, in true Elderkin fashion. You may choose, one day, to live among the Hurlorns – as a *Spirit Hurlorn* – or instead, pass on to whatever fate awaits you. It will be your choice. Those rare and unique Hurlorns who once walked the earth on two legs as you and I do now, who then cross over to become custodians of the forest, are the uncommon exception rather than the rule. They grow to become the keepers of our knowledge and history, captains of our forest guard, and may even become great leaders."

The idea seemed magical and wondrous.

"You mean... I can be a Forest King? A Tree King? King of Trees?"

"In a manner of speaking, but not so much a king. The King is in Gan, remember?"

I nodded.

"And there is no 'King of Trees.'" The woodsman shook his head and smiled. "Heavens no. But... in good time, among the Spirit Hurlorns one may grow to become *the Green Dragon of Deepweald.* I do not know how that happens."

"That's a myth," I said. I hadn't heard of Hurlorns before, but the Green Dragon was legendary.

Fyorn's eyes met mine in a steady gaze, his words unhindered by my doubts.

"And when the day finally comes to cross over," he continued, "your former life must be abandoned. That is the oath taken to receive the gift of renewal. There is no turning back once you decide to follow that path."

My uncle smiled and put his hand on my shoulder, then patted it.

"And one more thing," he said. "You can just call me Fyorn now. You are no longer a child. You do not need a made-up uncle."

I could not help but feel a little empty.

CHAPTER XVII

Interlude – The way around

What does it mean to wake up in the morning? Are you the same person that you were when you fell asleep? – of course you are. Your memories tell you so and your body is still your body. But what if one day you awaken in a body that is not your own and you still remember everything about yourself. Are "you" still "you"? Is that reincarnation?

I can't answer that yet. Little by little though, the pieces will come together. The recipe for Spirit Hurlorn Incarnation – or "tree-incarnation" for short – isn't something you just serve cold. You have to heat it up a bit, add sauce and spices, and then let the idea simmer for a while. Oh, how I miss a real meal cooked to perfection on a potbelly stove! As I said, it will all become clear, soon enough, in the telling.

You are probably wondering why I bothered to ask if there is such a thing as magic. Well, consider this: To take an incarnate form such as mine, you have to first perish… sort of… and then *transmute*. Magic didn't bring me here. It might look like magic and smell like magic, but it isn't magic – unless perhaps you're a savage. Then to you, magic is a good enough explanation. It's all you'll ever get out of me. Trying to explain more to a savage wouldn't be worth my time – precious time – a savage would never get it. But you're smarter than that, aren't you? Think about it. Magic would be kinder – like the good magic in faerie tales that wakes sleeping princesses and transforms animals and animated china back into the people they once were. Get those thoughts out of your head. It just looks that way.

Don't get me wrong – I am comfortable in my new form, or rather, "comfortable in my own bark" to butcher a common saying, but I have to say that I am not exactly sure what I am right now.

"Where does my soul reside?" – I can't answer that either. That's what really gets me.

"Am I still really me?" – yet another mystery to ponder.

"If not - who else could I be?" – well… no one, I suppose, to any observer apart from my former self. It all gets very confusing to my wood-warped brain.

Here comes the rain. I can hear it on the leaves. Wait… false alarm… that was only the angry front of a windy drizzle. Finally, our young storm is building! It's what we've been waiting for all along. Soon, I will have to forsake this grove and seek cover. Pardon any watermarks you might encounter on the coming pages.

CHAPTER XVIII

Treasure hunting

Before hitting the woodland trail, Fyorn aimed to deliver each of the boys another one of his famous handshakes. Pockets stuffed full of taffy, Bobbin lined up first. The woodsman hardly squeezed his hand before he squealed like a pig.

Kabor's hands were bloodied, so the two just bumped fists. "Hang in there," Fyorn told him. The Stout had taken a tumble while running through the bush.

Gariff challenged the woodsman by squeezing back with all his might. He twisted and contorted his body to lever into it, grunting ferociously. I don't think Fyorn even noticed. At least, that's how he acted. He even yawned and excused himself.

"Goodbye Sir Nud," he said when he got around to me. "You and Paplov should come by more often."

"Goodbye Uncle Fyorn," I said – a slip of the tongue.

"No need to call me 'uncle' anymore, right?" he said.

"Old habits are hard to break," I said.

"What?" said Holly. She had just stepped out of the cabin and into the conversation. She narrowed her eyes and shot me a sideways glance.

I shrugged, and sputtered. "I… ahh… well…"

"Humph," she huffed. "Well, Goodbye *Uncle* Fyorn," she said, and then gave him a gripping hug. "You can still be *my* uncle." I got the impression he was not completely comfortable with the idea.

Holly took a step back. "Is this the right one?" she said, holding up an old spotter's cloak. Fyorn had offered it to her for the trip back. In the evenings, conditions that time of year on the Mire Trail were either bug-free and cool or warm and buggy, with little in between. Either way, Holly was ill prepared.

"That's the one," said Fyorn. "It was made for someone about your size. Now, listen carefully. It's reversible. When worn one way it is a regular cloak, but wear it inside out and it camouflages – a simple redirecting of light to pass around you. There is also a melding quality... you will see. It usually takes young spotters a few weeks to get the hang of it."

Smiling, she draped it on. The dark material was light and flowy, yet strong, and with an unusual sheen to it.

"How does it look?" she said, and then spun around.

"Perfect," said Fyorn.

In truth, to my eyes the cloak seemed rather long for her and too thin to ward off flies. She donned the hood.

"Thank you Uncle Fyorn," she said in her best, polite Flipside voice.

As the woodsman waved us off, I felt small for not having come earlier. On my way down the path and away from the cabin, I thought to look back. I thought that maybe I should call out and ask him why he used to have a giant black spider boxed up in his attic. I did look back, but only to wave one last time. I turned to the path ahead and just kept on walking, silent. *The visit had gone well*, I decided.

*

The woodland part of the trail was hard-packed and rocky, but once we broke through the tree line and hit the mud flats, the going was softer. All three Pips meandered off the trail and squished their toes into the soft, cool mud underfoot. The Stouts stuck to higher, firmer ground.

Midday had come and gone and travel time alone would amount to a few hours if we kept a good sure-footed pace. That left half the afternoon or thereabouts for our search and claim staking. We would have to wrap up by early evening though, to make Webfoot by nightfall.

Holly began her chatter as soon as we hit the more open territory. I wondered if she had held her tongue on the notion that Fyorn would somehow hear everything she said as long as we remained in his woods.

"Did you see those high cheekbones and lean, chiseled features?" she started. "I could tell right away he wasn't related to you."

I shook my head. "Obviously," I said. "He's Elderkin."

"And those eyes… I could almost see the secrets behind them. So much inner strength… and thoughtfulness. He reminds me of Anexxander – Oh, you wouldn't know who he is. Anexxander is a woodland hero in one of the Elderkin stories I read."

I had no idea how to respond to any of that. I was glad Gariff interjected.

"Nevermind with all that Elderkin fancy now," he reminded her.

Fyorn's words at the cabin still clung to the back of my mind. What could be coming? What did the Hurlorns want with me?

"Holly," I said, "have you seen anything unusual at the Flipside lately?"

"Is this another 'Red Room' question?" she replied.

"No. And… sorry about that."

"All right then. Like what?"

"I don't know… any odd people or strange things, weird conversations maybe."

Holly smiled. "Really, Nud? You just described nearly everyone."

"True enough, I suppose." I tried to shake off the feeling.

After all, it could be that something completely different from what Fyorn was talking about is on the horizon – like finding the "mother load." That would change everything.

Before long, we had made our way to Blackmuk Creek, spilling out of a spruce bog just east of the Mire Trail. The watercourse wound ever southward, fed by crystal-clear headwaters cascading down a broad limestone staircase. The "muck" itself appeared sporadically as we followed its course, especially in areas where the creek bulged out into sediment rich holes, abundant in plant and insect life. After a short trek, we came to the site of the find. The woodland aroma of sodden leaves filled my lungs. Gariff led the way to the pit. I looked around. Something was not quite right.

"Are you sure this is the place?" I said.

"That's odd, coming from you," said Gariff.

"It's different," I said.

"Looks pretty much the same to me," he said.

"This is the same place we looked last time," said Kabor. He wasn't even wearing his glasses.

The Stouts were right – it was *mostly* the same. The pit had caved in some, the leaning tree had fallen over it, and the murky water had cleared a little, but it developed a green tinge. Wet leaves lined the sloping bottom, along with rotting branches and other forms of detached vegetation.

"It's the trees around it," I said. "These aren't the same trees. And the shape of the hole is different."

"Have you been into the barkwood again?" said Kabor. Everyone laughed. I wondered if that night at the Flipside could have messed up my recollection of the entire day as well. The fact that traumatic events were known to affect Pip memory also came to mind. I let it go.

"Just go into recall," suggested Bobbin.

"No thanks," I said. The whole bog-body experience was not something I cared to relive.

"I wonder if Mer made it here?" said Gariff.

"Look at the tracks in the mud," said Holly. "Someone's been here."

Kabor reached into his pocket and pulled out his specs. He put them on and gave the tracks a sideways look. "They're not all Mer's, that's for sure," said Kabor. "I don't know if any of them are. I'm no bogger, but it looks like Men or Outlanders to me."

"Well, no one's here now," said Bobbin.

We set our gear down near the creek. I pulled the stone out of my pocket to let everyone get a glimpse of it before starting the search.

"Can I hold it?" asked Holly.

Her request caught me off guard. I hesitated.

"I'll give it right back," she offered.

Despite my reservations, based on Fyorn's experience, I handed it to her.

"Careful," I told her, my voice overly alarming. "I mean… don't drop it."

Unless you have to. I watched closely as she cupped the bog stone in her hands, leaving only a small opening at the top to peer through. Everything seemed all right.

"The light gets brighter whenever you hold it," I said.

Holly looked at me with adoration. "Thank you," she replied, eyes smiling. Then I realized I might have just inadvertently complemented her. It was true though.

"That's weird," she said. "Look… it's gone steady now." Holly tilted the bog stone this way and that way in her hands. "And look, when I move it a little, the spark keeps to the edge, like it wants to go one way, but then it sort of hits the wall from the inside." Holly motioned to her left.

She opened her hands enough for me to see what was happening. Moving left to right, the spark hugged the left. Moving right to left, the spark would try to "catch up" to the left side.

"You're right… that is odd," I said. "Maybe it's like a compass, except it seems to like west better than north." There had also been times when it seemed to flash more energetically as well. It was all a mystery to me. She passed the stone over and I put it back in my pocket.

Gariff pulled out two shovels from his pack. He kept one for himself and lent the other to Holly. He passed Kabor a pan.

"Where do I dig?" asked Holly.

"That's up to you," said Gariff. "Before I dig anywhere, I'm visiting these outcrops here." One by one, Gariff pointed out three small hills where the ground was solid rock. "If Nud's bog stone is really ancient tree gum like Mer says, then it formed in the *ancient* landscape. D'em hills will tell me something about how it all looked back then, and just maybe where to dig."

"Sounds complicated," said Holly, a little deflated.

"I'm sticking to the creek," said Kabor. "The water already did most of the work for me – exposed areas and sand, like panning for gold."

"That might work," said Gariff.

"I like that idea," said Holly. "Nud, what about you?"

I thought for a long moment. "Tree roots," I said. "I'm going to look for exposed tree roots or ones that are easy to dig under, especially near the sinkhole."

"The one with the dead bodies?" she asked.

"I guess…"

Holly turned to Gariff's cousin. "Kabor, mind if I join you?"

"Nope. It'll be fun. I'll show you how to pan for gold," he said, "and old eyeballs."

Holly sent him off-balance with a hip check.

Bobbin's turn came next. He looked around and about, from the treetops to the ground. "I'm going to look under rocks," he said.

Gariff laughed.

Straight away, Bobbin stooped over and upturned a wide, flat rock. He pulled something from underneath with a bit of a shine to it.

"What's this?" he said.

"Give that to me," said Gariff, but it was Kabor who snatched it out of Bobbin's hand. He whisked it away to the creek.

With the rest of us looking over his shoulders, Kabor placed the item in his pan and washed the mud off, replacing the water as soon as it was dirty. After a few refills, when the water finally cleared, we could see that Bobbin had found a thin strip of curved metal, pitted and twisted out of its original shape. Gariff grabbed it. Piece in hand, he reached into his shirt pocket for an eyeglass that he had thought to bring along, much like the one Mer had shown me. He closed one eye and scrutinized with the other through the eyeglass.

"Old metal," he said, "pitting corrosion for sure. These boggish waters sure did a number on it."

"What is it?" said Holly.

"A bit of plate armor, I'd say," said Gariff. "A band from a... maybe a waist or hip fitting... broken away from the rest of it."

We all took our turns examining the piece, while Gariff explained what the original gear might have looked like. That got everyone's imagination leaping.

Encouraged by Bobbin's quick find, we all went our separate ways in search of more: Gariff and Holly with shovels, Kabor with his pan and thick spectacles, and me with a flat river stone for scraping and a good-sized stick for poking around in the mud. Bobbin carried his find around with him everywhere he went, overturning stones and pushing aside old logs.

We dug, poked and panned through mud, clay, and sand for hours as the day got hotter. We upturned rocks and dug around boulders and roots, and everyone tried sifting through sand on the banks. Many interesting stones were unearthed and even some plant and shell fossils locked in shale. Gariff found a few more bits of armor, including a visor, and a pitted blade from an old knife, its handle long corroded away. No one turned up any bog body parts, thankfully, and no one turned up anything like the stone I had found either.

All the while I searched, I pondered the relevance of our discoveries. It occurred to me that this could be the very site that Harrow was looking for.

Kabor eventually gave up on panning and came to join me on the grounds surrounding the sinkhole. I was near my limit by the time he arrived. Gariff, Holly and Bobbin had moved downstream to a fresh location and a similar looking formation, spotted by Gariff who has an eye for geologic detail.

"Be careful near the hole," I told Kabor. "The ground is quaky."

"I know," said Kabor. "I can feel it shiver once in awhile beneath me." He started digging, using his pan to scrape the mud aside.

"What were you and Holly doing at the market the other day?" I asked him, already in the process of overturning a large rock near the edge of the sinkhole.

"Buying books," he said, "Holly likes stories."

"What else did you do?"

"Nothing. Why?"

"No reason."

Kabor pulled up a roundish, fist-sized stone, rinsed it in the boggy water, and then tossed it aside. "There's always a reason."

I heard a stick snap nearby, a big one. I scanned the bog woods in the direction of the noise, but saw no movement.

"Did you hear that?" I said.

"Trying to change the subject?" replied Kabor.

"What subject?"

"Holly and me."

"No. There is no Holly and you... Is there?"

"Do you think she likes me?" he said. That annoying grin crept across his face again. "I think she likes me."

"What makes you say that?" I said.

Kabor just smiled wider and with overwhelming confidence. I hated it.

I pounded the ground harder than ever with my slate, grunting and growling with every thrust.

"Ahh!" growled Kabor as he slapped the back of his neck.

I looked up at the deer flies buzzing around my head and killed three in a row. That's the secret – to look up at them. They attack from the branches above and assume you are not looking.

"I'm done," I said. My arms needed a rest. "Let's get going."

"Did you hear that?" said Kabor. He wasn't talking about the buzzing.

I waited. Another stick snapped.

"Ya. I heard it too."

And another. "Who's there?" I called into the woods.

Kabor and I scanned the bank, but saw nothing moving. The Stout shrugged.

"You're right," he said. "We should go. No more of your stones are here anyway. Even if there were some, they could be a mile deep for all we know."

We soon abandoned the sinkhole and caught up with Gariff downstream, still digging alongside Bobbin.

"Find anything?" said Kabor, as we approached.

"Just one," said Bobbin. "But I let Holly find it. You should have seen her face!"

"A few odds and ends," said Gariff.

"Where is she now?" I asked.

"Nevermind Holly. Where's Mer when you need him?" complained Gariff.

"When I talked to him I thought we'd be here tomorrow or the next day," I said.

"Holly went to try her luck downstream," said Bobbin.

"I was just about to send her away," Gariff grumbled, "...the way she kept going on about Elderkin and all. She nearly talked my ear off. It's hard to concentrate with all that yapping."

"By the way, I found a stick in the ground," said Bobbin, cheeriness in his voice. "Gariff says we're in the clear because of it."

"You're lucky today," I told him.

"Yep," said Gariff. "Another claim post. They staked a property to the south. I already made four claim posts and I have a pretty good idea what territory to stake. It'll have to do 'til Mer gets here. And we'll have to pace it out so's we can mark it on the map fer 'im."

It was really happening. I looked to my companions and saw in them what I felt in myself – pure excitement. It lurked under every patch of earth we stood on, under every stone, at the bottom of the sinkhole, and hidden within the creek bed. Gariff promptly showed us how to pace distances accurately, to within one pace in twenty, and then gave us our bearings. We strode in giant-sized steps to our marks, checking, double-checking and cross-referencing with one another's positions as we went.

Bobbin and I mostly helped to set the posts, while Kabor sorted out exactly where to draw the boundaries on the map. It would be up to Mer to refine Gariff's estimate and add more posts if needed, and when the time came we would all help cut the claim boundary lines – blazing trees and cutting underbrush between posts. But only he among us, as a recognized prospector, could obtain the special metal tags needed and submit the technical paperwork.

Shortly after completing the task, Bobbin and I, eager to take advantage of the fair weather, made our way to a choice swimming hole nearby for a quick dip. Gariff and Kabor declined, as expected. I stripped down to short pants and dove into the cool, clear water where it was deepest. Kabor managed a seat amidst a cluster of egg-shaped boulders at the creek's edge where he could put away his specs, kick off his boots, and dangle his feet in the water. I knew he would never come in, but I'm sure he contemplated it. Hill Stouts and water just don't mix. Gariff, on the other hand, had decided to try out Bobbin's search tactic. He meandered along the shoreline overturning stones.

"Miss me?" called a voice. It was Holly. She had returned empty-handed.

"Claim's staked," said Gariff. Her face lit up.

"Oh good. I can't wait to talk to Mer about it," she responded.

"Watch this Holly," said Bobbin. He ran to the edge of the pool and jumped, backwards. At the height of his jump, the round Pip froze in a perfect nonchalant pose, as though he'd been resting up there all day in mid-air. At the last possible instant, he curled himself into a ball and barreled into the water with a tremendous splash. Kabor got soaked. Even Gariff put his hands up to protect himself from the spray.

Holly flung her cloak down on Kabor's rock, stepped along the creek to a spot where the bottom hadn't been stirred up yet, and then slipped underwater without so much as a splash. She swam over to where I was, and popped her head up. Soon, the swimming hole erupted in white water between us, with Bobbin joining in on the fun whole-heartedly.

Afterwards, laughing and refreshed, we set out to sun dry on a few boulders. As resting stones go, they were perfect, warmed by radiance and sheltered from the wind. We soaked up the last strong rays of the evening sun.

"I'm sorry we didn't find the 'mother load' today," I said to Holly.

"It's okay," said Bobbin, chewing on Uncle Fyorn's taffy. "I still had lots of fun. And now we have a claim!"

Holly rolled her eyes and smirked to herself. She lay on her river boulder, idly caressing the polished surface of a protected pool at her side. The caress became a sweep when she spread her fingers wide to stretch the thin lines of webbing between them.

Bobbin got up and brought his pack around to everyone so that each could grab a snack. Gariff had found himself a patch of shade away from everyone, but still well within earshot. He sat with his hat pulled down over his eyes, ready to doze off. Kabor continued to dangle his feet in the creek.

I sat up and leaned on one elbow. "Maybe there is only one of these in the whole wide world." I felt for the stone in my pocket and brought it out. It shone steady and brighter than usual, still hugging the left side.

"But if this spot is full of them, we'd be rich beyond belief," said Holly.

Kabor eyed the stone with a sideways glance, and then offered his own thoughts on the matter. "Even if there aren't any more bog stones here, there's still lots we could do with this spot. We could sell the whereabouts to a collector."

"Whoa," I said. It finally hit me. "We could sell it to Harrow. They're looking for the battleground where they fought the Jhinyari a long, long time ago. This might be it! They've been looking all over the bog lands and staking all kinds of claims."

"I can see where they might have went wrong," said Kabor. "The way the legend is told, you'd think it all happened in the middle of the bog. But there are deep pools right around here too, and it's all bog water. Maybe the Men from Fortune Bay skirted the edge of Deepweald and met the Jhinyari and the leviathan right here. It sort of makes sense – why go right through a bog where it's slow going and open, as opposed to along the tree line where there's hard ground and cover."

Gariff spoke up. "Are claims fer stuff like bog iron 'n gems different than claims fer stuff like swords and armor?"

"Not that I know of," I replied. "Some places do that, but not in Webfoot. You just have to state what you're going to pull out of the ground, and then pay a levy based on assessed value."

"We could be rich six different ways then!" said Gariff. "This is bigger than the mother load… it's the… it's the—" Bobbin interrupted.

"Grandmother load!" he said.

Holly's enthusiasm was uncontainable. "I'd take my share of the money and run away to Kel Faeriz. It's hot there all year long, and they are so sophisticated… with such lavish homes."

"Too close to 'the Scar' for me," said Kabor.

"You'd leave?" said Bobbin.

Holly shrugged. "What would you do Nud?"

Gariff answered, "We all know what Nud would do."

"Yep," Kabor interjected. "He'd be outta here. Where would you start looking, Nud? North to Dim Lake where they were last seen headed? Maybe the Western Tor. No one's looked there. You don't still have your sights set on Harrow do you? Only a fool would try that."

"I don't know where I'd start looking," I said, "somewhere like that, I guess. I can't wait to tell Paplov." I did not inform the others, but another plan had entered my thoughts. *Maybe this is just the sort of leverage Paplov needs to swing a deal and get my parents out, if they really are prisoners.*

Holly looked confused. "I thought you liked it here," she said.

"I do," I replied. "It's complicated."

"Great," said Bobbin. "So everyone would leave?"

"Not me," said Kabor. "I don't need to look for my parents. They're dead."

"Well, what would you do Bobbin?" asked Holly.

"That's easy. First, I would buy you that dress you were staring at the last time we went to the market. Then I would show you all the wonders of Webfoot so that you'd stay."

"All the wonders of Webfoot," Kabor repeated. "That shouldn't take long." He looked to his cousin. "Got a few minutes to kill?" Both he and Gariff laughed.

"Have you ever seen the bottom of Everdeep Pond?" retorted Bobbin. "Well I have. You'd never believe what's down there."

Gariff scoffed. "No one's been to the bottom. That's why she's *Everdeep*."

"I have," said Bobbin.

"Bobbin, you're the sweetest," said Holly. She stroked her hand through the young Pip's hair, then she gave him a big kiss on the cheek.

"Treasure's totally lost on you Pips and yer whimsical fancy." Gariff shook his head. "Us Stouts would put a fortune to more practical uses. That's fer sure."

"I would use my money to make more money," said Kabor. His scheming smile was back.

"It's getting late," I said, placing the stone back in my pocket. "We better head to the trail or we'll be mud-flapping in the dark." I sounded exactly like sensible Paplov. "We'll catch up with Mer first opportunity. That ole prospector gets around. Someone ought to have seen him – maybe the guards at the new post. When we find him, we can head back here with the right equipment, the right paperwork, and daylight to spare."

Bobbin packed the remnants of our snacks and finished off whatever he could stuff in his mouth. Holly and I put on our cloaks; then I grabbed my pack. Gariff upturned one last rock before departing.

I was the first to cross over to the homeward side of the creek. In the few waiting moments that I stood there, I pulled the stone out one last time to gaze at it. Curiously, the spark was still steady, but opposite.

"I guess it likes east better now," I said to Holly when she drew up beside me. I showed it to her.

She gazed into the light. "Some compass that turned out to be."

CHAPTER XIX

Stick'N Twine Outpost

L ate into evening, we finally arrived back at the "Stick'n Twine Outpost." Before long, the sun would descend upon the bog and our worries would double, if not triple. The site had already progressed, and now featured a manned gate that restricted access to the Mire Trail. In our absence, a thatched roof had been erected atop the hut, affording the guards refuge from the next rain – if it wasn't too serious a rain. Behind the hut on the east side, stables and a corral were in the works to accommodate more riding lizards. At the rate construction was proceeding, the crew might have something altogether functional by the end of the week.

The young guard that had caught Holly's eye on the way in was working hard, still shirtless and now swinging a sledgehammer. Noting our approach, he wiped his brow with the back of his hand and blinked from stinging sweat. He had been busy erecting a flimsy wall on the compound's west side, a "polite" security barrier to encourage travelers not to circumvent the gate.

The second guard – balding, middle-aged and well rounded – still rested on his log outside the hut, soaking in the withering sunshine. He seemed a little slow on the uptake and merely smiled dumbly at us. The third guard hammered away at a doorframe inside.

Leaning on his sledgehammer, the young Pip dolled out a sideways grin to Holly. Then he looked to our little round companion. He seemed eager to take a break and chat.

"Catch any glowfish lately?" the guard asked.

"Nope," said Bobbin, "we're sparkle free. And—"

Gariff was quick to cut-off Bobbin's revealing double-talk this time. "Has anyone left a message for us?" he said

"Like who?" said the guard.

Bobbin's quick tongue cut in before the Stout could answer. "Mer Andulus – looks and smells like Gariff here, 'cept older and not as sweaty. Mer likes sparkling fish too; wants us to show him where to find them."

Gariff folded his arms across his chest and drew in a slow, deep breath, nostrils flaring. He did well not to whack Bobbin. I know he wanted to.

"That ole rock-hound?" said the guard. "Sorry… not that I heard. Why? Was he supposed to show you the 'mother load'? That's all he ever talks about."

"He's the one," I said. "Can you give him a message for us, if he comes by?" I took out the map.

"A map? I don't see why not," said the guard. He called to the building. "Grof, did you hear that?"

"Yep," said a voice from within the structure. "They can leave it here."

I took out the town hall papers as well, which listed all of our names as partners in the claim, folded it in with the map, and then handed the bundle over. The young guard walked it over to his comrade on the log. Next, he looked to the empty corral, then addressed the lot of us.

"You just missed the handler," he said. "Wyatt set off with a load of merchants from Fort Abandon and he won't be back 'til morning. He's bringing us a fresh new load of sticks and twine."

The words stung my ears.

"Sounds about right to me," said Gariff, with a smug look on his face. Behind the guard's back, the Stout wiggled a nearby gatepost. It was tall and it moved easily, plus the wood was warped. Kabor stood in front of the post and tilted himself sideways to match its lean.

The young guard didn't seem to notice the Stouts' mockery. "It's nigh too late to cross on your own," he stated plainly. "As you know, by order of our own Lord Mayor Undle, I must insist that I accompany you back. Jory's the name."

"Pleased to finally make your acquaintance, Jory," said Holly, with a coy smile and a gentle handshake. Her wrist bent up ever so slightly. Jory's gaze met hers, and he held her hand longer than necessary. Holly could pass for an older teen, and she knew how to greet people and make them feel at ease. Not only did she give Jory her name, but Holly told him where she lived, her occupation, and went on to invite him to the Flipside for a free barkwood. The rest of us introduced ourselves in turn, with flat words by comparison.

Gariff pressed Jory for more information. "Why all the fuss?" he asked. "Is there a problem on the trail?"

"Nope," he replied. "Not unless you believe in the Boggyman. Truth is, I'm just sore all over and I'd rather sleep on a warm, comfortable bed in Webfoot than be stuck out here in the mud with these fly-bitten oafs." He waved a hand behind him at his fellow guards.

The guard on the log continued to smile dumbly. The one in the hut leaned out of a window and shook his hammer at Jory. He had thick white hair, cropped short, and his eyes were wide and round. He reminded me of a great gray owl.

"Did Undle really make that order?" said Gariff.

"Sure did," Jory replied. "The only exception being those who are judged capable of defending themselves… and that ain't yous."

Bobbin puffed out his chest at that, in jest. It only served to make him even rounder. Kabor imitated Bobbin. As far as I could tell though, it just looked like the Stout was standing up straight for a change.

"Is it thieves from Proudfoot?" I asked, recalling the innkeep's comments and Mayor Otis' concerns.

"Sounds about right," said Jory. "I haven't seen any signs of them myself though, so I'm sure it's just precautionary. Orders is to escort travelers and be on the lookout for anything suspicious."

For the most part, such "town orders" safely can be ignored without consequence, but with Holly keen on Jory we had no choice but to accept the guard's offer. Jory went into the hut, gathered his travel sack of belongings and tied it to a stick, located his pot helm and hung it on the end. He also took a canteen, which he sipped from often, and a horn that he fastened to his belt. And of course, he grabbed his long spear.

"You're in charge, Grof," he said to the 'owlish' guard inside.

Grof poked his head out of a window.

"I'm already in charge, Newt!" he spat back. "Don't get lost."

Jory laughed him off and shook his head, smiling.

"You're lucky," Grof added. "I'm letting you off easy today; tomorrow you'll pay double! Be back by dawn or I'll have yer hide."

We turned our backs on the trailhead and began the trek home.

I have to admit, Jory was pleasant and interesting company. He displayed practiced manners and had an easygoing way about him. It all made sense once I learned that his father was from Everdeep and his mother grew up in Watergarden. The first leg of the journey went quickly on account of all the stories Jory had to tell about strange sightings in the bog, people disappearing, and ghosts that drifted in the mist. On our side, we kept the day's events out of the conversation: meeting the Elderkin, Holly's cloak and the search for sparking – not sparkling – crystals. None mentioned the bog bodies, although at one point I was about ready to open my mouth and spill the story. I never had the chance to.

CHAPTER XX

The ruse

We were halfway to town and Jory was nearing the climax of yet another bog horror story. Gariff looked as wide-eyed as I had ever seen him. Bobbin and Holly hung on his every word. Our guard had a way of holding back the telling in such a way that you couldn't stop listening if you tried. Gariff had become his biggest fan on this journey, topping even Holly's enthusiasm. Maybe all the attention Jory was getting was the reason Kabor and I hung back, both hooded and pretending not to be overly interested. But for me, there was another reason.

"Kabor, I—"

"Shhh."

"I think something is following us," I said anyway.

Kabor shot me an irritated glance. "It's just the bog stories. You're as bad as Gariff. Now shut up. He's almost done with it and we're missing the ending." His voice became pleading. "The ending's always the best part."

There was no dismissing instinct though, even despite the fact that the telltale signs, like the usual snap of a twig, or footsteps, or wildlife scattering, were all absent. It was the little things that made me suspect we were being tracked: a soft shuffle in the rushes that didn't quite fit with the wind, a shadow seen out of the corner of the eye, a small splash. And then there was the gut feeling. The gut feeling sums up all the other little ways the mind opens up to the world that the conscious self doesn't even know about, the things that can't quite be put to words. Any one of the more subtle signs could be ignored, but together, and with a gut feeling on top, they could not. That would be foolish.

Finally, over Jory's talk, I caught the sound of an undeniably peculiar stir in the rushes off the trail. It was not alarming at first, but it was not the natural sort of rustling that a bird or a small animal was apt to make either. The sound was too quick-paced and there was something about it... a soft shaking trying to be loud, perhaps. I stopped and pricked my ears. The noise ceased. Kabor, hiking beside me, noticed the sudden change in my composure. He grimaced and followed my example. The others kept on ahead.

I whispered to Kabor. "Did you hear something?"

"I think so, that time," he whispered back.

For a brief moment, we stood in the middle of the trail, eyes searching far and near. On the horizon, the pale violet sky warned of the coming of dusk. Jory's voice still floated back to us, but suddenly it seemed half-empty. The mossy silence and stillness of the bog soaked up the other half.

At the end of Jory's story, Gariff made a loud gasp, followed by a nervous laugh. Bobbin and Holly groaned and guffawed. Kabor gave me a disappointed look – he hadn't caught the last of it.

In low tones, an unfamiliar sound began to build. It rose from underneath the chatter like a growing moan. It rose and filled the still, boggy air while the laughter of my friends turned uncertain, and teetered off. Then, without warning, the moan shot to the height of a decapitating wail. If pain had a voice, it would sound just that way. My ears hurt to hear it.

The group ahead shot accusing looks back to us. Bobbin was smirking. "Funny, guys," he said. "You can stop now."

But it was not us.

Kabor and I turned to scan the waterscape behind us: between the hummocks and the hollows, the grey standing dead wood and the hillocks crowded with alders, there were many places to hide.

"It wasn't them," said Holly.

Something slapped the water farther ahead, just off shore. Then another long and dreadful moan from behind us made my heart pump wildly. I watched and waited. *Silence.*

"It's probably just a fish," said Kabor, "or maybe a muskrat."

"A fish?" I was astonished. "How could it possibly be a fish? Do fish moan? It's NOT a fish."

"I meant the splash," he said.

Jory fixed his eyes on a grassy mound near where the splash came from. "I don't see how it could be a muskrat either," he called back. "Maybe some kind of bird though… or a big frog. I know a story about a giant frog—"

"You go first," Holly interjected, "I don't want to walk right into it, whatever it is."

Jory nodded. "Right… I'll scout up ahead a bit." Spear readied, he moved forward, alone. All eyes were on him. That left Bobbin with Holly and Gariff, me with Kabor, and Jory on his own: three positions spread over about ten paces, or fifty feet.

While Jory was off poking his spear into large, grassy hummocks, a crackled old voice called from behind, soft and muffled. The voice had a motherly quality, but there was something off about it, something wickedly off. I shivered as though touched by winter's chill.

"Over here l'il young'ns… ya, ya. <gurgle> I gots som'emm for you… I do, I do."

Against the dark blue of a freshly twilit sky, the silhouette of a hunched-over woman rose from behind a large, grassy clump, just beyond the trail's edge. She was not five paces from where we stood. Her bent frame stood head and shoulders above the tall rushes. Gariff came to join us right away as me and Kabor peered into the off-trail dimness.

"Who is it?" said Kabor. "I can't see." He reached into his pocket and pulled out his glasses. He put them on and gave the woman a sideways look.

The woman waved her long and bony arms at us to get our attention, as though not sure we had seen her. Long dark hair fell in loose tangles past her shoulders. Scant woven rushes were her only discernable clothes, barely concealing a waif body.

She beckoned us over. Gariff and I took a few steps closer.

"Are you hurt?" called Bobbin, from quite far back. He clung to Holly's arm.

"Yesums, yesums," said the woman in the bog, "but I'll be just fine now. I gots som'emm for you... I do, I do."

Gariff and I inched closer, Kabor a step behind.

I whispered to the cousins. "Can you see what it is?"

Gariff shook his head. I looked back to Kabor. He mouthed a "No." I saw Jory in the background. He had planted the butt end of his spear in the mud, and was fumbling for something at his side.

"What's going on over there?" Jory said. "Is everything all right?"

"Someone's here," replied Holly. "A woman."

"Be there in a minute. There's something..." Jory trailed off.

I turned my attention back to the woman in the rushes.

Bobbin called out to her. "We don't need anything, but thanks anyways." He sounded genuinely concerned, even sympathetic. "You shouldn't be out here on your own at nightfall. And you'll catch a draft if you don't dry off. It'll be pitched black before you know it."

There was no response.

"It isn't safe. Are you hungry?" he added.

Soaking wet, by rights the woman in the bog should have been feeling cold and plenty afraid right about then. Her sunken and shadowed eyes pleaded for compassion.

"Robbers gots to me, hurts me… <gurgle> they did, they did. They stoles everything. They even stoles my clotheses… ya, ya."

The woman in the bog hacked and coughed for a few broken moments, then cleared her throat. Her voice was raspy next she spoke.

"Only grasses for me to wear now… ya, ya, and I sneaks around in the water to gets away, I did, I did."

I whispered to Gariff. "If everything was stolen, how could she possibly have something for us?"

She heard. "Something special… ya, ya. Something special no one could *ever* steal."

The way she moved didn't look right. Every subtle motion came with an off twist or an unexpected jerk, and the surrounding rushes dithered with a dragging sound underneath, as though snakes lay coiling at her feet.

"Come into town with us," pleaded Bobbin. "You can have my cloak. We have a guard." He still played the gentleman, but just the same, he reminded her that we had protection. *Smart.* "You'll be safe with us," he added.

"Safe? Guard? <gurgle> Do you now… hmmm?" she said. Even in the falling darkness, she could not hide her sly smile.

And just like that, as if on cue, we heard another giant splash up ahead. We all turned to look. Then came a thrashing sound from the same direction, a muffled gasp, and the rushes jittered sharply.

Holly's shrill voice cut through the tension. "Jory!"

She grabbed Bobbin's arms, frantic. "Where's Jory? I don't see him anywhere!"

Something moved in the shallow water. For a long minute, I watched and waited as the disturbance came towards us, whipping reeds in its wake. Then it stopped.

Holly's voice rang out over the bog once more. "JORY!"

There was no response.

The woman in the grasses called to us again. She'd moved in while our attention was elsewhere.

"A little closer this way comes... ya, ya," the woman now begged, "come be safe with me... ya, ya. I'll protects you now, li'l ones."

Up close, we could see that the demented old woman was dripping wet and naught but skin and bones. Her hair was a tangled mess of mud, reeds and half-decayed twigs. But for an instant, I saw in her expression something youthful and pure, and there was something steady and unrelenting about her eyes. I took another step closer.

The Stouts stood their ground.

"That's right... ya, ya," urged the woman, "closer... closer." She opened her arms, her meek chest scantily clad in her roughly woven half-shirt.

"Protect you... I will, I will." Though the old crone's face was largely hidden in shadow, her eyes gleamed in the twilight. Arms wide, she invited me in to her embrace.

Gariff lurched forward and grabbed my arm. "We need to get out of here," he said. "*Now.*" He pulled me back. "Something's not right, Nud."

I felt hazy. I tried to walk towards her, without knowing why.

"Stop!" he boomed.

I shook my head and came to my senses.

Gariff pleaded with me. "That thing... it... she must be a bog queen... just look at her! She'll pull you under!"

Kabor was quick to agree. "Gariff's right Nud! Don't go any closer!"

"What's a... a... a bog queen?" asked Bobbin.

"Don't worry <gurgle>," the woman's voice called out again. "No worries for brave l'il Pips like you... no, no. No worries for

Stoutsies either," the woman assured us. "No worries for the l'il childrens... no, no."

"Something's on the road!" Holly screeched. Two hunched figures had stepped out of the darkness ahead, and onto the trail. Holly and Bobbin backed away.

The two newcomers planted themselves in plain view, blocking the trail where we last saw Jory. There was still no sign of him. Only the occasional ripple of water told me something still lurked in the deep pool.

The two figures ahead of us were also women, in the manner of the first: old crones, crooked and decrepit.

One of the two misshapen hags – taller and more hunched than her companion – cleared her throat three times before she spat onto the trail. Her shoulders bent in so drastically, they nearly touched one another. She spoke in a raspy gurgle.

"Give us something. <cough> Yes... give us a present for the Shadow in the Water, and <cough> we'll take it down with us, down, down to the gardens, for safekeeping, yes."

The hunched woman coughed, then spat, then coughed some more and had a coughing fit. When her throat finally cleared, the hag lifted one scrawny arm and pointed a boney finger at Kabor.

"Or maybe we'll take YOU," she said to the Stout, and then shifted her arm again, slowly. She pointed to Holly next. "Or YOU my l'il princess... you, you... take you where you can be safe, in the gardens."

The first hag, the one in the grasses, whined, shrill and accusing. Her body twisted and contorted as she scolded the others. "No, no... you fools, you FOOLS... you were supposed to wait. WAIT, I said." She sighed heavily and threw her arms down in despair.

Holly and Bobbin slowly backed away from the two hags to join the rest of us.

The hag who had not yet spoken opened her mouth to add

her piece. Only a shapeless gargle came out. She coughed and spat and heaved and gurgled and spat again. She shook her head and, finally, the words took form.

"What have you gots for us, l'il Pipses?"

I mouthed the word: "Thieves." I felt strangely relieved. The cousins heard me.

We all moved into a tight group and looked to one another. Bobbin checked his pockets and shrugged his shoulders at Holly.

"Come'on, give them *something*," said Holly. "Then they'll leave us be." She started searching through her pockets. Holly was trembling and her face was white.

"You're right," said Kabor, calmly, "we should give them something, whatever we can."

The two hags ahead of us whispered to one another, inaudibly.

Gariff took control. "Hold on," he called out to the whispering hags, "just give us a moment to collect our things." Stout level-headedness prevailed, despite Gariff's earlier fear of the mere *legend* of the bog queens. Strangely enough, he was actually more together when confronted with the real thing. That was his strength.

"You have to give Jory back," said Gariff. "Show him to us first, or you're getting nothing but a fight."

The lone hag writhed and twisted and gurgled in the rushes. I felt a light spray on my cheeks when she spat at us.

"Oh… give back?" said the hunched-in hag up ahead. She chuckled. "Hee hee… no, no, silly l'il ones."

"Silly, silly," said her companion. She wore a ridiculous flower that hung loosely from her hair. It was old and decayed, just like her.

Gariff kept us on task. "OK pipsqueaks, what'cha got? My pack has two small shovels, a clay jar, a pick-hammer, spare clothes… damn! My compass is in there too."

"I have nothing," said Bobbin, "We ate everything I brought…

see." He opened his pack to prove it, and then made a sick face as he glanced down at his ballooning stomach.

Kabor felt his pockets. "I have some change from the market and the stone Nud gave me, and..." Kabor pulled his knife out slightly.

Keep it, I thought. I couldn't say it straight out though, for fear of being heard, so I just looked at him and mouthed a subtle "Shhh." He closed his fist around the knife and slipped it back into his pocket.

"What about you, Holly?" Gariff asked.

"Well," she replied, hesitantly. Holly undid her necklace and passed it to him.

"What else?" he said.

She winced and felt at her side pouch. "I have a... I have a..." She searched and searched. "I have a brush, but I doubt they would use it."

"The cloak," said Bobbin.

"Don't be a fool!" snapped Kabor. "A thief with a cloak like that would be unstoppable." I cringed, fearing they heard every hushed word. Kabor didn't stop. "Holly, just turn it insi—"

"Shush!" I said.

Holly nodded her head and then handed the brush over to Gariff. He fumbled and dropped it.

"Let's put the loose stuff in your hat, Gariff," Kabor offered, "since you'll be handing it over anyway."

"Huh?" Gariff seemed a little taken aback by the suggestion, and I am sure he debated the offer internally. But with the hags waiting and the midges swarming, there was no point delaying any longer.

"Come on Gariff, we don't got much else," urged Kabor. "They might like it."

Gariff grit his teeth, took his hat by the rim and gave it one last farewell look before passing it around for the offerings. "I suppose... I guess you're right," he admitted.

Holly picked up her brush, wiped it on Bobbin's shirt, and placed it in. Then she pulled a clip out of her hair and dropped that in as well. Kabor's change jingled as he allowed each coin to slide out of his hand and into his cousin's hat. He took off his glasses and dropped them in as well.

"No way!" said Gariff, a little on the loud side. "D'ya know what Pops paid fer those?"

Kabor squirreled them away. Gariff just shook his head.

Bobbin put in a crust of bread after all. He found it at the very bottom of his pack. The hat still looked more empty than full though.

"What about you Nud, don't you have anything to offer?" asked Holly. "Stuff is practically spilling out of your pack."

"I have some wood... but what value would that be to them?" I said.

No one even suggested that I include it. There was also the short bow strapped to my pack. In the dark and unstrung, it was likely to be overlooked. I did not offer the remaining deepwood arrows either, for fear it would tip them off.

Satisfied we had given our all, Gariff called out to the hags. "We have your present, a REALLY good present... yes, yes... really good indeed, but you can't have it until you give us Jory... no, no."

The two hags blocking the trail exchanged confused looks, and then faced back our way.

Finally, the hunched hag replied. Her statement was abrupt.

"Him's gone," was all she said. A sinister grin crept across her face.

Her companion jerked her head to a sideways tilt. "All gone," she repeated, just as abruptly. She sounded the parrot and acted the bubbly clown.

The hunched hag shook her head slowly and spoke. Her face

was disfigured as well. "Him's not comin' back… no, no. Not from where him is."

"No, not comin' back, him's not," the other repeated.

All three cackled hysterically at the notion.

Holly scanned the trailside nervously. "What do you mean he's not coming back?"

"What did you do with him?" said Gariff.

"Us?" said the hunched hag.

"No. Not us," her companion assured.

Holly called out: "J-O-R-Y!"

The hags found Holly's antics amusing in the most sinister way, and a voluminous cackling echoed through the bog that evening. When the parrot hag finally regained her composure, she lifted a horn to her mouth and gave it a little toot, smiled, then tossed it aside. It was Jory's. The two hags ahead of us looked to one another and cackled madly. The parrot hag became so excited she fell over and rolled on the ground in a bout of cruel laughter.

Gariff turned back to us. "Let's just give them what we have and be done with it," he said. "Maybe we can't save Jory, but we can get out of this and send for help."

"They'll do the same to us," pleaded Holly.

Despite fears for the worst, we put the last of our belongings into Gariff's hat, but kept our pocketknives. Gariff snuck the rock pick out of his pack and stuffed it under his shirt. I kept the SPARX stone tucked away, the bow strapped to my pack, and Paplov's deepwood.

With slow, cautious steps, Gariff made his way towards the two hags on the trail ahead. Holly, Bobbin and Kabor stayed put, and I hung back to keep an eye on the other hag amidst the grasses, quiet as she was.

With an outstretched arm, Gariff offered them the hat and its contents. The two hags did not budge, so he ended up resting the offering on the ground in front of them, along with his pack. They watched with eager eyes.

"Here you are," said Gariff. "That's all we got that's worth anything… and you can keep the hat." He backed away.

The hunched-in hag looked into the hat and kicked it aside. "More. Need more… ya, ya, you gots to give us more." Then she spat in the hat.

"More, more" said the parrot hag, dead flower swaying with her stringy hair. She sucked back a huge glob of phlegm. She too spat in Gariff's hat.

Gariff flushed. "But that's all we got," he said through his teeth.

"Them's won't do… no, no. Won't do at all." The hunched-in hag shook her head and crossed her arms until it looked like they were on backwards. She looked to her partner who began shaking her head in unison.

The hunched over hag pointed to the reeds. "The Shadow in the Water won't let you pass… won't let you pass, he won't."

"More, more," said the parrot hag.

It was the hag in the grasses that spoke next. "The l'il girlsies," she started, then waved her hand at Holly *and* Kabor. "We want the l'il girlsies – that's all."

Kabor leapt toward her and raised his right fist. "Girl! Who are you calling girl you demented… swamp thing!"

Under different circumstances, the look of disgust on Kabor's face might have been humorous – a contorted blend of terror, disbelief and embarrassment, all rolled into one.

"I'll take *HER*! Take *HER*!" said the hunched hag as she raised her hand to Holly.

"HER, HER," mimicked the parrot.

"She pretty… she is, she is. Take her… ya, ya. Pretty for our garden beneath the moss." The hag in the grasses agreed.

Gariff gasped, "That's it! They are bog queens!"

"I'll take the other girlsie," the hag in the grasses continued, pointing to Kabor, "not so pretty though… a shame… ugly. Fix her up nice I will, ya ya, really nice. Take time, it will, she'll look pretty like the rest. Pretty pretty."

Kabor drew his knife. "I say we skin'em all. We can do it – there's five of us and only three of them."

"Wait Kabor, STOP!" pleaded Holly.

Gariff drew his pick. "I'm with ya, Cuz!" he said.

"No Kabor," pleaded Bobbin. "There *were* six of us, plus there's something in the water, that makes at least *four* of them, maybe more."

"Then stay out of the damn water," said Gariff.

The hags had finally grown tired of their ruse. Perhaps it was not quite working out the way they had hoped it would. The time had come to collect. Morbid playfulness at an end, the trio succumbed to their primal urges. In the battle that ensued, we found out that there is definitely more to hags than their old crone guise might suggest.

The hag in the grasses commanded the others. "Take 'em all… down, down. Save the li'l children… we will, we will." She looked directly to me. Her voice wilted. "Let me save you," she said. "Down, down deep to the safe cool waters. I must save you, my child, my promise."

That was all I could endure. The five of us clustered, standing back to back. The Stouts held their weapons defiantly. Bobbin brandished a butter knife. Holly picked up a stick.

I made a sideways glance at the quivering ball of flesh at my side, then at his utensil.

"Seriously?"

Bobbin shrugged.

I considered assembling my bow, but it would take too long to unhook from my pack, string, and then gather the arrows together. And I did not draw my knife as the boys had. Instead, it was the words of Fyorn that played back in my mind about the light of the stone, about the Hurlorns, and about the wise Elderkin. And how the Hurlorns had chosen *me* above all others for reasons even he did not understand. Was this to be the end the woodsman spoke of, as foreseen by trees? In my mind's eye, Fyorn's voice rationalized everything.

The Mark does nothing for the path ahead, but at the end is another journey waiting.

Those trees must know something we don't.

So, I let things happen the way I thought they must have been meant to happen. I reached into my pocket and pulled out the bog stone, the gift of the Hurlorns. I held it high, in full view of the crooked hag in the grasses. A spark of light flared bright for an instant, bright enough to be seen clearly by all. The light flashed and danced beneath the facets of the stone. I held the sparking stone in a manner so bold that anyone watching might have thought it to be a great weapon, and that it would flare up and strike the foul creature down. I truly believed it would do *something*. I believed in the mysterious power of a glowing hunk of ancient tree gum.

It flickered, as usual.

"Nud, what er ya doin'?" Gariff was baffled. "That won't do anything."

"Mine! All mine... MINE! I loses it!" cried the hag in the grasses as she dashed at me, reaching out for the stone. "My l'il one."

Knives flashed and Gariff's pick rose to halt her advance.

"I know what I'm doing," I said.

"You've got to be kidding. Put that thing away and take out yer knife! Are you daft?" said Gariff.

"Throw it away!" said Holly.

The hag in the grasses erupted in a hoarse shriek: "Give it to me!" She shifted back and forth, her gaze ever on the crystal.

Then she looked me in the eye, her voice full of ridicule.

"Listen, listen l'il pipses. Hear the children's whispers, ya, ya. *All the saved children like to whisper.*"

I heard the whispers. My heart froze.

The parrot hag repeated the words stupidly: "All the children's whispers."

"What does she mean, Nud?" said Gariff.

"I don't know," I said. Really, I knew. We all knew, but we didn't want to know.

The parrot hag and her hunched master crept closer, and once again the rushes betrayed the Shadow in the Water. My friends and I stood ready to fight in the middle of the trail. It was their move.

The hag in the grasses kept her distance at first, slithering to and fro and relaxing her stance. In a gentler tone, she began to speak. Her motherly tongue, forked as it might be, could have passed for reassuring. "Be a good l'il one… a good l'il one and give it to me… ya, ya. Save you I will. Save you from it. Your mother *wants* it. She asked me to tell you."

I closed my eyes and concentrated on a wish. *Strike them down.* I felt something, a surging energy. But there were no lightning bolts or blasts of magic arcing out from the electric spark in my stone, no matter how hard I tried, or thought I tried. The wind picked up, and in blew a gust so strong and concentrated that it rolled Gariff's hat over, emptying its contents, and then sent the monstrosity soaring over the bog waters.

The hag in the grasses watched curiously as the hat flew, tracking where it landed in the far off rushes. Then she turned her stare to me.

That's it? I wondered. My thoughts raced. *The stone is powerless.*

"You can have the pretty stone when you give Jory back to us," I told her flatly, "and if you don't leave us alone I'll smash it to pieces. SMASH IT!… I will, I will. Do you HEAR ME? I'll smash your l'il one." I posed as if to throw it against a half-buried stone.

In a dance full of anguish, the hunched-in hag squirmed and

writhed. "Them's lies to us... them's liars! LIARS!" she said to the parrot hag.

"Bad l'il ones. Bad children! Bad! BAD!" added her mimicking companion.

"Give them's one more chance," commanded the hag in the grasses. "Look into the heart of it... Tell us l'il ones, tell us what you see? Heh?... speak up. SPEAK UP!" She choked on a glob of phlegm, then wretched it up and expelled it into the moss.

I held the stone at eye level and stared into it, just like she asked. I don't know why I did it. The flashing was hypnotic, entrancing – just like that first day at the creek. Except this time, I remembered everything I saw. Tall grey towers rose against a grey cliff, and gargantuan trees grew beside them. Their topmost branches swayed in the breeze hundreds of feet above in a cool, starry sky. I drifted up into those branches. My ears filled with the familiar whisper of rustling leaves. The sound rose to a dull roar as the wind picked up, stronger and louder.

I don't know exactly how much time went by, but when I finally came to, all was in chaos. I felt Kabor's hand pushing at me. He had wedged himself between me and the hag in the grasses. The hag had me in her grips, but Kabor got between us, stabbing at her arms with his knife.

The rest had scattered by then. I lost track of their battles.

Kabor and I struggled against the hag in charge, with me in her clutches. The Stout whipped around and tried to pull me free. I became the rope in a deadly game of tug-of-war. A break finally came – as Kabor pulled I lurched forward and stumbled towards him, free at last.

I glanced up the trail in time to see a fallen hag push herself to her feet, then pull a long, pointed stick out of her belly. The disturbing sight caused me to miss a beat in my own battle. I just stood there and watched, half-dazed, as the two hags up ahead – including the wounded one – took chase after Gariff, Holly and

Bobbin. They moved with sudden and unnatural bursts of speed, stopping momentarily between leaps to look at one another. The parrot hag sought constant approval from her master.

Our part of the skirmish was not going well. The hag in the grasses was quicker than she looked for one so old and decrepit, and she could lash out at a distance. She snagged me and Kabor with vine-like tendrils. I fell into her entangling arms. Her rancid breath smelled like the bottom of the bog.

"Down now children, down we go," she whispered, "down to safety, down to rest."

Kabor and I kicked, and screamed, and bit to no avail. Kabor tried to slash the hag, but she held his arm firm. He managed to switch hands on the knife and swiped at the tendrils. But her tendrils were slippery, wood-strong, and tightly wound. It wasn't working. The hag had overtaken us. She dragged us knee deep into the bog waters.

Kabor kept the fight up and cut one tendril away. I wriggled an arm free, drew my knife, and stabbed her firmly in the shoulder. Her flesh was soft and unnatural. Still, she would not let go, so I cursed and stabbed the vicious witch repeatedly. Black liquid oozed out of every slit, but the wounds did little to impede her. The tendril roots and grasses that were somehow a part of her shot out repeatedly to twist around our limbs and trunks. I cut at them, but there were always more. They twisted together, tough as rope.

The worst was yet to come. That hag opened her mouth wide and even her tongue lashed out. It wrapped around my neck. My knife dropped, and with my free hands I did all I could to keep her leash from choking me.

With the two of us fully in her grips, the hag proceeded to drag us under. She was too strong to resist, an unsurpassed wiry strength. I looked to the others, half-expecting – fully hoping – to see Gariff charging to our rescue. But all I beheld was his entangled, sturdy bulk being pulled under as we were being pulled under. Both hags had bypassed the lumbering Bobbin to secure the faster prey. Holly screamed. I could not see where she was.

"Play dead," I whispered to Kabor, just before drawing my last breath. By his eyes I could see he thought I was mad. "Just do it and wait for my signal."

Down we went under the mosses; down into a cold, deep pool.

CHAPTER XXI

Queen of the garden under

So I let myself slip, deeper and deeper down the watery path to doom's end. I gave myself wholly to the woman in the bog and accepted the bitterness of defeat. There was no denying her victory. The hag's relentless grip and that twisty strength of hers is what caught me off-guard. Her tendrils not only held us firm, they latched onto debris at the bottom of the water pocket and pulled her along. She would have her way and I, Nud Leatherleaf, aspiring diplomat, seemed destined to adorn her cursed garden and roll with the bones of children from long ago – the lost innocents of Fortune Bay. I was to be her thing to put on display.

In return for giving in, she was to leave me there, alone, and not spend too many precious seconds lingering about in admiration of her prize decorations. That was the secret deal that I made with her.

A deathly chill engulfed me as we crossed into a layer of icy water and descended into a hidden drop-off. I bit my lip and tried hard not to flinch. She had to believe that I had drowned.

You don't have the right, you stupid hag. A voice echoed from within, from behind my brow.

"Wait," it told me.

The voice was reassuring. The voice was Paplov's.

As far as I could tell, Kabor had followed my lead. He was holding up well, for a Stout. That or he had already drowned. Kabor's chest had barely puffed out at all when he tried to imitate plump Bobbin – a less than encouraging sign.

The hag kept on with her undertaking, oblivious to my machinations.

Paplov's calm voice resounded again in my mind. "The moment will come."

Then something unexpected happened.

I felt a sharp tug forward, then a pause as the ropey tendrils slackened. Soon after came another tug. I bided my time. *She's testing my resolve,* I thought. It was the same way I might test a fishing line to see if the catch was still there, gauging the creature's will to survive by the fight left in it. I pulled back the next time, trying my best to imitate that last feeble trace of desperate resistance. I played the hooked fish, except I was baiting her instead of the other way around.

After a little more fight, just for show, I gave in and allowed myself to drift. The hag seemed satisfied enough with the performance. She even let loose her grip a little. The depth of water pressed against my ears.

I could break free, I thought. Pips are built for speed and quick dekes, and are semi-aquatic. I definitely could out-swim a blundering old woman, especially in an open stretch.

But I owed it to Kabor to stick it out.

I wanted to breathe, already, at only twenty counts. Nerves, I think. My record was one hundred and ten.

The hag crept farther into the hole, dragging us deeper than I had imagined possible anywhere in the bog lands, except perhaps Everdeep Hole. The pressure in my ears mounted. For Kabor, it would be worse. Our bodies bumped together as we were towed. I didn't feel him kicking or moving at all. Then again, he wasn't supposed to… not yet.

The hag changed course, abruptly, and sped up. She began to move sideways. My arm clipped something – a stump at the bottom of the hole. I half opened one eye as I skipped and spun along the bottom, stirring up mud and debris. I had counted to thirty in the time it took for the hag to bring us all the way down. At most, Kabor would have that much endurance in him again to spare.

I spotted the "garden" – not much of a garden at all; shallow mounds set within a ring of long-spears. Someone should have told the old woman that gardens are for living things. In hers, decaying things, long dead, drifted from the ends of sharpened poles. One pole skewered an oddly familiar, dark round mass, wrapped in reeds.

Still, Kabor had not flinched.

The hag slowed her pace, wrapped her tendrils around the bases of several posts, and carefully glided through the pike barrier. She coasted to a halt in the centre of the garden and set us down on the muddy bottom. The wood in my pack kept me floating back up. The hag kept a tendril on me at all times to force me down.

The Queen of the Garden Under never thought twice about the act of drowning us. Still, there seemed to be some hint of affection in the way she went about her gruesome task: the way she so delicately wrapped me in braided rushes like a spider wraps its tender prey in silk. And the way she so gently stroked my hair away from my forehead, like a mother might, to fully appreciate the precious face of her sleeping child. Kabor's death shroud was next.

To the hag, we were more than mere showpieces. We were her emotional treasures, to cherish and protect until the end of days. Nearly forty-five counts had passed and the hag had not yet honored our secret deal. She wasn't about to leave us alone any time soon. Worse, she started feeling at my pockets as she hoisted me up and floated me over the garden ring. What a lovely beacon my stone would make, flashing at the bottom of the bog for all eternity, a last sight for future victims.

It was Kabor's swift action that set us on our way. His reflexes bordered on precognition. I had just then gained my water lungs and comfortably suppressed the urge to breathe. All the while, the Stout had drifted death-like, just out of my reach, and loosely tethered to a pole. The time had come to make our move.

So when the hag's rearranging brought me close to Kabor, I thought to grope for an arm or a leg. But before even laying a hand on him, he sprung to life.

Something else stirred as well. The spiked round mass stuck to a pole began to quiver. Legs shot out, fan-like in all directions. Kabor shot upwards as the central mass of the dark ball spun about its axis. I had seen the thing before. Somehow, the hag had acquired Fyorn's spider – the prize attraction in her gruesome collection. And somehow, it was still alive.

Fear. Panic. I shot upwards after Kabor, kicking the hag square in the face. My braided bounds quickly became undone. Kabor tore at his bindings and set them adrift as he wriggled upwards. The hag batted at the spoiled ropes falling around her, hand over one eye. She let out an electrifying screech.

Barely into our escape, I felt a tremor in the water – the wake of the Shadow's passing. I caught sight of the tail of the hulking creature as it disappeared into the darkness.

The Shadow in the Water must have circled round, out of sight. It came back at us like a blur out of nowhere, crossing above and stifling our ascent. Then it swam out of sight again. The hag gained water on us in that moment, and her groping tendrils caught my ankle. Kabor was already snagged.

As we succumbed to her grip once more, the Shadow maneuvered to make a third advance, this time angled from below. Suddenly there was turbulence and mayhem, thrashing and swirling water. I was thrust aside. The Shadow had something in its jaws. "Kabor!" I screamed into the depths.

Then a muted wail of anguish reverberated through the water. I was released, flipped head over heels.

The Shadow had taken the wrong prey and disappeared into the inky depths. I felt for Kabor. He was with me.

But which way was up? I had lost track of time and direction. In the confusion, I went still for a moment and just let myself drift. The buoyancy of my backpack pointed the way, and off we went.

The two of us barreled straight into a mass of ropey vines. Although not fixed to anything solid, the vines were so entangled with one another that they opposed our every move, wrapping around arms and legs. I pushed up, at least I thought it was up, but it might have been sideways.

Nearly out of breath, I finally broke through to the surface. It was dark. I gulped at the air, foul air. It tasted bitter on the tongue, dank and decayed. But it was life.

Kabor should have been right behind me. Heavy breaths pulsed through the silence. My heart pounded. *He's not coming up.* I shook my head. Beaten, I removed my pack and tossed it to the dark shore. Maybe there was still time. Maybe.

Down into the tangles I dove, groping about frantically in complete darkness. I searched the water column around me, end to end and through and through.

Half a minute later, my leg brushed against what felt like a hand in the weeds. It was. I grabbed on and pulled, but there was no life pulling back. Kabor's limp body was caught in the tangles. I twisted, jolted and finally yanked him out, then dragged him to the surface, and to shore.

Exhausted, I laid my best friends' cousin on the cave floor. I fumbled in the darkness to find his chest. No rise, no fall. Nothing. I felt for his face, plugged his nose and gave him two short breaths.

I pushed down on his chest fast, repeatedly, to jumpstart his breathing. Nothing. I kept at it. Nothing. With every last bit of strength, I raised my fist up high and belted it down on Kabor.

I heard the spurt of water first; then coughing and a gasp for air. A long moment passed, and the Stout sucked in a single divine breath. He rolled over onto his stomach, retching. He was alive.

CHAPTER XXII

A hidden passage

The soggy and exhausted Stout lay face down on the dark, muddy shore, coughing and spouting bog water. Short, eager breaths regulated the urge to cough up a lung.

"I feel sick. <cough> Nud? Where am I?"

"A safe place," I said, scanning every direction. There wasn't a glint of light anywhere to break the darkness.

I collapsed beside him, smiling, breathing, and indulging in the rush of having just cheated death. It was a selfish moment. The air was stale and smelled of all things that crawl into the earth to die. I didn't care. A long, black minute of well-deserved tranquility floated by as my body normalized. Side by side, we lay still and speechless. Our breaths grew even and steady. Kabor cleared his throat.

"I… <cough> was trapped. I couldn't get out." The half-drowned Stout's fist thudded on his chest.

"I pulled you up," I said. There was a long silence. Breathing.

"Was that some kind of giant eel?" he said.

"Dunno," I said. In the long pause that followed, I waited for a milky "Thank you."

"This is all your fault," he spat. The acid water he swallowed must have turned his words sour. "You were supposed to fight with us, but you weren't even moving... you let her get a hold on you." His voice began to waver. "I tried to help... <cough>." Kabor's hands fumbled in the dark. He grabbed my arm. "What's the matter with you anyway?"

I was... seeing. But I couldn't tell him that. I couldn't say that the hag was not what made me act that way. I didn't know what to say.

"Let go," was all that came out. He did.

"Where is that damn rock of yours anyway? It would be nice if we could see down here. Did you *forget* to take it out?"

"No." I fumbled for words and fumbled through my pockets. I hadn't forgotten anything; I just hadn't put two and two together. One by one, I stretched my pockets wide open and felt through them.

"Well?" he said. "<cough> Cough it up."

"I don't know where it is." The stone just wasn't anywhere. I patted myself down.

Kabor let out an impatient sigh. "Did the ole crone take it?"

I snapped back. "I DON'T KNOW!"

I stopped what I was doing and thought through everything that had happened during the fight. The last thing I remembered about the stone was looking into it. It was unnerving, to say the least, to have a gap in my memory. It just doesn't happen very often to Pips. I started searching again, from the very beginning. Right pocket, left pocket, back pockets, shirt pocket...

Finally, I remembered the backpack. "I know..." When I undid the clasp and pulled back the flap, a pinch of pale red light filtered out between the soaked pieces of deepwood. Tucked away at the very bottom corner was the stone.

I breathed a sigh of relief. During the mayhem, I had half a mind to cast off the pack, for speed's sake. I don't even know how the piece got there – it started in my pocket, then I took it out, and then… no matter. I fished it out. In the palm of my hand, the light of the stone danced and pulsed, trapped in its gummy prison. There was scarcely a moment of calm between the flurries of red flashes. It seemed… excited, if unliving stones can be thought of that way.

I took a few minutes to empty the pack, shake the remaining water out, wring my cloak and dump the water out of my boots.

"You know we can't swim back," I told Kabor. By *we* I really meant *him*, mostly. I was surprised he could even swim at all. I repacked the wood and the boots, and left the flap open so everything inside would dry over time.

"We have to," said Kabor.

"I don't even know how to backtrack our way out," I said. "It was dark and I was disoriented. If we try, we could get turned around and lose our way underwater. And what's to say you won't get stuck again? You could get us both killed, even if we did figure it out. And then there's The Shadow…"

"I think it ate the hag," he said.

"Hope so," I replied.

Silence. The Stout shook his head.

"What about Cuz?" asked Kabor.

The last I seen of Gariff, he was in the process of being pulled under, just like us. The light of the stone steadied for a brief moment, and the Stout and I locked eyes. I didn't want to say it, or even to think it. The light vanished. When it returned, he was still staring. I didn't have to say anything. My lack of words spoke volumes.

Kabor let out a defeatist sigh.

In the uneasy silence that followed, I backed away and rested against the rock wall. A twisty tree root jabbed me in the back.

"Gariff's OK. They're all OK," I said, trying to convince myself that such words could be true. "The Shadow and one of the hags were tied up with us. That leaves two old ladies. Gariff is skinning one alive by now, and Bobbin's sipping tea with the other, exchanging turtle soup recipes."

Kabor smirked. "I believe the Gariff part. And either way, Bobbin's simply unsinkable."

As we sat deluding one another, and ourselves, chains of flickering light scattered off the cave walls to reveal the natural chamber around us. Fossil imprints of small, insignificant creatures from an ancient sea embossed the stone. We were at the mouth of an irregular, tube-like cave. A few feet away was the wide pool we had entered from. Above the pool was a pitted and well-rounded dome. The cave walls had an overall smoothness to them, and showed the elongated signs of shaping by water.

The tube-cave would be a tight fit. Dense mats of fine roots dangled from the ceiling, nearly blocking passage in some areas, and thicker roots hugged the curvature of the rock wall. The roots played host to a nest of old cobwebs and vermin sheddings. The floor was chunky gravel. Despite all the signs and sheddings of past life cycles, no living thing dwelled there.

"We could probably dig our way up and out," I said, examining where the roots punched through. I had no idea what I was talking about.

"I doubt it," said Kabor. "Roots work their way through small fissures in the rock and then expand into them. Besides, we could be underwater and underground at the same time."

"No. How is that even possible?" That did not seem right at all. "Wouldn't we still be underwater then?"

Kabor sized up the chamber carefully, repeatedly rubbing his scruffy chin as he closely examined the walls, the roots, and the floor. He put on his glasses, went right up to each feature and stared at it sideways, inches from his face. I described the dome to him.

"Water *used* to run down through that big conduit, that's for sure," commented Kabor.

"I know that," I said.

"And did you see the side openings? They're drains. They relieve pressure when she fills up."

"What stopped the water from coming?" I said, doubtful.

"The bog's ability to retain water, maybe. These tunnels are flooded regularly... a cycle. And I would guess we're near the end of that cycle."

That didn't sound good. "How long?" I said. "It's as wet as it's ever going to get in the bog right now. And that BIG rain we just had—"

Kabor bit his upper lip and started shaking his head.

"Dunno... years, decades. Maybe only during floods, or maybe it takes time to soak through. Or it could be that the geology shifted and there is no cycle to it anymore. Maybe..."

In the minutes that followed, Kabor came up with more maybes than I cared to count. After hearing half a dozen theories, I thought it best to move on. Young Pips are less than patient. I waited for a pause in his mental flatulations.

"We should get moving," I said.

With a tilt of his head, he motioned to the passage. "You really think that's our best bet?"

I nodded. "We can always come back."

Kabor had a grim look about him. "Humph," he said. "Lead the way then."

I peered ahead, into our would-be escape route. "It does seem to slope up a bit, right?"

"That's right," he assured me. He *sounded* like he knew what he was talking about.

The Stout seemed quite at home underground. He had experience working in one of the mines outside of the Bearded Hills. According to Gariff though, the younger of the two cousins was too easily distracted and never really accomplished anything productive on the job. In part, it was because he avoided any and all honest work. Gariff once commented that Kabor used up more energy trying to get out of work than he would have just doing it – always a workaround or a shortcut, never the straightforward and sensible way. At the mine, he spent his time roaming the drifts and getting into trouble, not to mention danger, until he was eventually let go. To his credit though, he did find a few stray mineral veins while picking away where others hadn't thought to look or had given up the search. But the network of caves under the bog was nothing like the organized, reinforced tunnels of a Stout mine. Water sculpted them, and water was a Pip's element.

I started along the passageway, gripping the SPARX stone in one hand. Every few yards I stopped, held it up, and waited for the flicker to reveal the way.

Kabor continually and repeatedly asked about what was coming, how tight the fit was going to be, and whether it looked safe. "The flashes are fast sometimes" he complained, or "The shadows are confusing."

"Just follow my lead," I told him.

We soon discovered that it made more sense to crawl and wriggle our way along the gravelly floor than to stoop continually, often having to resort to it anyway. After several long minutes, we reached a divide in the passage. The main course abruptly widened and leveled out. An offshoot tunnel veered off to one side, curved, then ran nearly parallel as far out as I could see.

A light breeze refreshed the air at the junction. It was a good sign. Our luck seemed to be turning. We kept on through the larger tunnel.

"Out in no time," I said, spirits raised. And as we crawled along on hands and knees, my mind began to drift towards the world above and the fate of our good friends.

Gradually, the passage gained in height and became high enough to walk along without stooping. Over time, the bed of gravel disappeared, replaced by larger, rounder river stones. Footing became an issue in the dim and fractured light, and I found myself wishing that I had my boots on. In one area, dark crevices loomed above, adding even more height, and a new odor was on the air. I stopped to rest by a small offshoot tunnel and hauled out my boots. That is when I noted the first signs of life – the floor was splotted with some kind of dung.

"Look Kabor," I said, pointing to the splotches.

"I ran into some a while back," he said. "They're all over the place."

"Bats?" I asked.

"Maybe. Hurry up with your flippers."

The boots were dripping wet, so I tied them upside-down to a shoulder strap for later use. Kabor still had his on – it's a wonder he had been able to swim at all. Of course, only a Stout would go swimming with his boots on, and leave them on afterwards.

Over the next leg of the journey, the scenery more-or-less repeated itself many times over – a dark, winding tube-like passage with smooth limestone walls and no major offshoots, small cracks and crevices here and there, and a stony path beneath our feet. At times, it was difficult to tell if we were traveling up or down. Certainly, there was no way to determine our bearing – we could have been directly under Webfoot for all I knew, or on our way to Proudfoot. Along the ceiling, fewer and fewer roots showed through until there were none at all.

So after a long crawl and a doubly long hike, we came upon a choke point in the passage. Rubble covered the ground and stacked up along the sides – a partial collapse. I inhaled the sweet air. It was high quality. The breeze had become stronger and it carried a pleasant water and mineral scent.

Kabor noted the change in my demeanor. "What is it?" he said.

"Water. Don't you smell it?"

"I hear it," he said. We stopped to poke at the fallen debris.

I found a weak point in the pile and punched through to the other side.

"Ahhh!" I yelled.

The floor gave way.

I felt myself drop.

I grabbed for the wall.

My heart pounded. Teetering in mid-air, half my body swung over a dark abyss. A mere two fingers gripped enough rock to keep me from toppling into it. I hung there for a suspended moment, and then gained a foothold.

I had come upon a large crevice of sorts in the rock. The passage opened up into it, and then fell off a cliff. Across the gap – no more than a few feet – a wet wall glistened. Water sprayed slippery doom from above. The mist chilled my cheeks and forehead. Below, a proven drop to sudden death beckoned. The gravity of the downward plunge drew me to the edge, as though inviting me to join the scattering of bones below. Kabor had halted behind me.

"What's the hold-up?" he said.

"Death by plummet, that's what." I waited for the next flurry of flashes then gestured to the drop. Kabor peered down from behind the rubble.

"Oh," he said. "Now that's a doozy."

A dozen feet up the far wall and offset to one side by another five feet, a second cave opened into the gap. By its size and shape, it appeared as though it once connected with the passage we stood in. A steady stream of water sputtered off the edge of the high opening and fell like red rain, glimmering in the light of the stone.

A knot developed in my stomach as I stood there, surveying the obstacle, a knot that told me we had gone the wrong way.

Kabor pushed me aside to get a better view. He was excited, and motivated.

"I never seen anything like this before." He stuck his head out and looked up. "We can scale it."

"I don't kn—" Kabor cut me off.

"There's only up or back down," he stated, leaning out dangerously to get a better view. He said it like it was an obvious, everyday problem, and went on to provide an equally obvious plan.

"There was that one side tunnel, not too far back," I reminded him. "That might be the way." It had been small, but we could have squeezed through.

"I say we go up," he insisted. "That's the way out. The crevice is narrow enough to wedge ourselves in as we climb."

"It's slippery," I said.

Kabor was either fearless, reckless or completely oblivious to the incredible peril that went along with his recommendation. I spent a moment pondering the situation, and tried to convince myself that *up* was what we were aiming for all along. *Up* was good – until I looked *down*.

"Are you mad?" I grabbed a loose stone and dropped it down the crevice. It fell for a count of two, then ricocheted several times before coming to rest at the bottom. "Why do you think there are bones down there?"

"They're probably ancient animal bones," he argued. Kabor ran his hand along the inside wall of the chasm. "Look at all the holds," he continued. "No able-bodied Stout – or even a Pip – should have any trouble scaling that wall. Just shimmy up where it pinches in."

"It's suicide," I said.

The argument continued, more for the sake of argument than for finding alternatives, but in the end, the choice was clear. Being the more agile climber, I went first, and the plan was that Kabor would catch my fall on the off chance I slipped. I would help to pull him up when it was his turn.

I held the SPARX stone with my teeth and braced myself for the climb. I started with a forward lunge, throwing my left foot into a small pocket on the far wall. I grabbed onto a small ledge jutting out above. I stayed in a near splits position for a second or two, and then shifted my weight wholly to the opposing side. Slowly, I began my ascent up the slimy wall.

"Wha ish som'ens up there?" I grumbled, jaw clenched on the SPARX stone to illuminate the gap as I climbed. "Wha ish I shlip and fall?"

"I told you I'll catch you," said Kabor. His voice echoed in the chasm. "I won't let you fall past me. Don't worry, there's nothing down here but you and me… and her."

"Wha?" I lost my foothold. Kabor's hand caught the sole of my foot; he was straddling the two walls just beneath me. Lucky for me, his hands were huge. They cupped around my foot as he gave me a boost.

Kabor laughed. "Be careful," he said.

"Vewy shfunny," I said, and took another step.

"That's good," said Kabor, cheering me on, "you're doing it. Just keep doing what you're doing."

When I reached the high cave, I peered into the opening. It was a sizable chamber, an empty chamber.

"That's right," said Kabor, "find a hold; a good hold."

I located a hold and pulled myself up and in. The grade sloped up and the floor was slippery. Slowly, I crept in, crouched on all fours. Rubble was everywhere, and the ceiling was high and dome shaped. Water poured in from above just two or three steps in, creating the stream and splashing into the crevice. A passage cut across the cave. It ran roughly parallel to the crevice. That tunnel was tall with smooth, straight walls – very different from anything we'd seen up until then.

I yelled back, over the edge to Kabor. "ALL CLEAR. And…"

Kabor was already right there. I grabbed his arm. "Man-made," I added. Bracing myself, I gave him one last pull to bring him up and in.

"You're not a bad climber," I said.

"I just followed the light. Did you notice the walls on your way up?" he said.

"What about them?"

"The other side is limestone, and this side is something else altogether. I can't quite place it." Kabor, like most Stouts, had an eye for structural detail, even half-blind and in near-darkness, it seemed.

"It all looks pretty much the same to me," I confessed.

Kabor's eyes were all over the new cave. He waved me over to a spot along the wall. He stood in front of it, eyes inches away from its surface. I brought the light down close to where he was crouched. Every flicker revealed something new.

"You're right, it's man-made," he said. "But this isn't mine construction – that's for sure," said Kabor. He pressed his index finger into a groove and ran it along the wall horizontally, then vertically. "There are bricks underneath the dirt and grime, and there's no such thing as a brick mine."

"Where do you think it leads? Maybe Men built it." I said.

"The ceiling height is about right," he said.

"It must lead out one way or the other." Kabor paused for a long moment. "Or just *in*. It could be some kind of displaced adit."

"Why would Men build way out here under a bog," I said. "And how did they keep the water out?"

"More importantly, why did they leave?" he said. Kabor just shrugged and shook his head.

Kabor judged the left passage to be up-sloping. I adjusted my pack and we started along it. Partially caved-in areas became commonplace along the way, and once we had to dig our way through a heavy choke point. Over time, new openings began to appear on either side. There were brick throughways, wide at the top and narrowing downward in a slow curve to the earthen floor, nearly to a point. To my untrained eye, it looked upside down to what it should be.

We kept to our path with few words. I thought back to the Mire Trail and the abandonment of good friends. *They're dead in the mud and I sure as put them there,* I told myself. I needed to say it, but I couldn't get the words out. Kabor's own thoughts were churning.

"Gariff abandoned us," he said, walking alongside me. "How could he do that? He's *your* best friend and *my* cousin. He should have been all over that old hag when she was dragging you in, and double when she had us both. The three of us could have pummeled her."

I took a deep breath.

"I don't know why things went down that way, they just did," I said. "We were all trying to get away. And those hags were more than a trifle cunning – they were *trying* to separate us. They were *scheming* to funnel us this way or that. They were good at it too. Gariff did what he could. We all did what we could. Nobody knew any better."

"We knew the legend," said Kabor.

"It was *just* a legend, back then," I reminded him.

It almost seemed prophetic how Kabor and I had only recently recited the "Legend of the Bog Queens," and were now hopelessly entangled in its inner workings. We had told the story and laughed hysterically at how frightened stuffy ole Gariff had become. Good Gariff. He probably had nightmares. Did the hags hear us that day? Was this some kind of punishment? Poetic justice? We went from telling the story to living it in a matter of days. A kind of morbid recurrence seemed to be at play in the world.

"What do you think happened to them?" I asked, solemnly. I knew Kabor was thinking about it.

He scrunched his shoulders once again, and then shook his head, his expression uncommonly blank. I left the conversation at that.

*

Further along, we came upon a new source of running water. Mist and the noise of random patter filtered into our passageway. Rounding a bend, the tunnel suddenly lost most of its man-made features and opened up into a large, airy chamber with a domed roof again. The original construction was fractured. Piles of rubble lay scattered about, and water poured through a gaping hole in the ceiling. It splashed into a pool that spanned the room from side to side. Water swirled in the centre and drained to unknown depths, and a gentle stream spilled out of the chamber on the far side.

"We're down-sloped," I said.

Kabor nodded. "Could be a temporary dip to get around something."

"Like what?"

"Another structure, a pond… the mayor's basement, hard rock… anything you wouldn't want to dig through or run into."

"I wouldn't mind running into the mayor's basement right about now."

Kabor laughed. "I bet he has some nice wine down there… *up* there, I mean."

Crossing the pool was easy enough, owing to the rubble that littered the floor. We stepped from pile-to-pile all the way to the rushing column of water. In that feat of dexterity, Kabor far surpassed the abilities of his cousin.

To complete the crossing, we had no choice but to get wet. Very wet. Before wading through the waist high water, we stopped to fill our waterskins.

"I need a quick dip," I said.

"I'll wait," said Kabor. "What choice do I have?"

I removed my pack, placed the bog stone gently on top, and suddenly became conscious of how filthy I was. With measured reluctance, I waded into the cold waters of the pool, dove under and swam to the bottom. I floated there, hovering, arms and legs spread wide apart, listening to the pacifying rush of the falling water. It was refreshing, and healing, and almost spiritual in the way the rest of the world just disappeared. The weight of the water surrounding me kept me bound, intact, and together, the way it gently pushed in from all sides. I appreciated the purity of it. If only I could live beneath the pool's rippled surface and forget the world, I would.

Eventually, I surfaced and ferried my pack to the other side. Dripping wet and more reluctant to leave than I had been to enter, I pulled myself out and shook myself dry as best I could. Kabor had tossed his clothes across, and was already on the other side putting his boots back on.

I gathered my things and we set out on our way without so much as a word between us. The events of the day replayed in my mind. Kabor seemed lost in thought and didn't say anything.

Once my thoughts were organized, I passed them on to Kabor. They weren't completely honest, but they broke the heavy silence.

"Gariff could have pulled free of the hags grip by brute strength alone," I started. "Holly could have avoided detection, plus she's tougher than she looks. If Bobbin got to the water, maybe he out-swam them. After all, he would never outrun them. And Jory, well, maybe he was just knocked out."

It was my way of saying, "They might be all right."

Kabor spilled the contents of his mind as well, having mulled over a different topic.

"You just can't trust bog queens – they're shifty creatures," he said. "Things might have turned out the same or worse even if we had given them all they asked for and did what they said to do."

I think it was his way of saying "I don't really blame you." And there was a glint of hope in his words.

But Kabor hadn't seen what I had seen, just before being pulled under. He couldn't have. I decided there was no point in flattening what little hope he could muster. I needed him to stay focused. I needed us both to stay focused.

So I could not find absolution in his words without knowing what had become of the good friends we left behind, for the sinking feeling in my gut and the echo of Holly's scream etched in my memory left me little doubt about their fate, and my role in it.

I wished I had never found that stupid stone.

CHAPTER XXiii

Flicker

In time, the schedule of flashes became so familiar that the intervening dead-times – the dark intervals – went by unnoticed. When I relaxed my eyes and let my mind wander, the gaps seemed to fill in all by themselves, phantom-like, smoothly morphing one illuminated scene into the next.

With the mystifying light as our only guide, our heavy feet fell into the monotony of a steady march through the underground cave system. The going was good and progress was even-paced for what seemed like hours. Spurious noises became commonplace: scratching, clicking, drips, drops, echoes and the hollow sounds of wind were all present. That meant life, food, water, and circulating air. Kabor took it as a sign that we were nearing the surface. "Cave dwelling animals don't venture far underground," he had said. I wasn't so convinced.

Again, my senses were on high alert, having picked up on a repetitive scratching sound, nearly hidden in the clutter of familiar cave noises. It was a rare and subtle thing, but distinctive, and only barely within earshot when it was there at all. If I stopped to listen, it would silence. I found myself questioning whether or not it was ever really there. But it was. The signature pattern of scratching persisted for long minutes at a time before disappearing for a while, only to return later.

Chk-chk-fwip… chk-chk-fwip.

Most times it came from behind us, but sometimes from ahead, and once, even from above after we had stopped to rest in yet another domed chamber – the fourth of our journey.

Our going was by no means direct. Three times along our course, debris-choked passages blocked our way and forced us to backtrack and take a side tunnel. With all the winding about, eventually we entered a new zone. The air seemed fresher again and there were less structural problems. Despite marginally lifted spirits, our souls were too weary to carry us much farther. We had gone too long without sleep, and all the swimming, climbing, worrying and decision-making had taken its toll on our minds and bodies.

At first, we talked to keep one another awake, mostly about the events that shaped our predicament: the chance meeting with Mer at the Flipside, the visit to Fyorn's, Jory's enthusiasm to accompany us, my decision to take out the stone… Mer – whatever happened to Mer? I wondered aloud if the hags had gotten to the prospector as well.

Kabor stumbled along for some time barely cognizant, having nearly fallen asleep at least once while walking (and mumbling incoherently). He tripped over his own feet. I caught him under one arm, mid-collapse.

"Time for a break," I said. "It's late. And you can't keep my eyes open…" I tried to shake the tiredness off.

"I mean, I can't keep your eyes open." I shook again.

"Whatever the specifics, our two pairs of eyes cannot remain open much longer," said Kabor, followed with a sleepy nod of agreement.

We took half a moment to settle into adequate, if not comfortable, resting places along one side of the passage. The floor was earthen with a few scattered stones and pieces of brick protruding.

I shrugged the backpack off my shoulders and slumped against a dry and plain looking section of wall. My body ached everywhere, and my shoulders were raw where the straps rubbed against my skin. The simple act of taking the load off my legs was absolute luxury though. I tucked the stone away and decided that I wouldn't be getting up again for a long, long time. As sleep began to wash over me, I pondered the prospects of endless days persisting on bugs for food – if it came to that – and imagined all of the places they might be hiding.

Kabor was already snoring by the time my dragging fatigue pulled me under the liquid gloom. I quickly succumbed to exhaustion and plummeted into a deep sleep. In the netherworld of dreams, I envisioned the vast wetlands outside of Webfoot, with fields of green reeds swaying in a light breeze on a drizzly day. Only a faint patch of light shone through the grey sky where the sun crouched over the horizon. It began to flicker.

I awoke startled, with the scent of bog water heavy in my nostrils and the sound of the whirring wind still in my ears. Except the scent wasn't bog water – it was the dampness of the cave. And the whirring sound was not wind – it was Kabor's raspy, early morning voice. The Stout's choppy speech suggested that he had not slept much either.

"Go away," I said. *How long was I asleep? A minute?*

The annoying noisemaker did not go away. *Is this another dream?* He kept on about something. *Who cares?* Unwilling, I spiraled up and away from imagination's abyss, through countless layers of cryptic illusion, and crashed through the paper wall of consciousness.

Kabor shook my shoulders. "I heard something," he whispered.

"You heard nothing," I countered, and promptly fell back to sleep.

He shook me again. "Nud, we're almost there. The way out is just ahead – we should go."

He was beginning to sound like a recurring nightmare: "just around the corner" or "maybe up that way" or "I can smell a Stout mine on the breeze" – I'd heard them all. And he wasn't the only one fool enough to proclaim we'd be out in no time. Wishful thinking – dangerous thinking – all of it.

I didn't open my eyes or say a word. I just shook my head.

"What if the hags are following us?" he pleaded. "We have to keep moving – we don't have much food – just a few berries I picked along the way and some maple candy from your uncle that I didn't tell Bobbin about."

"He's just Fyorn now," I said.

"Huh?"

"Those hags… just let me… think for a bit," I said. "If we run out of food we can… well… if we have to… I hear all kinds of scurrying sounds in the walls."

"Bugs and mice?" said Kabor. "Fine fair for a Pip maybe, but not for me."

Chk-chk-fwip… Chk-chk-fwip.

I sat up and took out the bog stone. In the first flash of light, something moved along the far wall. I pointed.

"There!"

A shadowy thing about a quarter my size scurried into the darkness.

The spider?

I scrambled to my feet and stared down the passage, holding the stone above my head. With dead eyes and a sideways look, Kabor stared too.

"Do you see anything?" he said.

I waited for the next burst.

"Nope… wait… nope," I said.

"Is it a hag, do you think?"

"Nope… it might be a giant spider."

"Shit," he said. "That's just great."

We both held our breath and listened intently. The air was dead and the passage deathly quiet... the regular noises that cave things make in the dark had subsided. Only the sound of water dripping into a shallow puddle persisted.

"I don't like this," I said. "You're right. What I'd do for a simple torch."

"What about your bow?"

"A shot in the dark?"

"Better than no shot."

I passed the bog stone to the Stout and unhooked my bow from the side of the pack. It took half a minute just to untangle the bowstring. In the mean time, Kabor picked up a rock and whipped it into the darkness.

He watched and he waited. Nothing. I strung my bow and notched an arrow. Still nothing. Slow and quiet, we turned away and footpadded deeper into the cave.

Kabor offered to take turns carrying the pack – I let him. He offered to carry the stone as well. Not that it was heavy, but holding it up in front of me the whole time was tiresome – I let him. I even kept an arrow notched and my bow slightly bent for a good long time as we continued on our way. Not surprisingly, the way out wasn't "just up ahead" as Kabor had thought. The air did shift again though. I couldn't quite place the difference. Kabor said it was a mine smell.

After that encounter, we spent a daylight's worth of hours exploring the network of tunnels.

Legs weary, we gave in to the notion that we'd be stuck underground at least one more "night," and so once again settled to rest. This time, we chose a section of passage that we had passed twice already and taken special note of. The area was home to a protected cubbyhole for sleeping.

I cleared a space to rest and lay my pack down as a pillow, then put my boots on before cocooning into my cloak. Kabor and I agreed to take watches. His was the first. The moment my head hit the pack was the moment I found myself somewhere in Deepweald, at least in spirit. A normal sleep just wouldn't do though, and so I slipped into recall. Having seen the spider-thing in the hag's garden had stirred up old memories.

CHAPTER XXIV

Heart of Darkness

Hatchet in one hand, box in the other, I made off towards a part of the woods that I knew would be clear of Fyorn and Paplov. The woodsman never brought us that way. "Best keep out of those thickets," he had once said. "There's no good wood that way, and the bugs'll eat you alive." But it was some hidden place that I sought, away from prying eyes, and the bugs were not out yet.

I trampled over the last remnants of melting snow. My heart quickened with anticipation. The buzz of old growth forest urged me on, alive with its earthy scents. Nature had just been jarred awake by a late rush of spring air and was making up for lost time. I sped up, faster. Small birds flitted from branch to branch as I passed, and foraging chipmunks scooted up tree trunks. Excitement seemed to loom beneath every strip of bark, behind every bush, and below every winter-trodden leaf. I didn't think much about where I was going.

I had never been alone in those woods before. Countless times, Fyorn had led me and Paplov along forest paths looking for wood salvage: branches or even entire trees felled by windstorms or lightning. He dragged the good pieces all the way back to his workshop, no matter how big they were, or how small. I thought I had been following one of the woodsman's paths, but when I looked behind it simply was not there. In fact, the forest looked nearly the same in every direction.

And that is how I came upon a clearing I had never seen before.

A rocky outcrop formed the foundation of the grove, surrounded by tall pines. It opened onto a small cliff that overlooked grassy lowlands, still snow-packed in the hollows. Middle ground, a crooked old oak tree stood sentry over a thick bed of fallen leaves. The tree's low, outstretched branches cupped a family of warblers, puffed up and warmly nestled in. Chilled air billowed up the precipice and into the grove, carrying with it the dank scent of wet earth.

Finally, the time had come. I set the axe down and weighed the box in both hands. After a long, examining look, I wedged my fingernails beneath the lid and pulled up firmly. Tap... tap... tap... came a sound from inside.

A cloud blocked out the sun, the temperature dropped sharply, and the warblers scattered in a whirling flurry.

Try as I might, the box would not open. There was no latch and there were no hinges, so I tried using the axe I had taken, gently forcing the blade under the lid. Working the keen edge inwards and twisting, I pried the lid up to the sound of wood screeching against nails.

Something cold oozed against my fingertips and a slithering, fleshy mass pushed out of the box with the uncanny strength of a coiled serpent. The lid bowed. A black tendril lashed out. I threw the box into the air and heard a splintering crack as it smashed against an overhanging branch. In my haste to get away, I tripped over a root, dropped the axe and fell. Something landed on my face.

It was the thing, sticky and oozing, its tendrils writhing over my face like fifty snakes. Two drilled into my ears, and another pair up my nostrils. More pressed into my eye sockets.

Frantic, I screamed and ripped the black mass off my face. I flung the creature and leapt to my feet. I grabbed my axe and watch as a blur shot across the ground, between sharp rocks and beneath patchy underbrush. I followed.

The creature stopped and perched itself on a mossy boulder at the edge of the clearing. It bore likeness to a giant spider, crouching in the way that jumping spiders crouch, as though poised for a spring attack.

The body of this thing was black and insect-like, but big. Its weight was borne on long, spindly legs – tens of them. The thing dripped black oil and the centre pulsed like a beating heart.

With a slight tilt and roll of its eyeless central ball, the thing measured my presence. We stood facing one another, the spider-thing and I, at an impasse it seemed, until a tremendous buzzing sound roared up from the earth. A cloud of flying insects swarmed all around – insects that should not have been there in the first place. All I could do to protect myself was to clench my mouth shut and wave my hands at the swarm. I ran like a madman, barely able to see where I was going. They landed on my arms. They got into my hair. Some crawled up my sleeves. I felt more crawling down the back of my neck and into my shirt. They bit and stung, repeatedly. Stupidly, I swung the axe at them.

Running in circles and flailing about, cursing and squishing bugs out of my hair, I found no practical way to defend myself against the swarm. And when I came to the edge of the drop, I froze, and for a foolish moment, considered making the treacherous leap off the rocky outcrop and down to the fractured ground below. I backed away instead.

Then something unexpected happened, as if enough of the unexpected had not happened already. That old oak tree in the middle of the clearing began to *move*. Not just by swaying in the breeze, mind you. It moved over the ground, from one place to another. The tree closed in on me before I could even think to dash away. And it wasn't alone. Slender conifers joined in from the sides, forcing me back towards the precipice. And the insects persisted. My next step would meet open air instead of solid earth or rock, and there was nowhere left to go but down. I reconsidered my odds of surviving the plummet to the rocky bed below.

No… instead, I planted my feet as firmly as I could in a wide stance. Precariously perched on the cliff's edge, I readied the axe with both hands. Bugs crawled over my face, but I ignored them. Sweat stung my eyes.

The crooked old oak tree led the advance. It bent down in front of me with a loud crackling sound. I swung Fyorn's axe, but missed my mark. The momentum of my swing nearly sent me spinning off the edge and I teetered for a long moment, but held my own.

The tree paused and made a deep, windy sound. A large hollow in its trunk opened wide like a gaping jaw, twisted and contorted. Black, pointed spikes made for jagged teeth.

My body tensed. I swallowed my breath. With a deep inhale and sudden burst of energy, I feigned to the left and lunged right, intent on making a run for the "real" tree line. But I was a beat too late, for in that very same instant a branch lashed out and struck me hard in the chest. It lifted me right off the ground and sent me flying backwards, out of the clearing and over the drop.

Up and then down I went in a rush of backwards acceleration, farther and faster. I waited for the back of my head to smash a tree, or a stray boulder, or hard ground.

Something went wrong with my recall at that point.

The sky flickered, and then went dark. When it flashed back on, I was in freefall, and a thousand disembodied eyes filled the space around me. They watched me as I fell, floating and swirling everywhere; they studied me and they studied everything. It went dark again, and in the flurry of red bursts that followed, they were gone.

I should have hit the ground in a pair of heartbeats after being thrown off the cliff, but I continued to plummet. A stinging branch whipped me on my way down, and then another. Soon I was crashing through a canopy of whipping branches. All at once, the foliage became so thick that it broke my fall. A branch caught me and I hung there, suspended, facing down.

A young woman with beautiful auburn hair stood on the ground. It was Holly, staring up at me from some fifty feet below. Except it wasn't Holly for long. The young woman looked to her feet before the next dark interval, and in the light of the next flash, she lifted her head and I saw she was a hag. Soothing olive eyes begged for affection in a motherly way. Her hair had turned stringy and dripping wet, and she was covered from head to toe in muck, moss and grasses. She started to regurgitate something, shuddering in the midst of her effort. On her second try, the young woman heaved and spouted bile. And while greyish fluid oozed down her chin and neck, gargled words rolled out from deep within her gut.

"Down ... down... down," she chanted in a drowning voice. "Down... down... down..."

With a rising roar, the wind shook the branches and flung me off. Flailing, I grabbed at anything, and landed solid on a spread of thick branches. At that moment, I locked eyes with a gnarled face set in the very trunk of the colossal tree that held me in its grip. I let go. The face glared after me as I began my third descent. It was Fyorn's. Again, the branches whipped past me, until I landed in a giant web. The black spider-thing scurried out of its nest and rushed me. I twitched and jerked and slashed at the strands, and broke free. But there was nothing left to cushion my final descent.

The inevitable happened; my back struck the ground with a tremendous CLUNK! I heard my spine snap. I felt my body crumple. There could be no denial.

Then all went black, and in the instant that followed, I beheld a grim figure of death looming over me. He stood at my feet, tall and dark as a long shadow, and he wore a thick, hooded cloak. The grim figure grasped a long scythe taller than he was. The tip of the wicked blade was a hook for the unwilling. His face – if indeed he had one – lay shrouded in the black cloud of his cowled hood. Death stood there, judging. And... flat, as though lacking depth. My heart seized, my chest tightened.

I am dead and the Grim Reaper has come to claim my soul.

In the flurry of that realization, the budding of that free and rational thought, the dark apparition began to dissolve. First, he flickered, and then faded into tiny specks of patchy, utter blackness. One by one, the dots disappeared until there was nothing left to see of the Reaper. Nothing but empty space.

CHAPTER XXV

He who holds the light is King

Many years would pass before knowledge of the strange creature unleashed in the forest ever came my way. It was not a mere spider. The thing, the *Heart of Darkness*, was a danger to us all, returned to the hands of its maker for destruction. Just possessing it violated the Treaty of Nature. My uncle would have to answer for that, eventually.

I opened my eyes. Slowly the pale glow and familiar flicker of the crystal melted into view. My head was spinning, my mind charged. It had only been a recall, but the transition to reality had not been without doubt. And some of it, at least, had been false.

I lay frozen in a cold sweat, afraid to stir. My neck was stiff and sore. I found myself wishing that I had flattened out the lengths of deepwood in my pack before resting on them.

I reminded myself that what I had just relived was not an accurate portrayal of how the events really unfolded. I reminded myself that the gaping maw in the oak tree had opened a second time and swallowed the spider-thing, that I had landed far afield on a bed of thick moss, with only slight injuries, and that I had fled back to the cabin.

Kabor lay beside me breathing shallow and steady, fast asleep

– so much for guard duty. The bog stone rested between us. I lay still for some time, staring into the shadowy red void, pondering my dream and the notion of death. I hadn't really thought much about death before. Sure, in recent memory I had known Pips and Stouts with relatives who had passed on. I just never really thought much past it. I was too young when I lost my parents and when my grandfather, Paplov, had taken on their roles. Apart from a few scraps of distant, but fond, imprints from the earliest times, all that really stuck with me about them was a feeling… kindness. I can still see the blur of light behind my father's head as he stood tall above me, looking down kindly. "Little Newt," he would say as he patted my head. But I can never see the face. And Mother…

I shook it off. Morning or night, we would have to measure our time by the number of "sleeps," which got me wondering about just how many sleeps we could last. And what if the light…

No one will ever find us here.

I woke Kabor from his slumber, nudging him until he finally retaliated with a push back.

"Where… What is it?" he said, rubbing his eyes.

"Wake up. Get your stuff together; we have to go back… we have to go back and swim out. This was a mistake."

Kabor responded by closing his eyes. Gently, I shook him again until he was awake.

"We might not last if we continue this way."

"Go back?" said Kabor. "But you said we can't swim back – you can't just flip sides like that, not now."

"We tried, OK. We tried but now it's taking too long and we're just getting deeper and deeper into this system. Who knows where it ends, or if it ever ends."

"But the animals… we can't be too far from the surface. We could live off them, like you said."

"What if the light goes out Kabor? What if it just stops? Then what?"

"It won't go out."

"How do you know that?"

"I just know. Have you forgotten about the bog queens?"

"I don't forget."

"That doesn't mean you know what you're talking about, Nud. And this tunnel leads out. I can feel it in my bones."

"We don't know where it goes or what's waiting for us. Worse things than bog queens could be skulking about in these forsaken caves. Besides, in broad daylight with people looking for us all over the bog, the hags will make themselves scarce."

"Who's looking?" he said.

"Well… Paplov knows we're overdue, and Gariff's father, and the Numbits. The guards at the trailhead would be wondering what happened to Jory. They *must* all be looking for us."

I stood up, determined to get moving. I hooked in my bow and slung my backpack over my shoulders.

"If we leave right now," I continued, "we can get there for day-light – I think. I can make it to the surface; I know I can. Once I'm back on the trail, I'll fetch help to bring you up… and maybe a long rope would be all we need to guide you. You could follow it and—"

"No. I'm going with you from start to finish."

"You'll drown. I don't know the way, and I don't want to have to babysit you trying to find it."

"You want to leave me alone down here? I'll need the stone to see."

"You're half blind anyway, just sit in the dark and wait."

"I'm not half blind. If it's daylight like you say, you won't need it. Just swim towards the light."

"I'll need it to see through the dark water, and to get back to you."

"You have a perfect memory, just use it."

"I can't remember my way through the dark."

"At least if I have the bog stone, you can just swim to the light again to find me."

"If I have the light with me, I can probably remember my way."

"Probably? Weeds are weeds, Nud. And if you don't find your way back, what then? I'm left here to die, alone and in the dark."

Neither of us said anything for a long moment. When the light flickered on, Kabor turned his head sideways to fix his gaze directly on the stone. I sensed a scheme forming behind those dull eyes, lurking. He broke the silence.

"Maybe we can bust it into two pieces," he said, "and each take one."

"That's the surest way to snuff it out," I retorted, "and way too risky. You'll just have to wait in the dark for a little while. Like I said, I'm sure someone's already looking for us. All I need is some rope and…"

"No. I'd rather take my chances moving forward than backtracking. Up is up, it's not that complicated."

"We're lost down here. There's only one way out! We have to go back."

"I'll make it on my own then," he said.

Stubborn Stout.

"If we stick together, we stand a better chance," I said. "And you won't be able to see, remember?"

"Something's following us," he countered. "You saw it last night. No way. I'd rather take my chances with whatever's up ahead than be left in the dark wondering who will find my bones."

"I'm done arguing. We're going back and that's final."

I had the light, which gave me the upper hand, so I turned to go back the way we came. But before retracing a single step, Kabor grabbed for the SPARX stone with a sleight of hand so fast I didn't know what hit me. He swiped it and stepped back deftly.

"What are you doing? Give it back!"

"No."

"It's mine! Give it back!"

"You stu—," he started, before I cut him off with a surprise cuff to the head.

Kabor lurched backwards.

"Filcher! Liar!" I grabbed for the stone. He pushed back, holding it out of reach behind him. I muscled my way in closer, swiping to regain my prized possession.

"You… would just leave me here?" he said.

Kabor executed a swift maneuver and wriggled free. He backed away. "You need my help to get—"

I cut him off.

"You're the only one that needs help," I shot back.

"We'll see about that," Kabor replied. "So what will it be?"

The chamber went dark, and stayed dark. I took advantage of the moment and charged at Kabor before the stone lit up again. But he wasn't where I thought he would be. Kabor had sidestepped. I tumbled to the floor of the cave. Scraped and bruised, I brushed the dirt off and regained my footing. The light shone again. But it had grown dull and barely flickered for long at all. Kabor stood in front of an undiscovered section of passage. He was panting.

"I'm getting out of here," he said. "If you don't like it… TOUGH!" A kind of venom began to seep into his words. "And if you try to take the stone, I'll cover it up and bolt. I'll try smashing it into two before I give it up. You might never find your way out unless you follow me."

I burned like fire inside. *I never should have turned my back on the filcher. How dare he, after all I did for him.* I didn't rat out Kabor when he stole from the town, I introduced him to an Elderkin, I cut him in on our claim, and I saved his skin when he was drowning. I was stupid to think he was selfless back at the Mire Trail. *He just wanted the stone for himself, all along – my stone.*

"Last chance," he taunted, poised for a sprint.

Kabor knew I could easily outrun him. But with his blind

sense, he could cover the light and disappear in the dark tunnels. He could even hide in plain sight, or double back while I fumbled for him in the dark.

"The light is getting dimmer," I said. "It doesn't like you."

He hesitated.

"It's just a *thing*," he said. "It doesn't like or dislike anyone. And I'm not kidding about what I said. You'll get your stone back when we reach the surface. Until then, it's mine."

"It doesn't belong to you. Give it back. You're making it go out. Then we're dead meat."

"Oh ya?"

All went black. Long, lightless seconds passed. A shuffling noise sounded away in the tunnel, away in the dark.

Chk-chk-fwip… chk-chk-fwip.

I screamed at him. "STOP!" I had the eeriest sensation that this wasn't going to end well.

Kabor did not respond at all. The shuffling sounded again.

Chk-chk-fwip… chk-chk-fwip.

Then silence.

I spun around, searching for a glimmer of light.

"Open your hand! It's coming closer!"

Kabor made me wait for it. He made sure I understood what it meant to be alone in the dark with the lurking presence of danger nearby. He made sure I understood who was in control. Finally, after a long minute, he opened his palm. The light erupted into view.

"This place is full of strange noises in the dark," he said. "Do you want to be one of them?"

I said nothing. The anger burned inside.

"Well, do you?"

"No," I said. "OK then. We'll do it your way. Give me back my stone and we'll see what's up the passage."

"You'll get your stone back when we reach the surface."

It was worth a shot, but there would be no swaying him.

"Fine," I said, but my compliance was a thin veil. In bitter silence, I vowed to retrieve my gift from the Hurlorn's at any cost, the first chance I got. I also vowed never to trust Kabor again.

"One more thing," added Kabor.

"What now?" I said.

"Promise you won't try to take the stone back before we get to the surface."

"But it's mine."

"Just promise," he repeated firmly. He knew.

I crossed my fingers behind my back. "Fine, I PRO-MISE," I said, drawing out the syllables to the point of mispronunciation. "We'll do it your way, BUT... it's my stone and don't you EVER forget it."

The matter was settled. I gathered my gear again that had become scattered during the scuffle, and then adjusted my back-pack, belt and pouch fittings. Kabor didn't have much of anything to collect, but the one thing he did have was everything.

In utter darkness, he who holds the light is king.

CHAPTER XXVI

Interlude - Dark daemons

D oes it matter if you break a vow that you were forced into? I didn't really know the answer to that, at the time. Had I not surrendered to Kabor's demands and had the Stout followed through with his threat, I might have been left to flounder in the dark, cursed to die in those tunnels. I wasn't sure if he was capable of doing that to me, but I wasn't about to test the waters one way or the other either. So I forced myself to follow the footsteps of my new master faithfully. Naught but a faint flickering glow led the way. And with each desperate step, my mind raced, and my rage multiplied. There are at least a hundred ways to take someone down.

With that, the steps forward became easier, but an uneasy calm came over me as I plotted. In an odd way, I reveled in the notion that I would get back at Kabor. I began to imagine all sorts of machinations about exactly how his demise might come about by my hand. But one thing nagged at me. I had once taken something that wasn't mine to take, something of great importance. I was very young when I did it, but that was no excuse, and the reasons were not as grand…

After some speechless wandering and ample time to cool off,

I concluded that the best way to inflict revenge on Kabor was to bide my time and let Paplov know about what happened when I got home. He would bring in the town guard and Kabor would be in a mess of trouble when it came time to answer for his actions. Of course, there was one flaw in that plan – it would mean that he had been right and that his way led out, making him impossible to criticize. He would be a hero for sticking to his guns. Webfoot folk liked that sort of thing and Stouts idolized it.

Kabor held the stone tight in his thick fingers the whole way, as though it were a gold nugget. His mason-like hands were typical of Stouts from the Hills – like his uncle's, they were honest hands built for honest work, not for thieving.

And yes, in the perpetual night of the underground world, he who held the light was king. But even a king must sleep, eventually...

CHAPTER XXVII

Forsaken

The passage leading to a way out was brick-lined, just like all of the other subterranean halls in the area. And in the tinted glow cast by the stone, the walls flickered as red and pale as any we had stumbled upon. Nevertheless, a brief excursion inside was enough to confirm that we had entered into a new zone, and that something was very different.

For starters, the air seemed vaguely familiar. It had an earthy scent to it, more like that of the original point of entry than of the intervening cave system, but pleasant – without the underlying stench of decay. There was even a hint of freshness. On the wall, signs and markings began to appear in an unfamiliar script. Directions of some kind, it seemed, combined with arrows pointing to side tunnels or down. The down arrows were a mystery, drawing attention to unremarkable sections of the debris-laden floor. We cleared the area beneath the first few, searching for covered openings, more signs or hidden doors, but found nothing of the sort. It wasn't much of a concern, really – we were on the lookout for ways up, not down.

It wasn't until we came upon another dead-end that our prospects heightened. Cave fill from a ceiling collapse fully blocked passage from top to bottom. On the face of it, the dead-end was just another disappointment. The automatic thing to do was to backtrack and find a suitable side passage to try instead. And that is exactly what happened, or began to happen. But as I gazed back into the dim, empty tunnel, something compelled me not to abandon the area just yet. Call it a gut feeling. Whatever it was, something about that spot gently tugged at my instincts.

"Wait," I called out to Kabor, already well on his way back. "The ceiling."

His shoulders slumped, and then he turned around. After so much effort that had yielded so little, I didn't fault Kabor for his lack of enthusiasm. The fatigued Stout had already forsaken the blocked passage and seemed reluctant to linger any longer. Annoyed, he dragged his heavy feet the whole way over. It seemed to take all the strength he could muster to humor my bog-wild notions.

"All right," he said. "What is it?"

"Just a minute," I told him, and climbed to the top of the pile.

Water trickled down from a cavity in the ceiling, above the blockage. It wept onto the jumble of shale and clay and ran down the side of the pile, settling in a shallow puddle at the bottom.

While on top, I cleared enough debris from beneath the cavity to stick my head inside. It was too dark to see anything.

"Kabor, have a look," I said, and climbed down. I would have done it, but the Stout still held the stone and was loath to part with it. The Stout sniffed at the drafty air.

"Do you smell that?" he said.

"I know," I responded. "That's *real* bog air, I'd recognize it anywhere... I know the place... it's... it's..." I trailed off. Unfortunately for Pips, smell is the sense least linked to memory. I couldn't quite place it.

Kabor climbed the pile and stuck his head right up into the hole. Light in one hand and eyes an inch from the inner surface, he examined it closely. He said nothing for an excruciating minute.

"Well… what is it?" I said. "What do you see?"

"Ahh!" he screeched and jerked back. "Damn it! Right in my eyes." Muck covered the Stout's face. He rubbed his eyes to clean it off. A sly grin crept across his lips.

"What?" I asked.

"Look for yourself." The Stout moved aside and held the light up to the cavity so I could see.

It was more than just a gap in the ceiling; it was a natural shaft extending nearly straight up into the darkness. It was round and tubular in shape, with a glistening surface of wet clay. I felt a pulse of air pass by my face – definitely boggy.

The wave of realization hit me. I laughed and cried out. "We found it!"

"Hold on." Kabor nudged me aside and began to inspect the shaft acutely. He took on that engineering look that Gariff sometimes gets when sizing up a job.

"I don't know… might be a blind shaft," he said, still peering into it. "Plus those walls are slippery and unstable. If we fall—"

"We're dead and buried if the wall gives," I said.

"But on the upside," he offered, "the sides are soft enough to dig your hands and feet into. On the downside, even you barely fit."

We stood pondering for a long minute.

"Sometimes you have to follow a blind passage to know that it's blind," I said.

Kabor nodded in agreement.

"I can chimney up," he said at last. "I've done this sort of thing before in some of the old workings. There were some really narrow shafts in there – downright dangerous if you didn't know what you were doing."

"We have to go up one at a time though," he continued. "There's no sense in you having your head stuck up my rear. I'll go first and find solid holds and footings. I'll dig them in a bit so you can use them on your turn."

"I bet I can squeeze through the tight spots easier."

"Maybe so, but I'm going first anyway. If I can get through, you'll be sure to and we'll both make it out."

"It's a good thing Bobbin isn't with us," I said, not thinking. The words didn't sound right to my ears, and a sick feeling came over me for saying them.

Head askance, Kabor looked me in the eye.

"That is the plan, right?" he said. "That we *both* get out."

I nodded, feeling somewhat selfish about my earlier notion to abandon him to the dark and return later. The flag incident came to mind, suddenly. Truth is, I wanted to be the one to climb that time as well, but fear had gotten the better of me. Fear of climbing to the top of the flagpole and fear of being caught in broad daylight. It wasn't even the flag I wanted – it was the adventure. Once again, I let him take the risk.

"How am I supposed to see the walls when it's my turn?"

"Follow the light. Don't worry, I won't leave you behind. 'Never leave a hand behind.' That's as much a sacred code of honor as you'll ever find in the Bearded Hills. And that's not just for Stouts either. It applies to anyone – even boggy-smelling Pips."

"What if the shaft isn't straight, or what if it's too long?"

The pile shifted and Kabor braced himself as debris slid beneath his feet, and him along with it. When it settled, he stroked the wispy whiskers on his chin where his beard rightly should be, at least by Stout standards. As he stood there, a blob of runny muck splatted onto his head. He shook it out of his hair.

"I'll drop the stone down to you," he said.

"What?"

"We're in this together, right?"

"It might hit something hard or get stuck along the way," I said. "I'm not sure about this."

"Do you have a better idea?"

"Not really."

"Look, I'll call before I drop it down. It'll be up to you to catch it. You can't miss it – it's the only thing lit up around here. Have a little faith. Look for the glow."

Kabor was convincing, not just in his words but also in the conviction of his voice and the confidence that emanated from every pore. There would be no stopping him.

"OK." I surrendered. "Good luck."

"I could use a little luck today. This would be a lot easier with rope. If we had—"

"We don't. Get going. I don't want to be down here any longer than needed."

"I was just saying... ah, forget it." Kabor brushed a few mud-soaked strands of hair away from his face.

"Stay clear of the shaft at first or you might be sorry for it," he said.

With those words, Kabor clenched the stone in his teeth. He began his ascent, leveraging the walls to pull, push and twist his way up. I stood back as mud splattered down onto the pile.

"Don't swallow the spark!" I called. Not long ago, I would have wished he'd choke on it so I could rip it out of his throat. But I watched with hope as the wiry Stout slowly scaled the shaft, up and away, until the red glimmer of the stone grew dim in the distance.

I removed my pack – it would be too cumbersome for such a narrow climb. I was reluctant to leave my bow and the deepwood arrows behind, but bows and arrows are replaceable.

Kabor grunted and groaned about the climb, but made fair progress nonetheless. Judging roughly, he must have chimneyed a good twenty feet before disappearing around a slow bend, out of direct sight.

"Can you see daylight yet?" I yelled up the shaft.

"I'm not sure," he yelled back. "It's hard to see anything up here. There are roots and—"

That was the last of it, those final words lost to echoes in the dark.

A tremendous crash followed. I scrambled back. A pulse of water shot out of the hole. I backed away farther. The pile became drenched. The next instant, a loud sloshing sound funneled through from above, and the opening sighed with a strong rush of air.

Something big was coming. I began to run, but stumbled and fell. A muddy mess came crashing down behind me. A long moment passed in the dark before I processed what had just happened. And then it was quiet.

I tried to feel my way back to the opening, but cave fill blocked the passage. I couldn't get through. Kabor was nowhere to be found.

"KABOR!" I screamed.

I threw myself at the debris. Desperate, I clawed and dug my way in with my bare hands. I groped for a rock that could help and found a suitable piece of shale.

"KABOR, ARE YOU THERE? CAN YOU HEAR ME?"

Silence.

"KABOR!"

Scraping at the cave fill with my rock, I managed to gouge out a space. I tried digging up where I thought the hole might have been, but my efforts were repeatedly undone as runny sludge seeped down. *I can't see. I need to see.* I called out.

"KABOR, ARE YOU THERE?"

There was no answer.

I plunged my fists deep into the soft regions of muck, reaching and grasping for a limb, hair, clothes… anything. It was no use. The sludge was overwhelming. I dug and clawed and scratched at the earth until my arms went weak and my hands began to shake.

Soaked in sweat, fingers raw and stinging, I crumpled against the wall of the passage, exhausted. Warm blood trickled down along my battered knees as I caught my breath.

A minute went by way too fast. I forced myself to my feet and returned to the pile. I tried tapping rocks on the ceiling, hoping the sound would carry through – that he might be in a cavity.

There was nothing in response.

Then a horrible thought occurred to me. I had to stop.

I had to stop and shake my head.

I had to walk in circles, shake my head some more, and mutter "No" as I did so.

"NO!" I screamed, to stifle that unfeeling, inner voice.

"no…" I said quietly.

I will not think or ever say that he had it coming.

That was for everyone else to say. And they would, if only they knew.

CHAPTER XXVIII

Cloaked

So deep underground and so far away from everything that matters, at times I welcomed the idea of transmuting skin to bark, even begged for it. No more pain or weary limbs or pangs of hunger to dampen the mortal spirit, no infections or maladies of the flesh, no need for sleep, increased resilience as opposed to infirmity over the centuries, and less mortal concerns altogether, I suspected.

But if the inevitable were to occur while still trapped underground, the re-becoming's leaves would have no choice but to unfurl in utter darkness. Would they sustain the new being? I think not. Trees need light, but do Hurlorns? I didn't have the answer.

Such was the doom and gloom that consumed me as I paced in the dark hallway of the collapse.

No respectable Stout would leave someone behind to perish underground. But what is a Pip to do about a Stout that might already be dead, was *likely* dead? Did they all perish... all of my friends? Am I the last?

Back and forth... back and forth... the monotony was strangely reassuring, a diversion from all the mulling over things I couldn't possibly control. Pacing, even if it produced nothing, was better than pure inaction. Pure inaction would have been unbearable. Somehow, the motion kept a part of me busy that just wanted to curl up and die, or scream, or do something drastic... something *extreme*.

And it seemed that as long as I continued to pace, some grand idea lurking in the back of my mind might take shape, propelled into being by the sheer momentum of my stride and the sharpness of my turns. But nothing brilliant came of those dark minutes, and the gray matter of my intellect left me holding a black list of sad alternatives to choose from instead.

"A hard choice," Paplov would have said. He warned me about having to face situations where there were no right choices or easy answers. "There's value in waiting," he said on one occasion. That meant do nothing until you know what to do. Years later, on another occasion, he told me to "just choose *something*, follow through with it, and hope for the best." He never gave his reasons.

I bowed my head for several long minutes and prayed to the nameless gods of my father. It was more of a complaint, really. I promised to be good. Praying was not something I did very often.

Somehow, the exchange left me feeling refreshed. I revisited the blocked shaft and tried to reach Kabor again. After all, he might be stuck in an air pocket. I quickly settled into a routine: dig, tap, listen; dig, tap, listen; and so forth. And every so often, I took a break to resume pacing. Through it all, I pondered the situation at hand.

Kabor should have come out with the initial rush of water. He must have either dug in his heels – a typical stubborn Stout thing to do – or become stuck on his way down. Either way, if the collapse started higher in the shaft, he should have come down with the cave fill, otherwise there would be a lot less of it because the space was too cramped to let that much material pass around him. Since I did not find him in the pile, odds seemed not terrible that the collapse started *beneath* Kabor, perhaps in a spot he had disturbed that took some time to react, or maybe he started an avalanche with his foot.

With Kabor's chances of survival stabilizing in my mind, I began to consider my own prospects. In utter darkness, it would take every bit of razor sharp memory and every pinprick of heightened awareness to have a chance of making it back to the entry cave. And this wasn't some ordinary game of "Green Ghost." If I messed up, I couldn't just open the blinds and end the game. There were enough turns, dead ends, pits, and circling paths to make the darkened course deathly treacherous. The hard choice was clear. I had to try.

I will not wait here much longer.

But suppose Kabor did make it to the surface, got help, dug his way back down through the shaft and didn't find me waiting. Then what? He would still know the general layout of the caves, and he would have brought with him lanterns and loud horns and certainly experienced miners.

Perhaps the others made it to safety as well. Then a search party might have already discovered the entry cave. Help might be on its way, trudging through the caves. Would they know which way to go? A good bogger should be able to track our course.

No one is coming, warned a small voice inside.

I continued to dig, making fair progress for a time. I managed to excavate an arm's length into the cavity without provoking another collapse. But the stability was short-lived. A minute later more sludge slid down the neck of the cavity and jammed it up again. It was hopeless.

Defeated, I decided to finish up with one last round of tapping, rock on rock. Finally, I got a reply. But it wasn't the one I was hoping for.

Chk-chk-fwip… chk-chk-fwip.

My heart skipped a beat. I didn't dare breathe. The scraping sound was near. It was *really* near. Emboldened by the dark, I heard the creature scuffle overhead and then down along the opposite wall. All became silent. I thanked The Nameless that whatever it was had backed off a bit.

Back against the wall, I blindly squatted to the ground and felt through the rubble until I found a sharp, fist-sized rock. I lifted it high above my head. Muscles tensed as I waited in the dark, ears pricked, and breaths thin.

But I needed more air.

I breathed heavy once.

The silence and waiting amplified my fears. *Can the thing somehow see me?* My heart raced and pumped so quickly, so violently, that it hurt my chest. It resonated in my ears so loud, I feared the thing would hear the wild thumping.

The noise started up again, but softer.

Shsh-shsh-fwiph… shsh-shsh-fwiph.

It slowed, and even crept – a disciplined and willful motion like the careful, muted footfalls of a cat stalking oblivious prey… just before the pounce. I could barely discern the sound over the pounding of my own heartbeat. Again, there came an awful silence.

I had decided to take another normal breath, but in that instant of anticipation, it was stolen from me.

A moist, sticky mass slapped me in the face and stuck there like a wet towel. I couldn't breathe.

I felt for the thing. The body was incredibly thin and flat, but solid like pure muscle. I tried to pull it off, but its back was slippery and coated with slime. I dropped the rock and tried to pry the creature free, but it was clamped on tight.

I can't breathe.

Frantic, I dropped to the ground and rolled, pulling and clawing at the thing on my face. But I could not get a good hold on it. Under the slime lay stony flesh, impervious to my nails. The beast wrapped its long, winding tail around my neck and began to squeeze. Grunting and struggling, I rolled onto my face and shook my head violently, scraping the creature against the roughness of the floor. But the mud was too slick and the thing only squeezed tighter.

I felt the smothering creature's mouth open, near to mine. A ring of razor sharp teeth pressed against my cheek, and a rough tongue – rough enough, I reckon, to lick the flesh right off my face, down to the bone. A head butt to the wall caused the teeth to retract.

Reeling, I tried to peel the creature off again. It just wasn't working, so I tried another head butt. The thing reeled back and emitted a shrill screech. It came partially undone. I tore it off.

Free at last, I gasped for air and fell against the pile. I swept my hands through the debris, searching for another rock. All at once, the darkness lifted. The mud suddenly lit up, and then went dark again. My wayward crystal had found its way back to me. When it lit up again, I grabbed the stone and gave it a quick wipe against my shirt. I held it like a burning torch.

I scanned the area. At the first set of flashes, the passage appeared empty: the walls were blank and fill covered the floor. During the next flurry of sparks, a thick glob dropped next to me. I looked up. The creature was there. Its skin matched the color and texture of the ceiling so perfectly it looked like part of the rock. The light went out. I stepped away. On the next flash, I noticed a flap of black skin that seemed out of place on the thing, loose and hanging with fluid dripping down – the damage I inflicted.

The stone went dark for a long moment.

Chk-chk-fwip… Chk-chk-fwip.

"YAAW!" I yelled, waving my arms wildly in the dark, "GET OUT! BE OFF!"

I picked up a rock. The creature was an easy target, wide and flat, and far too confident in its disguise. I waited patiently for the light to return. When it did, I flung the rock – a solid hit, square on the back. The creature jerked and fell. It twisted and contorted in mid air as it plummeted, reminding me of a falling cloak. But that cloak never hit the ground. Rather, the thing spread itself out in an arc and *flew* away down the tunnel with the pulsed grace of a bat – long, smooth glides punctuated with abrupt shifts in height and bearing.

I groped for another rock and tried my luck once more. It sailed through the air and missed by a wide margin. The flying thing accelerated around a corner and out of sight.

I gathered my pack. It was half-buried in cave fill. I readied my bow as well and crouched with my back to the pile. Arrow notched, for a very long time I watched, waited, and listened for the creature's return. My head pulsed as my heart pounded at my chest.

Once I realized that the creature was truly gone, I relaxed my stance. My face felt sticky.

I made one last feeble attempt to find Kabor before turning to leave. In a small way, I was glad not to find him. Not finding him meant he could still be alive… but without the stone.

I hauled on my pack, slung the bow over one shoulder, then turned to the open passage and started along it.

I thought about something Kabor had said. He had been right; it wasn't beyond me to abandon him, alone in the dark.

CHAPTER XXIX

Interlude - That stupid hag

Now I set out to tell you the tale of how I became the gnarly beast that I am, and ere I have brought you to the very time and place when and where I felt less deciduous than ever before or ever after... at least in that life. A world away from sunshine, rain and the free wind that carries it, deep within the element of earth, so deep even roots chance not to go, I sat skulking in the dark, my only company retched vermin and once animated fossils locked in shale, long ago having met inevitability. I contemplated the notion that I would never see the true blue sky again; and that my bones might one day be found amongst those fossils, encased in a silt sarcophagus with evidence of being gnawed upon.

The storm has finally arrived and Amot is off making preparations. He has more Fyorn in him than he cares to admit. I have taken shelter in a west-facing crevice. It is cramped, but dry and the old ranger set me up with enough light to see by and enough ink to mark the pages. May these words find the right reader when the need is greatest.

Back to what's important. Never lose sight of what's important.

I have somewhat spoiled my own tale, the story of my great adventure, in the way I have dished it out. Dishes... Ha! My dish is the massive granite formation that cups the overburden. I eat dirt now.

You must have reasoned that *somehow* I escaped the recesses of the dark zone in order to be here, writing this. The only real mystery is how and when I met my fate. For the time being, I continue to reserve the telling of that part of the adventure, while you continue to wonder – if you are the type to wonder about such things.

I will no longer hold back that which is rightfully yours for having read this far – the tale of Holly, Bobbin, Gariff, and Jory on the Mire Trail in the sights of the dreadful bog queens. For this compilation I borrow the collective accounts of all those who were able to speak of the incident afterwards. It is not an adventure, sadly, so much as a tragedy, and the sap runs free whenever I must think it through and through. If you abhor sad tales, skip this part. You have been warned.

*

The mangled mass that was once easy-going Jory lay half-sunk in the bog water, wrapped in half-decayed grasses and moss.

The search crew was quick to find the first of the missing teens and their guardian. But with such a distressing discovery, their optimism for finding the others in good health withered. Mer Andulus was among the volunteers.

"What could have done such a thing?" Mer said, shaking his head as he reached out with his walking stick to comb through some brush.

An air of impatience still lingered in Holly's voice, and worry kept the skin tight around her eyes.

"I told you all a thousand times already," she said, "we were ambushed… bog queens… remember?"

"There is no such thing as bog queens, child." Mer sighed, eyes fixed on the horizon, the grey in them reflecting the morning sky. The old Stout prospector took in the wideness of the scene for a long minute. He always thought the bog was beautiful. He also thought he'd seen it all.

Mer reached over to lay a hand on Holly's shoulder, to comfort her. But Holly would not be comforted. She spurned him, turned aside and left him hanging.

"I believe you experienced something treacherous. Of that there's no doubt. Thieves out of Proudfoot, or so I hear." Mer's voice trailed off into stoutish mumblings and inaudible curses.

Holly did her best to tone down her whimpering. She had heard the rumors. There were many, many rumors, ranging from the mundane to the extreme.

Indeed, "thieves out of Proudfoot" was one of the more sensible speculations.

"Ya know," some folks said, "sometimes them bog lights is swamp gas and sometimes they's wicked spirits." For all Holly knew, there might have been some truth to that one.

"The Numbit boy went mad and ran away. He's always been a little off. The others got lost trying to find him." That one, at least, was quickly set straight by Mrs. Numbit, proud owner of the Flipside rumor mill, along with her husband. No one dared say "He got so hungry he ates them" to her face. Mrs. Numbit was always great that way. She pushes her nose right into people's business and gets the better of them. Holly received more support from the Numbit family than she ever got at home. And when hurtful whispers arose out of Proudfoot about Holly's upbringing, Mrs. Numbit was there to put a stop to it.

Holly tried not to think of poor Jory. Jory was young, and good, and charming and handsome and brave. *Was.* She never got a good look at the body that was found. She was glad for that. Though the corpse was mangled beyond recognition, the crew had been able to surmise it was that of the young guard. Shredded remnants of a once dapper uniform, found scattered in the near vicinity, made the identification certain.

It had been two days since the disappearance of her friends. Determined to do whatever she could to find them, Holly had insisted on joining the search crew during the day. It was tiresome recanting the events to official, after official, after official as volunteers rotated on and off the job. None of them fully believed her. And she didn't like the looks they gave her. Some offered pitiful stares; some looked at her as though she'd gone mad. Others, she thought, glanced and pointed as they conspired with one another, whispering that she was holding something back and that her version of events had been falsified, or that she was purposely leading them astray. *Let them think what they want. They're just stupid.* All these things she imagined as she meandered about the site.

Even Fyorn had heard the news and showed up to help. He was a marvel to behold in his tall helm and leather armor, with an impressive sword strapped over one shoulder as if he expected to do battle. As out of place as he appeared, Fyorn at least had believed her, Holly was sure of it. He'd gone out with the boggers in their small watercrafts and even down under with the divers where Bobbin was last seen.

The woodsman was up the trail a ways at the moment, pointing across the bog waters as he conversed with volunteers in his mild Elderkin accent. He insisted there was a trail in the grasses they could follow, if they looked hard enough. The boggers were skeptical.

"There are two distinct trails," he said, pointing into the bog, "but they break off out that way… there and there." Fyorn's hand chopped at the air in one direction and then the other. The outdoorsmen continued on about that topic for some time.

Rumor had it that Nud's grandfather had immediately set out to join the search when he heard the news. "Not again," he was heard saying, as he gathered his hat and cane.

Mayor Undle delivered the ill tidings personally, and had assured the aging Pip that everything possible was being done to find the missing teens. "Then why are you here?" he had said to the mayor, "You should be out there too."

Despite Undle's insistence that he stay in bed, while still in his night robe Paplov shushed the mayor and stormed out of his hut. He collapsed before even reaching the gate, far too ill to exert himself.

Such information had come to Holly through eavesdropping – an activity she would never have even considered were it not for the spotter's cloak and the prevailing circumstances. In the course of her information gathering, Holly learned many other useful and interesting things about Webfooters, some of which were exceedingly private and unsettling.

One of the councillors had a mistress and another, Mrello, accepted bribes; a group of Stouts from the Hills (not Gariff's clan) were charging double the fair price to straighten out a sinking building that they built purposely deficient years earlier and, to make matters worse, they were cutting corners. As a server at the Flipside, Holly was used to overhearing such talk and, for the most part, looked the other way or, on occasion, might drop just the right hint to a patron she sympathized with. But with the power of wild elderkin camouflage, she found darker secrets too, either too disturbing or too damaging to repeat.

Holly Hopkins paused by the tree where she had donned her cloak, searching for signs of the bog queen's passing. There was nothing. Up ahead she could see Gariff and his father talking with Pip divers near the last known location of Nud and Kabor.

The events of that dreadful day consumed Holly. *It was dark and we were divided. The witches planned it. Where are my friends? What am I missing?*

*

Holly grew frantic when she saw the hag pull Kabor and Nud underwater. She couldn't believe what she saw, what she thought she saw. Her dear friends just gave up without a struggle. *The hag has them by a spell,* she thought. *They won't take me like that,* she assured herself.

Gariff fought on relentlessly. Hopeless or not, he would never give in – stubborn and Stout to the bone he was. Pushed under repeatedly, arms flailing, he kept bobbing back up for air. He desperately tried to land a punch, grabbing and pulling at anything he could get his hands on. Even when underwater, Holly could hear his muffled grunts of determination – overtaken, but not yet beaten.

The parrot hag had been the one to chase Holly down. She tackled the serving girl and pulled her into the bog water. The Pip's wide feet were all that kept her from sinking into the moss.

"Let me go you stupid witch!" cried Holly.

She scratched at the wretch's face. The hag didn't seem to notice, or care, and squealed in delight as she forced Holly's head down with ease, like a mother dunking a stubborn child in the bathtub – except the hag held her there.

On the brink of suffocation, and without known cause or warning, the parrot hag relaxed her grip. Holly pushed and wriggled her way above the waterline. She gulped for air too soon and took in a mouthful of the quaggy water, and heard a voice over the sounds of her own sputtering – a singing voice, and the source of the hag's hesitation. It was not a change of heart or feeling of pity that saved her; it was Bobbin. At the Flipside, the baker boy sang all the while when preparing food. Apparently, he did the same when seeking a hag's attention.

The still air echoed with his taunting. He stood at the trailside on a patch of moss, waving his arms and mocking them. He explained by melody exactly how they became so ugly, and why they had to steal children – "because no man would ever have them." Abruptly, he stopped, and pulled something out of his pocket.

"Na-na-na-na-na… I-have-your-sparkle-stone." The immature

Pip wiggled his mid-section foolishly and pointed at the hag that held Holly in her wiry grasp.

He plugged his nose. "You-oo-oo sti-ink... bog breath!" Then Bobbin lifted one hand high above his head, with the palm opened just enough to reveal that he held a stone there, obscured by the dim light and completely unrecognizable at a distance. It was not even flashing.

"Want a kiss?" said the parrot hag.

"Come and get it you dirty old bag of weeds... I-know-you-want-it."

The dim-witted parrot hag shook her head twice, dropped all that she was doing and looked around. She seemed confused, as though she did not know where she was.

Then she glared back at Bobbin, fixated on the stone he held. A sudden crazed look came over her. The blank, stupid expression, ever present on her face, was ripped away by maniacal rage. The hunched-in hag noted the change and scolded her for it.

"No, no! <gurgle> Stay! Stay!" she spat. "Lose them both, you will. Stuu—pid."

Bobbin noted the shift in character as well, and in the way that he stumbled back there was a hint of lost nerve. He carefully shuffled farther out onto the floating moss, to the very edge of the water.

But the hag who was no longer a mere parrot had set her sights on Bobbin. She must have taken his subtle retreat as a sign of weakness. Immediately, she let go of Holly and bounded towards the uncertain Bobbin like a wolf on a scared rabbit. A scared, pudgy rabbit. And a really ugly wolf.

In the time taken to snap at her disobedient accomplice, the hunched-in hag had turned her attention away from the struggling Stout. That was a mistake. Gariff had been pushed around, dragged underwater and was short on breath, but he was determined like no other.

Taking full advantage of the distraction orchestrated by

Bobbin, the burly Stout ducked under the hunched-in hag and lifted her right up out of the water. She gurgled and writhed and squirmed in protest, and it wasn't long before she had twisted her way back down. But Gariff had gained a few steps towards the trail, tethered as he was to her. It was all he needed to gain solid footing.

Holly, free at last, gasped, coughed and spat out bog water as eloquently as her nemesis. With one hand beating on her chest, she cleared her throat and called out.

"No Bobbin! <cough, cough> What are you doing?"

But it was too late to change the sequence of events that he had initiated. The parrot hag ignored her master, took the bait and closed in on the gentle Pip with alarming vigor.

"Catch me if you can!" Bobbin squealed, just before hitting the water in a ripping dive. The adept swimmer propelled himself under with the grace of a bullfrog. In the blink of an eye, only the slowly rising depression in the moss and wide ripples in the water betrayed that he was ever there. Holly staggered to shore, hunched over and gagging.

The parrot hag screeched and plunged in after Bobbin, a tangled mess of flowing grass and flailing limbs. As far as Holly could tell, no one was looking when she turned her cloak inside out. Just before closing the hood, she glared at the hideous leader, still battling Gariff.

The unmovable Stout had his heels dug in, braced for a wrestle. And when the hunched-in hag turned back to him, with firm quickness Gariff diverted her grapple, and when she fell, with solid leverage he lifted her right up out of the water again. In the air, she was off balance.

"Uggh!" she screeched, unable to contain her frustration. Gariff used the hag's own tether on him to keep her twisting, writhing body in check. But before he could take full advantage of the situation, more tendrils wrapped around his face and neck, even creeping inside his mouth, his ears, and his nose. She would have him suffocate, above or below the boggy water. She was determined to have her way.

Holly slipped into the water and the mayhem. A new demeanor washed over her, cold and placid. Moments later, the Stout looked down in terror at the strangely swirling water and the subtle splashes around him, unnerving and phantom-like. A ghastly whiteness spread across his face.

The hag looked about, uncertain.

From behind the hag, Holly raised a waterlogged stick, long and jagged. It was especially solid, and the jagged edge especially sharp. She took careful aim and plunged it through the wretch's back. Gariff observed the stick punch through, beneath the hag's ribs. She arched backwards and screamed. Gariff stumbled back as the hag released the tendrils around his face and neck. She fell into the shallow bog water. The old woman's eyes went wide in disbelief. She stared, gaping, at the ooze-coated point of Holly's stick protruding from her belly. The hag spun her head around to face her attacker. It was the only time she ever appeared fearful, for all that she beheld was the serving girl's disembodied face set atop a blurred, dripping form. Holly wrenched the stick free and stabbed the hag again, and then many more times for good measure. Holly could not have stopped herself if she tried. Each time the wretch jerked and writhed. After a flurry of piercings, exhausted, the Flipside girl ended it all with one final thrust to the neck, then she let go of the stick. Her arms dropped.

It was Gariff's turn. The Stout took over and grabbed the beaten creature with strong, determined hands. She still had tendrils on him. He carried her as she writhed and moaned. She tried to pull the stick out of her neck. Held fast by a knot in the wood that had passed straight through the wound, the stick would not draw free. Eyes glazed, and in senseless desperation, the dying hag rolled the stick in small circles, inscribing an invisible cone in the open air.

Stretching the hole only served to open the wound. Thick, dark liquid pulsed out.

"She's not done fer yet," said Gariff. A level of sternness that only Stouts possess infused him. He laid her down and tore at the hag's twisted tendrils, severing the last remnants of her hold on him. Then he lifted her above his head and firmly carried her to a half-submerged log, spiked with a rat's mouth of jagged old branches. Gariff thrust her down upon the broken tips, impaling the wretch. The despicable bog thing did not so much as twitch after the impact.

Full of battle rage and with one opponent down, the Stout turned his aggression to the remaining hag, the parrot, and charged after her. But that hag was still within the pool where Bobbin had disappeared, continuing her dives to find him. When she caught sight of the berserking barbarian, and after she beheld the dismal fate of her sister, the parrot-no-more hag slipped under the mosses and disappeared. Gariff stopped at the edge of the bog pool and stared into the moss-filled depths. He knew better than to enter. The ripples in the water faded with Gariff still standing there watching, waiting. He looked back to where he'd last seen Holly; she was gone too. Gariff jumped a nervous jump when he heard a girl's voice so near.

"Come here," said the voice.

Gariff spun left, then right, then all the way around. It sounded like she was standing right next to him, but where?

"Holly?" he said to the wind.

He spotted the eyes first. On meeting her floating gaze, he realized it could only be Holly in her elderkin cloak.

The serving girl had already gained a full appreciation of the benefits of invisibility. As long as she kept the hood closed, everything about her was hidden. But if she wanted to see the outside world, she had to reveal at least her eyes. And the cloak worked in water as well as air, apart from the displacement of fluid around her physical being, which could not be helped.

Holly Hopkins opened her cloak to Gariff and revealed herself fully, beckoning him to join her in the safety of its confines. She was shivering.

"Wow, that really works," said Gariff, dumbly.

Holly nodded. "We have to hide. Hurry, come in."

Gariff obliged. They crouched down and hid together for a time, and fixed their eyes upon the scene where Bobbin had dove in. Together, they peeked through the hood of the cloak. There was plenty of room for two in there. He kept her warm. She kept him hidden.

The impaled hag remained motionless, and the other never returned. Bobbin never came up for air either. Kabor, Nud and Jory were long gone. The Shadow in the Water was nowhere to be seen either. It was almost *too* calm, eerily calm, with only the gentle drone of insects breaking the twilit silence. The two waited together a bit longer.

After a time, they convinced themselves that there were no more dangers lurking anywhere near. Holly and Gariff abandoned their hiding place. Gariff emerged from the cloak, and both scanned the bog from the trail's edge to the horizon for signs of those gone missing. They saw little evidence that their friends had even been there.

There were many tufts of grass, mounds and stumps to provide hiding places, so they called out for their companions as well, mindful of the possible consequences of drawing attention to themselves. Their voices bellowed out into the quaggy expanse and were lost on the absorbing mosses. There was no response.

Defeated, Holly bowed her head and walked along the trailside to where Bobbin had dove in. She stepped out onto the moss and gazed into the night-shimmering pool.

"We have to go back to town for help now," said Gariff, "We've done all we can. I can't cross the water or search underneath it."

"I can," said Holly. Gariff took her hand.

"No," was all he said.

Holly looked to the skewered hag, then up at Gariff, sobbing. "We as good as killed her, didn't we?" she said.

"We did what needed to be done... besides, she looked half dead already, right? I mean, she wasn't really alive to begin with... a bog queen from down under is unnatural. She couldn't have been a *regular* living thing," said Gariff. "And I'm the one that finished her off. Remember?"

Holly nodded and wiped her eyes. "That stupid hag," she said, then painted her face with a forced smile.

"We have to mark the spot," said Gariff.

Under the darkness of a new moon, the two survivors set out for Webfoot together and reported the incident to the first guard they met at the Long Wall. A search party was quickly organized, and many hands deployed to the bog even before the rising sun burned off the mists of the new morning.

PART II:
Order of the Undying

It was the Orbweaver who created the universes for Her own consumption, but only after they produced Knowledge. So She infused a strand into every single thing and wove them all together, like a great web, to track the production of Knowledge. One man learned the secret of the Orbweaver. One man realized when it was time for the Orbweaver to reap what She had sown. And when She came for him, he rolled dice for all humankind, and won.

And this man devised a way to make peace with the Orbweaver, or so he thought. His people had to be disciplined though, and obedient, giving, and most importantly, forever creators of new Knowledge.

But the man was wrong. The only way to beat Her was to out-learn Her.

- The Diviner

CHAPTER XXX

Retreat

Paplov was in the den plotting his next course when the news came. Old Mayor Flosh had sent his condolences, along with word that the search could not be kept up any longer: The town had done everything it could, and it was time for people to get on with their lives. The volunteer search crew would be disbanded after an extensive, three-week investigation that had turned up nothing.

The decision did not sit well with Paplov, and half the town was still fuming over the incident. The Bearded Hills and Proudfoot had offered help that Council largely ignored, stating that their own people were best equipped to handle the situation and that bringing in outsiders would just cause more problems. Then came "volunteer" searchers from Harrow – soldiers. They received a hero's welcome. Yet, less than a day in, the Harrow crew had announced that the search was hopeless. Sadly, the entire operation was a mess, and badly handled.

Paplov had his own ideas about where the group was last seen and their heading. Why there had been no sign of my parents or the other delegates was puzzling to the point that he suspected foul play. Harrow claimed they never received their "guests," but not all Webfooters trusted the word of the dominating power, especially Paplov.

When the town officials arrived, I was waiting on the stepping stone path outside our hut, as I had done each and every day since my parents' disappearance. I had hoped to be the first to hear the good news that they had been found; that they had taken a wrong turn, gotten lost, and ended up in the Western Tor or some other unlikely place. After the officials left, I lingered there under the willow for what must have been hours. I didn't go inside for lunch and Paplov didn't make me eat any dinner... both dishes sat full, nothing touched.

The days that followed were very quiet. Paplov spent a lot of time out and about, while I stayed home and ate meals with the neighbors. They were especially kind to me, and they were always so sure that my parents and the others soon would be found – the next day, the day after that, and the day after that. But I could see their smiles wearing thin as the days rolled by, and I caught how their expressions changed when they looked away after saying it.

I never stopped believing that one day they would come back – that Mother would come running to me with arms wide and a big smile and give me the biggest hug and tell me how much she missed me. She would never leave me alone... I suppose I was never quite alone though. I always had Paplov. He'd always lived with us.

Even he wouldn't think to look down here. Who would? – no one I know.

Here, beneath the bog, I have no one. I am really, truly, alone.

A Pip's sharp mind can become confused in a maze with so many twists and turns and obstacles along the way, and in such poor illumination. Nevertheless, finding the entry cave *should* have been straightforward because Kabor *should* have been there to help. I needed his discerning eye for geologic detail and good instincts for direction and slope, if not stability. Working together, the path would have been obvious, one filling in the gaps where the other faltered. But Kabor would never go that way. He would never go back. Without the Stout to lean on, I had to think of some new way to better my odds.

I dumped the contents of my pack and rummaged through the sticks of deepwood and the odds and ends until I located my deepwood box. Flipping up the lid, I nodded with a grin at what I saw. Inside, everything was dry and intact: a folded piece of parchment, a pen and two ink bottles, one quarter-full and the other full – all leftovers from Proudfoot that I didn't bother to remove.

"Perfect," I said to the box, and perhaps the lurking cloaker – my name for the face-sucking creature that had attacked me and probably was still tracking my every move. "I'll map my way back, which is half as good as having mapped my way here. And you, *Cloaker*, if you're listening, will make a fine welcome mat some day."

Just having a plan set my mind at ease. It would make for slow going, but slow and steady progress towards a reasonable goal beats going nowhere fast and just getting more and more lost. I gathered my scattered belongings together and set out once more, sketching as I went.

Right away, there were difficulties with the map. There was no way of knowing what direction I started off in, or subsequent directions except by reference to the most recent bearing. Paplov's compass, which I had inherited simply by never bothering to return, was safely at home and neatly stashed away in the drawer of my night table. So I made another vow that I could never keep, with the walls and with the vermin and with the face-sucking cloaker to bear witness.

"Never again will I leave without my compass…"

That just opened the floodgates. I couldn't stop there.

"…and a lantern… and a small shovel… and food… and clean water… plus a change of clothes."

The list went on.

"…some soap… a toothbrush… matches."

And there were many emergencies and unexpected turns for the worse to consider, and so the list expanded.

In the end, it seemed impractical to carry everything that might be needed. The sorts of things Mer Andulus carried were probably more than enough. He went into the wild for weeks on end and returned none the worse for it. All the prospector had on him that morning we met in Webfoot was a small pack with pots and pans tied on, an axe handle sticking out one side, something rolled up and roped on top of the pack (probably bedding or a small tent), a pick and a hunting knife on his belt, a pair of good, solid boots, light clothes brown and beige and tan in color, and a full brimmed hat with bug netting.

I kept on with what little I had until I came to a part of the cave system where the path split into three forward directions, fanning out in a wide arc. None of them looked familiar. A short walk down each did nothing to confirm which one we had originally taken. I stood at their junction, staring at each in turn. The walls pulsed in an angry red glow with the flicker of the light-bearing bog stone. The throbbing in my head began to pulse along with it.

This is hopeless. I cursed the old tree gum that brought me to that place, and I cursed its former bearer.

I sat there for a long minute feeling sorry for myself, until I felt a small, tickling patter across the back of my neck. In a frenzy, I brushed the culprit away and rubbed my skin vigorously, then ran my fingers through my hair. A large centipede dropped from my sleeve and scurried off along the floor. I won't say what I did with it.

The entire situation infuriated me to no end. I shook my fists at the cave roof and pulled at my hair. I hurled curses at Kabor for not listening, at Gariff for not helping as much as he could have, at Bobbin for being utterly useless, and at Jory for not defending us the way he said he would. No blame could I assign to Holly. I finished deflated, and hollow, rhythmically thumping the back of my head against the stone-block wall. The mind-numbing pain flooded my senses. And as I sat there exhausted, having expelled all of my untamed demons, the strangest chill came over me. It was a chill that told me I was not alone – speaking ill of the dead while the dead listened in. An icy tremor shot up my spine. *But would the dead hear my unkind words? Of course not – they're dead.* It was a silly, superstitious thought.

And as the trailing guilt swept over me, the fury that had taken me at unawares began to pass. A minute later, it was gone. I relaxed my arm and my grip on the stone, and then sighed deeply. Tantrums can be exhausting.

Focus on the problem, I told myself. A fact is a fact. I was lost and lost is lost, no matter whose fault it was. Somehow, on the way in, I had failed to notice the funneling in of three passages into one while following Kabor. Maybe I was half-asleep at the time, or distracted, or maybe the shadows painted the illusion of a single passage. *Deal with it.*

"Holly. Bobbin... Jory." In my mind's eye, I could see all three faces, plain as day. Bobbin's was round and smiling and mischievous; Holly's coy expression drew me in; Jory's steadiness inspired confidence.

I looked up and scouted around. *It's left.* I have no idea how I knew.

With loose stones, I created an arrow-shaped marker to show which direction I planned to take. Then, flattening the map out on the ground, I traced out my path as best I could, having kept track of paces to record distances and estimating the angles by eye.

After what must have been hours trekking through tunnels, I began tripping over my feet, and nodding off mid-stride. I made it to a familiar chamber, beside the whirlpool Kabor and I had stopped at on the way in. Eyes barely open, I drank deep and refilled my waterskin. An opportunity for food presented itself. I won't mention what I ate. Then I found a place to get comfortable, and looked over my map.

As I sorted out the bearings and slopes, something about the architecture kept nagging at me. The man-made caves looked more like ruins than anything else I had seen. But what really struck me was that everything looked better upside down. Archways should close in at the top, not the bottom, to better support their load. Gariff had taught me about keystones. It's no wonder the tunnels were littered by cave-ins if the ceiling was meant to be the floor.

The idea was intriguing, but sleep weighs down your eyelids regardless of the bright ideas behind them. So I slumped down and settled in for a rest with my back against the wall. I tucked the map away in its box and the stone in my pocket, and then finally closed my eyes and began to nod off.

No, the cloakers. I jarred myself awake. *I will not let them suffocate me in my sleep.* Kabor and I had caught our first glimpse of a cloaker in that very chamber.

I fumbled for my pack in the dark and dumped out its contents one more time. Then I slipped the leather loosely over my head and closed my eyes once more. I drifted off imagining Kabor talking it up with the townsfolk and figuring out how to free me from my entombment. I could literally hear his voice. It was a pleasant thought and I wanted to hang onto it. *Nevermind that Kabor dropped the stone and has no light to see by. Nevermind that if I really believed he was alive, I would still be at the pile, waiting, not here…*

*

I was taken aback when I found myself approaching the entry cave, in such short order that the travel time seemed to have just melted away. Everything seemed closed in as I crawled on hands and knees through the low tunnel to get there. Near the waterline, I noticed something not there before… a lump of weeds… no… a person… a wet person tangled in weeds. The person was lying down as though sleeping. *Has someone else come to the air pocket?* I wondered. *Holly?*

I crept over slowly, carefully, so as not to disturb. It was a woman, wrapped not only in weeds, but also in the long rushes of the bog lands above. She lay on her back, arms folded across her meager chest. Water pooled under her drenched hair. As I drew close, I could see bare bones jutting out of her rib cage. Remnants of cloth and flesh clung to those bones.

She sat up abruptly, eyes wide. I froze. The woman's chest heaved as she sucked in air like it was her last breath, wheezing and gurgling all at once. She leaned over to one side and spat, and then turned to glare right at me. Wet, knotted hair clung to her cheeks. Her voice was the soothing murmur of a gentle brook.

"I'll take care of you now, I will, I will. No worries, my lovie."

I could hardly believe it.

"But... Mother?" I said. It was her. I could see it in her eyes. She pulled me in close. I let her. She stroked my scalp, running her fingers through my hair like she used to and kissing the top of my head.

"I missed you so, Nud, I did, I did," she said as she squeezed me tight – too tight. I couldn't breathe. She was soaked, and she made me all wet. But it still felt good... for a minute... for a long minute – until I really needed to breathe. *I... I... I can't breathe. My lungs are flat.* I struggled and shook, and tried to push her away.

She whispered into my ear. "You must RUN!"

What? Where?

Finally, I remembered where I was.

The cloaker. No the pack... it's just the pack.

I woke up sweating.

Every muscle was sore. Dark thoughts lingered in the back of my mind; dark thoughts for dark places. I rubbed the sleep from my eyes and took out the stone. The cavern was clear – good. No cloakers, no hags. I stood up, feeling drawn and thin and lacking in color or substance, like the leached blade of a fallen leaf – a dry leaf. I sipped from my waterskin and swished the refreshment around in my mouth. It wasn't enough to wash away the bitter taste of last night's supper. It would be slow to fade. The smaller bits, the hard parts that broke off the main body so easily, resurfaced regularly in my mouth. I launched them into the air from the tip of my tongue.

The next leg of the journey actually did go by faster than anticipated. I crossed the chasm into the natural caves with little difficulty. Striding through the dark passages, I dwelled on simple thoughts about the bog and the Mire Trail, Mer and Webfoot, Oda, and clouds floating high in the sky of the world above; light thoughts for dark places.

And as I hiked on, I grew to appreciate how the walls of the limestone passages were like natural works of art, sculpted by time, water and gravity. The ceiling held a rat's jaw of cave icicles, dripping wet with the cement of their spiky, ground dwelling counterparts. *I remember this place*, I thought, for it bore some of the first images I saw after leaving the entry cave on that ill-fated night. I was getting close.

By the time I came to a certain tunnel – the last stretch before the crawlspace to the entry cave – my pulse had quickened and, despite everything bad that had happened, a sliver of optimism shone through to my bleak, desperate soul. *There would be no "lump" near the waterline on the other side*, I told myself. Mechanically, and more for completeness than necessity, I paused and added a reference to the map.

When I looked up from my map, my heart sank into my stomach. The pen dropped with the inkbottle. The clash of the bottle against the stone floor might as well have been a clap of thunder.

They hung from the ceiling and clung to the walls. Some dangled by a ropey tail jammed into a crack, others lay flat against the surface. I had stumbled upon an entire nest of the vile, face-sucking cloakers. They were everywhere.

They weren't there before!

I took a step back. My foot crunched on a piece of broken glass. A stir spread among the hive. The walls and ceiling suddenly came to life. One after another, cloakers let themselves drop. They dropped and twisted into arcing glides and headed straight for me. *Too many, too fast.* There was no time to ready my bow. I turned and bolted down the tunnel to the sound of a hundred shrill calls behind me. I ran hunched over, and looked back over my shoulder. The cave had erupted into a flurry of flapping wings.

A swarm of the fastest face-suckers shot past me, then spun around to fly at me head-on. I veered off the known course into an unexplored side tunnel. Some hot pursuers missed the turn, but many others followed. They screeched and flapped behind me. I sped along a downslope – steeper than I was prepared for. I nearly overran it and lost my balance. I stumbled. Another swarm flew past me.

The cloakers ahead spun about in a coordinated effort. They spread themselves out fully in mid-air and at face height. *Smart. Too smart.* I ducked and dodged to get around them. I batted them aside as I charged through their ranks. The largest latched on to my arm. Still running, I tied to shake it off. A few crazed moments later, I tore it loose. But I had taken my eyes – and attention – off the uncertain path ahead. *A big mistake.*

The drop was as sudden as it was unexpected.

The ground beneath my feet simply disappeared. Had I known the pit was there, I easily could have cleared it. As my legs crumpled into the far side, waves of pain reverberated through me. The impact knocked me backwards. I fell, crashing to the other side. Then I bounced, tumbled, and slid down the pit-side as I plummeted, stirring up dust and rocks in my wake.

In a split moment of suspended time, I broke free of this world, unconfined, and in perfect free fall. I "remembered" how I use to fly, and I "remembered" the feeling of open air around me. The whole of me tingled as I floated euphoric and helpless, eyes on the receding hole in the ceiling above. The cool air prickled the back of my neck. It rushed past my ears. I breathed in its freshness. I probably had a dumb smile on my face.

Then it happened – the inevitable. I hit the ground with a thud, a roll, and a splash. The world went fuzzy and then black.

*

When I came to, everything felt wrong – my arms, my back, my head. They all felt terribly wrong. I was wet, partly submerged. A current of shallow water rushed past me.

I opened my eyes. It was dark… wait… light, muted… flashing.

CHAPTER XXXI

Water dancing

The high hiss of rushing water filled the hollow belly of the cavern I had fallen into. Droplets ignited in the mist around me like tiny dots of iridescent flame, sparkling with the fractured light of the flickering bog stone. Truly, the cavern possessed an otherworldly quality.

Lightheaded and dazed, my wits slowly came into focus. The events of the epic chase replayed in my mind – the discovery, the run, the fight, and the fall. I stared at the hollow eye in the broken ceiling that I fell through. *How did I not see it?* Heading back that way was not an option, not without wings.

I tried to stand, but rolling to one side was as far as my bruised and beaten body would take me. Numbness vibrated through every limb. Blood soaked through my hair, trickled down my neck and dripped into the water. I watched as the stream caught the droplets and whisked them away.

Cloakers.

Panic gripped my chest as I scanned the cavern urgently. I listened for their beating wings.

Nothing. Maybe they don't come down here.

The air smelled like the sea. I licked my lips and tasted the salt.

In all ways, the winding stream I lay in appeared to be seawater, or near to it. I propped myself up on one elbow and felt my bruised forehead – sticky. The inflated wound was tender and it stung like mad. I felt my lower back beneath the cold water – bruised and cut.

The bog stone flickered away, underwater and within arm's reach. I fished it out and placed it on a jagged rock beside me. In pulsed images, it revealed a chamber wide beyond the measure of the light's reach. I surveyed the area around the mound of cave fill that had broken my fall, or redirected it, more like. It was rocky everywhere, except where the slope of the mound met the stream… except where I had fallen. *Had I tumbled a slightly different way, I very well could have smashed into that rock,* I realized. *It would have broken me in two.* I took a deep breath and thanked luck.

Get up, I urged myself, and tried to stand again. Pain shot up one leg and a wrong twist sent me toppling back. On the next try, I staggered to my feet and steadied my weight against the surrounding rocks. I immediately got to work. First, I took care of my wounds, washing them in the salt water and bandaging what I could with strips of cloth torn from my already-frayed clothing. Next, I fished my waterlogged backpack out of the stream and emptied it onto the shore. *I need to lessen the load.* I grabbed a handful of deepwood, tossed it into the stream, and watched as the torrent swept it into darkness. I wasn't sure what to do about the rest, so I just left it for the time being. Last, I readied the bow in case the cloakers found me. I set it against a rock and jabbed three arrows into the ground next to it.

The remaining inkbottle – the full one – had shattered inside the pack. *So much for mapping.* Worse still, huddled in the bottom corner, nicked and blotched with ink, I found the crow Paplov had carved for my eleventh birthday. I had made a complete mess of it. In my mind, I could almost hear my grandfather's voice like it was just yesterday: "A mysterious creature of the forest lies hidden within the grain of each piece of deepwood, just waiting to reveal itself to the world, and all I have to do is to let it out." I cleaned the carving as best I could and put it back where it belonged.

Chk-chk-fwip… chk-chk-fwip.

Damn. Another cloaker.

Slowly and carefully, I reached for my bow. On the next pulse of light, I watched for it, near the ceiling. *There it is.* The creature fluttered to a nearby rock. *Not far… maybe twenty feet… clear shot… alone.* The light went out.

I pulled an arrow out of the ground, notched it, and drew it some weight. In darkness I aimed, and waited. *I can't let it get away*, I told myself, *it will only bring more.*

When the light flickered on, the thing screeched and flew off towards the hole. I tracked its flight, canted the bow, and aimed slightly ahead of its course. The light flickered off.

I let loose the arrow anyway. "Thwunk."

Half a moment later, something hit the ground with a thud. On the next flash, I saw that my arrow had found its mark.

Now what? I wondered, breathing a sigh of relief.

I stared downstream as far as the light extended, and then upstream.

I have to get away from that hole, I decided.

"Which way out?" I said to the salty stream. At first, only echoes responded. A simple gurgle from the stream would have sufficed as an answer. Instead, a far-off "SNAP!" like thunder shook the ground and the rocks overhead, followed by a cascade of splitting and crackling. Debris fell from the sides of the pit, and then one large piece broke off and came crashing down. I dove for cover.

Collapse, I feared for a tense moment. I gazed up at the tons of rock looming overhead, anticipating the next fall. But the crackling and splitting sounds quickly subsided in the distance, and the dust thrown up around the pit soon cleared. Only the burbling of running water broke the silence. I rose to my feet.

"Which way?" I said again, to myself.

Water flows down and deeper, I reasoned, *my least favorite direction, so upstream to find the source seems like a good choice.*

I looked to my belongings still scattered on the shore, and reconsidered leaving all the deepwood behind. An odd-shaped piece caught my attention – club-like. It broadened at one end with a heavy burl, and the other end tapered to a natural, curved handle. Fyorn had pointed that one out specifically, I recalled. I picked it up, weighing the burl-wood in my hand. I practiced a swing, then another. The weight of the wood felt right: well-balanced and sturdy enough to deliver a good, solid hit to any face-sucking cloaker that dared to show itself. "Shatters," I declared, calling it by name. I loosened my belt-rope a notch and hung the club at my side. It hooked in rather naturally.

A second noteworthy shaft of deepwood stood out as well, but for different reasons. It had been troublesome to carry all along due to its length, sticking out of the pack well above the others. But it was straight as an arrow and the grain was flawless. Using a thin string of leather taken from my pack, I fixed a sharp rock to one end of the shaft and made a decent short spear of it. "Sliver," I declared, calling it by name. And just like that, I was as ready as ever to fight off cloakers. I opted to keep the remaining deepwood after all. Paplov would be happy.

I decided to carry *Sliver* in one hand to support walking and for quick protection when needed. That would tie up both hands though – one for the stone and one for the short spear. So I undid a leather tie from my backpack and worked it into a crude chord and setting with which to hang the stone around my neck, or even to wear like a headband. I added a flap to block the light on demand.

Satisfied with my creation, I gathered the archery gear and slung my pack. I scanned the area for my waterskin and found it hooked on a rock. It had taken a beating in the fall and the leather was scuffed, but it was still intact. From that point on, I would have to ration drinking water.

Water all around but nothing to drink – such a cruel curse.

*

The going was not easy – constant climbing over mounds and stepping through piles of sharp rocks. And it was not fast on account of the state I was in. Evidence of roof collapse was everywhere. As time wore on and as I followed the watercourse, my wounds did not hurt so much, that or I became numb to them, overtaken by hunger and fatigue. I had contemplated the felled cloaker as a food source, but worries about the uncooked meat of such a vile creature buried that notion.

Apart from the stream and the rubble, the landscape was dark and barren with no life at all. There were no cobwebs or sheddings of any kind, and no pawprints or signs whatsoever that life had ever visited the cavern.

Over time, the ceiling began to change height. Slowly, it rose, and eventually, its bland features disappeared beyond the reach of the light that guided me. For what might have been a day or two, I followed the path of the stream. Half in a trance, I kept my pace, shutting down as many mental and physical facilities as possible while I stumbled on: Minimize navigation. Minimize ups and downs. Minimize exertion. Look only where needed, and minimize thought. It was like conserving energy during a long, deep dive. Every so often, I stopped to salt my wounds and sip from my waterskin.

Eventually, the debris piles grew enormous, and signs that Men had once been in the area began to show through in the rubble. Among the scattered rocks were bricks, twisted metal, broken glass and other manufactured bits and pieces. I stopped to pick up a few of the small, glassy tablets that littered the floor, here and there. *Devices of old Fortune Bay*, I surmised, and probably illegal by the

Treaty of Nature. *There is no treaty down here*, I decided, and put them in my pack.

The ruins differed greatly from those of old Akeda. The shores of Abandon Bay held partial structures you could enter and explore, wells you could lower yourself into, and outlines of buildings that ignited one's imagination about who once lived there, how they lived, and how they might have faced death. These ruins were just a giant, crumbled mess.

*

On what might have been the second or third day in the cavern, after having slept on beds of rocks, rationed my water supply to the very limits of discipline and endurance, and ate nothing, a distant glimmer caught my eye. It was off my path though.

Nevermind; keep going; stay focused. I walked past, huffed, and then halted.

No. Stop. Investigate.

I turned toward the sight, and made my way to it. As I approached, the reflection appeared to waver. Closer still, it began to spread out. Slowly, surely, it spread wide and tall into a shimmering veil of light. Tiny, stretched droplets of water rained down from unseen heights and pattered the surface of a small pool with soft, tingly splashes. *Water... fresh water.*

Gently, I placed *Sliver* down, climbed the small plateau that the pool sat on, and crouched over it. A depression in the rock had trapped the water there. I cupped the precious liquid in my hands. It was cool and clear. I let it run through my fingers, then cupped some more and splashed it over my face. A trickle ran down my cheek to the corner of my mouth – no salt. Slurping up a long draught, smooth and golden, it slid down my throat and bled into my chest. I felt the coolness pool in the bottom of my stomach. I closed my eyes in revelry, then accelerated into a euphoric moment of simple pleasure. Just then, something extraordinary happened.

It was something that compounded the good feelings sweeping over me.

The stone around my neck began to flicker wildly until the light steadied into a single beam. It brightened. I stood up, amazed, and the darkness receded in all directions. I held the light up high. The stone burned so bright I had to shield my eyes from its brilliance. Something more was happening though – something *inside* of me; something not at all normal. I felt a light within, and as the stone grew brighter, my consciousness seemed to inflate right along with it. The sensation stacked mental rush upon mental rush, high upon high, and drove pure elation to new plateaus. It was dizzying and dazzling all at once. I nearly passed out at the height of it.

Then it all changed, like falling. A gentle fall though, with a wide, slow spin to it. I floated into fond memories: good times and laughter kidding around with my friends, blue skies, lazing on a hot boulder after a refreshing swim, tall pines buzzing with harvest flies, a barbeque in our yard, a table near the hearth at the Flipside with a tall tankard of barkwood ale gripped in one hand. Easy times…

A sudden, peaceful light flared up inside, warm and comforting and reassuring. *I did my best. I outsmarted the bog queen and made a good fight of it. I tried to save Kabor. I tried to get home. I fought off the cloakers. I did everything right. Fyorn would appreciate those sorts of things. He was a fighter and tough as nails. He would never give up.*

Fuzzy at first, my eyes adjusted to the day-brightness and the layout of the cavern revealed itself fully for the first time. The roof was most bizarre and unexpected, for what I saw, by rights, should have been… right-side up, if indeed it belonged anywhere on this earth. Like giant, broken spikes, the vestiges of a once great city dangled from the sloped roof of the cavern – a wedge of land violently cut out, overturned, and set to lean on its side.

Remnants of buildings, roads, tall towers and the skeletons of long dead trees dangled precariously. I could see how debris on the cavern floor lined up with barren spots on the overturned landscape that had given way. Together, top and bottom could be pieced together to make an entire city, a city of the kind only Men might have endeavored to build, long ago.

Farther out, the tallest buildings of the Hanging City spanned from ceiling to floor like pillars of ruin, windows smashed and large sections missing.

Despite the new limits on vision, still, only ruins surrounded me. There were no cave walls, and no end to the stream or debris either. Out of the corner of my eye, I chanced to witness a large section of building material snap and release from the ceiling. It struck the ground with a resounding thunderclap, and sent a bulging cloud of dust billowing up.

Abruptly, the world shrank to nothingness. The light had flickered out. I waited patiently in the dark, anticipating the usual pause before start-up. But the darkness persisted. A chill sank into me. First through my skin, then it crawled under my flesh. After the normal downtime between flashes had long passed, the chill soaked into my bones.

That's it; I am going to die down here. At least I saw it though. At least I saw the Hanging City.

I shook the stone – it did not help. I knocked it with my knuckles and lightly tapped it on the rock floor to no avail. Immersing it in water proved just as fruitless. Nothing happened, no matter what I tried. I put the stone back around my neck. Doom had finally arrived. It had been lingering from the start.

The pool seemed as good a spot to die as any, I supposed. *Maybe someone, someday, would discover it and my remains alongside, and name the cavern after me. "Ole Pip's Drip" perhaps, since they might not know my name or that I was young when I died. It has a nice ring to it.*

I dumped the last few swallows of water from the waterskin

and refilled it. More defeated than ever, I removed much of the remaining deepwood from my pack and stacked it neatly beside the pool, forming the word "Nud" so that one day, someone might know the bones there were mine.

When I finished, a strange tingling sensation began in my left hand, especially the fingertips. I tried to pass it off as a circulation issue at first, perhaps related to the way I was sitting or had stooped over, but after a few minutes of persistence, I began to believe otherwise – something unpleasant was imminent. I lay down and broke into a cold sweat. *What goes up, must come down*, I thought. The same is true in the world as is true in the mind.

It started with a single, hopeless thought. *I'm never getting out.* Then came the crash. *Even the Mark of the Hurlorn is useless here.* Then came the crash upon the crash. My heart began to race. My chest felt tight. *What is happening?*

The worries escalated, and they, in turn, fed on more worries. A wave of anxiety rushed over me and held me fast in its grip. Unable to take it any longer, I rose to my knees. Hands shaking, I ran my tingling fingers through the pool and tried to distract myself from despair. The water felt cool to the touch, but it wasn't enough. I traced small concentric circles, then larger ones, faster and faster. *Here it comes…*

The final crash was the worst. It flooded me with despair. *Everyone died because of me.* I thrashed at the water violently and sent handfuls of it soaring into the air. A part of me wished that the old gods of my father would just be done with me. If they still had power anywhere, it would be in the deep recesses of the world, lost but not completely forgotten. *Like me.*

Even darker thoughts worked their way inward; the darkest thoughts for the darkest places. Tired and sore and mentally drained, idle hours slipped by in anguish. I dozed off, and later awoke with some semblance of logic regained. I had given up on the light. With or without it though, the time had come to make a decision: die here or get moving.

I can still make a go of following the stream, I decided. *It might yet lead me out.*

Out of nowhere, water noises filled my ears. They came from the pool. *A creature in the dark*, I thought.

My body tensed. I slipped on my pack, stood up, and grabbed for *Sliver*. I held it defensively towards the pool, and backed away.

Without warning, the bog stone flared up. A blinding flash of light lit up the cavern. But the light was not alone in its coming. As my eyes adjusted, I stared at the water with grim fascination, for it began to move as though I were tracing circles in the pool, but without my hand to guide it. My heartbeat erupted as circles once traced were traced anew, and thrashing waves once made were made again – every motion of mine duplicated like an echo, not of sound but of deeds done. I stumbled back. At once, the animation halted. Within moments, the bog stone resumed its normal pattern of flicker, as though nothing had happened.

"Madness!" I screamed at the dancing pool.

"Are the old gods really down here?" I yelled to the rock ceiling.

I motioned to the pool, still looking up. "Are these the ghosts of a dead city?"

Ghosts!

Wild with fear, I turned and bolted. I ran to the stream and slid into a watery crevice. I hid from the noises in the dark and I hid from the water spirits in the pool. My muscles tensed as I waited, silently… listening… and trying not to breathe too loud.

In time, I gathered enough nerve to come out of hiding and resume my chosen path. Less than an hour into the hike, my ears honed in on the faintest hiss. It grew louder as I approached, spilling over the random gurgles of the stream. I picked up my pace. The roar of rapids intensified. Finally, at long last, I arrived at a sidewall of the great black cavern that had held me captive for so long.

There, a roaring torrent poured down and out of a gaping cave mouth, set between two massive columns built solidly into the rock, and intricately carved. With the frothing water came a steady breeze of salty air.

The columns depicted the forms of dark mermaids with sultry expressions, and with hair that flowed above and around the arched cave opening. The mermaids' tails curled in and flattened beneath the falls, dolphin-like, to catch the rushing water and flip it on its way.

Something peculiar struck me about the inner depths of that cave. I sheathed the bog stone and peered inside. In the distance, ever so rarely, a misty glint of blue-green light flickered. Literally, at long last, I beheld the light at the end of the tunnel.

The way out.

CHAPTER XXXII

The Dim Sea

Many Stouts mistook the rare, light-giving cave moss for signs that Gnomes lived in the deep places of the earth, taunting and luring goodly passersby with glittering gems and gold they could never possess. Any beguiled person who reached for the treasures found only dust, and if particularly unlucky or offensive to the Gnomes, a knife in the back. It had been Kabor who told the story of the moss, only observed to grow in the mouths of a precious few caves and the entrances to old mines. He heard more whispers than a rover and seemed to know a great many things about secret places. But even he knew nothing of this secret place.

The grand cavern I had entered possessed its own sources of illumination, shining from above and reflecting off the water's glassy surface that stretched out before me. I strolled casually along the seashore from the stream head where I had gained entry, to a stretch of land that jutted out into the water. Across the wide expanse, colossal spires rose out of the liquid glass like island pyramids, and natural columns braced the netherworld sky. A greater darkness, high above, was speckled with green patches of light – the hazy stars of a faerie twilight. I covered the SPARX stone.

In the distance, a thin curtain of natural light beamed down through daylight holes, igniting the whitewater of a long line of waterfalls that arced out of sight and into a bay. Bulging cliffs blocked the view in the foreground. Some falls cascaded down steep slopes, while others appeared as gushing columns that followed no course but gravity. Their far off roar melded with the dull rumble of the nearby outflow rapids. Beyond, the channel was shrouded in mist.

I breathed deep and filled my lungs with sea air. In it, I tasted a hint of freshness that only could have come from the world above. There had to be many openings to the surface – light doesn't just spark up out of nowhere in caves... not normally, at least. Even glowing moss needs some access to natural light for sustenance, however minimal. There was no question in my mind... I had found the way out. *If only Kabor could have seen this.*

All at once, my head began to ache in an unfamiliar way. And it throbbed like never before.

What's happening? I wondered.

Overtiredness?

Hunger?

Dehydration?

As I gazed over the waters, an uncomfortable clicking noise sounded in my head. The disturbance grew in volume and wormed its way through my skull at all angles. It tunneled into the hidden depths of my mind. I shook my head violently, as though it were something that could be flung off, but the pressure mounted. I dropped my spear and covered my ears. The clicking became too loud, piercing. I stumbled backwards and nearly toppled over.

Then, without warning, the noise ceased. Slowly, I let my hands drop. A muffled silence filled the audible void, like being underwater. It only lasted a moment though, but a long moment. Out of the prolonged hush arose a deep and cavernous voice. It called out to me like an old friend. The voice seemed to come from all around, nowhere and everywhere all at once, near and far, here and there, permeating like resonance.

"HUUM haa," boomed the cavernous voice. It was paced and rhythmic, like waves crashing onto shore. "I have been waiting a long time for one like you to arrive." And strangely disconnected and hollow. "You are Nud, if I am not mistaken."

I did not answer.

"Nud, is that you?" said the voice, seeking confirmation. The tone was suddenly different, almost too familiar. *Father?... No.* I couldn't quite place it.

"HUUM haa. Tell me, have you come to me for something? What is it you want most?"

What do I want most? I thought. *My parents... my friends... out... I'm hungry.*

In my most respectful tone, I answered.

"Yes... my name is Nud, Nud Leatherleaf of Webfoot, and I just want out," I said to the thin air, then looked about. Nothing in plain sight gave away the source of the voice.

"I don't want any trouble – food if you have any to spare."

I looked up, behind.

"But mostly I just want out – through the cave roof... Sir."

"Sir" seemed like an awkward way to address the voice. I normally reserved "Sir" for councillors and diplomats. This voice seemed larger. Pressing on, I pointed to a sizable clump of the glowing moss residing on the roof of the cavern, one that might be accessible from a nearby column, impossible to climb. I knew that the moss only grew near sources of natural light, so that a way out had to be near.

"Out through one of those daylight holes, Your Highness Sir," I continued. "Do you know the way?... How do you know my name?"

The voice resounded back in reassuring tones. "I know *all*

children of the dark. And I know *the Way*. I can get you *what you Want*."

There was a long pause after that, and when next he spoke, it was in a matter-of-fact manner.

"HUUM haa," the voice went on. "I know *all* the ways and all the names of all the ways and all the names of all the things you're apt to meet along all the ways."

I stood quietly, waiting for him to continue, to explain further, but nothing more was forthcoming. Nothing more was offered by the hollow voice that only seemed to exist inside my own head.

A breeze blew up in the moments that passed, and the lightest of wavelets caressed the twilit shore. I called out.

"Hello?" I said. "Are you still there?"

Were you ever there?

Time passed and normal sounds crept back into my ears, mostly wind sighing in the cavern heights and small waves lapping against the rocks. I turned my attention back to the starry sky and the daylight holes. Then I peered out to the waterscape and noted a subtle blackness where waves were lacking.

It wasn't a protruding rock, but something was definitely out there. It fluttered… no, not quite… I shook my head, blinked, and peered again into the dimness. The second look told a different story: there were two shapes, long and curved, like a pair of giant bull horns. I unsheathed the bog stone for a better view. The light cooperated and flashed on, a long and steady pulse.

They *were* horns, two of them, slowly gliding my way and each producing its own thin wake. I sheathed the stone and backed away from the water. The horns were deathly white and as tall as a man. Fleshy and flexible, they swayed this way and that way like trained snakes.

With an abrupt "POP!" the horns fanned out like a lizard's frills, thin and pale and white.

Aggression? I wondered, and shifted to a low stance, ready to spring back if I had to. The sounds of the world grew muted again. Every muscle tensed.

Yet, when things started to happen, I stayed put. Lulled by its slow and steady rise, I gazed in wonder as a massive, writhing form broke the water's surface. It was the size of a whale. The fans appeared little more than fixtures on the colossal forehead of the great beast, dwarfed by the creature's sheer bulk and ample length. The beast was a true leviathan out of stories of old. It rose and rose until it towered high above the water's surface, glistening white. A torrent of water drained down its imposing frame and crashed alongside it.

The body of it was long and thick, and I glimpsed a whale's flat tail. Spiny ridges covered the head and back. The forebody propped up in an odd manner – too high, it seemed.

A sudden movement – the leviathan twitched and curled. I hopped back and nearly bolted. But there wasn't much to run to other than loneliness, starvation and the prospect of being suffocated in my sleep, so I stayed put.

The thing may have laughed at that point, or scoffed, or maybe it just blew something out of its blowhole that needed blowing out. After the spray was lost to the breeze, the leviathan raised its bulk even higher out of the water and shuffled landward. I thought the beast might crawl up onto shore. Three great, red eyes faced me, the eyes of an albino, fixed to one side of its huge whale-head. Three more were on the other side as well.

What I did next was out of character, and stupid: compelled, I made my approach, in sure knowledge that I would be safe. I stepped forward to meet the abomination and find out what he would have of me. I stopped at the water's edge and looked into that triplet of eyes of his, searching for something friendly, familiar; searching for something I had heard in that voice. I saw only my smaller self, set against the deepest red and encircled by tiny specs of light that shone like knowledge; nothing more. Slowly, persistently, my senses recovered from a certain numbness and complacency that is difficult to describe. A cautious step back seemed in order.

The leviathan spoke at last, with a low and devouring growl in his voice. Yet his jaw did not move.

"HUUM haa… daylight holes… not the way 'Little Newt'… this side a fall, the other side savage creatures will tear you to shreds."

The fanned out horns rippled in slow vibrations; the words echoed in my head. *"Little Newt" – my father used to call me that.*

"HUUM," he bellowed, "HAA… there is another way. I know the Way; I can get you what you Want. First, tell me 'everything.' What brings you here?"

"Where am I?" I said.

The leviathan's voice rolled in response. The rumbling sound that rolled along with it was not quite a laugh, *per se*, but the embedded inflection could have passed for amusement.

"HUUM haa," he boomed, "You have come to my shores, Outlander. Leggy beasts call this place the 'Dim Sea.'"

"A Dim Sea indeed," I said, looking about. Obviously, this thing, whatever it was, did not know a lot about surface people. I looked nothing like an Outlander. I mulled over what to say next. I couldn't get it out straight.

"I would like to find my friend Kabor, if he is alive, and I want for us – me and him – to return to the surface… the bog, that is. The bog is where I live. I'm from Webfoot, you see."

There was a long, awkward silence, during which, the eyes of the leviathan seemed to stare through me. At one point, I thought to speak, but the moment I opened my mouth a low and subdued thrumming noise began to build in my head, cutting-off at just the right level to scramble my thoughts. It was a warning – a precursor to a loud blast. The words froze to my tongue.

The voice returned, at normal volume.

"HUUM haa," it said, "I can help you. Let us talk first

though… It is lonely down here. Let us roll along the shore as we become… better acquainted, HUUM? I dislike sitting still. I must say that I feel I know you quite well already. HUUM haa… Walk alongside as I sail the shores of this great and cavernous sea."

I felt pity for the beast, for I had never been so utterly alone as during my time underground. Perhaps he'd spent his entire life that way. And this magnificent creature was not only sentient, he seemed inviting enough, in his own way. My single, greatest fear evaporated, only to condense as a triad of hope, admiration, and awe.

A new source of energy overtook me. I spritely hopped from stone to stone as I kept pace with the leviathan. We exchanged news and facts about a great many things. Ecstatic to have someone to talk to, I opened up completely to him. I told him *everything*: my life from early on, all about Paplov – whom he seemed already to know a great deal about and wanted to meet, my parents, the bog, and Webfoot. I went into detail about the Flipside, the menu at the Flipside (indeed, I was incredibly hungry), Proudfoot, the Bearded Hills, the Akedan ruins, and Deepweald. He seemed to be quite familiar with those topics. But then I told him of things he knew little or nothing about: the Hurlorns, the giant black spider I discovered in a box, deepwood (at which time I promptly showed him my club), my friends, the bog queens (which caused a grumble), and even the discovery of the bog stone. These last few, above all else, clearly sparked his interest, and he prodded me to tell all and leave out nothing. For the most part, I obliged the beast, but I avoided talk of Fyorn. The woodsman, as a Kith ranger, prefers to keep to himself.

Without warning, the *White Whale* – my name for the beast – furled his two fans into horns and made a shallow dive. I watched and waited as he swam out to open water, and then slowly looped back in a wide circuit. He surfaced not far from where he had started, but oriented the other way – back the way we came.

"HUUM haa," he started. "You must be starving."

I had gone on and on about the Flipside menu.

The leviathan unfurled his horns. Moments later, a scattering of small white fish began to appear, dead ones, drifting sideways. They were blind cavefish, of the catfish variety, longer and more slender than their darker cousins in the upper world. A minute later, there were more than a dozen.

"Please, help yourself," offered the beast. "They are perfectly edible to leggy ones like you."

And so I did. In the star-shadow of the beast, I scooped up a handful of the small morsels. The leviathan's casual thoughtfulness had put him into my good books. It had been so long since I had eaten much of anything. The raw fish felt soft and slimy in my mouth, but the flesh strangely sweet. My stomach couldn't take so much at once though. I stashed some away in my backpack, wrapped in a strip of cloth torn from my cloak.

Once finished, the White Whale addressed me. "HUUM haa," he said, "may I see this sparkling stone of yours?" he said.

Something in my gut did not feel quite right just then. I thought it might be the small white fish, but it could have been the bigger one. Reluctantly, I brought the stone out and held it for him to see, in all its glory around my neck. At first, he just stared at it with those red eyes of his. He did not flinch – no motion, no words, nothing. All the while, his eyes sparkled in the flicker of the bog stone. I grew to anticipate such long pauses, having come to the conclusion that the leviathan liked to take his time at examining things, or thinking them through first before speaking on them. Or maybe he just had slow ways.

"Do you know what it is?" I said, breaking the silence between him and the stone.

He did not answer. Much time went by and he became... fidgety, if ever a whale could be fidgety – rolling and displaying subtle shivers. Something was wrong. I sheathed the stone. Soon, he was back to normal.

"Huum. Huum. Where did you find such a wonder?"

I told him straight out. I certainly did not want to raise the ire of this one. There was a long pause after I finished.

"Exotic," was all he said. All three eyes on one side fixated on the stone dangling in its sheath around my neck. After a good long look, the leviathan began to speak once again. He seemed to believe that his turn at telling had come. He recited many old stories and some recent ones about the lightless caves, which he called *Everdark*, and the Dim Sea caverns, which he called *Everdim*. Most of what he told me I understood plainly, but some of the events he spoke of were beyond my comprehension at the time, for I did not recognize all of the terms he referred to just then, and explaining them to me all at once would have proved far too laborious. His bass voice was calm, slow between words, and most steady. There was power in it. In true Pip form, I committed all he told to memory, if not understanding, for later pondering.

I looked to the fans and then to the eyes for some inkling of emotion or bodily response, but nothing of the sort was forthcoming. His body was a cold shell. All of the White Whale's life was in his voice. Conversing with him differed greatly from conversations with people – the looks, the body language, the intonations – all different or absent. I just got used to not seeing any lips move, or smiles, or frowns, or eyebrows rising, or any intense wrinkling of the brow or shrugging of shoulders.

However, over time I began to see that the fans actually gave him away ever so subtly, in small wavers or ripples, and seemed to vibrate or curl up slightly, at times, in response to stress or excitement, or upon making certain intellectual points.

I did not question the things that I did not understand as much as I should have – a poor performance on my part, given the once-in-a-lifetime opportunity presented to me, to have any and all questions answered. This creature seemed to know nearly everything about everything. He spoke of the First Men on Fortune Bay – now Abandon Bay, the native Abindohns, the Elderkin, and the plight of Harrow. He spoke of the coming of new plants, animals, and peoples, and of Outlanders, the Treaty of Nature, and the decline of mechanization.

He said friends of his lived on the shores of the Dim Sea. When I asked if I could meet them, he said: "HUUM haa, you will in good time."

Many hours passed before the conversation began to wane. I could only absorb so much information at once. It seemed I had told him everything I knew and heard all that I could take. Drowsily, I lay down between the rocks and just listened for a time as his voice rolled on. I rested my eyes and soaked my barely conscious soul in the leviathan's poetry of knowledge.

There was a long silence at one point, that or I dozed off. When I opened my eyes again, the leviathan was still at my side, as close as he could be while in water deep enough to support his bulk.

He spoke to begin the end of our meeting. "HUUM haa. I will help you, but I must ask a small favor in return."

I tensed. "What would you have me do?" I said.

"When one comes to you in my name, you must help him or her."

"Just one?" I said.

"Any one," he replied. "But only ever one at a time."

The offer seemed agreeable, under the circumstances. Quite open ended, really. How much help I needed to provide was not specified, and time lines were only implicit. The White Whale may have known many things, but he was not so well versed in diplomacy, conditions, or the finer points of contractual arrangements. He really did need to speak with Paplov.

"Agreed," I said.

"HUUM… now you are one of the smaller ones, aren't you?

HAA... Pip you called yourself? You seem to have a good memory. That will serve me – I mean you – very well indeed. HUUM... you must listen carefully to every detail. I will tell you the precise way to follow. HAA... follow my words and they will lead you to what you seek."

My colossal friend detailed exactly where I should go and exactly what I should do when I arrived there. When he finished, I was pleased, and I believe he was pleased as well, somehow, and we parted on those terms. Well, almost. He swam out to sea.

The White Whale luminesced as he propelled himself through open water, glowing from deep within and along his spiny ridges. He was not alone. Just beyond the breaking water, five long, slender figures appeared from the depths on all sides. I blinked slowly in the face of what I beheld. They were female, and human-sized.

Bog queens? Really?

One of the figures that trailed behind the beast shot back a blank, lifeless stare. I recognized the look. Undoubtedly, she was one of their ilk – bog queen or something related. But where the hags were disheveled and crude, she was fresh looking and elegant, with long golden hair flowing through the water behind her. Her lean body undulated with the energetic grace of a porpoise.

With heavy eyes, I watched the sea creatures glide out of sight. Every so often, I observed the leviathan expelling a great cloud of vapor from his blowhole. With a content stomach and a mind full of wonder, I wrapped myself in my cloak and slept a deep and dreamful sleep.

When I awoke again, many hours had passed. How many exactly, I could not know. I should have asked the White Whale what day it was, assuming days were counted in such dark places. Strangely, the green stars had disappeared. The water was placid again; the air, still. The persistent drone of rushing water filled the emptiness.

I reached for my faithful SPARX stone and pulled it out of its sheath. The sea reposed under the broken glow of its gentle light.

Was it all just a dream? The events of the day seemed too impossible to be true. I had polite conversation with a creature out of legend. It could not have been a dream though – I recalled the stories he told me and I recalled the plan. A Pip remembers many things perfectly, but recalls dreams as poorly as Men and Stouts and Outlanders alike. Dreams are not memories; they are a sorting out of the day's happenings.

The plan of the leviathan included essentials such as where to find food, where to find Kabor (more like how to find him) and, of course, how to get out. That last part was vague though, as it relied on someone else finding me, in *his* name. But I trusted that it would all work out, somehow. I trusted the White Whale. I called him friend.

I gathered more catfish that I had somehow missed, and recovered my short spear that I had left near the outflow tunnel. I said my goodbyes to the Dim Sea, and set forth on the path laid out for me. And as I passed through the tunnel's misty veil, I realized that I had not thought to ask for the leviathan's actual name. I shrugged my shoulders and leapt from stone to stone alongside the rapids, all the way through to the other side.

I will know the name, when I hear it, I reassured myself.

CHAPTER XXXIII

Interlude - The trapper's cabin

On the edge of Deepweald, the storm builds and the rain pours down in sheets. Troops gather on the east line of Harrow. Already, the lightning strikes. I must hurry or lose my opportunity. My limbs are whipping through pages like you wouldn't believe. Terrifying giants, I am told, are near ready to march. They are Men bred of the wild fiends that thrive and multiply in the Western Tor. I can hear their drums beating in the distance, loud enough to drown the very thunder rumbling in. Amot is certain they will lead a foray outside the city walls. Such beasts are not permitted within the city proper, and yet they are permitted to serve the Iron Tower with their lives. Outnumbered many times over, the Queen's Guardsmen have only their unproven strikers to defend them in a confrontation. If the giants reach the forest and break the Elderkin lines, all could be lost.

Time is wasting. We must get back to the story before the storm front rolls in.

As you must have gathered, the White Whale was none other than *the* White Whale from the tale of the First King's flight from Fortune Bay, while pursued by the brutal Jhinyari. And as you may recall, according to Kabor's account of the legend, the White Whale made a deal with the desperate Men to save them, an arrangement that no one ever spoke of. Let me tell you, the leviathan is not as poor a dealmaker as I initially made him out to be. You shall see before the end. But before I divulge any more details, there are a few more items of interest that must be brought to light.

So, in order to provide you with a full appreciation of the intricacies of the powers at work, what was at stake, and what *is* at stake, I must now turn your attention to the events that transpired on the surface during the time that I wandered through the lightless limbo of Everdark. As before, they are reconstructed from pristine Pip memories of all that happened as it happened, and so are as complete as they possibly can be.

*

It rained the morning Bobbin showed up at the inn. The night before, Mr. Numbit had bragged to the crowd gathered there in vigil that Bobbin would find his way back. The bystanders, freeloaders and genuinely concerned alike, drowning their shared sorrows in spirits and ale, responded with little more than a few cautious words and a sympathetic hush. The very next morning, to the town's surprise and delight, Mr. Numbit showed them all.

"I told you so," he said with a grin to just about everyone that came by that day. "Free barkwood ale, on the house! Tonight we celebrate!"

Some celebrated, others still mourned; one confirmed dead, two remained lost.

Holly returned to the Flipside that morning as well, not to work her shift, but to gather news from the inn's breakfast patrons. She had free reign to come and go as she pleased, ever since showing up there a young girl with no place to stay and nothing but the clothes on her back, looking for work. "I need a job. Any job, anywhere that is not Proudfoot," she had said. Mr. and Mrs. Numbit have soft hearts and so took her in, no questions asked. Holly overheard Mrs. Numbit pressing her husband to find out what was wrong. The woman wanted to help just a little too much.

"Sometimes," said Mr. Numbit in response, "it is better not to ever know the answers, or have to tell them." Holly was grateful for that. Although eternally indebted to the Numbits, she lived under her own rules: never theirs… never anyone's but her own.

Holly hung her dripping wet cloak on one of many pegs in the foyer. The typical morning crowd had gathered in the great room. She looked in and there he was, just like that, sitting at the table in front of the hearth, stuffing his face with cheese and bread. Holly ran over and embraced Bobbin immediately. She smoothed his thick, curly hair with her practiced fingers. She squished his rolls and gave them a scolding shake.

"You stupid fool. You could've been killed!"

Bobbin continued to chew on his bread as he hugged her, smiling bits of cheese.

"How did you get here?"

"I swam," was the muffled response.

"For three days? Nobody swims for three days." Holly crouched beside the young Pip, looking directly into his lively brown eyes.

"I got lost, <gulp> I got bug-bitten, I even <swallow> ate bugs – unspiced and unsteamed! How's that for a story?" Bobbin sipped from a tankard of barkwood ale. "<belch> Want some?"

Holly turned her head away for a moment to avoid the worst of the bad air. She could smell the beer. She turned back to face him. "Do the searchers know? We looked for you. After you dove in you… you never came back up."

"I didn't need too… It took a while to shake that dirty old hag though. When I finally did, I tried coming back. It was dark… I got lost."

"Three days?"

"Three days. One underwater."

"You're lying."

"<belch>" Bobbin shook his head while pounding his chest.

"Who knows you're here?" said Holly.

He took another sip from the tankard. "News travels fast. Any sign of Nud, or Kabor?"

"No. Jory was horribly…"

Bobbin looked down at the table and shook his head. "I know. I heard it all." He faced Holly and swallowed the lump in his throat. "What do we do now?"

Holly felt the water building behind her eyes. The rain outside shifted from heavy to a steady patter. One hand on the table, she pushed herself up from her crouch, reached into her pocket and pulled out a pendant on a corroded chain. "Oh," she said, surprised when she looked at it.

Bobbin wiped his lips with his sleeve. "Where did you get that?"

"I found it on the trail. I think one of the bog queens lost it."

Bobbin's eyes lit up when the stone on Holly's pendant flickered just barely, almost hidden. He coughed when a piece of ham caught in his throat.

"Ahem," he began. Even blearier-eyed than Holly and slapping his chest, Bobbin cleared his throat. "So there are more!"

"At least one," replied Holly.

The light radiated green instead of red and was faint compared to Nud's, but otherwise the two stones shared the same pattern of light bringing.

"That's a lot different from the bit of quartz I was teasing the bog queen with," said Bobbin.

"That hag was as dumb as a post," said Holly.

A familiar voice interjected. "She's efficient." It was Fyorn, leaning against the entrance to the great room. A small puddle had formed at his boots. "She only knows what she needs to know. If a hag has too much on her mind, she starts to get confused."

Holly lit up. "What are you doing here?" she said.

"I was just about to head for the trail when I heard about Bobbin," said Fyorn. Even the woodsman's eyes seemed to smile as he looked to the young Pip. "I came to see if it was true." Fyorn strode over and messed up the Pip's hair as though he were a toddler. "Bobbin, glad to see you're safe."

"Not as glad as I am," said Bobbin, just before quickly stuffing in the last of the cheese. A sizable chunk of ham dangled on the end of the fork, held in his other hand.

Fyorn made a passing glance at the morsel, but seemed to have other concerns on his mind. "I just spoke with Nud's papa," he said. "He isn't doing very well and he can't leave home. I fear the boy's disappearance is worsening his health out of pure worry."

"Who's taking care of Paplov?" said Bobbin.

"For one, he's about as good a healer as you'll find in these parts. And he has friends that can help. I asked a neighbor to keep a close eye on him too. I'll drop by when I can." Fyorn extended his palm to Holly: "May I?" He motioned to the necklace.

"I'll bring some food over," said Bobbin, eyeing the stone as well. Fyorn gave him a nod in appreciation.

Holly tilted her head and gazed at Bobbin. "You're so thoughtful," she said, and messed up his hair again.

"Why do people keep doing that?" he complained.

The Flipside girl handed the woodsman her find. Fyorn held the pendant by the chain and examined it closely. There was no denying its likeness to Nud's bog stone, but a skilled jeweler had cut it and cast it in a metallic blue setting, worn and smoothed over time. The setting resembled a large coin, except with a hole in the middle to fit the stone and a wave motif impressed along its edge. Fyorn cupped Holly's stone in his hand, and as he ran his thumb over the design, his nostrils flared, his lips pursed, and he shook his head. His broad hand tightened its grip on the stone's setting to the point Holly feared he might crush it.

"What is it?" she said.

He did not respond.

Bobbin, whose eyes were on his plate, missed the display

entirely. "We have to get back out there and find them," he said, oblivious to the woodsman's sudden rage.

"They're not in the bog," said Fyorn. "We looked everywhere twice."

Bobbin shrugged in a show of mild disagreement, then promptly stuck out his belly and rubbed it.

"If they're not in the bog, then where?" said Holly. "Do you think they're still alive?"

Fyorn paused. "Of course," he said.

Holly could see in his eyes that the answer he gave was not fully genuine. The woodsman dangled the newfound stone in front of her eyes.

"Do you see the warrior in the waves?" he said.

She took the pendant, examined the setting briefly and gave him a quick nod.

"The frothing wave is the sigil of Harrow," he continued, "dating back to the days of old Akeda." He paused. "Those hags answer to the Iron Tower." Fyorn casually made his way to the picture window, took a deep breath and exhaled as he peered out onto the veranda. Heavy water drops fell from the leaky eaves in front of the window.

"We won't find any more answers here," he said.

Holly shifted her stance, bracing herself with one arm on a chair. "Are you going to search Harrow?" she said.

Fyorn returned to the table and sat down with Bobbin. He sunk back into his chair, legs sprawled and arms folded, tired eyes fixated on the tabletop. He appeared drawn and thin, having kept on with the grueling search at the expense of his own nourishment. The woodsman shifted his gaze to Bobbin – who was in the midst of a slurp – and then to Holly's expecting eyes. When she sat down beside him, the woodsman patted the two Pips on the back and then rested his arms on their shoulders.

"No," he replied, looking to one and then the other. He

pulled the two towards him, almost in a huddle. Holly could smell the outdoors on him. The outdoors mixed with old leather, newly crushed grass and something wet. It wasn't a bad smell; it was natural.

"No, you are, Holly," he said. "You and Bobbin and Gariff."

"Wha—" Bobbin looked up, his plate licked clean. He wiped his face with his forearm.

"I'll start packing the food," he said, excited. In the blink of an eye, Bobbin was up and en route to the kitchen.

"Wait," said Holly. Bobbin ignored her raised hand and continued on his way.

"Let him go," said Fyorn.

Holly looked to the woodsman. "Why us?"

"I can't be seen anywhere near Dim Lake. Don't ask – it's a long story. No ranger can, not without starting a war. They'd sniff me out and call me spy, and with good reason. And Harrow is not kind to spies. You and your friends, however, are all quite innocently looking for lost friends and family. None of you are a cause for concern to Harrow."

Fyorn stroked his chin and looked up. His hazel eyes met her gaze. He was unkempt. His hair was windswept, his skin well tanned for so early in the season, and he hadn't shaved in days. "I won't tell the search party, but I'll keep tabs on them," he said. "They might yet turn up something useful. I'll contact the mayor to send diplomats, but we can't hang our hats on Webfoot's expediency or Harrow's cooperation. We should leave by mid-morning the day after tomorrow – that should give Bobbin a chance to get plenty of rest and for me to make the necessary arrangements."

"So we're going to Harrow?" said Holly.

"We have to," said Fyorn. "The food's already on order. Besides, I know the perfect place to make camp. I'll send word for help to meet us there."

*

They were right to go to Harrow. But the reasons were all wrong.

Hurlorns are now forming a line in front of the Elderkin. They will be the first to clash against the giants. The forest is expanding towards the lake. I should be with them...

No, my place is here. There is more yet to tell... so much more... and I've already done my part in this battle. On top of everything, someone has to prepare for the unthinkable, the inevitable.

*

"Karna?" said Bobbin, suddenly interested. A moment later, he nearly tripped over an exposed root in the middle of the game trail. The trampled grass was slick from the morning rain. If the afternoon sun came out at all, it went unseen from beneath the dense crown cover of the mixed forest.

Holly thought herself clever. "It would be easier if you could see the ground." She grabbed Bobbin's flabby waist and gave the handful a teasing tug. Bobbin jerked away and pushed her hand gently.

"Yes, Karna," Fyorn repeated, before himself stumbling on a root. The long-strider kept his composure well.

"What's your excuse?" said Holly. She reached to grab his stomach. He deftly out-maneuvered her, and then grimaced.

"How do you know she's false?" said Gariff. The Stout looked to the woodsman for an answer as eagerly as Bobbin did. They had been waiting a long time.

Fyorn started over again. "The First King's so-called Karna, the Mother of Rejuvenation, is the reason we're all here."

"She's not my mother," said Bobbin.

"Are you 'Rejuvenation'?" said Holly. Gariff laughed.

The woodsman fumbled for the right words. "What I mean is... we were not supposed to be here. You all must have heard the story of the First King. It's more than just some ordinary faerie tale. He led the First Men out of Karna's all-consuming, destructive path, on a long journey that ended on the shores of Fortune Bay."

"Yes," said Bobbin, who proceeded to recite the meat of the story as though he'd just heard it told yesterday. "The Orbweaver was consuming the Universe, and by doing so she gained more and more knowledge. She wanted to know *everything*, but she could only know the nature of things by eating them. She consumed nearly everything, but when she arrived one day at the hall of the First King, he cheated the Orbweaver out of her prize in a game of dice. He rigged the game so that no matter what the roll, the Orbweaver could eat everything *except* the First King and his followers, and yet believe that she had actually eaten them a thousand times over."

"In a sense," said Fyorn. He let out a soft chuckle. "That's an interesting twist on it." The woodsman stopped for a moment to clear the way, chopping at branches with his axe where the trail had become overgrown.

Gariff added the next part. "Yep. But the Orbweaver eventually became aware of the ruse, and now relentlessly searches for the First Men and their descendants to—"

Bobbin and Holly chimed in to form the chorus, "...consume them all and claim that final grain of knowledge, Hers at last."

There were many variants of the story, but they all ended with that familiar phrase.

The woodsman chuckled once again, nodding his head in acknowledgement of a tale well told. "Very interesting... and highly symbolic, but it captures the essence nonetheless."

"Karna is the Orbweaver?" Gariff asked, rhetorically.

Fyorn nodded. "Quite literally," he continued, "but not a spider in the normal sense. Everything we know about Karna suggests she is the *consumer* and *destroyer* of all material things, not something to be worshipped. Karna bleeds knowledge and delivers death to mankind. She is a mechanical thing, a self-replicating doomsday construct."

"That doesn't make sense," said Gariff. "How could the First King get things so opposite? How could she be the Mother of Rejuvenation if she destroys everything?"

Holly had an answer. "The circle of life," she said. "Death feeds new life. Life leads to death. It's everywhere in nature. Maybe after dying and being rejuvenated, The First King came to the conclusion that Karna – the Orbweaver, or whatever, would somehow renew all life and make it better."

Fyorn looked at her, shaking his head. "No," he said. "The man went mad." The woodsman swiped an overhanging branch aside, and then another. "Damn it," he said. "I missed the mark." He backtracked a ways and cursed when he couldn't find the trail. After walking in circles for a minute, he cut away a larger branch with his axe, and then followed up with a blaze on the same tree. "This way," he beckoned, with a sideways nod.

The woodsman picked up the conversation where he had left off. "But I believe you are right in your way of thinking," he went on. "The First King believed – believes – that his people were spared by Karna because they showed such promise at creating new knowledge and, realizing She could never truly know everything until all knowledge was created, he deduced that She needed them to feed Her appetite, or solve the Final Puzzle. That is why Harrowians sacrifice their leading intellects to Karna. They believe it feeds Karna's hunger and keeps Her at bay, until the time comes for complete rejuvenation and unification – the day when all that can be known is known, and all is brought together as one to begin anew in perfect balance."

"They sacrifice people?" asked Gariff.

"Don't worry," said Bobbin, "You heard him – only the smart ones." That won him a solid punch in the arm. Fyorn ignored the antics.

"They hold the ceremony in a sacred cave during the Solstice and Equinox festivals," he said. "The Summer Solstice is being celebrated right now, in fact."

Holly looked to Fyorn, her skepticism obvious. "The story of the First King is just a myth… something grown-ups tell their kids as a fun scare."

Bobbin nodded. Gariff shook his head.

"Indeed," the woodsman admitted, "but all legends and myths come from somewhere, and some hold more truths than others."

After a steady climb up a high hill, the forest thinned and, whenever the clouds gave way, rays of sunlight streamed through the overhanging branches. The game trail they were following ended at an old road overgrown with weeds, wildflowers, and small shrubs. Boulders covered in white and rusty red lichen lined the roadside. Pine warblers sent their penetrating trills and slurred chips through the treetops, and a raven could not help but to caw at them.

Pine scent was in the air. After a quick drink, Fyorn resealed his waterskin and pointed up the road, north-east.

"The cabin's just up ahead," he said.

Twinkling sunlight on water flashed through the tall pines. A short, brisk walk later, the hikers broke through the tree line. Fresh winds whipped off the sparkling blue narrows of the small lake – their destination. Across the water, a plunging ridge of folding rock formed the opposing shoreline. The trail ended abruptly at a pebble beach that stretched to the mouth of a quiet brook. Inland from the beach and nestled among tall pines sat the trapper's cabin.

It was a humble and submissive cabin, with a low roof, covered porch, and walls made of greyed over logs once kin to the surrounding trees. The windows were shuttered and the only door was barred shut. Firewood had been stacked in a neat pile under the porch.

"Last one in is bog bait!" said Bobbin. The rollicking Pip

dropped his pack and cloak, flung off his shoes and the remainder of his clothes. Off he dashed, leafless as they say, giggling and jiggling ridiculously in all directions as his little legs sped him towards the lake.

"He has no shame," said Gariff, shaking his head.

Holly cried after him, yet looked away. "That's not funny!"

Unable to resist a challenge, she shrugged her shoulders and sprinted to the lake after him, shedding clothes and gear behind her as she ran. At least she kept her underclothes on; conveniently made for water sports.

Holly looked back as she ran, laughing. "Come on, Fyorn," she said. He respectfully declined.

Gariff looked to Fyorn and rolled his eyes. "Froglings."

Holly gained on Bobbin easily and the two frolicking Pips crossed over the beach together, with him laughing and her screaming. Each claimed victory over the other when they finally hit the water, erupting into a frenzy of splashing and falling over themselves.

"Wild time," said the woodsman. "We all need it. Time to do what you want when you want." If he didn't feel the beguiling draw of the cool lake water himself, he sure looked it.

Soon, both swimmers stood soaked and shivering. Bobbin dove to deeper water, and then popped his head out.

"Come on," he said to Holly. "It's warmer once you're all in."

Somewhat reluctantly, she followed.

Having seen enough entertainment, Fyorn turned to open up the night's lodgings with Gariff at his side. Before getting far into it, he called out to the lake.

"Hey Bobbin," he said, interrupting the Pips chatter. They were half way out to the opposite shore.

"Boat's upstream in the brush," said Fyorn. Bobbin looked confused. "B-O-A-T," he continued. "Fish'n hole too." Bobbin's blank look froze onto his face.

The woodsman spoke slowly and clearly. "S-P-E-C-K-S."

The bobbing Pip finally got the message, and his eyes went wide at the suggestion. With unseemly grace, he dipped underwater and propelled himself back towards the beach like a pike on a minnow. The markings on his back and neck shone orange and red through the sunlit water. Holly changed her position to a peaceful back float, and slowly drifted to shore.

Bobbin arrived, dripping wet. "Hooks and line are in the cabin," said Fyorn.

The Pip shivered as he dabbed the water off with his cloak. Besides the hooks and line, Fyorn outfitted him with a proper knife that he kept in the cabin, pointed to where he might find some bait worms, and then pointed him in the direction of an old rowboat, partially hidden under some branches.

While Bobbin was out fishing, Gariff built a fire out in front of the porch and Fyorn tinkered away in the cabin. Holly explored the grounds.

By the time Bobbin rowed in with his catch, a moderate wind had blown up, sending flames reaching out of the fire pit towards the porch steps.

"That boat has a leak," Bobbin said to Fyorn.

"Really?" said Fyorn. He raised an eyebrow to Gariff. Gariff smirked.

Chest out and puffed, the proud Pip held three trout on strings, as far out in front of him as his arms would allow. They were a good size, with the largest maybe a three-pounder. After receiving high praise from Holly, attesting to his greatness in all things culinary, Bobbin went to work boning and filleting the catch of the day.

Even Gariff had to admit that the meal Bobbin concocted was the best fish fry ever.

As the firelight dimmed to the glow of burning embers, fueled by a skin of wine Bobbin had thought to bring, Fyorn spun a night-shimmering web of war stories. Strand after strand of tall tales he wove: Narrow escapes, lucky shots, lucky misses, good instincts, those with bad instincts, and superstition. Those who didn't make it, but should have. Those who made it, but shouldn't have.

When he was done, Holly called him on the sum of it all. "These stories," she began, "are not believable. I enjoyed them greatly – don't get me wrong – but you'll have to come up with something better than that."

Fyorn stared at the burning embers for a long moment, a thousand miles away. He looked to her, grimly.

"Death was ever present. Life a gift or a curse, depending." Fyorn paused, and then looked to each in turn.

"Those I fought with who survived only did so by outside chances – a day too sick to fight, a moment's privacy to relieve oneself, a well-timed stumble to dodge an arrow – killing the man next to him, or a blow to the head that knocks one out of a losing battle. It was that bad."

"And so many of them – the Outlanders – so many of them were like us. They could have been us. They could have passed as Men. All lost. We won, but we all lost. We were disciplined. They were learning. We stopped them in time – just in time – before they gained too much."

Holly, for once, curbed her curiosity at that juncture. *It's the wine speaking*, she thought. Fyorn soon became drowsy and they decided to call it a night.

*

The next morning, Holly was the second-last to wake up. She awoke to clinking and clanking, and set her eyes on Bobbin stirring a pot on the woodstove. A smile crept across her face as her eyes widened. She tilted her head up from the pack pillowing her head. Gariff was even slower to rise. Fyorn was nowhere to be seen.

"Bobbin... is that for me?" she said in a playful tone, rolling her blanket around her body like a personal cocoon.

"But of course, who else? You're the one I'm trying to impress.

This oaf doesn't deserve any." Bobbin motioned to the bundled up lump of Stout flesh still sprawled out in his bunk.

Holly laughed. "Fine by me," she said. "And I expect service with a smile, if you're hoping for a gratuity."

"What sort of gratuity did you have in mind, fair lady?" said Bobbin, winking.

"My secret," said Holly, eyes smiling.

Holly's delighted state and Bobbin's banter soon stirred a grumpy Gariff. He rubbed his eyes and aimed to sample Bobbin's cooking as well. Bobbin gave in. He had found the time to gather slate tablets from a rocky outcrop not far from the cabin, which he rinsed in the stream and warmed on the woodstove. They served well as platters. Before long, Fyorn returned and all enjoyed fair portions, together with a swig of leftover wine and a roll of thin bread that Bobbin had packed. Sweetened sausage, taken from the Flipside stores, made for a tasteful main course.

After breakfast, Fyorn told the others his plan. Simply put, Fyorn and Holly would search the outlying areas while Gariff and Bobbin went into Harrow to gather information.

Fyorn turned to address the young Numbit. "Bobbin—" The Pip nodded at the sound of his name. "Take the old loggers' road north and then cut west to the edge of town when you see the lake."

"OK," said Bobbin. Fyorn laid out the young Pip's tasks. "I need you to find out what you can about talk on the street."

"OK."

"Find out what people are saying about the disappearances, and general sentiments about the leadership in Harrow. Strike up conversations with the locals, starting at the docks. Also, keep an eye on the tower and report anything that might be important."

"OK."

Bobbin was easy going and a fast talker. It was the perfect assignment for him.

"How do I get the information to you?" he said.

"I'll send Janhurl – a 'listener' to shadow your movements. Just speak the message while out of doors, and she will hear. I don't have time to explain."

Fyorn turned to Gariff, who looked surprised to be included. "Gariff, you go with Bobbin. Don't say anything, just keep watch and be there for him. Keep him out of trouble."

"Too easy," said Gariff.

Gariff and Bobbin gathered their gear. Once everything had been collected and packed away tight, Bobbin said his good-byes with big, long hugs. Gariff held back a moment longer. He appeared somewhat drained, disheartened.

"Good luck," said the woodsman. He put his hand on Gariff's shoulder. "We'll find your cousin, one way or another, and your best friend too."

The burly Stout nodded and shook the woodsman's hand goodbye, then gave Holly an awkward hug. Eyes down-looking, he backed up a few steps before turning around to follow Bobbin.

Later that morning, Fyorn set out with Holly to search the forest on the off chance Nud and Kabor had entered Deepweald at night and become lost. The woodsman taught Holly how to pace and direction-find. The two kept about a hundred feet apart and walked traverses bearing north-south for the better part of the day, calling out as they went, and stopping at the lake in late afternoon for a quick drink and a bite to eat.

By evening, while still searching for signs and calling out names, a breeze blew up. It was light at first, but it grew strong and gusty. Hidden in the rush of the wind and the rustling of leaves was a *whisper*, quiet but clear to the woodsman's trained ear. Fyorn mouthed the words.

It was from Bobbin, compliments of Janhurl, of course. "Mineral rights: Harrow has the right to exercise mineral claims in the bog and provide any security deemed necessary to protect the claim area – a technicality. It's in the Treaty."

"What does that mean?" said Holly.

The woodsman shrugged. "I'm not sure. But it was important enough to whisper," he said. Fyorn contemplated his thoughts for a long moment. "Could be related to a loophole in the Non-aggression Treaty."

"What about Nud and Kabor?" said Holly, frustration in her eyes. "Isn't she supposed to send us information about Nud and Kabor? Who cares about a stupid treaty?"

"No, nothing yet," said Fyorn. "The Hurlorns have their ways about them."

"Hurlorns?"

Fyorn delicately explained that Janhurl, for all intents and purposes, was basically a tree.

Holly wondered a great many things, as can be expected, including where Janhurl, Bobbin and Gariff had gotten too.

CHAPTER XXXIV

Dromeron Odoon

Kabor's last known location was crucial. "Chimneying up a narrow shaft" was the way I put it. More so, I had described how the shaft dropped drown from the bog into a network of tunnels that lay *above* the city chamber. The waters around the leviathan churned in response to my words. And I had depicted Kabor as a hardy Stout, about my size and age, with experience in mines and a knack for spelunking. By the glint in his many eyes, the great beast seemed most interested in that as well, but nothing so much as the last bit of news I told him, the part I kept in reserve. The last bit changed everything, according to the leviathan. He nearly rolled over when I explained that Kabor was half-blind.

The leviathan had taken over from there onwards, pointing out just where such an individual might have ended up on a string of chance events: given that he survived the cave-in; given that he did not reach the surface; given that he was not trapped; given that he had followed all of the obvious signs and that he knew where to search for fresh water; and so on, and so forth. On those assumptions, the oversized lore master had reasoned that Kabor would have made his way to Dromeron Odoon, if anywhere. "He should be there by now, or soon, Huum haa," is how he put it, "…if all went well, as it should."

"As it should" was comforting to hear – words to cling to, if not to fully believe.

Of course, the leviathan's assumptions did not go unchallenged. The great beast grumbled unintelligibly and rolled to and fro in the water when forced to explain himself. From the waves he made, I surmised he was not fond of being questioned, or did not like to bother with explanations, or did not take kindly to the urgency of being put on the spot. I did not ask so many questions or press him for details after that, fearing what might become of me if I raised his ire.

Once settled again, he gathered his composure. "HUUM haa… all roads in Everdark lead to Dromeron Odoon, eventually," he boomed, "and if anyone found your friend, or if he had followed any one of the many paths available, he would have ended up either there or here. Do you see him here? – No. Neither do I. Since he is not and never was here – for I would know if he were ever here – he can only be there, in transit, or nowhere accessible to you without further aid."

As I trod on, I wondered how a conversation between the leviathan, with his slow and careful ways, and Bobbin, with his fast and looping double-talk, might have gone. I laughed in spite of myself.

Now the casual mention of one particular point of interest was a revelation to me: The leviathan did specifically say that any*one* meaning any*body* and meaning some *person*, of sorts, wandering through these lightless caves, could possibly have happened upon Kabor. Just knowing such people existed gave me great relief. And at least some of these people must live in the place called Dromeron Odoon, for which I had a mental map to its location. I could only imagine what they must look like – pale, hairless albinos perhaps, with large, bulbous eyes and skittish demeanors, climbing from holes and peering at me, cat-like, out of shadows cast by imported light.

The leviathan had been especially vague about the settlement and its inhabitants, but quite specific about the location. I paced my steps accordingly, mentally following every instruction to line and letter – another advantage of Pip memory. Given proper directions and accurate descriptions of landmarks along the way, any self-respecting Pip worth his salt didn't need a paper map. I never thought to question how the leviathan knew the cavern paths so well, being a marine mammal.

Travel through the dark zone was more bearable than ever with a full stomach, a wet waterskin, and best of all, a good lead on a way out. I had become less the prisoner and more the explorer. To top it off, the way was lit steady and bright. Gone were the endless hours of fumbling through the dark and navigating by quick flashes. It wasn't that torches had suddenly sprung up out of the walls or that daylight holes now illuminated the way. No, it was the SPARX stone. Something had changed, something important. And it was the leviathan who had tipped me off about how to bring about that change.

After describing the strange behavior of the stone at the dancing pool, the leviathan suspected a connection between something I did and how the stone reacted. I knew it had to be true, based on all the strange things that had happened since finding it in the bog. He also had suspicions about the mechanism at work, and none of them involved the sorts of spooks that had gripped me with unfounded fear and caused me to bolt in the first place.

"Huum haa," he had said, thoughtfully. "The bare facts suggest that you experienced the following sequence: thirst-hope-fulfillment-brightness. Try recreating that experience." The whale's glossy skin shimmered in the grey-green light. He swayed gently in the water. "If you have to, go back to the pool and step through everything again."

A return to the pool was unthinkable. However, I did spend the first leg of the journey pondering about how thirsty I had been when I arrived there, how much I had hoped the water was drinkable, and how relieved I was to experience the hope coming true.

So, in my mind, I put myself in that very same situation, and imagined stepping through the very same actions. I concentrated long and hard. At first, there was no focus: the emotions and the sensations that I had felt back at the pool were all over the place, evasive. Remembering simply wasn't enough. The events had to be *re-experienced*, like a recall. And so they were. Three times I recalled the events, and three times I analyzed each and every step of the process that led to illumination. Eventually, painstakingly, I found the secret combination, the key to unlocking the stone. And to my utter amazement, on cue, the SPARX stone flared up steady and bright. After a moment's burn, it even went white, untainted: the true colors of the underground finally revealed.

At first, the light did not last. It dwindled as the mind wandered to other thoughts. The key to sustainment was to hold on to that very specific thought while otherwise engaged – a threading, if you will, of the mind's tasks, weaving them in and out of focus so that they could proceed together, without cancellation and without one dominating the other. If I could keep it up, the light would shine forth. When I lapsed, so too did the light.

The solution wasn't perfect. In particular, there was one long and stubborn blackout, same as at the pool. Thinking back to the original experience and focusing on good memories to bring back the light, I fondly recalled times well spent with friends and family, happy events, and moments of glory. But darker times always pushed their way in and interrupted the flow: When I thought of sweet Holly, her face became that of a bog queen. When I thought of my friends, they morphed into pole-mounted bodies drifting at the bottom of the bog. Even Uncle Fyorn was not immune; he shifted into a rabid wolverine. Focus collapsed, and no light came forth. Only the dark. Even the normal pattern of flickering was lost, and the degenerate thoughts turned in on themselves to make the stone cold and lightless. It took the better part of an hour to coax it to flare up again. Afterwards, there were still sporadic intervals of pitch-black, now and again. Distractions helped to reset my thoughts and remedy the situation, as did rest.

When it was time to rest, I simply returned the SPARX stone to its natural state with a mere absence of thought, and sheathed it. Over the course of a day, control became automatic. One small part of my mind became devoted to keeping the necessary thought train active, while the remainder was free to pursue other tasks.

Continuing on my way, I kept close to the left-hand side of the cavern wall as instructed, measuring step-by-step over a thousand paces from the Dim Sea entrance. The settlement should have been at eight hundred paces. Now a pace is roughly the span of two man-steps, but because of my stature, I corrected my distancing by taking extra-large steps. Counting paces was complicated by another factor though – the terrain, and having to clamber over piles of debris or pass around them.

I never stopped toying with the SPARX stone as I walked, attempting to change the brightness through subtle variations in thought. The response was limited at first, as the variations seemed more random than anything else and mostly modulated the flicker speed or color. But if I covered all but one facet and concentrated on embracing one, single-minded thought, a more concentrated light was emitted – a narrow, penetrating beam. That beam was red. Why did a stone care about what I was thinking? Surely, the leviathan had the answer. I sure didn't.

Over time, the air slowly turned heavy and sulphurous with a sharp, biting taste to it that settled behind the tongue, dry and metallic. It reminded me of an odor on the wind that blew in from the Bearded Hills every so often: smelters teasing out metal from raw ore and puffing out the waste smoke, except much stronger.

Farther along, at nearly double the expected distance, I began to suspect that somehow I had missed my turn. "On your left," the White Whale had boomed, "you will come upon a firelit haze and roads all leading into a large cave with much activity about it. You must bear towards the fires of Dromeron Odoon at that juncture, and ask those you come upon about your friend – news travels fast among the inhabitants there."

After rounding a long bend, sheer and jagged bluffs rose up on either side as the ground began to slope downwards, slowly descending into a deep, open gorge. Cracks and small caves gashed and gutted the bluffs, and rock splits allowed for passage between the standing fragments. In the distance, on the edge of a deeper darkness, a smeary red haze emerged against the rock wall at the bottom of the gorge, illuminated by a strange and uncertain light.

I dampened my thoughts to dim my own light source and better appreciate what was coming into view. A few tens of paces more and the faint outline of a low, wide opening could be seen there – just as the leviathan had said – hemmed in by a cluster of rocky spires that rose out of the ground like the jutting teeth of some great, stony beast. An orangey-red, diffuse glow spilled out of it, scattered by swirling clouds of shifting smoke that billowed to unseen heights. Dark shapes in the air, almost triangular, dashed in and out of the opening and spiraled through the smoke at its thickest, almost playfully. A small cluster of the shadowy forms flew out together and then scattered erratically, like a cloud of bats vacating their ancestral cave.

As I continued down the slope, noises arose as well; an underlying drone welled up and the far off banging and clinking of metal on metal rang through the air. At one point, a horn blasted out so loud I felt the resonance in my chest cavity. But there was something else, something nearby. I pricked my ears to the faint sound. *Conversation?* I wondered. *No... not in a normal sense...*

Insect-like clicks and chirrs filtered into earshot, with varying tones, slow and rapid tempos, rising and falling volumes, and streams of varied and complex patterns. Some parts sounded like tapping; others mimicked the trill of a blackbird, the drone of a harvest fly, or the chirp of a cricket. The echoes played off the sheer terrain. *Ahead and to the right*, I surmised as best I could. By the changing volume of sound created, I also concluded that the source must be moving, and close. I needed a better view

I scaled a rocky hill to its summit, uncovered the SPARX stone and held it high above my head. I wove my thoughts into a strong thirst: I thirsted to be found; I thirsted to know what had happened to my companions; I thirsted to reunite with family and everyday life in the bog. For hope and fulfillment, I imagined being found and brought to the surface, and I imagined seeing everyone I missed. And then I thought of Holly, and multiplied that longing by the sum of many longings. The light flared up brighter than ever, a star in the palm of my hand for all to behold. I gasped at its brilliance.

I am the bringer of light to this dark underworld!

And with the cavern lit up so, I caught a glimpse of the cave dwellers – a small group – making their way through the tor and heaps of rocky debris that littered the cavern floor. They were *people* – no question. A rush of elation surged through me. Head dizzy with delight, I called out.

"Hello there," I said, waving my arms and the bog stone frantically. They kept going, so I slid down the rock face and ran towards them, winding my way between precipices and rocky mounds. I came to an open area with an unobstructed view and there they were, on the other side, about fifteen strong at a hundred and fifty feet. They seemed on the small side, but stocky like a Stout with rounded, hunched over shoulders.

"Over here," I said, raising my voice. That got their attention. Heads finally turned. "The light! Look to the light!" A flurry of clicks, ticks and chirps erupted. They honed in on my position.

"Yes, I'm right here," I said. I wove through more debris, making my way towards the cave dwellers. *Maybe they speak another language*, I thought. As I got closer, I noted they were medium-grey in color, not albino like the ones I had imagined, and garbed in drab clothing. They looked filthy too, with matted hair and dirt-strewn faces. But so what? Stout miners coming up after a shift underground didn't look much different.

One carrying something over his shoulder seemed to take a long, examining look at me. He blasted out a stream of chirrs to his companions and a heightened commotion arose among them. Fingers pointed in my direction.

Yes… Yes! That's right. I waved again. "I'm lost," I called. "Can you help me find my way?"

After my question, without warning two of the underground dwellers bolted in the opposite direction. I halted. I heard a sickening thud as one among the crew bludgeoned a runner to the ground before he could get far. He knocked him hard with some kind of short club and followed up with a flurry of bashes. The beaten runner cowered under the blows.

What the heck? This doesn't look good. I put the stone back around my neck.

Another in the crew cracked a whip and chased after the second runner, taking the cave dweller down after a few strides. Others beat heavily on that one as well, unrelenting. All the while, they exchanged heightened clicks among themselves – a discussion, it seemed, or perhaps orders.

No, not good at all.

Uneasy about these new developments and still a good distance away, I took a few steps back and watched intently as the cave dweller that had been carrying something over his shoulder erected a tripod. Another of them unslung a heavy device from his shoulders and mounted it on top. It swiveled.

What is that? What are they doing?

A moment later came a metallic cranking sound, then a soft "thwunk," and then the answer to my question. Before I knew what had happened, I lay upon the ground, the wind knocked out of me. At my side, a projectile... spear-like, but with a heavy, pear-shaped ball on the end. I rolled to my side. My chest hurt. I tried to get up.

Thwunk.

Hit again. This time by a ball... netting... I'm caught in a net, hooked in.

Several hunched over individuals broke off from the main group and hobbled my way, ticking and clicking in a particular sort of pattern. It was a regular beat with a varying pitch that cycled back every eight ticks.

I fought to regain my breath. I pulled and tore at the net, yanking its hooks from my clothes. I wriggled my way free, stood up, then backed away towards the nearest bluff. Climbing to its summit, I turned to face the approaching attackers. They had fanned out to better cover their angles of approach and limit my options for escape. The chirrs and clicks grew louder, faster and more coordinated with every step. The sounds they made had a cold and calculated feel to them.

The light flickered.

Don't lose it now, I told myself, and redoubled my focus. I saw that they had weapons – a whip for the one in the middle, who was also the largest, and clubs for four others. The clubs appeared flexible and leathery as their bearers swung them in their arms, in stride. And there was something awfully wrong about their eyes.

Thwunk.

I dodged the next shot from the tripod device, and then set *Sliver* down beside me. I readied my bow and took careful aim at the tripod operator, in the midst of loading another round. I aimed low, and released. The arrow found its mark on the operator's leg. He fell back and rolled, chirruping in pain. Another took his place.

The approaching segment was nearly upon me. Hands trembling, I dropped my bow and picked up *Sliver*.

I can outrun them, I thought. I dimmed the light, crouched and prepared to dart.

Which is the slowest? I wondered. *None of them look like great runners. Avoid the whip.*

The tripod device operators loaded something new.

Thwunk.

I lunged left and heard a smash like broken glass. A waft of foul air assailed me. I felt dizzy. I stumbled, off-balance. I could hear them climbing the cliff face.

Without warning, in that staggering moment, a giant bat with the wingspan of a rooftop dropped out of the black heights. Like a blur, it flew straight at me. Worse, I was seeing double.

As the beast swooped in, I dropped hard to the ground. The dwarvish aggressors cringed. My heart raced as a rush of air blew past and the thing that raced by arced up and away into the darkness above. I tracked its course. It was not a bat. Rather, it was a *giant cloaker*.

Like a bounding rodent, one of the mad dwarfs scaled the bluff, brandishing a club. His face was deformed and terrifying. With lightning speed, he lashed out at my head, but whacked my left arm instead as I raised it in defense. The hit was solid, but the material was not hard or rigid – meant for a knockdown, like being hit with a sand bag.

I stabbed at the assailant with *Sliver*. It felt as though my spear hit something solid. It did not penetrate, but was enough to push him back down the ledge.

Weak and light-headed, I collapsed on the summit.

There I lay, helpless, alone and seconds away from attack by a troupe of mad dwarves and a monstrous flying beast bent on suffocating its prey. If the cloaker were to spit fire at me, I would not have been surprised.

I heard the flap of giant wings and felt a great push of air.

Desperate, I pointed Sliver straight into the air with a mind to impale the beast as it descended upon me. At the last possible instant, the swooping cloaker abruptly changed course. Instead, it flew over the heads of my attackers. The mad dwarves cowered as the beast made a second approach and hovered over them, beating its massive wings. They backed away with a flurry of clicking protests. Then the oddest thing happened – the face sucking cloaker called me by name as it veered towards me.

"Nud!" said the voice in the air. "It *is* you!"

Thwunk.

A balled spear went flying past the cloaker.

I could hardly believe my ears. The cloaker's great flaps ballooned as they caught air and the creature descended to the summit. The span of it blocked out the cavern heights while it floated to a landing. The creature's flaps fluttered when it made full contact with the ground, and then conformed to it.

Again, the voice called out.

"Get on, 'frog legs!' It's me!"

I could barely move.

"Kabor?" I said.

Thwunk. Another miss.

"Nud, hurry!"

Barely lucid, I dragged myself closer and looked up. It really was him. And there was another at his side – one of *them*, with grey skin and bat-like ears. Something else was odd about his face, but before I could take a closer look, Kabor's hand grabbed my arm just under the shoulder. Another hand, from his mad dwarf companion, grabbed my other arm the same way. Together they hoisted me up and hauled me onto the back of the cloaker beast.

"Hold tight," said Kabor, "especially on the spins." His companion, who seemed to be in control of the creature, chirred in agreement.

"Spins?" I nodded and promptly clinched onto the straps of some kind of flat-backed saddle.

"Wrap your feet in too," Kabor advised, glancing back.

Thwunk.

It was a net this time and it struck the cloaker, partially fouling one wing. Kabor's companion quickly unhooked it and tossed the net aside.

The giant cloaker's wings raised and beat fiercely as we lifted off. As it gained height, the pilot directed the beast away, bearing towards the hazy lights of Dromeron Odoon. We glided like magic carpet riders out of a faerie tale, speeding off into the chamber heights to a chorus of shaking fists, stomping feet, thrown stones and throttled curses in our wake.

I felt the wind on my face and flowing through my hair while we rode the air currents, as though in a dream. Our mount swooped up, down and sideways as it cut through billowing smoke and ascended to the upper chamber. In the ambient light from the cave mouth leading to Dromeron Odoon, I caught glimpses of the fires within, but little more. Speeding away, our mount effortlessly weaved a path between inverted structures like the ones I seen in the Hanging City, at one point twisting along like a corkscrew before rolling into a steep dive.

My stomach felt like something quite separate from the rest of me, with its own distinct inertia and resistance to every turn. Still weak, I redoubled my white-knuckled grip and kept my eyes shut for the most part. At times, I heaved uncontrollably.

A few long minutes later, the beast righted itself and coasted to a steady glide – the most pleasing part of the flight. The motion felt a little like being on a boat ride along a fast river. When my dizziness subsided to some degree, I brightened the light for a brief stint and watched as the ruins raced by. Some time after, the pilot gave the cloaker a few coaxing churrs and sharp tugs. In response, the giant cloaker spun into a shallow dive, righted itself again, and then floated to the cave floor on a cushion of air. I could smell water and hear it too as we neared the landing zone. My ears popped.

When the cloaker finally came to rest, crouching low and hugging the stone floor, the whole world began to spin. I let go my grip and rolled down a flap until I hit the ground. I must have passed out then; I have no idea for how long.

CHAPTER XXXV

The way

I awoke to the hollow sounds of Kabor busily minding his gear and muttering to himself. He didn't have much, only what he could stuff in his pockets that day we left the Flipside. More than you might think though, and every item counted in the dark zone.

I opened my eyes to the flicker of the bog stone, still in its place around my neck. Kabor must have unsheathed it to see by. When I lifted my head, the world spun. The giant cloaker was gone. That was fine by me.

My voice was weak and raspy, my vision blurred. "Kabor," I said.

The Stout turned to me. "Good morning," he replied. "Or 'Good evening,' Or maybe 'Good afternoon.'"

I smiled. "I suppose you didn't make it out then, like we planned," I said. "Unless this is part of some grand rescue scheme…"

Kabor chuckled and shook his head. "Nope."

"At least we're both all right," I said.

"Yep." He was still busily messing with something… his glasses, all bent out of shape. A long moment of silence passed as Kabor perfected the bend and tried them on. He looked me up and down and spoke earnestly. They were still crooked.

"I never thought I'd see you again," he said. "Thought maybe you got caught in the cave-in. I tried diggin'…" He trailed off.

"How did you find this place?" I said.

He smiled.

I wondered how I must have looked to him. Dirty, thin, ragged and bruised, like I had been through hell, yet still carrying a load of useless wood on my back. Not to mention the makeshift spear at my side. I quickly looked about. *Damn… my bow.* I had left it behind.

"Slid and flew here," he said, a touch of pride in his voice. "How about you?"

"Kabor. Where am I?" I said.

"You know as much as I do. But we're getting out soon," he said.

"Where's the pilot and the…?" I trailed off. "Are you preparing for a trip to Dromeron Odoon?"

The flashing light was hard on my eyes and my head, so I steadied it. Kabor looked down at the stone. He was so taken aback that his "answer" came out slow and soft, barely spoken.

"Dromadoon? Where the heck is that?" The Stout pointed behind him with his thumb. "You must mean that despicable trash heap, thataway."

I nodded.

He looked back to the stone. "The flashing – how did you fix the light?" said Kabor.

"I didn't *fix* it," I said. "I just figured out how it works."

"How does it work?" he said.

"I mean, I just figured out how to control it," I corrected.

Kabor just stared at me, face cut and scraped, hair matted and his cloak torn and soiled. He stood with his hands in his pockets, looking more ragged and battered than I had ever seen anyone look. *I can't possibly look worse than him*, I thought.

"How do you control it?" he asked.

"I just think of being thirsty."

Kabor looked confused. "Can I try?"

"I don't know…"

"I'll give it back, promise."

"Sure."

I hesitated a moment, and then handed him the stone.

Try as he might, the light continued to flicker on and off in the usual way. Frustrated, he returned it to my hand.

"I guess it just doesn't work for you," I said, replacing it around my neck.

I never told Kabor that at one point, he nearly had it – the stone had initiated a steady light. Amazing, really. And so soon. But I crushed his emerging glimmer with a single dark thought. He had nearly dropped the pendant, and passed off the slightly long flash as part of the normal pattern. One thing was for certain, his lackluster performance put the possession issue to rest once and for all; the stone was mine and mine alone.

I rephrased my unanswered question: "What about Dromeron Odoon?"

"You wouldn't last a day in there, Nud."

I stood up and leaned against a boulder. "Why not? The lev—" I stopped myself. Kabor didn't waste any time speaking his mind over my fragmented speech.

"Your *kind* belongs in a bog. Day in and day out, Pips hop around in the mud, but… how do I say this… not *delicate*…" The Stout sighed. "The whole lot of you get bent out of shape about fumes and bad air and impure water and such. The topic of your… *sensitivities*… yes, that's the word, comes up quite a bit in the Hills."

"What are you getting at?" I asked.

"It's too dirty, in every way and every sense of the word. Nud, they're not civil folks that live down here in the dark. Not most of them anyway. Some yes, but not most. We can't go there."

"But Dromeron Odoon is the way out."

Kabor shook his head. "What makes you say that? No Nud. We have to go this way." He gestured upstream.

"But the White Whale said…" I lost my train of thought.

"White Whale? I don't think your head is right, Nud. And if that's the place you were heading to, Dromodoon or whatever, then you're nuts for trying. They enslave anything that walks on two legs or hops on one. They even sell 'em to the highest bidder. I know because I saw my fill of what happens down here and talked enough about it with… the pilot, as you say."

"Did you go there?" I asked.

"No," he replied, "but I heard all I need to hear about it."

I was in no condition to argue. Plus the encounter and my brief glimpse at the city supported everything he was saying. *Then why would the leviathan send me there?* The question lingered in the back of my mind. I felt dizzy still, light-headed. The light began to flicker again. I sat down on a large rock. Kabor sat next to me.

"So, what happened to you?" he said.

"OK," I began. "Well, first I was chased down a tunnel by smaller versions of the beast that brought us here – cloakers, I call them. One was following us the whole way before… and it tried to smother me – that's what we saw near the pool, remember?"

Kabor nodded. "Stone ghosts," he said.

"What?"

"I've heard old miner's tales about them. They call them 'stone ghosts.'"

"Well I call them 'cloakers,'" I said.

I continued the story of what had happened to me, but omitted any specific details about my encounter with the leviathan. When I was done, Kabor started his own story in a hushed tone. There was a waver in his voice.

"When the shaft caved in under me, I lost my footing and slid down with it a ways. The light-stone just popped out of my mouth while I was scrambling to stay above it all."

"Anyhow, I dug into the sides with my boots. The walls started falling apart above me too, and it got real slurpy. I had to move my arms like this." He began waving his arms frantically in the horizontal direction. "Like the butterfly – that time you showed me how to tread water, except tighter."

I nodded, eager to hear more.

"Well, the sloppy earth rose right up to my shoulders before it stopped filling in. Once it settled, I had to push myself up just a little farther, but it was pitch black. I tried digging to find the crystal and get back to you, but it was no use – too much earth and clay blocked the way."

"Then what?" I said.

"I couldn't go down, so I tried to go up, but I didn't get far – dead end. I didn't know what to do, so I started feeling the walls. I felt a really soft spot and started to push and dig. It was soaked through and gave way real easy." Kabor held his hands up and showed them to me. Several fingernails were worn off and the tips of his fingers were red and raw.

I shuddered at the sight. "You *dug* your way all the way here with your bare hands?" I said.

"Not quite. More like I poked my way into a parallel shaft, except it didn't lead to the same cave system. It took forever to make an opening big enough to get my whole body through, but eventually I forced my way in, pushing and clawing at the earth until it all gave way."

"Then what did you do?" I said.

Kabor took a moment to compose himself. He sucked back a few deep breaths.

"Anyhow," he continued, "I pretty much crept, wriggled and slid after that, right down into this cave system. It's a rabbit warren up there – little tunnels leading every which way. When I heard rushing water, I headed for it – thirsty as Bone Hill in a drought for the digging. I rinsed off and rested by the river, taking my fill o' water, but not for long – had to keep moving. Had to get out. I felt like something was watching me the whole time. It's odd when you think about it. What can watch you in the dark?"

Kabor paused, waiting for some acknowledgement that I was following his story. He was sounding more and more like his cousin. When you strip away Kabor's nonsense and back-handedness, what you are left with is pure Stout, which pretty much describes Gariff.

I nodded to him, letting the obvious pass – many animals use scent to track their prey, which works perfectly well in darkness.

"My biggest problem was that I couldn't see anything. I tried hitting two rocks together to make them spark so I could light up some cloth, but that didn't work. Just made lots of noise and attracted attention. I called your name, but..." Kabor's voice began to falter a little. "I thought maybe you were buried alive when the shaft collapsed."

"Anyhow," he continued, "I started hearing noises in the dark. It scared the heck out of me at first. I followed the river upstream and stumbled upon an odd sort of fellow – heard him banging on some rocks with a pick, a familiar sound. I couldn't see him in the dark and right from the start I could tell he was... different, but he seemed decent enough. Spoke with a Dim Lake accent, but with lots of weird beeps in between words. He knew what torches were, but didn't see the need for them apart from setting fires for cooking and metalwork and such. I got a better look at him later when we passed near Dromadoon and something appeared off – all deformed, and his eyes were... I don't know. He was so dirty it was hard to tell."

Kabor turned away and peered into the vast darkness. He took a deep breath, and then continued with his story. "Anyway, this fellow gave me the run-down of the place and all the crazy things happening down here in the dark. It's like a separate little universe. I was so happy to be talking to someone. Said he was a 'slave driver.' Saved my life, no doubt."

Then he laughed to himself. "I thought he meant he was in charge of slaves. You know, with a whip and all that, but after talkin' and ridin' with him, I find out he's a driver that happens to be a slave – he drives other slaves from place to place on his stone ghost – 'cloaker' as you say – and gets'em to their work. Does some prospecting on the sly too, hoping to one day buy his freedom. There's whole flocks of them flying carpets in these caves, and lots of drivers – pilots – working for their freedom. Sometimes though, the stone ghosts *eat* their riders. It's a dangerous business to be in."

"You could have maybe mentioned that when you picked me up," I said.

"What choice did you have?" he retorted.

Kabor seemed to have trouble deciding what to say next. For a long moment, he looked up to the ceiling of darkness before shifting his gaze back to me.

"Anyhow," he went on, "I told him about you and he said I should try some place he called 'clickity clackity something-or-other,' but he said I couldn't go alone because of the slavers, so he was nice enough to bring me there and… I had already given up."

I mouthed the word "Yep" and nodded. *Me too, for a while.*

"You see," he continued, "like I said, that one's a slave too. I told 'Clickety-clack' – the pilot – to come out with me to the Hills, but he says they need him. Not his masters, mind you, but the other slaves he helps out. For some reason he gets lots of freedom and privileges compared to some, and that includes air riding."

"Unbelievable. You were lucky to find Clickety-clack when you did," I said.

"Anyhow, then I couldn't believe my eyes when I saw the bright light and… I guess it was the right thing to do because here you are and we're getting out now. By the way, that Clickity-clack told me about a way out, sort of. I would never have found it alone in the dark though. But with your light, it should be easy to sort out."

"What was his real name?" I asked. My head was still throbbing. "The slave driver?"

Kabor thought for a long moment and cleared up his voice. "Clack-click jitter-jit snap something-or-other pop," he said with a smirk, "…really. But he could speak our tongue as good as some foreigners, except like I said he kept clickity-clacking between words, which was distracting at first, but I got used to it."

There was a long pause. I could smell the vomit on my shirt.

I stood up and went to the river, filled up my waterskin, then took a small sip. It had a metallic taste to it, but at least it wasn't salty.

"This water isn't very clean," I said, as I took off my shirt and started washing it.

"You're right. Water's no good for drinking unless you'd die otherwise," said Kabor. "It's slurry: polluted runoff from a mine. That's what made me wonder if miners were down here. There might be arsenic and all kinds of chemicals and minerals in that water."

"Thanks for the tip," I said.

With my toes in the water, small blind fish gathered around my feet, chasing little bits of debris that I had stirred up from the bottom. They went so far as to nibble at my skin and toenails. The brave little fish were different from the ones in the Dim Sea, smaller and thinner for starters. They had no idea what I was – just random potential food to them, I imagined. Straight away, I set out to steer as many as possible into a shallow area, closing off their escape.

"We'll see who's food!" I said.

The naive fish were easily cornered and I scooped out a handful. Kabor noticed and tried his own hand at trapping them. Without the cover of darkness, their evasive maneuvers were useless against our herding tactics. The small fish were white, eyeless, and probably tasteful. I stopped short of swallowing one whole though, thanks to Kabor.

"Don't eat the fish either," said Kabor. "Toxic."

I released my spoiled meal back into the river. We didn't linger long afterwards. The toxicity of food and water sources and the threat of slavers in the area inspired us to move on immediately.

"Did your gloomy friend say where this river leads?" I said.

Kabor shook his head. "He just said 'falls.' There was never time enough to get into the nitty-gritty details. But I'd bet Gariff's hat that it leads to a mine."

I smirked at the thought of ending up at a familiar waterfall, but I knew what he was saying meant we could no longer be anywhere near the bog. The closest "real" falls lay north, spilling out of Dim Lake.

Putting our worries behind us, we headed upstream with renewed hope. I brightened the light to its maximum intensity just once, stopped, and took one final look back at the way we had journeyed.

CHAPTER XXXVI

Spears of the gods

"The jaws of gloom," I said, more to myself than to Kabor. Indeed, the thought of entering gave me the shivers.

"What is it?" said Kabor.

"Leviathan – it can only be a leviathan," I said.

"They're just myths," said Kabor.

"No. I saw one," I countered. "I spoke with one – he knew everything about everything and he sent me to Dromeron Odoon to find you."

"Well, I wasn't there, was I?" was his snide remark.

We clambered up and over the edge of the plateau that bore the massive skull. From inside of it, giant, empty eye sockets kept watch over the cavern we came from. The skull must have been the size of the entire Flipside Inn – larger even than the White Whale's. Our river cut through the maw of it, peaceful but strong.

"Leviathan, aye?" said Kabor.

"I think it was the White Whale – same as in the story."

"Have you ever heard of a mirage?" said Kabor.

"I know what a mirage is. It wasn't a mirage. Mirages don't talk."

"They do if you've gone batty."

"I'm not… I didn't… it *was* real."

"Stop blubbering and bring the light this way," said Kabor, squinting as he examined the inner wall of the jaw closely. He ran his fingers along its edge.

"Humph," was all he said, and then pointed to a smooth, wet section of the riverbank.

"See that surface?" he continued. "That there is solid limestone – the stuff of the first cave."

It looked like normal rock to me.

"I couldn't care less if it were diamonds," I said. "I just want out… does it mean this is the way out?"

"Maybe."

Next, the Stout ran his entire hand along the inside wall. "This here is not the petrified innards of a dead animal. The skull was put here to mark the cave entrance, and the local stone shaped to make it fit in perfectly."

I examined a section of the jaw carefully – where the transition was. There was definitely a subtle difference in shade and grain where, presumably, bone met stone, just as he said. We turned our attention to the tunnel.

Deeper inside, the natural cave narrowed and the river running down its middle became spirited. Bones littered the shore. Someone or something had stacked most of them into three piles. They were of the animal variety, identifiable by the nature of their teeth, the outline of their jaws, and some by their antlers. Bear, deer, and ox were all present, and some others less familiar. Elsewhere in the cave were bones mixed in with silt that had settled in pits and dips on the rock surface.

The way forward was clear. The river cut a passable tunnel through the rock. Beyond the skull chamber, smooth furrows, like rolls in a carpet, ran lengthwise along the ceiling. Water noise from the tunnel suggested rapids might be upstream and out of sight. I adjusted the straps of my pack and followed Kabor in. He seemed more interested in studying the rock than anything else, until an odd question popped into his head.

"Have you ever wondered what you would do if your light went out?" asked Kabor.

"Good question," I replied. "It has, but usually – make that always, so far – I can start the thing up again. Sometimes it takes a while though."

"Like a fire?" he said.

"Sort of like that, I guess. Sparked by… imagination, fueled by…"

"But a fire needs new wood when it burns low," he added. "What would you throw into this flame if it went low? A new thought?"

"I don't know," I said. "I'd certainly try, I guess…" That particular idea stayed with me, in the back of my mind, for a very long time.

The farther in we pushed, the heavier the mist. In what seemed the opposite thing to do, I had to dim the light to see ahead better – too much scatter otherwise. As we made our way, the shape of the cave began to change as well: narrowing in, yet still tall. The current became stronger, and the rush of it grew louder in the confined space. Kabor raised his voice.

"We need to figure out a back-up, just in case…" he said. The Stout wiped droplets of mist away from his eyes. "…while we can still see."

I nodded, but without a single idea to offer.

The tunnel pinched in even more and we were forced to wade. The ceiling dropped as well, and the waters ran swift and deep. We braced ourselves against the sides of the tunnel to push forward until we came upon a rushing wall of water. Something about the air and the feel of the current made me itchy. Kabor saw me scratching.

"That's probably the slurry," he said, and smiled. "Frogs don't like it."

"Ha ha," I replied. "This might be our exit. But we can't get through that mess."

The two of us stood there staring at the water and the mist, dumbfounded. Deflated, I hoisted myself up on a small ledge to get out of the current, where I fully satisfied my itch. I pulled out the last of the Dim Sea albino fish and split it with the Stout, who had pulled himself up on the other side.

"We can try the Dim Sea cave," I offered, chewing. "There might be a way we can climb to the ceiling, to a daylight hole."

Kabor continued to stare at the water, then cocked his head and went still. A long moment passed. He pointed to a spot in the torrent ahead of us.

"Look there," he said. "The water sounds funny over there."

It was difficult to see what he was talking about. I adjusted the light and gauged its brightness for the best view. Then I toyed with the color, and found that it only made things worse or the same. Defaulting to red light, I tried an intense, narrow beam, but that didn't really help either. I settled on the way I had it with my first idea – straight up white light at a slightly lower intensity than before.

"It's just a wall of whitewater at that spot," I said. "And some of the mist kind of swirls upwards."

"I bet there are two streams that collide right in that spot," he said, "a weak one from above and a stronger one straight along the tunnel. Let's check it out."

We slipped into the water.

"Wait here," I said. Arms braced against the tunnel wall, I ducked my head under and pushed my way through the water column.

On the other side, I wiped my eyes. Kabor was right; there were two streams. I looked up and saw a shaft. Water ran down half of it – the part separating me from Kabor. The other half was open to air. On that side, the shaft appeared to be climbable. I reached through the falling water, grabbed Kabor by the shirt on his chest and pulled him through.

"Look," I said, and made a narrow beam directed up the shaft. He rubbed his eyes and peered inside.

"How far does it go?" he said.

"It's not that far to the top," I said. "Maybe ten feet."

"Out of the way," he said.

"No way," I replied. "The last time you did this, it nearly killed us both."

"This one's easy, and its solid rock the whole way."

"I'm going first this time," I insisted, "for luck."

There was an awkward pause, and then he offered me a hoist. Before stepping into his locked hands, I untied the leather strap holding the stone and wrapped it around my forehead like a head-band. Kabor boosted me up.

Once inside the shaft, the many rock ledges made for an easy ascent. I braced myself and then pulled the Stout up beneath me. As we climbed, the shaft widened, and as we neared the top Kabor was more beside me than below. At the highpoint, a ring of stacked rocks lined the shaft's rim. One side had partially collapsed and the water poured through. I lifted myself up and out on the dry side, sat on the stack of rocks, and grabbed the SPARX stone. I raised it above my head. Situated in the midst of a sparkling pool of water, I invoked the stone's steady glow. Around me, the chamber lit up like diamonds in the sun. So bright, I had to shield my eyes.

"Whoa," said Kabor, as he felt out the final grip holds he needed.

The stone's luminescence found new and vigorous life in the glittering cave, dancing and playing on the moving water and complex cave surfaces of the wall and ceiling. Long, jutting crystals crisscrossed and collided in every direction, and the light seemed to converge at their tips, flashing like pinpoint stars.

Kabor pushed himself up through the hole and sat beside me

on the stack. Squinty-eyed, he scanned the chamber. To one side, a thick column of glistening water gushed from the ceiling and into the pool. It crashed onto a pile of melded crystals that shot out like icicles, frozen in time. The walls sparkled and sent rainbows of refracted light scattering all around.

"Holly should see this place!" I said. Why I thought of her right away, I don't know.

"Ya, this is amazing," he said. "We'll never see anything like this again in our entire lives, guaranteed."

"Too bad, she would really appreciate it," I said.

"Holly doesn't need something this elaborate," said Kabor.

"What do you mean?" I said.

"A borrowed carriage and a picnic in a nice spot on a nice day would do the trick. It's easier and she'll appreciate the attention and convenience. She just needs enough romance to gab to her friends about – nothing so fanciful as an underground cave that you have to tread through miles of tunnels to get to."

"How the heck would you know?"

"She as much as told me to do it."

"She didn't."

"She did."

I closed my eyes and generated a blinding flash.

"Ahh!" cried Kabor.

When I opened my eyes again, he was rubbing his.

"What was that for?" he said.

"Oops," I said, apologetically. "It got away from me."

"You did that on purpose!" he shot back.

I brought the light to a mid-range brightness and let my eyes casually soak in the sights. Wide ochre veins stained the walls in sideways bands, while pure white crystals descended vertically from the ceiling, hanging like thin, squared-off icicles.

"A cave of giant spears," I said.

Kabor stood up on the wall of stacked rocks, reached out and ran one hand down the length of an inclined crystal the size of a young tree.

"Spears of the gods," he corrected.

There was more beauty and wonder to behold in that chamber than could be appreciated at once, like stepping suddenly into a room holding all the world's most fantastic art, but all crowded together, covering every square inch of wall space, ceiling and floor, one blocking the other. Kabor cupped a palmful of water to his mouth and slurped it down. He grinned.

"This water is good," he said. "The slurry must have come from the other river."

At his urging, I drank deeply. The water felt cool and soft inside. We both took the opportunity to fill our waterskins.

Muscles sore from the climb and fighting the current, I waded though the pool to dry ground, set my pack down, and found a comfortable place to sit. I took to playing with the flicker and brightness of the stone, and stepped through the color spectrum. Kabor and I admired the show and the unusual geometry of the crystals, hypnotized by patterns of sparkle and shadow cast throughout the cave.

On a more practical note, there were no notable exits other than the one we came through and the hole in the ceiling, which was impassable. After some time searching for an alternate way out, Kabor followed his instincts and began rummaging around a caved-in portion on one side of the chamber. I agreed with his assessment that it had a suspicious look to it. The debris there was mostly crystalline, and the ceiling above was bare. Kabor waved me over.

"More bones," he said, pointing to the ground.

Some careful digging revealed scraps of cloth and the complete skeleton of a smallish person, boney fingers still clutching a pick.

"Pour soul," I said.

Kabor pushed away more of the debris, and then donned his

spectacles. With sideways glances, he put his face right up to the skeleton and examined it carefully.

"It looks all twisted out of shape," I said.

"You got that right," said Kabor. "Could be the forces of impact."

"Well," he continued, scratching the top of his head, "that's a heavy miner's pick he's got there. An old one too, but a good one." He examined it closely. "This is Stout-made."

"He's a Stout?"

"I dunno about that… 'bout the right size though… maybe. I think he was deformed. I'd say this fellow broke through the wall from a connecting cave or mine tunnel, took one look, and thought he'd found the 'mother load,' as Mer would put it. Then WHAM! That was it for him."

Kabor pointed to a long, broken crystal that pierced the skeleton's rib cage.

"Spiked by a giant spear," he said. "Poor bugger."

"The gods here had it in for him," I said. There was a moment of silence. "Do you think the rest of this cave is stable? Could it fall on us?"

"Best be careful and not bang around too much," said Kabor. "Half this cave is like to shatter. But we still need to move the pile aside and see if there's an opening in behind."

Kabor undid the skeleton's boney grip on the pick handle and took the tool for himself, then put away his glasses. We set our minds to clearing away the cave fill, stuffing our pockets and the pack with choice crystals as we worked. Although loose on top, the pile became hard-packed near the bottom and near the wall. Kabor raised the pick for a solid swing. I grabbed the handle.

"Shush!" I said, and pointed up. "The ceiling."

"Oh ya… I forgot," said Kabor.

The Stout tapped lightly on the compacted material. It gave away little by little, and I removed the debris. After a long while, we swapped places. But it took painstaking chipping and many swaps between us to carve out a narrow lane that breached the wall. Kabor paused at that point and, leaning on the pick, wiped the sweat from his brow.

"There it is," he said. "Just like I said."

Sure enough, behind the pile was the outline of a roughly hewn crawlspace that could pass as a mining tunnel. But the way was still blocked.

"It can't be totally caved in, can it?" I said.

"Doubt it," he replied. "But it could have filled up some. And cemented like the stuff we just chipped through."

"Do you want to switch?" I offered.

"Nope. I'll finish this," he said, and raised the pick.

When he swung, he did so a bit hard; a bit hard and a bit high. He hit the rock wall.

SNAP!

CRASH!

I raised my arm to shield my face from flying shards. The rain of crystals pelted Kabor so forcefully it knocked him over.

"Whoa," I said. Not ten feet away, a good-sized chunk of the ceiling had broken off and exploded when it hit the cave floor. "That was close."

There was no answer.

"Kabor?" I said.

"I'm all right," he replied. He stood up and brushed himself off.

"A little gentler this time?" I said.

"A little gentler," he agreed, and tapped away.

"Maybe this isn't such a great place to bring Holly after all," I conceded.

"Ya think?"

A few minutes later, he broke through to the other side. We peered in – it would be a tight squeeze, but we could wiggle our way through. While Kabor picked away at the last of the blockage, I grabbed my pack and my spear and stood behind him.

"Out of the way," I said. Kabor obliged. I crawled in first, guided by the light of the stone. The Stout followed on my heels. I came to an opening on the other side, partially blocked.

"What's this?" I said.

"You tell me," replied Kabor.

I forced my way past the debris, crawled out, and stood up. The Stout poked his head out of the crawlspace and scanned the passage beyond. He sniffed at the air.

"It's a mine all right," said Kabor, grinning widely as he looked up at me. I never beheld a sight so fine as the grin on his face that very moment and the sureness of his step as he rose to his feet and brushed off his pants. He was on familiar turf.

"We're on the home stretch now," he said.

No doubt, it was darker and gloomier than any other mine. Not one torch or lantern lit the way. But a mine has a clear way in and, more importantly, a clear way out. We chose a direction and began to make our way along the tunnel, single file and down the middle where the path was clearest. Our footsteps echoed ahead of us.

Before getting far, there was a clicking sound…

CHAPTER XXXVII

The eyeless Glooms and Isotopia

The strange noises began to fill the passageway. I had heard them once before.

I backed away. Kabor, behind me, pressed his hand against my spine.

"Hold it," he urged. "Maybe they can help."

"No," I said. There would be no giant cloaker to drop out of the heights and whisk me away from danger this time. This time, I would have to deal with the inhabitants of this gloomy underworld face to face.

The stream of sharp clicks grew louder. The noise mingled with the patter of soft footfalls. They were getting closer.

"They're probably just a bunch of miners," pleaded Kabor, "you know, slaves… nothing like the mad dwarfs that you met up with."

"Who do you think keeps them in line?" I said.

Kabor shrugged his shoulders and provided his best counterpoint. "Probably a few guards at the surface and a dozen or so patrolling the whole mine. I don't know what they're going on about, but all the chatter sounds a little lively for security."

I pricked my ears to the chatter. There did seem to be a kind of excitement or thrill in the rise and fall of the exchanges between them. If birds and crickets could engage in banter, it might sound very much the same.

"I guess you're right," I conceded.

And so we waited.

We waited as the twisted and deformed shapes slowly came into view, hobbling in from the edge of darkness. And we waited for the nightmarish and malformed faces to take note of us. But they didn't, at first. At first, they just continued towards us, preoccupied with their conversational chirps and beeps to one another. The creatures stood vaguely Stout-like, nearly a dozen in all, although Kabor will swear they appeared nothing like his kinsmen. They carried picks, shovels, and hammers; and dressed in long, drab, dirty robes that nearly matched the color of their skin. Most were without footwear and some wore leather sandals.

Remembering the others didn't react to light, I brightened the stone and focused on their eyes. They had no eyes. All of the other normal features of a face were present – nose, mouth, ears and hair, but unkempt and lacking in basic symmetry.

Suddenly, they stopped. Their clicking erupted into a chorus of startled clicks and trills.

"YAW! STAY BACK," I yelled, threatening with the spear.

"Nud! Put that thing down!" said Kabor.

The miners chirred and trilled in heightened tones. They pointed at us, clicking and clacking in rapid bursts. The crooked creatures waved their arms and shook their tools, until one trilled so loud my eardrums nearly burst. Then, for a long moment, there was silence. One among them advanced a few cautious steps. Hairy, bat-like ears angled this way and that. My spear kept the cave dwellers at bay.

"Kabor," I said, pulling at his arm, "we should go now. They look angry at us." There was still a good chance we could make it back through the crawlspace and escape down the shaft.

Kabor seemed unsure, but he did not protest. We edged back

to the opening. The creatures of the gloom followed in step. When we reached it, their chatter rose alarmingly. They shook their heads and waved their hands frantically.

"Nud, they want us to stay with them," said Kabor. I stopped, undecided.

"Nud, look at what they're carrying – work tools," continued Kabor. "These are the slave sorts, like Clickity-clack. And they're not armed... nothing to worry about."

He had a point. Sheer ugliness is not considered a weapon under most circumstances. Even I got the sense they were trying to protect us from entering a dangerous area.

The "slaves" studied us with quizzical looks, incessantly chittering until the same triller let out another ear-piercing blast. The others hushed. All faced us, expectant. I lowered my spear.

Kabor whispered: "Do you think they're waiting for us to tell them what to do? After all, they are trained slaves."

"That's just stupid," I said.

The creatures stood and waited. Each was badly hunched over, warped in limb and dullish grey in the flesh. Loose, wrinkled skin marked where eyelids, lashes, and eyeballs all should have been – as though grown over. Bristly hair grew over the vacant eye patches. Indeed, they were the epitome of utter gloom, and pitiful to behold. But they were not monsters. They were people.

"Put down your spear," said Kabor.

"No," I said.

Kabor raised his voice. "PUT IT DOWN!"

"This better work," I huffed, and laid down my spear. I took a step back from it.

The gesture excited the gloomy onlookers. They waved us down to a hunched position... to their own crooked height. I'd say "eye to eye" if it made any sense to.

"See," said Kabor. "They don't want a fight." Kabor put on his spectacles.

The loud triller of the lot, who appeared to have status, spoke in a sonorous, guttural voice. He used common words.

"Isotopia?" he said, amidst a series of clicks and ticks.

"Isotopia?" repeated another, sprinkled with the same sounds.

Others joined in, each repeating the same word again and again, louder and louder to be heard above the others. They crowded in closer until we put our hands up to stave them off.

Neither one of us tried to answer, or even knew how to.

Slowly, I reached into my pack and offered up a piece of deepwood as a token of friendship. They went quiet again. The triller reached out and ran his hands along the wood, grasped it, and then tested its sturdiness against his thigh. He nodded his head in approval. I gave out two more pieces and a handful of cave crystals. The offerings seemed to please them.

"Can you lead us out?" I said to the triller, now that they appeared to be somewhat charmed. "We live above the ground… outside… under the sky, the sun and the moon."

"And clouds," said Kabor. "And rain and stars."

"And comets," I said.

"Comets? <click>" said a cave dweller.

Some of the others chirped attentively. One of them, identifiable by his oddly spotted head, seemed to have acquired some measure of understanding. Another, the smallest, appeared attentive. I focused my efforts on those two and presented them with a close view of the SPARX stone. I lit it up with the thought of cool water from a spring near Fyorn's cabin. They carried on as if nothing had changed.

"The sun," I said. There was no reaction.

"What are you doing Nud?" said Kabor. "It's obvious they can't see."

"Just checking," I said, wondering exactly how to describe the sun to them.

I held my hands above my head. "Warmth above," I said. They

tracked my moving hands, but otherwise the expressions on their faces were flat. I closed my fist around the stone. In the darkness, I moved the same hand to one side and then unveiled the light. Both of them focused on my hand in its new position, faces still expressionless, and clicking softly amongst themselves.

I turned to Kabor. "They notice how we move – they seem to know something is in my hand – and they can hear, but they can't 'see' brightness or dimness."

"You're right," said Kabor. "They can't see. But they don't seem to really need to see either."

After an exchange of chitter, several of the more outgoing members stepped forward. The triller and the one with the spotted head ever so cautiously grabbed onto my arms. The small one and another grabbed Kabor's arms as well. They tugged at us gently – to follow. I did not resist wholly, and neither did Kabor. One picked up *Sliver* and carried it along, another relieved Kabor of the pick. The "Glooms," as we began to call them, did not appear to have any interest in harming us. In our stretched states, we were simply too exhausted to put up a fuss anyway. I could only hope that they understood we were surface dwellers, and I could only hope that they would lead us to a place where we could find the sun that they had never seen; would never see.

*

The Glooms had much to discuss, but not with us. All attempts to make small talk came up short. And as they shepherded us through the dark maze of cramped mine workings, once again their conversations took on a lively character. Sensing our willingness to follow, they let go their holds and, as a group, simply adjusted their walking speed so that we were always in their midst. Kabor and I openly discussed our predicament.

"They click to talk and they click to see, don't they?" I said.

"That might be it – something like bats," said Kabor. "But I don't know if we can hear all the sounds they make… just look at those ears."

We stared at the pointed, active ears of the nearest Gloom, angling about.

"That's sort of like turning sounds into pictures, isn't it?" I said.

"Maybe," said Kabor. "And they might be able to mix words and pictures when they talk by imitating the reflected sounds."

"I don't know how that would work, really," I said. "Just because I hear a sound, it doesn't mean I can imitate it perfectly when I try to tell you about it. So when they 'hear' a picture, they still might not be able to convey exactly what they 'heard.'"

"I didn't say it was perfect," he said.

Kabor's idea got me thinking though. "I wonder if they get mixed up. Like if their words bounce off things and then get twisted into pictures in their minds, muddling up the conversation."

"Or if sometimes one can't 'see' because the other won't shut up," said Kabor. We laughed at the thought of it.

A Gloom passed us a disapproving look. Already, I had learned to read the mouth and brow for signs of emotion, as opposed to the eyes. Not quite sure what we might have done wrong, Kabor and I simply trudged alongside the miners without words for a long while, soaking in the lulling drone of their chatter and examining the passages carefully as we passed.

"What is that ring for?" I said to Kabor, pointing to a simple iron ring on the wall. He took a close look at it as we passed by.

"It's meant to support a torch," he said. "I guess somebody needed light down here, at one time."

"These are very old workings," he continued. "Those sconces are from the Hills, but no one makes them like that anymore. I can't think of any mine that would be quite like this one. I think we're deep, really deep, and that we've strayed north."

"What makes you think we're so deep?"

"The rock," he replied. "I've only ever seen anything like it once."

Kabor went on to describe the geology of the Bearded Hills, and precisely how the rock we were walking through might fit in. I didn't quite understand what he was saying at the time – his terms and language were all foreign to me. I got the impression though that the layer of rock we were situated in somehow intruded into a layer he'd seen on the deepest level of a Stout mine he use to work in, and that the angle of intrusion told him something about the direction it came from. So, by his reckoning, we were down and north of that part of the mine – towards Harrow.

As he talked, the Glooms led us on through many low and dark passages, with wet walls and piles of rubble at every turn. The arched ceilings were high enough for my liking, but full-sized Men or Elderkin would have had to stoop. Three could walk abreast in the widest areas.

Cross-tunnels were common and on occasion, the group steered us into one. At one point, we were forced to crawl past a rubbled section of the mine – a partial cave in. Kabor mentioned that, although we went up and down regularly, it seemed to him there was more up than down lately, and overall we were getting closer to the surface. That simple fact gave me a great feeling of relief, especially after hearing how deep we must be.

For the first time since our flight from the bog queens, I really felt like every step was one step closer to home. I clung to the hope that the Glooms leading us through the black tunnels were wending their way to the surface, where we belonged. I found myself wondering what Paplov was doing back in Webfoot, and how my friends had faired against the hags. I made a wish that they would all be fine and waiting for us when we got there. I could see them in my mind: the trio of Gariff, Bobbin and Holly at the Flipside, along with Pops, the innkeeper and his wife, laughing and cheering as we entered through the great room door; and Paplov in his workshop looking up and smiling when he saw me, relief on his face.

Eventually, we reached an area of the mine where it looked as though the tunnel came to a dead end. On one side, it turned out, was a small, vertical crevice in the rock, which we entered. It was a tight squeeze, but we managed, and worked our way to an opening at the other end. Passing through, we entered a wider and taller section of the mine. I could now hear activity in the distance – metal on stone clanging and the faint clicking voices of what must have been Gloom miners busy at work. We hadn't heard any activity or seen any other workers up until that point.

Spirits were high between Kabor and me. Finally, an easy task that actually was not a waste of time or precious resources. We didn't even have to guess which way to turn, or which tunnel to take – our guides through the secret paths of the underground did it all for us. I felt a pang in my stomach in anticipation of fresh air and the warm light of day, or perhaps a crisp starry night lit by a half moon. Either way was fine with me.

Kabor had a noticeable spring in his step. The dream was nice while it lasted.

As we were about to round a corner, our escorts suddenly went silent and dropped flat to the ground, face down. Glooms tugged at our arms and legs, urging us to do likewise, but soon covered their heads with their hands.

"I have a very bad feeling about this," was all Kabor had time to whisper. We crept towards the wall and shrunk down against it. I sheathed the bog stone.

CHAPTER XXXVIII

Never forget, never forgive

Torchlight filtered from around the bend in the old workings, a host to dark shapes in the shadows it cast. The walkers were silent.

The first to come into view was a tall, hooded figure garbed in black, head to toe. Long, clawed fingers jutted out of his wide-sleeved robe. I recognized him from my dream. He carried a long scythe in one hand, like the Grim Reaper would, with a shaft that rose above his stooped frame. The black metal blade at its tip was long and narrow with a wicked curve. It gleamed in the firelight.

The figure halted when he saw the Glooms, prone and vulnerable. He raised a hand to the others, still shadows on the wall to my eyes. They waited for his signal. Heads turned among them and hissed words passed between them in an unfamiliar tongue. After a long moment, he beckoned one forth – the torchbearer, who lit a second torch and set it on the nearest sconce. Three others glided past him as they entered. An icy sort of presence chilled the hallway.

The grim leader spoke. His voice soaked the air with venomous pleasantries. "Now this is just lucky," he remarked, surveying the

Glooms and us as well, "as I am famished." He sneered at his companions. "How long since we last feasted?"

The four reveled in the implications of his words. Glooms whimpered and squirmed.

"Too long," said the torchbearer, his voice hoarse. "Our slaves have been too obedient of late… until now."

The leader, clearly a slave master, nodded. "Too long indeed," he said, and then raised his voice to address the Glooms. "Is that what you think, Gropers? I believe it is true, you have all been too obedient."

He looked to his vile companions. "And my own congregation – you have also served so very well of late, like true masters of vengeance. Where does the balance lie?"

He pondered the thought for a long moment, until the answer came to him.

"Gentlemen, you must show restraint nonetheless," he said.

A wave of relief-laden chitter spread among the Glooms. But in tandem, a subtle kind of anticipation began to grow among the leader's ghastly crew.

The torchbearer raised a single, dagger-length claw, and added to the gesture an approval-seeking nod.

"Oh very well then," said the slave master. "Each may take ONE for their pleasure and sustenance. But leave the tag-alongs for me." He looked to my Stout companion, and then to me. But before our eyes could meet, I turned away.

"Yes, little ones… I have noticed you there. You cannot meld into the wall."

"Who are they?" hissed one of the four.

"So sweeet," said another.

One Gloom responded with a flurry of clicks – the smallest of them. He frantically waved a stick of deepwood above his head.

"Curious," said the torchbearer, "This one is trying to tell us something. He's being… helpful. Yes, very helpful indeed. These items were found on the Outlanders, weren't they, Groper?... I'll bet they stole them."

But we are not Outlanders, I felt like saying. Instead, I said nothing, and kept my head down and my eyes low.

The Gloom responded with more clicks and chirrs, accompanied with nods of his head.

"Yes... they might know something important," said the leader.

The creatures proved themselves truly evil and merciless; for what happened next was that and more – undeniably despicable. I never fully recovered from the events that transpired, or understood their connection to my darkest dreams. It started when the torchbearer set his torch on a second sconce. The leader then raised his viperous voice to the Glooms, smooth and penetrating.

"Slaves! Mongrels! Listen up! Those whom I spare shall take these prisoners to Taeglin at once, or suffer the fate of those whom I do not spare. You must take ALL of the items along with them – I have made note of that old pick, the makeshift spear, and the stolen crystals bulging out of the Outlander's pack. Let Taradin know of your insolence as well. Any disobedience will mean a feast – ten of your brothers to every one of you that crosses me!"

Although I could not see his face, by his voice I imagined a wicked smile creeping across it.

"In return for your obedient service," the leader continued, "we promise to take no more of you than we absolutely need this day."

Why don't they run? Scatter? I thought. But I knew in my heart that the Glooms were too slow on their feet, and that at least one for each of the shadowy beasts would be caught. Although it sounded like Kabor and I would be spared, I did not wholly trust their intentions.

The four nodded in agreement before sizing up their prey. One immediately turned its head towards me. And although the creature's grim visage remained veiled in the darkness of its cowled hood, I still felt the presence of its probing eyes visually gorging on my flesh. The hairs on the back of my neck stood straight on end. Ice filled my veins, and my pounding heart sent the chill to every part of my body. I looked away for a moment, in the same way you might look away from an animal so as not to raise its aggression. But I could still feel the biting gaze. Slowly, the figure began to sway left and right in a rhythmic, fluid motion. The body swayed, but the head remained fixed, as though floating above it. My heart stopped when it took a step towards me, just as the others began to close in on their chosen game.

I heard the whisper. "Sweeet," said the shadowy form, nearly under its breath.

The slave master responded in a calm, but firm, tone. "Not that one."

"So sweeet," repeated the aggressor, "so tenn-der, so sweeet."

The dark figure took another step in my direction. Kabor glanced over, pity in his eyes for I'm sure he thought I was doomed. But the grim master would not stand to be disrespected. He raised his black metal blade in warning.

"NOT THAT ONE!" he screeched.

His voice was murder, torture and defilement all in consonance. Angered, he turned back to the cowering Glooms, who redoubled their cowering. They shrunk into small, quivering mounds.

The shadowy, insubordinate figure backed off, but his torturous desires could not be quelled. He immediately turned to glare at another would-be victim – the closest Gloom to where I was crouched.

"I am glad you found these wretches," the leader said to the small Gloom that had waved the stick of deepwood. "But you should not have come so deep. There is no active mining this way… I know where you've been, you fools."

His last words hung thick in the air. I could not be certain whether he was angry or glad, or what it might mean either way for the fate of my new companions. This beast seemed to revel in dangling kindness over the Glooms' heads, while at the same time keeping terror close at hand, never further than a black whim away.

"Now I will spare you, and I mean you only, due to your tremendous good fortune and good sense in bringing the Outlanders to us. But, unfortunately, someone must pay... no... many must pay dearly for this insult."

Please don't harm them, I begged to the gods, old and new. But this was not a negotiation. An urge to voice my opposition welled up inside.

What good would come of it – drawing attention to myself? What good would come of defiance, other than to get myself killed? I wanted to fade into the wall or sink through the floor. *Any place but here.*

In my deluded state of mind, I did sink into the wall... just a bit, having felt out a crevice. But I found no comfort there.

The slave master's voice lashed out once again, loud and harsh and commanding, with a promise of doom for any who would dare question his word.

"NO ONE IS TO COME DOWN TO THIS LEVEL. IS THAT CLEAR? Take that message to your sneaking brethren!"

The shadowy figure that had chosen me played a sick mind game. He abandoned the Gloom closest to me and pointed at one quivering miner after another, looking to me for approval as he pondered each selection. I did not move or even flinch. In no way could I bear responsibility for the insinuated authority that he put upon me. But each time, he shook his head, as though I had responded. In the end, he shrugged his shoulders and settled on his original choice – the one closest. It was cruel. He was cruel. My club, my spear – useless to me. A stone that lit up... just as useless. Simply outclassed, we were unfit to stand against such terror.

That one would be the first to bear down upon a Gloom.

A simple touch was all it took to subdue his prey. Even then, the vile thing continued to fix its gaze upon me. Up until that point, I had watched fearing it would choose me, despite the warnings received. Finally, I hid my eyes, fearing what might come next, unable to bear the everlasting impression it would leave on me. Pips never forget that which they witness, even when they want to, and so as a general rule make every effort to avoid seeing such horrors.

Then Kabor did something stupid.

He stood up.

He shouldn't have done that, but he did. He didn't even have a weapon. Well, he had a rock.

I had no choice but to stand with him, so I did, reaching for *Shatters* as I rose. But one swipe from the taunting aggressor and it was over; the rebellion quelled the moment it had started. He drew blood from the two of us in one swift strike. Numbness set in almost instantly. I felt a tingling in my hands, and watched as blood dripped from my elbow to the floor. My heart wasn't right… racing, erratic. We both stumbled. Kabor fell to one side and I fell backwards and slid to the floor, back against the wall.

The tingling rush flew through my entire body. I lay propped up against the wall, unable to move. I couldn't see Kabor even though he was right beside me. I couldn't even close my eyes.

"Enough!" scolded the leader.

The thing complied, turned his back on us and continued to work his prey. Sounds of ripping and tearing into flesh with claw and fang stung my ears. Barely more than a subdued peep came from the unfortunate Gloom. The thing dragged the carcass in front of me. Still, I could not move, and my eyes bore witness to unimaginable gore. By the Gloom's twitching, I believe he had passed the endurance threshold of pain and had fallen into unconsciousness. For mercy's sake, I could only hope that he was no longer aware of what was happening to him. I could only hope that he did not understand that he was half devoured.

I wanted to look away as two of the four shadowy forms took a more cool and calculated approach, going so far as to court their victims. They each stroked their chosen one on the back of the neck gently, as though scritching the family pet, before lifting gently and neatly gorging. The last fed in a rough, whirlwind frenzy. Blood and guts flew in every direction.

I wished for darkness, but the torchlight was not mine. The wraith consumed the twitching Gloom right in front of me. I was helpless, spattered in blood. I am not sure how much Kabor seen of it. We never discussed the particulars afterwards.

Of the original eleven, only seven Glooms survived first contact in the encounter, as each foul creature took one to devour, each save the leader. Scythe in hand, he waited patiently while the others fed. He seemed to take pleasure in the show of blood and guts and gore. And when it was over, the sinister captain took his time to step carefully among the surviving Glooms, still prone and cowering, tapping each one with the butt end of his scythe, and prodding in a way that spoke to testing plumpness. He settled on the innermost Gloom of the group. I watched in horror as the leader set his scythe down beside him and stooped. I wished I could run and grab it, and then swing it upon him. I did nothing but twitch a single finger.

The paralysis is starting to wear off, I thought.

The leader crouched to the ground, gently reaching to his chosen one with an outstretched hand.

I tried to open my mouth and scream "NO!" but only a bubbling "Ahhh" wheezed out. The grim master looked our way. And at just that very moment, I noticed a faint flicker on the wall. *My stone.* It must have shifted in the fall and was about to slip into full view.

So to quaff the light, I raised my darkest thoughts and dwelled upon them, thoughts I dare not repeat. The stone burned cold against my chest. And even though it was not the SPARX light that lit the tunnel and brought the grizzly scene to my eyes, the entire room flickered. All went dark around us. It only lasted an instant, like a flash of darkness instead of light. When it was over, the torches still burned with their usual glow.

The foul creature glared back at the torches on the wall, shook his head, and then returned to his foul business. The others looked this way and that way for a brief moment, but soon carried on. The leader returned to stroking the neck of his chosen miner in long, slow draws. I knew what was coming. I fought to close my eyes. It was no use. I thought the right thoughts to dampen the stone so it would not flicker. That much worked. I dared not risk utter darkness again.

Lifting the compliant Gloom gently in his arms, the slave master whipped his head back. The motion threw back his hood. His face was corpse-like. Long, thin fangs pierced the flesh of the helpless victim. He simply tore the poor, obedient thing apart. *Lambs among wolves.*

Blood and bits of flesh splattered the remaining Glooms, cringing below. Some whimpered as the frenzy played out – horrified, but subdued. When it was over, the leader wiped his mouth clean with his sleeve. He pulled the hood back over his withered skull and called to the others.

Smooth as silk, the grim walkers retreated the way they had come. Their shadows shrunk into the receding torchlight.

Those Glooms spared from the dreadful feast took leave to mourn over the dead for a time. With heavy footsteps and dull chatter, they collected the remains to a heap in the middle of the tunnel. Dragging his feet, the Gloom with the spotted head felt out the location of a torch left behind on the wall sconce. He proceeded to ignite his fallen comrades, all the while emitting low, muffled clicks and taps.

"Isotopia," said one Gloom angrily to another, when the deed was done. Smoke began to choke the hallway. With his fist, he pelted the other right in the eye socket. The injured Gloom yelped as he dropped to the ground, hands covering the vacant patch.

He rolled back and forth in agony, and then sat still for a time. Without so much as a click or a clack or a tick in apology, the fallen Gloom stammered to his feet and wandered off listlessly, bumping once into the wall before setting himself straight, back the way we had come.

The remaining Glooms gathered their belongings quickly and left before the fire burned high and the smoke became too thick. Kabor and I leaned heavily on two Glooms each as they lead us onward and upward, as instructed. My feet dragged at first, but eventually fell into a proper step. The level of chatter, once lively and full, had reduced to almost nil. Only the occasional low volume, sporadic burst broke their muted silence. I surmised that it was just enough to allow for minimal navigation and little or no conversation. Eventually, we passed through a doorway with a heavy stone door and a rusty bar latch. The mechanism allowed for the bar to be raised and lowered from either side. Once through, the rearmost Gloom slammed the door shut behind us and dropped the latch.

Kabor was the first to regain his ability to speak. "Wha' were w'ey?" he said.

My own mouth was too numb to form words.

"Wraiths," said a Gloom, between muted clicks. It was the same one that had first inquired about Isotopia – the triller. The one with the spots on his head nodded in agreement.

CHAPTER XXXIX

Interlude - Nekenezitter

Nekenezitter was a Gloom with eyes. It happened every few generations.

He was born in as common a manner as any other of his kin, amidst the choking fumes and perpetual darkness of Dromeron Odoon. But as he matured, it became obvious something was different about him. Nekenezitter perceived things others did not. At first, he could not even begin to convey his perceptions in terms any would understand. What he described was nothing like a voice, or the sound of footsteps, or the gurgle of flowing water, or the clank of hammer on anvil. Nor was it anything like the echo of a column, boulder, cave icicle, or of an opening in the wall. It had no feel, smell or taste to it. The closest sensation he could give them was that of heat, for he first perceived of light in the burning forges where his father and brothers labored, one mere rise above the status of Bound One. "I can *hear* the heat," he would say.

After first making contact with the Men of Dim Lake, it took years for the Glooms to learn about this extra sense. Those Glooms who believe in extra-sensory perception call it "The Fifth." Of course, this refers to a fifth sense. Those who would deny the ability call it nonsense.

Nekenezitter seemed destined to become a great teacher and leader of his people. Already a vocalary, philosopher and prophet in their minds ear, he was encouraged by his elders to travel the world above, a world sounded out as a veritable Hell in traditional teachings. The recent experiences of slaves returning from Harrow after being sold into service – the so-called "Bound Ones" – only reinforced such notions. They spoke of Taradin's demons in the Catacombs under the Iron Tower – beasts of the upper world who kept the order and wreaked havoc among them.

Yet, as decreed by the elders of his society, "he must learn the way of The Fifth, and this, he must do alone." Nekenezitter received the finest education before embarking on his solo journey, including teachings of all the known peoples of the upper world, their ways, customs, and languages. These were limited, though, by what could be gleaned from his people's interactions with Harrow, underground activities that the Glooms had spied upon, and lost or abandoned items in their possession. For the most part, the latter only served to confuse them.

It became evident to the elders that none among the Glooms truly could prepare Nekenezitter for his quest, and so they turned to the being they held as divine. "Kechekenibek" heard their request and agreed to provide the additional tutelage. He proclaimed, however, that the entire undertaking was to be held in the utmost of secrecy, for sanctioning a journey to "Hell" and back would meet resistance and could cause unrest among the worshipping populace. "Huum haa, change must be gradual," he boomed.

Now there was an ulterior motive to the mission, which Nekenezitter also kept secret – nearly secret that is. The gifted Gloom also took on a personal quest to discover the truth about another great mystery of his people. It was the Bound Ones who often whispered of a land they called Isotopia. To them, it represented Heaven in Earth. They held to the prophecy that someday, one with The Fifth will deliver their people to its bountiful caves.

Some said slavers fabricated the notion of an underground paradise as an instrument of control to prevent the Bound Ones from committing suicide. It gave them hope for a better life, so they would never succumb to ending their dismal lives and thereby decrease productivity. Indeed, stories and excitement about Isotopia would spread throughout the slave population in waves that were often coincident with some of the hardest times the group ever faced. The logic of the theory held that as long as the slavers gave false hope, there would be no loss in productivity apart from the odd straggler sent off to find Isotopia, who either died trying or returned empty-handed.

The day finally came when, armed with knowledge and burdened with duty, Nekenezitter departed Kechekenibek's side on the turbulent shores of Gusher Run, on a personal path of discovery and enlightenment. It happened to occur only a short time after my own visit to the Dim Sea.

I recall asking Nekenezitter a simple question about his search. This was some time after Kabor and I had reached the surface and watched, through watery eyes, the magnificent sun sinking over green, rolling hills. The forgotten music of birdsong and buzzing insects filled our ears. Fresh air filled our lungs. I heard the wind in the treetops.

"Why would you go aboveground to find something that is supposed to be underground?" I asked naively, all the while savoring the last hints of daylight.

The Gloom paused for a brief moment, as though in perfect stasis. He was curious to watch, standing so still he might have been a statue. He did not shuffle, or breathe or fidget while he searched for the right words in our awkward tongue. His expression mirrored the placidness of a lake on a windless morning when the water is glassy.

"I <click> begin <clack> search where no one <click> look before," he said. It was that simple.

Nekenezitter looked at me squarely with large, unseemly eyes, and chirred. "I do this <click> for Bound Ones. <tick> They are my brothers and sisters <trill>."

He went on to explain that the dream of Isotopia emerged decades ago, maybe longer, but that no true evidence of its existence had ever been found, despite "many, many costly attempts." A disconcerting outcome, for if anyone knows where to look for a hidden underground city, it would be the slave miners.

"How I hope do better than they?" he continued. "So, <click> I take different approach <clack>; one they never take themselves <chirr>."

I learned all of this about Nekenezitter because of the small part I played in his journey, and because of the time we spent exchanging views. He asked many questions too lowly to ask of the grand Kechekenibek. I was the first to teach him the meaning of dawn and dusk, and the names of the colors of the rainbow. We discussed common uses of words on paper, and the notion of "capturing" a scene on canvas as a painting, and of maps for navigation. The notions of light reflection and scattering were familiar to him, even the fact that some objects reflect better than others. Transparency was also somewhat familiar, in as much as it related to the soundproofing qualities of certain materials.

All of this happened over too brief a time. My quick lessons about life above ground were but a trifle considering the debt that I owed, for who knows what would have become of us if Nekenezitter had not acquired clothing and a spare cell key from his brethren, and suddenly appeared to lead us outside by a secret way, beyond Harrow's wall. I might have been wrapped in bark much sooner, were it not for him.

"What your names <click><chirr>?" he had asked through the cell bars, a fist full of keys in hand.

Kabor and I had been sitting on the floor. I stood up.

"I am Nud," I said. "Nud Leatherleaf of Webfoot… from out the way of the bog lands. And this is Kabor Ram. He is from the Bearded Hills."

Before I even finished answering, the lock had been sprung.

"Kechekenibek <tick> sent me," he said. "His <click> design we help one another <clack>." He extended a handful of robes through the bars – Gloom robes. "I am <click> Nekenezitter," he continued. "Put these on. Hurry <chirr>."

Kabor and I donned the clothes and followed him out, reclaiming our belongings from behind an unmanned desk along the way, but minus the cave crystals that were nowhere to be seen. It was a small price to pay, considering.

I knew that the intervention could only be the work of the leviathan, and that the name of the loremaster I had met must be Kechekenibek.

As we stood in the twilight of the world above, ready to part, Nekenezitter had some final advice for us. It came in part from the leviathan and in part from him. When he spoke, the usual Gloom noises punctuated his words.

"Steer clear of crowds <click> on way home <clack>. Half city search for you <chirr> when wraiths <click> learn of escape <clack>. Label you thieves, assassins; they will <tick> <tick>. Hunt your blood <tick> until Kechekenibek's word <click> reaches Taradin, they will <chirr>. Be watchful, ready."

The leviathan was more connected and helpful than I ever could have imagined.

In return for his advice, Kabor and I gave Nekenezitter some of our own. We pointed him in the direction of a good place to begin his travels. I used a stick to draw a quick map in the earth, and then directed him towards the Bearded Hills. The miners and prospectors there might be able to help him. I even gave him the name "Mer Andulus," and told him to tell Mer that Nud Leatherleaf and Kabor Ram sent him.

The bog lands were also on the map that I had drawn for him, and east to Gan, south to Fort Abandon, and west. "Wherever you go, do not go west," Kabor told him.

Nekenezitter looked up from the scratchings. He gave me a concerned look. "You say you live in a bog <chirr>?" he said.

"That's right. Born and raised," I said.

"Hmm <chirr>." He sighed heavily.

"What is it?" I said.

"In Iron Tower <click>, hushed talk about bog <clack> overheard. Men not know how good are Il'kinik ears. Taeglin <click> ordered <clack> Tor Lord to drain bog <trill>… dig out for mining. Equipment <click> gathered <tock> Western Tor."

I knew the name "Taeglin" from Paplov's political circles. Fyorn had mentioned him as well and both regarded him with contempt.

Kabor and I exchanged glances.

"Why would he want to do that?" I said.

"And who was he talking to?" said Kabor. "Nothing's there 'cept bog iron and bog bodies."

I glared at Kabor, but held my tongue in the presence of our companion.

"I <click> don't know," said Nekenezitter. "But he wants <tick> something buried there <clack>. More, <chirr> I cannot say, except sounded… urgent talk."

"I don't think they can do it," I said, remembering my lessons on treaties and agreements. "The Non-aggression Treaty clearly states that neither Harrow nor Gan can occupy the Triland region – that covers Webfoot to Proudfoot to the Bearded Hills." But even as I said the words, I knew they were empty. *Harrow takes what Harrow wants.*

Just before parting, I tried to explain a bit more about directions. Nekenezitter was not accustomed to having so much choice in the matter. He showed me his compass though, and demonstrated that he was well versed in the use of a lodestone, and that he knew which way was north. That helped; otherwise, it would have been far more difficult to explain how the sun moved.

Kabor and I hadn't much time; daylight had faded and the wraiths would be on our trail soon, if not already. The tower light of Harrow had been lit for an hour and already burned bright in the distance. We had to make a run for Deepweald.

CHAPTER XL

A sacred grove

Kabor was as good as dead and the one that struck him down was gaining on me – the price paid for having lingered too long with Nekenezitter.

Gasping for breath and legs nearly spent, I bounded along the narrow forest path in a last ditch effort to evade the vicious creature. Before the sun was even fully down the wraiths had our bearing or had guessed it, informed by either spies or good sense or *Lady Luck*. They moved unseen and near crossed our path on the eastern edge of Harrow, where the long piers of the city finger out into Dim Lake. Kabor and I had a good head start, but the wraiths were bigger, faster, and their persistence is legendary. They pursued us into the forest with cold determination.

Only the subtle axe blazing on a young maple suggested I hadn't lost the trail. Tall trees loomed over the up-sloping path, bearing an uncanny resemblance to the Hurlorns from many years back. It was difficult to know just how close the wraiths were. *The base of the hill? Ten paces? Are they on my heels? How many?* Wraiths did not move like regular Men. Their motions were fluid, silent – only the whipping sounds of branches in dense bush confirmed their presence. I did not look back. Dead ahead, a thick stand of cedars blocked passage. I barreled through and hoped for the best. It could lead off a cliff, for all I knew.

The cedars parted to allow passage, and after I dove through, they sprung back into place. I found myself in a wide clearing at the crest of the hill. Standing before me was a warrior, facing from the heart of the grove – no, stationed there – stationed beside a mammoth stone monument with runes inscribed upon it. Ordered rows of maples, elms and oaks stood behind him like troops in reserve.

The warrior did not quite look like kind old Uncle Fyorn, the one that I had known for so many years, for the light of the Elderkin shone from his fierce, wild eyes. He stood tall and straight in a mail vest that shimmered in the moonlight. And he wore a silvered helm in likeness to a ferocious wolverine. A great tree insignia covered the front of his vest, with silvered branches and shining green oak leaves. I darted to one side, not knowing exactly what to make of him.

The woodsman unsheathed a large sword and his trusty hatchet. The hatchet I recognized well. The sword I had never seen. The white metal of his weaponry gave off a pale sheen in the night.

Fyorn shifted into a readied stance – bent knees, left foot ahead of the right, eyes focused on where the branches had closed behind me. He raised the bastard sword high above his head. My heart skipped a beat and I feared his rage, but for a moment. With a sharp "fvit-fwit" and a quick shake of the axe, he gestured me out of the way.

I scrambled aside as a wraith fought through the barrier of branches, hissing and clawing and pushing aside the grabbing twigs. I glanced back to see one of its hands holding the shaft of a long scythe and the other balancing a crouched pose. The thing looked to me first, but quickly turned its burning attention to the armored Elderkin.

The foul creature sniffed at the air in Fyorn's direction. From behind its dark hood, a liquid voice poured out into the grove, cold and fluid and hateful. The words surged through my spine in a shiver and permeated my torso, my neck, and my limbs.

"Mut!" slashed the terrible voice. The thing began to pace slowly back and forth in a smooth, gliding motion, "You don't fool me. I've smelled your false flesh before; the stench you left behind at Harrow's Gate."

Fyorn's stone cold expression broke, his jaw clenched, and his eyes went wide and dark. The woodsman – Kith ranger – tilted his head slightly to one side, lips pursed, defiant.

The wraith worked his forked tongue. "Yes, I was there so long ago now," he hissed, "I know… I know… I am the one you should hate."

The vile creature then pointed a long, clawed finger my way. "There's no more life in a mut like you than there is in this half-sized wretch, or his wretch of a father, or brother. But his mother… now she was fine wine. So I'll take this wretch's life just the same and yours too, if only to savor the sweet intoxication of it."

Mother? Father? I don't have a brother.

Fyorn roared as he charged at the beast with unchanneled aggression, bearing the sword down hard in a wide arc. He followed through with a quick swipe of the axe. The wraith dodged the attacks with effortless gliding motions. The dark, loose robe it donned flowed like a trailing shadow.

"Look out!" I yelled when a second wraith appeared at Fyorn's side, stepping out of long shadows. In a flash, the woodsman turned and cut the creature down with his long blade. At the same instant, with his axe, he parried a would-be deathblow from the other's swiping scythe.

Turning his attention to the remaining wraith, axe spinning in his off-hand, Fyorn rushed at the wraith repeatedly. But fast, two-handed blows from the scythe kept him at bay. The wraith was being cautious, taking advantage of the extended reach of his weapon to wear down the woodsman's aggression. And the wraith never stood its ground for an instant. Neither did my uncle for that matter. Each tried to outwit and out maneuver the other in a swift and deadly dance to gain the upper hand.

I tried to warn my uncle several times when I saw a strike coming, but each time he reacted before I could even get a word out. He was in the heat of the moment, the battle rage. I was just an out-of-breath onlooker. I raced over the possibilities. Maybe I could sneak in and attack the wraith from behind, or flank the beast, or if it fell, I could bash it with *Shatters* before it got up. I took the club out and watched in awe the foot movements, the feigns, the precision of thrust and slash. I witnessed subtle lures not fallen for, and missed opportunities. Time seemed to slow seconds to heartbeats.

My reach was less than half that of the long-limbed, lanky creature. I was an easy target, a liability, and I knew it. My direct involvement would only bring greater risk to the woodsman. *Think. What can I do?* Fury welled up inside me.

It was the axe that made first contact, cutting into the shoulder of the wraith and flashing green sparks where white metal met flesh. The creature had been blind-sided as scythe and sword had clashed, which I attributed to the hood the wraith wore, obstructing its peripheral vision. But the axe did not pull freely from the flesh when Fyorn tugged it back, and the wraith did not seem to care that it was there. Rather, he used it.

The hold-up afforded that vengeful beast with an opportunity to catch Fyorn's leg, causing him to stumble. The woodsman maintained his balance, partly leveraging the axe still embedded in the wraith's shoulder, even as the creature writhed to break free.

But the Elderkin had made a fatal mistake in the duel that left him vulnerable. The wraith bit at Fyorn's outstretched arm, sinking its teeth deep into his wrist. The woodsman jerked back and screamed in pain. The wraith let go its hold, favoring a new tactic.

Fyorn had retrieved his axe at the cost of a bite. The wraith lashed out at my uncle's face with one clawed hand, while the other kept a firm hold on the scythe bracing against the woodsman's sword and tying it up. Long black nails scratched beneath the protection of the helm. Trails of blood streaked across Fyorn's chin and neck.

I gasped, thinking it might all be over. *The touch...*

Fyorn had spun with the wraith's strike, and in that motion he freed the entangled bastard sword. Leveraging the weight of the spin, from his crouched position he stole another swing. He met his mark, but the mark had since moved. The wraith sprung back and avoided the cutting force of the blow. The follow through of that failed attack put the woodsman in a vulnerable position. To make matters worse, he stumbled. The wraith gained the advantage it had been so patiently waiting for. In a flash, the scythe rose high against the bulging moon, and the creature readied a death-blow against the sprawling Wild Elderkin.

Anger surged, I focused my mind to a point, and my blood began to boil. Time seemed to stand still. Kabor had already suffered the wraith's deathly touch, and now Fyorn was to be slaughtered. It was my fault for bringing this terrible demon to his forest grove.

Under normal circumstances, the sum total of what I did next would have amounted to nothing. But I saw that the two masters of combat were skirmishing near the tree line. At that pivotal moment, beyond any doubt, I experienced a sudden rush of energy. First, a wide pulse tingled up my spine. Then it fanned out, coursing through my trunk and every limb, finger and toe. It was the energy of the living forest. And as it spread, the light of the SPARX stone around my neck flickered faster and faster, in pale red pulses. I felt as though I had made *the connection* – with the trees, the grass, the insects, animals large and small, the monument, and even the moon and the stars that speckled the sky.

In that internally tumultuous moment, I had a desperate, simple thought – a pure wish.

I sensed that many of the nearby trees were Hurlorns – Sleepers, the regular sort that grow throughout Deepweald. I knew them to do little more than pass whispers, and occasionally bend to ease the passage of rangers, and fleeing Pips for that matter. I thought of my hand tracing out circles on the pool under the Hanging City, and how later the water had danced. I remembered how helpless I felt back then, and traced the desired motion with *Shatters*. I imagined the trees lashing out in vengeful fury. The memory, the motion and the *e*motion all intertwined in a split second to become one.

I whispered into the wind: "Strike."

It happened.

Branches whirred out and lashed at the wraith from behind, knocking him off balance. He hissed as the force hurled him directly into Fyorn, just as the scythe was bearing down. The disruption was all that the Wild Elderkin needed. The wraith attempted to adjust his swing, but missed a beat, giving Fyorn just enough lead-time to dodge the plunging scythe. The woodsman threw himself to one side and then rolled. The scythe dug into bare earth and clanged on a buried stone.

On all fours, Fyorn scrambled towards the monument and leapt over it to the other side, landing squarely on his feet. In that time, the wraith had pried the scythe out of the ground, and then launched a flying attack at the woodsman. But Fyorn was fluid and quick to counter. He toyed with his opponent around the stone slab, playing a child's game of elusion that kept the rock between them. It seemed as though he could have danced merrily around the monument all night until sunrise, if need be.

A mischievous grin appeared on Fyorn's face during that dance with death. I had seen the look many times before – the moment he knew the game was his.

But the wraith was not impressed or amused, and grew angry

and impatient at Fyorn's mockery. The shadow in the night threw up its arms and shrieked in frustration at the hopelessness of the chase, while Fyorn spun his axe tauntingly.

The fight turned, unexpected. In a move of cold cunning, the wraith threw back its hood and looked to me instead, unleashing a horrific hiss before lunging my way.

I gasped, and braced myself. I readied the deepwood club, defiant. My heart pounded. But Fyorn came upon the wraith so hard and fast, the timing of it bordered on precognition.

The woodsman had made his own lunge with lightning speed and immeasurable ferocity. In a flash, he had sheathed his sword and vaulted over the edge of the monument, tackling the charging wraith. As one they rolled along the forest floor until Fyorn gained the upper hand and pinned his foe to the ground. The wraith dropped the scythe in the scuffle. Desperate, the creature grabbed for the handle of the axe and wrestled for control. Raging, hissing, and cursing, the vile thing jerked violently to be free of Fyorn's heavy-handed grip. But the woodsman would not relent. He would never give in.

The shadowy form was slick though, and in a wiry way managed to twist free and stand. It reached to regain the scythe, one hand staying the axe. But during the tussle, Fyorn had found a moment to draw his sword. And with what looked to be an awkward swing that started with the sword lying flat on the ground, he slashed into the wraith's mid-section from the right flank. The wraith's body bent into the blow, and its clawed grip on the woodsman's axe went limp. The sword dropped to the ground as Fyorn regained his footing and moved into a low, balanced squat. Without hesitation, he raised his hefty axe in two hands and hacked down on the wraith's exposed neck, severing it. It dangled, bloodless, held by a mere thread of flesh. And when the creature fell to its knees in front of me, the body remained upright. The head spun freely and the eyes rolled to and fro, mouth open wide in a silent scream. I backed away.

Fyorn took a step back as well when the headless body began to flail about. It twitched and spun wildly in what could have been a morbid dance, until stopping abruptly in place. The creature's own hands cradled the dangling head, and held the face so the eyes could gaze directly at me.

And then the thing's lips formed a grim, half-crazed smile. Dark eyes dug deep into my soul, and tore away a piece of it. The wraith had chosen to mock me in its final moments, as though somehow it sensed I was doomed anyways. The smile drew thin into a silent laugh. One hand reached out with long, skeletal fingers to pull me in close. It was slow moving, and I easily sidestepped the out-stretched arm. Having had enough of this wicked beast, I lunged at it and swung with all my might. I bashed the head with *Shatters*. The tether snapped, and the hoodless skull went flying into the night. It sailed across the grove and crashed into the brush beyond. The body fell forward and landed with a thud.

A wave of relief washed over Fyorn's face. Then he gave me an odd look, a sense of urgency upon him. "We have to burn the bod-ies now," he said. "NOW!" he shouted when I did not move within half a heartbeat.

I fumbled through the pockets of the robe Nekenezitter had given me, and produced a handful of sulphur sticks. *He knew*, I thought. Too shaken to start the flames myself, I tossed them over to Fyorn.

"Here," was all I could manage to say.

My uncle handled the deed, first setting the wraith's robe on fire and then adding dry wood to the flames.

"Get the head," Fyorn said as he fussed over the fire. He left his handiwork to gather the second wraith.

With *Shatters* tight in my grip, I made way to the edge of the grove and peered into the brush. Dark shapes and darker shadows met my eyes. Anything could be lurking amongst the thick foliage. I feared stepping in, but knowing the importance of my task, I called on the SPARX stone. A narrow beam focused ahead of me as it had under the Hanging City. I spotted the disembodied head almost immediately, only a few steps in. It wasn't moving and seemed dead enough, so I went over, reached out and grabbed the head by its stringy hair. I raised it up high and held it out and away from my person, to the limits that my outstretched arm would permit. Stepping back into the grove, I called to Fyorn.

"Head's up!" I said, and then bowled the head to him. It was a good enough roll, stopping only a few feet short of the woodsman's boot. He gave me a steady look, and then side-kicked the head into the fire. Exhausted, I sheathed the stone and lumbered back to the fire to rest. The air soon became thick with billowing dark smoke and the smell of burning flesh as the fire crackled on. Flames danced merrily over their rich sustenance.

A gradual movement in the dark caught my eye – it was the trees. Rows of maples on the far side closed in, ever so slowly. Eventually, they formed concentric rings around us, beginning a safe distance out from the fire and extending to the edge of the clearing. Branches intertwined into a contorted mesh. From above, the light of the moon filtered in, illuminating the rising column of smoke that passed through an accommodating gap in the crown canopy.

The deed was done. And of the remaining wraith or wraiths in the woods – naught to worry…

CHAPTER XLI

Janhurl

I took a step back from the burning corpses to gain my bearings. If the wraiths left Kabor alone, he could not be far. I had entered the grove only minutes after we parted ways.

"We should split up," Kabor had puffed. The situation was hopeless. We both saw what had been done to the Glooms. Splitting up gave us the best odds. *I was faster.* The decision was not faulty. By sticking together, we could only pray for swift deaths. *I was faster, and he knew it.* "Hide," I said as I veered one way and he the other. *Goodbye.* The wraiths were gaining ground on us – the three that we knew of.

Kabor's frantic crashing through the bush cut through the night. Then came a loud "thunk" and sounds of rolling, followed by screams in the dark. I kept running. Last came the ominous silence, heavy as though the night had mass.

The wraiths on Kabor did not linger long with their catch. To them, a bird in the hand was not worth two in the bush. In short order, they were whipping through the bushes again.

I wanted to dash out of the grove and find Kabor, but common sense reminded me there was at least one more wraith in the woods. And it was still dark.

Flames roared and the fire crackled violently, taking deeper root in the blackening remains. Fyorn threw in more wood to keep it steady – larger pieces of dried maple. A loud hiss rose from the fire. No doubt, it would consume the remains through and through.

"There are more wraiths in the woods," I said.

"There was only one," he assured me, "and you sent him running home with his tail between his legs, and less an eye."

I did not question how he knew. He always knew. Fyorn had more to say. "Kabor has been found," he said. "He's safe and in good han – limbs."

The woodsman's face was drawn and he looked sick at heart. I think he knew more and feared the worst for it. He took a few steps towards the edge of the grove, raised his head to the branches above and whispered Elderkin words into the night. The rustling of leaves grew louder as he spoke, and the trees – the Hurlorns – parted in front of him. He stood perfectly still for a time afterwards, eyes closed and palms raised. He took a deep breath and held it.

A wave of relief poured across the woodsman's face as he expelled the air from his lungs. He turned to speak.

"The Stout will be brought to us," he announced, "and he is not seriously harmed."

I breathed my own sigh of relief.

Fyorn continued, "He is being tended to first though. It will take some time. Best to carry on until he is brought to us."

By whom? I wondered.

For a long minute, I just leaned against the monument and stared at the building fire. The dry heat bade me to stay put, get comfortable, and take a load off. My body ached and sweat stung the many scratches and scrapes that I had suffered while running through the woods. The prison guard had offered one small meal during our short incarceration. It would take many more to make up for the trials underground. At least there was the fire – bright, warm and inviting, in as much as a wraith can be, I suppose.

The woodsman spaced out the new fuel with a makeshift poker. I could still discern the contents of the fire, and found great satisfaction in its permanency. The Glooms were avenged, and there would be no fiery demons in the night.

My uncle came over and flopped down. With my back to the massive rock, I slid down onto the grasses next to him. The woodsman-turned-warrior removed his helm and wiped the sweat from his brow with the back of his sleeve. His sword had returned to its scabbard, left to lean casually against the monument, and his axe lay flat on top of the roughly hewn surface. Fyorn said nothing, drawing in deep breaths and gazing up through the smoke hole to the starry sky above, legs sprawled out in front of him. I suspected that he pondered his mortality, as did I. It had been a narrow escape.

"Thanks," I said.

Fyorn only nodded. I had never seen him so winded.

"One less eye? Really?"

Fyorn nodded again, in between breaths, this time with a silent "Yep" on his lips.

In a desperate attempt to foil my pursuers, I had stopped half a moment to throw *Sliver*. I did not even wait to see where it landed: halt, turn, throw, turn back, keep running.

"Lucky shot," I said.

"That wasn't luck. *That* was deepwood."

"Lucky I found this place, then."

"No, Nud. Not much luck there either, I'm afraid," he said. "The Hurlorns guided you here. I know because I told them to."

"Holly, Gariff, Bobbin—"

Fyorn cut me off. "They're all safe," he said.

More relief welled over me.

"How—" I began to ask.

"I read the rustling of the leaves and whispers in the wind," he said, smiling. That was always his answer.

His smile turned sour. The woodsman looked down and shook his head, then found my staring eyes. "Tragically, your lost guard was not so lucky."

We sat together silent and still, taking in the cool, night air with heavy breaths, lost in thought. Eventually, after twice refueling the fire, Fyorn broke the silence.

"Where did you pick up the wraiths? And how was the Stout when you last seen him?" he said.

"You don't know?" I asked. "Kabor was being pursued... we split up."

"Dire times indeed are upon us when wraiths walk the woods," replied Fyorn. My uncle put his arm on my shoulder. "We'll make your friend better."

"He'll tough it out," I said, hoping it was true.

Thinking back to what happened on the trail, I blurted out: "And the bog queens... the bog queens are on the Mire trail."

"I've known about the bog queens for a very long time," he said. "There are even worse things in the bog nowadays. They never bothered anyone before now. Something has changed."

The words were less than comforting. I was reminded of the shadow in the water. Someone in Webfoot must have known as well – why else would we have a new guard post on the Mire Trail?

Fyorn stood up to go, looking, again, very much like the *Uncle* Fyorn I knew. He turned to face me.

"You did good," he said. "Bravery and good sense in a pinch are hard to come by. You have it in you to make your mark on the world, on the strength of those pillars alone."

I flushed at the praise. Paplov would have been proud to hear that. Fyorn suddenly froze, lifting his hand to me in a hush signal. I stayed still. His head cocked, followed by a sideways glance while he listened intently.

"Kabor?" I whispered, and then stood up.

Fyorn shook his head. "Holly," he muttered, nearly to himself.

I perked my own ears, but heard only the wind and the rustling of leaves. They did not speak to me the way they spoke to Fyorn.

"She must have followed me here," he said. There was a commotion in the surrounding woods… a struggle.

Sure enough, the trees parted and sweet Holly strode into the grove as though she owned the place. She wore a worried look on her face, and carried her exceptional cloak in one hand. Her hair shone and sweat streamed down her cheeks. She looked radiant in the smoky moonlight, as radiant as the first night I saw her at the Flipside Inn.

"They wouldn't let me in here until I took off the cloak," she said, pointing to the trees. She tugged on the shoulder of her shirt. "They kept hooking it." She brushed leaves and crud off her shirt and pants.

"Perverts," she said. "I'm just glad they stopped there."

Fyorn rolled his eyes.

Holly sent me an easy smile and rushed over. Her embrace was long and sweet and heavenly. She smelled of lavender. Afterwards, she stepped back to face me, grasping my hands and squeezing them tight. Her eyes were the forest moss and her hair the finest silk.

But it was Fyorn's voice I heard instead of hers, speaking in a firm, fatherly tone, blending annoyance with concern. "You were supposed to stay at the camp and await my return," he said, glaring at Holly.

We broke off our greeting, all too soon in my mind. Holly returned his stare with guilty eyes.

"I know, I know," she said. "But you told me there was trouble and… I just had to know what was happening. I'm not useless in a fight you know, especially now. I can sneak up behind someone and—"

"I regret ever giving you that cloak. I've created a monster." Fyorn's tone was less than serious.

"Besides," she continued, "I'd rather be here with someone who knows what he's doing than be out there alone. And it's eerie... there are all kinds of *noises*."

"No doubt, you were the loudest of them. I could hear sticks cracking under your feet a mile away." The woodsman and I looked at one another, both shaking our heads.

"It's more than a little eerie right here," I said, gesturing to the burning corpses. By that time, the flames had consumed the bulk of the bodies and, with all the wood stacked on top, they were unrecognizable.

Holly closed her eyes, turned her head away from the fire and held one hand up. "UGH... Don't even tell me what that is – I don't want to know. I heard all the clanging and grunting." She looked around the grove. "Is Kabor...?"

"He's still in the woods," I said. "We split up when the wraiths... I mean... sorry... were gaining on us, but they all went for him first."

Fyorn gave me a quizzical look. "I wonder why," he said. "Their tactic is to seek out the high value target first... hmm."

I refrained from mentioning that he was the easier target – louder and slower.

Holly shook her head vehemently and interrupted straight away. "Why are we all standing around here then? We have to find him."

She took a step toward the trees, and then stopped herself. "Wait a minute. Wraiths? Tell me you didn't say wraiths. The Grim Reaper and all? They aren't real... are they? Those are just stories to scare children." Holly's voice cracked. "I told you *not* to tell me."

I was shaking my head. "Kabor's all right. He's on his way and taken care of."

Fyorn confirmed with a nod when Holly looked to him.

"Nevermind about the wraiths." Fyorn planted one hand firmly on Holly's shoulder, with the other he pointed to the flames. "Your Nud here finished this one off and sent another running with one less eye to see with. We're roasting two of the buggers now."

She looked to the fire in disgust.

"There are more? Nud killed a wraith?" A look of disbelief crossed Holly's face when Fyorn nodded.

"You owe him a debt of gratitude. Yes… Nud slew the wraith and sent another running. If he hadn't, something might have sniffed you out on your way here. They are all too familiar with the sweet scent of Pip blood."

Holly shivered at the thought. She looked me over, as if trying to see something that wasn't there before. I didn't correct Fyorn's account of things, or try to be modest. Surely, knowing Holly she would eventually pry every detail out of me or my uncle anyway. For the time being, I simply basked in the glory of borrowed victory.

Thereafter, I was known throughout Webfoot as the young Pip who had slain a ferocious beast in the wild. I didn't mind the rumors, and the fact that Fyorn deserved most of the credit didn't bother me either – he was one hundred and two, had fought in countless battles and was already *Courser*, the highest rank of the Wild Elderkin rangers in Deepweald. What's one measly wraith to his credit? He didn't need another win. From what I knew of Uncle Fyorn, by his very nature he valued anonymity above fame anyways.

"What happened to Gariff and Bobbin? Couldn't they come along too?" I said.

"They went looking for you two lost pups in Harrow," said Holly. "Fyorn thought you might have gotten lost and ended up there."

Oddly, he had been right. When I looked to Fyorn, he nodded, but something about the way his eyes sparkled told me he knew more than he let on to Holly.

"We'll meet up with them back at the camp tomorrow morning," said Fyorn. "I gave them enough coin to live it up at a certain inn tonight."

While we waited by the fire, I recounted the details of the chase, and the last thing I saw. I explained how we had come upon the wraiths in the mine, and of the premonition that I had earlier in a dream. But I could not do so without recounting nearly everything about our adventure in the Hanging City, the Catacombs, and the Iron Tower. They both listened intently as the fire burned low, nodding and shaking their heads. Holly even sobbed when I mentioned how I thought that Kabor had been buried alive. I left out the White Whale for the time being, saying only that a solitary and very knowledgeable underground dweller helped guide my way. There were no questions. By the time I finished, Kabor and I were heroes in their minds.

After the tale had settled and our stares had fallen into the fire, a loud crashing sound startled us. A thirty-foot tree – yes a tree – just strode into the clearing. Fyorn leapt up as it approached. The tree's long strides whipped curled roots over the ground and stirred up leafy debris. Unlike the normal sorts of Hurlorns that grew in these parts, this one had a kind of face – all knots and burl wood, twisted in on itself to form eyebrows, a nose and lips around a hollow. Black knotty eyes shone like polished ebony from inset eye sockets.

Fyorn greeted the tree with a nod of his head. "Janhurl," he said.

"Fyor-yor-yor-yorn," the tree replied, like a flute in the wind.

The tree bore Kabor, wrapped in a cocoon of leaves and a nest of woven branches. The Stout was pallid and shivering as though feverish, but alive and well otherwise. She laid him down as close as she dared go to the fire. Holly ran to Kabor's side and, down on one knee, placed her cloak over the Stout's trembling body.

The rest of the conversation was strictly in Elderkin, which I did not understand at the time. The Hurlorn's voice rang out mellifluously as a rich, resonant buzzing of notes. Some of them might have been syllables of the immortal tongue. It wasn't proper speech by any stretch of the imagination, but Fyorn understood.

He looked up and nodded in acknowledgement at whatever was being said, taking a few steps back though to give her roots some space while she winded on, and on, and on. Holly and I kept our distance, eyeing the talking tree-creature in utter disbelief.

Janhurl bore one final message, which she passed to Fyorn before returning to the woods. It was dark news – a whisper out of the alders, rushes and reeds of Webfoot. The woodsman and the Hurlorn said goodbye to one another in the customary way of the woods, as I would later learn.

Janhurl fluted her part, incomprehensibly.

"By sun, wind, rain and earth," repeated Fyorn.

The woodsman later explained how Janhurl was one of the few fully animate Hurlorns – a spirit reborn – and that she had great concerns about the slaying of a wraith in *her* woods. He also said Hurlorns have a round about way of getting to the point, and that in just such a round about way, Janhurl had requested that we bury the charred remains deep on a high hill, but not the grove itself. She also asked that we promise not to *speak* of it to anyone, ever again. As far as I know, we all kept that promise, although I walk a fine line to have *written* of the event here.

We watched as the tall Hurlorn strode across the grove on a heading west, stopping for a brief moment to look back. Janhurl's measuring gaze found mine for a long moment. She turned back to her route and with one giant stride stepped out of the grove and out of sight. Fyorn walked over to me and stooped to eye level. His huge hands gripped my shoulders firmly. He faced me and his bright eyes met mine. His irises were vessels of amber bleeding into a calm sea of blue, his pupils sparked with flames from the bonfire.

"I'm sorry to be the one to have to tell you this," he began. "Bad news – your papa is seriously ailing; he may not make it through the night."

It came out of nowhere.

The words gripped my chest.

I think there was some mention of a long and successful life, and something about using his time well. And Fyorn handed me a rolled sheet of black leather. The scroll looked vaguely familiar; it was some kind of official document from Paplov's desk.

I turned and stared into the heat of the fire. The flames danced on what was left of the burning wraiths. My heartbeat quickened, my lifeblood pumped nervously. I felt the sanguine fluid suck in and spill out in its vital rhythm, the body fully aware of what the mind had willed away by denial. Flames consume all. *Things will never be the same.* Paplov had been sick on and off for some time. The Proudfoot trip did him in. *I should have carried more of the load. I should not have given him such a hard time.*

The tightness in my chest squeezed full force. I mulled over how much Paplov had stayed in lately, curled up in his chair with a blanket and a book. I recalled how he had missed some meetings lately too, and how he had passed important duties to other council members, and how he had tried to do the same to me. *I could have done more.* The signs were all there, I just never put them together. *I didn't care enough.*

Time was short between that and the next setback.

"That's not all," said Fyorn. "Holly, you need to hear this too." He waved her in closer. Kabor was in no condition to be a part of the conversation. "I don't want to alarm anyone, but Bobbin and Gariff have not been heard from since early evening. At this point, Janhurl is optimistic, but she is being cautious nonetheless. She'll look into it and we'll know more in the morning. Hurlorns are on the watch tonight."

"They probably just took a meal and a room for the night, that's all," said Holly.

"Probably," said Fyorn.

It never rains, but it pours, I thought. Paplov said that all the time when worries were multiplying.

CHAPTER XLII

The Watch

I t wasn't until I focused on the notion that things had to get normal again, the notion that everything still could be the way it used to be, that I finally relaxed, breathed deep, and allowed the night air to stretch the fabric of my lungs.

Fyorn sat near the fire on a well-hacked stump, normally reserved for wood chopping. He looked the tired old man, washed out and heavy hearted. Dried sweat matted his hair and dried blood streaked his chin. The woodsman's years showed in his face and in the way he slumped. The sharpness of his features, so striking on livelier days, gave way to a long and somber expression in the red-tinged glow of the fire. Years take their toll on people, even when the body retains its virile strength. Fyorn fixed his eyes on the crackling fire and did not even flinch when it flared up high right in front of him. Paplov had always been a close friend to him. On top of that, it had been a long and complicated day after a long and complicated week, and the day coming wasn't shaping up to be short and simple. I felt as heavy as the Elderkin looked.

"How did he seem to you?" I said to him.

"He's a tough old bugger," replied Fyorn. "I'll give him that, but he never looked so… grave." *A poor choice of words*, I thought. There was more. "Your papa insisted we keep up the search…"

I closed my eyes and let my chest heave, and then relax.

The woodsman's gaze never left the wraith's fire. "I'll send him word that you and the Stout have been found alive and well," he said. "Your papa will hear the words tonight. That will put his mind at ease and lift his spirits. He never gave up hope."

I unraveled the scroll slowly, near enough to the fire to read by its unsteady light. The leather was soft and worn. I recognized it fully by then; Paplov traveled everywhere with it. To open the scroll, he would hold one roller and let the other drop – let gravity do the work. On official business, Paplov showed it to gain entry at town gates or guarded meeting halls. He kept it in a double bone tube, corked at both ends.

"When I spoke with your dear old papa last, he insisted you keep that safe for him," offered the woodsman.

I held in my hand one of Paplov's personal belongings, something he had never before parted with.

"He still needs his colors!" I said, stopping short of blurting out "He's not dead yet!" I took a deep breath, held it for a moment as I briefly closed my eyes, then let the air out slowly.

Fyorn sighed heavily. By the way he paused and by his blank stare, it was obvious he chose the words that followed carefully. And he should have, he was walking on thin ice as far as I was concerned.

"Until then, you'd better take them, Nud. Your papa wanted you to know that you are ready for this. You know the issues, you know the processes, you know the people, and you know how to negotiate. You can always return the colors to him yourself… when he's better. Until then…" He trailed off.

I nodded. Whatever came to pass, I should be the one to hold onto it.

The first section proudly laid out Paplov's diplomatic colors and those of Webfoot. Further down were the emblems: stamped in the usual reserved corner was the tree frog – upper right. The tree frog was the family emblem on my mother's side, a source of unbounded teasing from my Stout friends. The town emblem on the upper left corner was a bog scene, skillfully embroidered. Deep red circles for bog berries dangled from slender brown stems with tiny, oval leaves. The branches crept along cushions of moss and wound their way down the left margin. A silhouetted hill with huts on the horizon marked Webfoot. Other sections of the document recorded Paplov's responsibilities, authorities and jurisdiction. Near the very bottom was an embroidered version of his personal seal and that of the mayor in the name of the Council, complete with signatures.

I don't know why, but I blurted out an idea that popped into my head; the only sure way I knew to beat death at the time. "The Mark!" I said, and wondered why I hadn't thought of it beforehand. "Janhurl can just give him the Mark and—" Fyorn was shaking his head.

"Hurlorns choose their own," he said. "It is not for us to dictate. I do not know what drives their ways. They just do what they do." He stood up stiffly and walked off to the edge of the grove, alone. He had that look about him – nothing more would be said of the matter and something important demanded his attention. Where he stood, the Hurlorns parted again, as though to avoid his burning stare. His field of view unobstructed, the woodsman surveyed the wide expanse of lowland forest below, little more than shadows in the faded light of a starry horizon.

Soon enough, Fyorn was on to other business and it was high time that I did likewise. I kept busy to take my mind off things, tending to a fire that needed no tending and organizing things that didn't need organizing. All the while, Holly had been making herself useful. Finally, she grabbed my wrist.

"Just relax," she said. "Maybe tomorrow talk it through, once you've cleared your head. And I'm sure Bobbin and Gariff are just in some cozy inn, ya' think?"

I nodded. "Yep. I wonder if they serve barkwood ale."

She smiled. "Hope not, or we won't see either of them until noon if they get to arguing like last time."

"I never heard Gariff talk so much," I said.

"Or so loud," said Holly.

Relaxation was not an option for me, but Holly did set me on a task that actually did require immediate attention. It was time to lick our wounds, so to speak. I joined the woodsman, already one step ahead on that aspect. He had pulled his pack out from a stash under some thick bushes. It lay open beside the fire, contents spilling out onto the trampled grass. A small iron pot, filled with wine, hung over the flames from a makeshift tripod.

Holly went off to check on Kabor. The Stout was trembling and white as a ghost. He sat leaning against the monument on the fringes of the fire's warmth. Holly was made for the job of keeping a conversation lively, and only had to remind herself to let Kabor get a word in edgewise every so often, to make sure he was still lucid. Whenever his eyes fluttered or his head nodded, she had no problem delivering a polite shake or a cuff to startle him awake.

When the contents of the pot were good and hot, Fyorn bathed my scratches and scrapes in the hot wine. He mulled over one gash in particular, on my thigh. Eventually he decided it needed stitches.

The steel burned red hot alongside the flame, but was quick to regain its gentle hue. A quick prick followed by a gentle tug. The thread glided through my skin, almost softly. It was not painful, not really. I watched as the needle zigzagged across the gash, each stitch measuring a careful finger's width distance from the last to leave room for the wound to drain. The stitching took only a few minutes. When the deed was done, the woodsman applied a waxy healing salve and wrapped the area in a sticky, shimmering fabric. It luminesced with a patchy green glow.

"Spiderweave," he said while rolling up what was left. He must have caught me eyeing the fabric.

Fyorn also checked the injuries that I had sustained underground. When he seemed satisfied that every wound was set to heal as it should, he told me that I would end up with scars on the back of my head and my lower back, plus the gash he just stitched. Nothing serious though.

The woodsman spooned some hot wine over his own wounds next, separating the skin to help it seep in underneath. He would finish dressing them later. Kabor needed tending to. The Stout showed only minor scrapes and puncture wounds, but Fyorn whispered his concerns to Holly about him. Kabor had endured an injury of a kind I did not quite understand at the time. I overheard my uncle say that the deep touch of the wraith might yet cause serious harm in days to come.

After finishing with Kabor, the woodsman made his way back to the fire and continued our conversation where it had left off, long after I thought it had fallen off a cliff. By then the fire actually did need tending, and I had just honed in on a small stash of cut wood and put an armful down against the rock.

"Wild Elderkin are the sole producers of the weave – even Gan is not privy to its manufacture. We trade with them, but they sure as hell can't produce it and they don't use this stuff much. There are only so many ways you can get a paper cut or jab yourself with a pen, or bump yourself when you nod off and your head hits the desk." He was referring to the High Elderkin that lived there and their academic obsession. The woodsman had always portrayed them as less than practical.

Fyorn passed a strip of the weave over to me, and then went on to clean and dress the scratches on his chin and neck. A small metallic mirror helped him to guide his actions. The fabric was a mesh, and one side was sticky.

"A spider made this?" I said, holding the strip by the edges and stroking the non-stick side. I tried to pull it apart, tear it and push my nail through. It would not damage that easily. The fibers were strong and tightly woven. I wondered if the spider was anything like the one I found in my uncle's attic.

"Not exactly... more like a silkworm actually; it's an old art from days long forgotten." A warm, familiar smile came across his face. "I carry the pads for their healing properties, but some weaves will turn an arrow." Fyorn winked at me as he lifted the bottom of his chainmail vest, revealing a thin suit of shimmering silk underneath.

"Even arrows coated with the same stuff?" I said.

"Sure," he replied. "It's the give in the fabric that does the trick, not the hardness. It can't even defeat itself."

I chuckled.

Once again, Fyorn and Holly checked Kabor over thoroughly to see how he was fairing; particularly with regard to the puncture wounds he received on the back of his neck. The Stout's breaths were short and shallow. The wraiths had done something to him, but as far as the woodsman could tell, it was safe for Kabor to sleep, so long as someone kept an eye on him. The Stout rested his eyes.

Holly returned from her watch on Kabor with regularity to check up on me, offering her caring blend of polite consolation and advice. We seemed an unlucky bunch, the four of us together: Holly dealt with more than her share of tragedy before the Numbits had taken her in. And then there was Kabor, taken in by his aunt and uncle after his parents were murdered. Fyorn was no stranger to hardship and loss, having fought against the Jhinyari slavers. And then there was me. *The world is a messed up place when you piece it all together. All the more reason to make the most of what little of it is good*, I thought.

Those final minutes of solace flew by; we all had tasks to attend to, save Kabor. Sorrow tugged down at my gut like a heavy weight in my stomach, but I would deal with the bulk of it later. Holly had passed Fyorn's news to the Stout. It hadn't really fazed him in his state.

Despite all that had happened, at the first opportunity Holly stole some time from Fyorn to feed her curiosity. There always seemed to be some puzzle that required immediate resolution – the questing mind of a know-it-all. "What is this place?" She sounded sweetly naive. Holly played that card often with adults when vying for attention or trying to pry information out of them. It never failed her.

If talk of the spiderweave had awakened the woodsman's pride, describing the grove made him downright boastful. "You are standing in a most hallowed place," he began. "Important ceremonies are held here." He pointed. "That rune stone in the centre is more than it appears. It is a symbol of our connection to nature."

"Who do you mean by *our*?" she returned.

An innocent question, but it proved less than easy for the woodsman to answer. His eyes dropped as he searched for the right words. He looked up and met Holly's eager gaze.

"Those who take *and hold* the oath," said Fyorn – a vague answer at best. I settled in to eavesdrop on a long-winded explanation, carefully worded, but without pause my uncle was up and away again, busy with a new task that I could only guess at. It was almost rude. Surprisingly, Holly didn't push for more at the time. Somewhat contrary to what Fyorn had told me at his cabin, I learned later that members of the woodsman's order had been chosen not only from the ranks of heroes and sages, but also scoundrels and even villains; some were relics from the distant past and others came from far away lands or were taken from the here and now. More in line with what he had said though, each member was chosen for what that individual could contribute to the whole. Most were Hurlorns by the time they joined. Some were Wild Elderkin. None were anything else.

Kabor jolted awake, still shivering and visibly annoyed at something. He stood up and steadied himself against the monument, dropped Holly's cloak, then shakily scuttled off to a more secluded location. He found comfort within the confines of the gnarled roots of the grove's tallest tree. Once settled, Kabor wrapped himself tight in a heavy blanket that Holly brought over to him from Fyorn's stash. The Stout nodded off almost immediately. Fyorn, who had returned to the task of making sure every last bit of the wraith was charred, kept a watchful eye on the Stout as he worked. Every now and again, he went over to Kabor, smeared the back of his hand with a few drops of water from his canteen, and held the hand under Kabor's mouth or nose to feel the Stout's breath.

After a small, shared meal of dried meat and warm wine, cooked over a new and separate fire from the one disposing of wraiths, the three of us that were mobile made preparations for the night. Holly tried waking Kabor up to eat, but he would have none of it. I had dug a small pit for the new fire and lined it with stones, locating it purposely close to the tree Kabor had chosen, but not so close as to scare it off. Then I gathered enough wood to fuel a blaze through 'til morning. It was a compact fire, but deep and hot burning. Fyorn, with weary, heavy eyes, asked me to keep the first watch for as long as I could stay awake, and then to wake him. He reminded me not to let the fire burn too low and called upon Holly to keep a close eye on Kabor. "Let him sleep through the night if he can. He may gain some strength by morning, but monitor his breathing and keep him bundled up," he advised.

Holly and I chatted late into the night. Kabor received less attention than he ought to have, but no harm came of it. We wondered openly how the watch for Bobbin and Gariff was going.

With Fyorn asleep, there was no one to receive any whispers. Holly insisted he would wake up anyway if one came, but kept her ears pricked just in case she heard something. *Wishful thinking,* I thought.

"So… how did you escape the bog queens?" I asked her.

Holly's eyes lit up as she recanted the ordeal in superb pip-pish detail, mimicking the motions and imitating the hags' voices a little too well for comfort.

"…that witch screamed and cursed and spat something terrible at him the whole time," she finished.

"So Bobbin saved the day. Hmm… go figure." I could not help but to smile at that.

"As much as could be saved. There's still Jory…" She looked away.

"You screamed," I said. "It was the last thing I heard."

"There was a lot of screaming," she said. "Me and Gariff thought you were both as good as dead, so we ran back to town for help. Gariff and his 'Pops' had half of Webfoot out looking in no time. They were great at getting everyone riled up in a hurry."

Holly caught the look on my face. She nodded. "Ya, I was impressed too," she said. "And your uncle must have caught wind of what happened, the way he always seems to. He met the search party on the Mire Trail and tried to get some answers too, but I'd say the whispers were silent on the matter. He said we might have to look where no one would ever think to look – I guess he was right."

"How did you know I was coming to the grove?" I asked.

Holly shrugged her rounded shoulders. "You'll have to ask your uncle about that," she said. "He sent Gariff and Bobbin to Harrow to find out if anyone at the local inns had seen or heard anything. Your uncle and I searched along the edge of the forest thinking that you might have broken free and ran for the tree line, then got lost or had injuries to contend with. He didn't know you'd just pop

up the way you did, out of nowhere with wraiths on your tail."
Holly was quiet for a moment, peering up through the dark stand
of Hurlorns to a piece of the night sky beyond.

"It was weird," she continued. "At one point he just tilted his
head in a funny way and said you two were coming. He told me to
get back to the cabin with my cloak on until he returned, and then
he just took off. The armor he wore in battle and his big sword
were just hanging on a tree nearby, in the middle of nowhere. I
spied him through the trees, putting them on. Then off he went,
bee-lining it for the grove. It was bizarre – I could hardly believe
my eyes."

"Maybe it was another whisper," I said.

"I suppose," said Holly, "but I didn't hear anything and I have
especially sharp ears."

Apart from a few suspicious branches cracking somewhere in
the dark perimeter, nothing of concern interrupted our watch over
one another. Holly sat close by, gripping my arm or thigh at every
snap, which I did not mind one bit. She quizzed me in her usual
manner, until her eyes went heavy and her speech became choppy.
I kept the fire burning steady until the Flipside girl finally nodded off on my shoulder. Dreadfully tired myself, I tucked her in
and gently shook my uncle awake, then took my place by the fire,
wrapped securely in my trusty cloak. It was a cool night. The soft
earth was far more comfortable than what I had become accustomed to, and the fresh air cleansed my lungs. A sense of relief
filled me. And with it, openness. All in all, I had no qualms about
being exactly where I was, protected and with the whole of the
underground ordeal behind me, and the bit about the wraiths settled. I was happy to be on the other side of things. I drifted off
without another thought.

CHAPTER XLiii

Interlude - The Hurlorns' stride

For the most part Hurlorns appear to be regular trees, at least at first glance. But to a discerning eye, a certain simplicity in form might be noticed. They tend to have fewer, thicker branches than their fully natural counterparts, and the leaves or needles tend to grow in rich clusters rather than spread out evenly. As long as a Hurlorn lives, it carries no dead wood on its limbs, and rarely have Hurlorns been observed to look sickly in any way. The noblest of the great Hurlorns – those with spirits instilled in them – have burl wood features somewhere up high in the trunk that, with a little imagination, resemble a face. Burls might be found in other areas of the tree as well, giving the appearance of shoulders or elbows or other vaguely man-like features. A precious few – one in a generation – from among the Spirit Hurlorns forgo even their tree-like forms, to become a lumbering colossus such as myself, with scales of bark, a long, whipping tail like a giant vine, and a neck that stretches high above the treetops. They become what I am now, the Green Dragon of Deepweald.

Either way, Hurlorn roots must be contended with. In stride, they are long and whip-like, and do more than simply flail about during locomotion – they feel out the ground. And so, a Hurlorn has intimate knowledge of the terrain trodden upon. In particular, a former Pip transmuted to a Spirit Hurlorn would recall every detail.

In any case, it is best to steer clear of a Hurlorn's approach and give the creature plenty of room, or risk being lashed at, or worse, trampled upon. But when Hurlorns are still, as they nearly always are, their roots twist deep into the living soil. And at the base of the trunk, they tend to curl up in such a manner as to give the impression of toes on giant feet – a fitting signature for trees that stroll through the woodlands. If you happen to come across roots that appear to be two very large feet at the base of a very large tree, you may have just stumbled on a dormant Hurlorn.

CHAPTER XLIV

Who's who

I n the grey shades of early morning, the apparitions that haunted the grove in the night stood tall and silent. So proper in their place and so lasting in their presence, the advance of the hardwoods had seemed more the fabric of dreams than the substance of reality.

I stood and stretched at the very crest of the Wild Elderkins' sacred hill, and through the trees glimpsed a pale magenta light ascending over wooded hills and beneath blue-grey clouds. To the southwest, fog had settled in the low-lying areas, punctured by the sharp skeletons of suffocated pine and spruce trees.

"Good morning," I said to the Hurlorn sentinels in the grove. None responded. None were like Janhurl, or maybe they were still sleeping.

Holly was the next to wake up, groggy. She looked to the dead fire pit and then to me. Her auburn hair was tousled, and the smile of acknowledgment she flashed my way was soon conquered by a long-faced yawn. Fyorn was nowhere to be seen. Kabor slept soundly, but twitched violently every now and again. The other fire – the wraith fire – had been dug out and the foul ashes removed.

"What's for breakfast?" said Holly.

I replied in my best snobbish accent – Fort Abandon elite. "I have acquired a taste for vermin and blind fish of late. Allow me to serve you."

Holly graced me with a full view of her wide, flat tongue. She moaned and made an awful face before burying her head deep into a stuffed hood posing as a pillow. The Flipside girl sighed heavily, and then spoke into her pillow. "Where's Bobbin when you need him?"

Tagged with the responsibility to provide, I rummaged through Fyorn's pack and found more dried meat, some dried fruit and, yes, several rather large chunks of taffy – bone dry and hard as a rock. Anyone who knew Fyorn at all also knew that he had to have sweets on him somewhere, at all times.

After we consumed a fair portion of the meat and it was time to help ourselves to the taffy, Fyorn stepped into the clearing. He was sooty and sweaty, carrying a small shovel and a large, empty sack. It was no mystery what he'd been up to. Nor was it any mystery to him what we were up to. His sudden entrance had caught us off guard and with our hands in the cookie jar, so to speak. He grinned as I shattered a chunk of taffy between two rocks and divided the pieces as equally as I could, four ways.

"Would you like my axe?" he said.

I shook my head. "Not after last night," I replied.

Kabor awoke and sat up. A shimmering line of drivel ran down from the corner of his mouth, which he promptly wiped with his sleeve.

"How about a bite?" I asked him, showing him the candy morsels.

Kabor made a sick face and shook his head. Holly was quick to claim his portions. The Stout thirsted greatly though, and downed the contents of a watering can that the woodsman had set beside him in the night.

Fyorn took his bits before Holly got to them. "We'll see rain by evening," he said, and then proceeded to recite his plans for the day. "Once we rendezvous with Bobbin and Gariff, you should all head for Webfoot together. Stay at the trapper's cabin if..." He glanced at Kabor. "...stay there if the going is slow. Holly knows where the key is. Lock up when you leave."

"I have big concerns about Harrow," he continued, "so I'll be veering off to the Hidden City to report what I have seen and heard, and to seek council on recent events. I'll let them know everything that's been happening, if they don't already know more than I do."

The woodsman fixed his eyes on Kabor and then me. "Harrow will have to answer for incarcerating the two of you," he said.

Fyorn paused and looked to each of us in turn, inviting questions. It was too early for questions though.

"Good, now that's settled. Time for a *real* breakfast," he said. "We have a big day ahead. Holly, you're in charge." He was teasing her, but she didn't seem to catch on.

Holly opened her mouth in protest. Her jaw moved, but she said nothing. She was a great server, but never claimed to be a cook. It seemed she would let it pass, until her voice rang out. "Just because I work in a tavern doesn't mean I know how to cook," she said.

"You must have learned something," teased Fyorn.

"Ya, like who's cheap and who's not, who'll try to cop a feel, who tries to pick a fight, and who'll stand up for you. Then there's who talks about their wife all the time, who cheats, who works hard all day, who tries to pick you up, who likes to have fun and who likes to drown their sorrows and forget. That's what I learned: who's who."

My uncle shook his head and grimaced. "Knowing who's who is important," he said.

Holly's eyes went wide with enthusiasm. "MMM... but it's fun though too," she said, "like on special occasions when everyone's happy. And out-of-towners are amazed when they order a big meal and I remember every little detail without writing anything down. Offerings are good sometimes."

She continued on and on about the Flipside and her patrons, delving into lively accounts of events and incidents. While she spoke, Fyorn began tidying up the campsite and packing his belongings. When he came to the cooking gear, Holly interrupted his progress.

"You're not putting that away, are you? What about breakfast?" she said.

Fyorn smiled thinly. "Of course not," he said. "Just getting to it." I could see he was drawn, but my uncle was nothing if not a good host. To Holly's delight, he stoked the fire, got his cooking gear together, and put his pan over the heat. I threw some fresh wood underneath.

The woodsman sent me off to a cold storage space that he maintained, down the hill in a glen. I found it easily enough, set beneath rocks deeply shaded by tall pines. Winter ice, doped with pine needles, had persisted through spring and probably would into early summer. Under the rocks and the blocks of ice, I pulled out a few black sausages spiced with garlic that he had stowed away, and fresh crow eggs as well. It suffices to say my uncle whipped us up a quick and satisfying breakfast.

My shrunken stomach was already satisfied going in, so I found myself nibbling at the fixings for the sheer pleasure of it. He also started a pot of tea of some unknown variety, tearing apart small, spiky leaves and dropping them into boiling water. The tea came out pleasantly weak, and sipping it imparted a tightening sensation that soothed the throat. Kabor, in his first gesture of non-grumpiness that day, made his appreciation of the beverage known to all.

As we ate, I filled in more details about my travel underground. Fyorn listened intently while he busied himself. Every so often, he halted what he was doing to focus in on a topic. Holly was just as enamored by my tales as she had been the previous night. Once again, I omitted the part about the leviathan. In particular, Fyorn seemed quite interested in the strange race of underground dwellers I encountered.

"…and one of the Glooms, named Nekenezitter, can see. He led us out." I told him.

"Gropers," Fyorn stated matter-of-factly. "They're called Gropers, not Glooms."

"Actually, they call themselves the Il'kinik," I said.

"Il'kinik?" he repeated. "I never heard that before."

"But, Gropers sounds about right," I said. "The oddest people I've ever met. They do more than work the mines though." I went through my pack and pulled out one of the smooth, glassy tablets I had found. "Under the tower, I saw some working on these."

While being led to my cell, I had glimpsed tablets of the sort that I found in the Hanging City, this time through an open doorway in the Catacombs. They were laid out on a long, metal table along with other… interesting items. A man was in the room as well, richly dressed, and the constant chirring of Gloom chatter spilled into the hallway. For a brief moment, I observed how the Glooms handled the tablets and other gadgets with gliding hands and deft fingers. And the way they seemed to *study* what they held had me wondering if somehow they could "see" *better* than we could, at least in some ways.

Fyorn stopped what he was doing for a quick glance at the tablet. He held it up to the light, and grimaced. "Harrow will have to answer for this as well. Sorry Nud, but I need to hang on to it."

"Keep it," I said. I nearly volunteered the other one that I had stashed away, but thought better of it. Fyorn wrapped the tablet in cloth and carefully packed it away.

Thunder rumbled in the distance. Kabor, who had dozed off sometime during the discussion, was startled awake.

While Holly and I cleaned up and Fyorn reorganized his pack so everything would fit neatly, I went over the bit about Taeglin's plans for the bog, as told by Nekenezitter. Fyorn seemed irked at the mention of the Harrowian. Then he spilled his taffy. It scattered into the fire pit.

"Taeglin is like a spoiled child," he said, clearly agitated. "Everyone knows that officially, he is the rightful King of Harrow, but he seldom acts the part and few respect his rule while the First King still lingers beyond death. Taeglin shuns all responsibility, but will not hesitate to take what he wants, when he wants it. It is difficult to believe that he came from the same stock as his proud forefather, Taradin."

Holly pieced together the puzzle rolling around in her head. "Taradin is the *First* King – the one who led the First Men away from the shores of Fortune Bay?"

Fyorn responded with an iffy nod. "That man died a great hero long ago. Unfortunately, he should have stayed that way. Taradin would have been far better off without all those abominations he surrounds himself with – wraiths included."

Kabor tried to drink from his empty watering can. The woodsman tossed him a skin from his pack, which the Stout accepted with a long swig.

My uncle continued. "In Taeglin's stead, the city master runs everything, while he spends his days hidden away in that impenetrable tower of his."

I knew from experience the trouble that Taeglin had caused, routinely overstepping the boundaries of his official jurisdiction to force his will on the surrounding territories. Fort Abandon tended to fall in line. The Trilands that included Webfoot, Proudfoot and the Bearded Hills resisted, but in reality, all three districts were subject to his every whim unless Gan took issue. The Outlands and the Scarsands are lawless lands, powerless to resist any incursion and not capable of organized defiance. Only the might of the Elderkin steadied the balance of power in the region.

I had my own thoughts about Taeglin's interest in the bog. "I think he wants something the Jhinyari left behind from the battle long ago, or maybe he knows about the stones—"

Holly interjected, "They're not his! He can't just take them. That's *our* claim! *Our* bog!"

"No one said he was taking our claim," I said.

"That is something we will have to discuss," said Fyorn. He went back to packing, but severing eye contact was not enough to stop Holly from arguing her point. Not for a minute.

CHAPTER XLV

Strange attractor

I only noticed there had been a breeze when it vanished. An eerie stillness took its place as I stood next to the Rune Stone. And such a fine rain fell not a drop of it could be seen, but it tingled on the surface of my skin. A lone puff of wind sent a large elm leaf up the hill to circle around me. Something in the hush and the agitated movement of the leaf set me on guard. Fyorn and Holly, still carrying on a spirited conversation about what is right versus what rights are, abruptly went silent. Fyorn looked to the treetops.

I heard the heavy gust before it came bearing down on us – branches snapped and leaves flapped violently. Above the trees, debris swirled about. The rogue cushion of air that had frolicked in our midst suddenly was overwhelmed and the leaf whisked away, out of sight. I lifted my arm to shield myself from the onset of high winds. Dirt, leaves and small twigs blasted past.

The gust of wind did not last long, and when it subsided, the strangest sensation came over me… to go back to Harrow, a compulsion really. Perhaps that was my first whisper. Or maybe it was my second, or maybe it was nothing but a gust of wind that triggered a feeling. I could not be sure.

"But why?" I said to the blowing wind. There was no response.

My uncle's creased and scrinching brow mapped out a concerned look. He glared at me squarely, suspicion in his eyes. "Why what?" he said.

I wasn't sure what to say, so I just shrugged, climbed on top of the monument and found a dry enough spot to sit. I watched as the Hurlorns redefined the grove, backing away into their ordered rows. In so doing, they opened up the sky to us, grey and foreboding. Fyorn decided not to pursue the matter of my question any further. He went to check Kabor's wounds, and then exited the grove on some minor mission, perhaps to seek out a healing herb or fresh water.

A break in the clouds above released a sliver of morning sunshine into the clearing. I closed my eyes for a moment's solace, soaking up the elusive rays. I knew it wouldn't last long. For a few precious minutes, I put aside the Dim Sea and the demands of the leviathan. I put aside wraiths, Glooms, and whispers. Instead, I found myself thinking of home, and Paplov. It was short-lived though. Holly came to join me. She sat an arm's length away – an arm's length too far in my mind.

"Want to see?" she said, dangling her pendant in front of my eyes, the one she had found that disastrous day on the Mire Trail back when we had crossed paths with the miserable hags. I took it. She explained everything.

"It's brighter now than ever before," said Holly, almost apologetically. Initially, she had told me the spark was "tiny" compared to mine.

"You're right," I said, letting the stone spin at the end of the chain as it dangled and dazzled in the sunlight. "It's a lot like mine, except the color, of course, and the grey rock mixed in. Mer would know for sure if it's the same stuff."

"Fyorn says the markings are from Harrow," she said.

I unsheathed my stone and removed it from my neck. It was

brighter than usual too, and the familiar red luminescence glowed forth. The look and feel of the green portion of Holly's stone was the same as mine, except hers showed more fracture planes on the inside and was a different shape. Mine was more round than oblong, and the chipped facets less regular in size and shape. The spark in Holly's was more constant than what I had become accustomed to, fading in and out in a slow course. I noticed mine now displayed the same constancy.

Out of the corner of my eye, I caught Kabor's quizzical, sideways look as he eyed us from where he was resting. A light rain began to fall again, this time with the sun still out. Holly and I slid off the monument. Placing the green piece into Holly's small, cupped hand, I gazed into her green eyes and smiled. They were bright in the sunlit drizzle, and flecked with molten gold.

"Stay right there," I said, and made her wait until a cloud blocked the sun. It wasn't long. "Now back away – slowly, and hold your stone in front where I can see it." As I suspected, the sparks in the two stones grew dimmer and out of synch the farther she went.

"Now walk towards me," I said. And as she approached, the lights brightened and the flickers synchronized.

"The creek—" she started, eyes dancing.

I nodded. "There might be more. And now we know how to find them."

"Closer," I said. She advanced a cautious step. We were face to face. I set my stone against hers. Holly's eyes went wide as the two lights became one, shining bright and yellow and steady. In that moment, I felt that I touched her mind, her thoughts. Abruptly, she pulled away and broke eye contact, looking to the ground. Holly put on her necklace and swept her hair so that it draped over the chain.

When she looked up, a mischievous smile came across her face. "Try to find me," she said. Playfully, Holly reversed her cloak and donned the camouflaged pattern, minus the hood. Her body shimmered like a blur as she dashed into the surrounding woods, blending into the scenery.

She pulled the hood over her head. "Find me!" she called again, wholly translucent. I closed my eyes for ten counts, and then scanned the woods with a narrow, red beam. I caused the light to flash when I found her.

"That's cheating," she called, completely hidden.

"You have to learn to throw your voice too," Kabor called out to Holly from under his tree.

I put the stone away and she tried again. That time I couldn't find her. But after another few minutes of the game, I got better at figuring out where Holly was, especially if she kept sneaking about.

"You need to be really quiet too," I said.

"I am quiet," she replied.

Fyorn happened by and took note of the Flipside girl's antics on his way through the grove. He carried a bundle of sturdy sticks in his arms. Holly, gregarious as always, abandoned the game with a "humph" and took the opportunity to grab his attention. She flipped back her hood, and, as he walked on, spoke more to his broad shoulders and the back of his head than anything else.

"How do the Elderkin become undying?" she probed.

The woodsman stopped and looked over his shoulder, eyes smiling. He grinned widely and then winked at Holly. "Just like everyone else," he said, "and it all starts with the twinkle in a lady's eye."

I chuckled.

Holly smirked, rolled her eyes and shook her head. "Mine aren't twinkling," she said. There was a long, easy silence, during which Fyorn strode over to Kabor and began sorting through the sticks that he had gathered, gauging the size of each one against Kabor's build. Holly trailed behind him like an expectant puppy, practicing quiet steps.

She moved next to the woodsman and peered around his shoulders. "Is Taradin undying?" she said.

Fyorn jolted back. "Turn that thing normal-side out!" he said. "You don't let up, do you?" My uncle paused and turned to face her. Holly just looked at him, still expecting. He couldn't be mad at that face.

"The answer is yes and no," he began. "Taradin is undying like the Elderkin, but the roots of immortality did not take well with him, or his ilk."

"What about the wraiths?" I said, casually strolling over and wedging my way into the conversation.

"They look like they're half-dead," I continued, "and the smell..." I made an awful face. "...and they most definitely are mad."

"Now the wraiths are different," explained Fyorn. "First of all, they despise all that fully live and especially those who are free to walk under the sun... but none more than the three Eternal Races. Even the touch of a wraith can be as cold as death itself. Taradin was never that way."

"The wraiths came before Taradin," he continued, "the result of even earlier experimentation with undeath. Yes... they are madder still, but serve the Old King and only the Old King. After losing him to the Jhinyari, and after the many years of toil and struggle that went with that loss, the wraiths recovered Taradin's body and raised him from the bog. They were outcasts at the time, banished from Harrow and the cities of Men."

"I'll vouch for the despising part," said Kabor. He looked a little more like himself again. "If they hate us more than they hate the Gropers, I can only imagine..."

"That's exactly right," said Fyorn. "They put themselves above everyone, but they still need others. You catch on fast."

The woodsman suddenly became distracted. I was about to speak when he raised his hand and halted my words.

"A whispering wind is blowing," he said.

My jaw hung half-open with the words still stuck there, not knowing where to go. The woodsman faced the steady westerly rising up the hill slope, and stared blankly down the rocky path to the lowlands. Stunted evergreens kept watch over the hillside like rough skinned guardians. Whether or not some were Hurlorns I could only guess. Our Hurlorns, the ones that had encircled us in the grove, stood in their former ranks atop the hill, tall and proud and deciduous. Fyorn didn't look right.

I had seen him "fly off the handle" a few times over little things, and I also seen him calm and collective in the heat of battle. This was something else. Something was terribly wrong.

The woodsman began to shake his head. In a sudden fit of anger, he threw down the sticks. His tongue lashed out so vile the words made me cringe. Holly gripped my forearm. His arms flailed as he paced back and forth and cursed some more. It would have been enough to curl even a sailor's ears.

"What is it?" I said, dreading what the answer might be. *I don't want to hear it.* My heartbeat quickened. *Paplov…*

Fyorn's tone came off somewhat accusing. "Bobbin and Gariff have been taken prisoner," he said bluntly. "Apparently, there was a generous reward out for the capture of a *certain escaped Pip* and his *Stout companion,* caught thieving in the Iron Tower. Ring any bells?"

I felt my ears flatten with the way he said the words. My expression tightened. *Thief?* My lips trembled as I tried to shape a response. I muddled several consonants. "I dit… it's shust… what bad luck," I sputtered.

"Nud, it isn't luck," he said, irritation in his voice. The woodsman stooped over and began recovering the discarded sticks.

"I'm not mad at *you,*" he said at last. "This just complicates things. You don't know how much it complicates things."

Holly confronted Fyorn. "You said it would be safe."

The woodsman shook his head in disbelief, holding the sticks.

"I never imagined… I mean… no one could have predicted something like this could happen."

Except maybe Hurlorns, I thought.

The Flipside girl stepped aside and gave me an odd look.

"I can't even go to Harrow to put a stop to this. Damn it!" said Fyorn. He tossed one of the sticks to Kabor, who caught it in one hand. "Sending word to Gan is hopeless. They'll debate for days and then decide to act after the consequences have already played out." He looked to me. "You certainly can't go with your papa sick the way he is, and…" He trailed off.

"Webfoot is obligated to negotiate," Holly offered. She addressed Fyorn directly. "Did you talk to Mayor Undle about sending diplomats before you left, like you said you would?"

"I did," said Fyorn. "We'll need to have a word with them, if we can catch them before they enter the valley."

Kabor chimed in. "The Webfoot Council will be either too slow or too accommodating – can't be counted on either way."

"Even if they did get their act together they would just send Councillor Mrello," I said. "Besides being completely useless, he's completely under Harrow's thumb."

"How do you know this?" said Fyorn.

"It's true, just ask Holly," I replied.

Holly nodded, and the notion seemed to make her worry even more. "Nud, *you* have to go," she said. "You have to get them out. They're on the chopping block because of you, y'know."

I wanted to volunteer and straighten things out. I wanted to impress Holly. Bobbin and Gariff were imprisoned because they were trying to help me. But I could not abandon Paplov. I might never get to see him again. I didn't know what to do. Not yet.

Fyorn sighed and nodded his head. "Not good," Fyorn explained, "Not good at all. They could be put to work in the mines, or worse."

"What about the ritual?" said Holly.

Fyorn took a deep breath, but did not reply.

"Ritual?" I said.

Holly huffed, and then explained the details. "A ritual where they sacrifice people, Nud," she said. "What if they sacrifice Bobbin or Gariff? You have to get them out!"

"They do that in Harrow?" I said.

"That's not going to happen," said Fyorn. "That *honor* is traditionally reserved for intellects and high achievers – the best of the best among the city populace, excluding the ruling class, of course."

Kabor shook his head in disgust.

"Nud," said Holly, "you have your colors now. Isn't it your obligation to negotiate? You're the closest representative from Webfoot, and the colors—"

I shook my head. "As long as Paplov is gravely ill I *must* go home, *that* is my obligation," I said. "The Council is better equipped to handle this sort of thing anyway. We just have to make sure they send someone other than Mrello."

Holly gasped in disbelief. "Ya right, the Council," she said. "There's more who are crooked than just Mrello. Gariff and Bobbin came here to get *you*, Nud. We all did." Holly stormed off.

"What about the Bearded Hills, or the Triland Council?" I said.

"How do we know they're not just as crooked?" said Kabor.

"He's right," said Fyorn. "If what you say is true about Mrello, there is no trusting any liaison to Harrow from any of the councils."

"There's no other option," Holly called to the rest of us. "Nud has to go straighten this out."

The woodsman sighed and scanned the grove, studying the treetops. A light, swirling breeze blew up. He grabbed my shoulder and spoke in a hushed tone. "More news is on the way. Nud, come with me this time. I sense it has much to do with you. Everything hangs in the balance for you right now." We hurried to the northwest section of the grove.

Holly called after us. "I'm coming too," she said.

Kabor stayed behind. With the woodsman's back turned, the sickly Stout whipped the stick my uncle had given him over the edge of the hill. He searched through the pile and chose another instead. With all the strength he could muster, Kabor pushed himself to his feet, supporting his weight with his new walking stick. I recognized the grain – deepwood. He hobbled after us.

Fyorn and I stopped at the summit's edge. We stopped and just stood there. I was not sure what to expect. The woodsman went completely still. "I hear it," he whispered. He crouched down and addressed me at eye level, the way he did whenever he was trying to teach me something important or show me a wild animal that I had failed to notice. "Nud, you have to be open to it. Relax your eyes like there is nothing to focus on. Then relax your ears the same way. Relax all of your senses. Let them go. Let them go and your mind will follow."

"What about me?" said Holly.

"Shush," said Fyorn. "Do the same. No talking, any of you."

The wind rose up stronger and the leaves began to rustle more urgently. If the whisper was not in the wind, it sure sounded like it could be. And so very faint, I had to strain my ears. There were many whispering noises it seemed, streaming in and out and softly padding over one another. I tried to focus on one among them, but there were too many layers. I cocked my head one way, and then the next. Nothing changed. I plugged one ear, then the next, then both. Nothing changed.

I closed my eyes, inhaled deep, and let out a calming sigh. Then it came to me. I heard my second whisper, or maybe it was my first, but either way it was definitely a whisper.

It was a quiet rhythm of syllables, fully immersed among the other gentle sounds of morning. It was not smooth, like the whisper of a secret from one giggling girl to the next, but was as grainy a sound as the rustling of leaves. The words formed imparted a good feeling, or *sense*. "Better. All better," is what I heard.

I turned to Fyorn. "Did you hear that?"

He smiled and nodded. "Your papa is going to be fine."

Holly gasped. "I heard something too," she said. "I don't know what it was, but it *felt* good."

By all accounts, the whisper was positive. Paplov seemed to be on the road to recovery.

"That's odd… truly remarkable really, considering his condition when I last saw him," said Fyorn. He looked introspective for a moment, and then snapped out of it. "Did you hear that part about the old gaffer being spotted up and about early this morning, tending to his garden?"

Evidently, I still had much to learn about whispers. "No," I said. Holly shook her head.

"How about the fact that no one from Council has been sent to Harrow yet?" said Fyorn.

"Nope," I said. "But I'm not surprised."

I waited for Kabor to say something, like "It figures," but he held his tongue. He had made it as far as the dug out fire pit.

"There is a lesson here," said Fyorn, looking to me. "The whisper also picks up something of what it finds along the way. Do not think you have heard it all just because you picked out one intended message. The whispers collect as they propagate and the sources multiply."

Holly looked to me. Her eyes lit up with anticipation. "Nud, that means you can go to Harrow and get Bobbin and Gariff out. You're free to negotiate."

The good news about Paplov and Holly's pleading eyes were enough to seal my decision: I would go to Harrow. Webfoot was lagging, Gan ineffective, the need was desperate, Paplov was fine, and I had full diplomatic authority as long as the Webfoot Council did not oppose – and they wouldn't. They couldn't. And with the authority granted, I could negotiate for everyone's release – even my parents, assuming they were actually prisoners. *Paplov would be ecstatic.*

It gets better. Holly would see me as a hero if I saved my friends – doubly so if I put a stop to Taeglin's plans to mine the bog. I might even challenge the Iron Tower on the Treaty of Nature, for Fyorn's sake. He'd like that. Paplov, of course, would be proud of me. The Hurlorns might even be proud of me. People would gossip, and when they spoke my name they would say "Nud Leatherleaf the wraith slayer, defender of the wrongfully accused, and protector of the bog."

Kabor was silent on the matter. He caught me glancing over to him and seemed annoyed, or in pain, or some combination of the two.

"You're right," I said to Holly. I turned to my uncle. "I have to go back to Harrow, it's the only way to make things right. Bobbin and Gariff are there because of me. And I think the Hurlorns want me to go as well. I think they whispered it."

Fyorn raised his eyebrows and tilted his head sideways. "The Hurlorns are not sending you back," he said. I knew then that he was wrong though.

"Bobbin and Gariff need me," I went on, "Webfoot needs me – I can convince Harrow that they don't need to drain the whole bog to find what they want. And I need to know… I need to know what happened to my parents. I think I heard a whisper telling me to go back. It happened when the wind came, before any of this. Did you hear it?"

"No," said Fyorn. "There was no such whisper. And you don't know if you can accomplish any of that."

I didn't argue the point. Maybe he was right.

"And this business about the bog is nonsense," Fyorn scoffed. "They can't mine it."

"What about what Janhurl said?" responded Holly-miss-know-it-all.

"You said there was a loophole about mineral rights and that for some reason it *must* be important."

"Neither Harrow nor Gan are permitted to occupy the Trilands," said Fyorn, "It's a veritable no-man's land according to the Non-aggression Treaty – Pips and Stouts exempt, of course."

"Yes, it's true," I said. "Proudfoot had similar clauses in their dealings with Fort Abandon concerning the Flats – a rich agricultural borderland. There, a complicated land lease agreement has been in effect for decades."

"But mineral rights are different," I continued. "If we can't deny them somehow, then Harrow might be permitted to initiate and maintain a strong, practical presence in the bog that includes 'protection' for their assets."

Kabor interjected. "That matches up with those 'HME' claim posts we found along Blackmuk, right Nud?"

"HME… Harrow Mineral and Exploration," I explained to Fyorn, "is state-owned and run by the Tor Lords. I know because it was in one of the legal documents for the deal with Proudfoot."

"So," said Fyorn, piecing it together, "you're saying that if they staked claims all over the place and then started mining them out, Harrow might try to justify large troop deployments to protect their assets?"

"Something like that," I replied. "HME already has several claims in the bog lands and around Proudfoot."

"They can't just send in troops like that. Harrow would need a strong basis to do such a thing," said Fyorn.

Holly cut in, excited. "Well, get this: to justify the added security, all they have to do is make the bog lands a more dangerous place to conduct business."

"Whoa. That explains the raiders on the Outland Trail, and worse things that have been happening," I said. "It used to be safe, but now everyone in the Trilands worries about the dangers of traveling."

"That's dirty," said Kabor.

"You can't say that for sure," said Fyorn.

"Harrow takes what Harrow wants," I replied, repeating the common saying and remembering the frustration expressed by Mayor Otis. My uncle did nothing to deny that fact.

"They have their ways," he admitted. "And Janhurl did find it important enough to whisper… hmm."

Holly looked to me. "I'm going with you," she said. I smiled at her. She smiled back, shyly.

Clearly frustrated, Fyorn shook his head at Holly. "You're not going anywhere," he said.

Holly ignored his words, which only served to frustrate him more. "I can help," she said.

Fyorn crossed his arms. "Oh?" he said. "And what are you going to do when you get there?"

"They'll kill you both," rasped Kabor, who had taken to stirring up what little remained of the wraith's ashes with his stick. "The wraiths will kill you and feast on your flesh."

"Not if I can get to the gate first, with my diplomatic colors in hand," I said. "I will have diplomatic immunity."

"True enough… *in theory*," said Fyorn. A complex look washed over him. He spoke to Kabor next. "Nud and any assistants of his would be protected by code of law. Harrow goes by the book on that, at least. Wraiths do not come out in the light of day and they do not eat diplomats. Thieves maybe…"

It was the Stout's turn to scoff. I know what he was thinking. He saw what I saw.

I hadn't thought everything through, but I couldn't back down now, not with Holly behind me all the way and my uncle warming up to my way of thinking. "Maybe Taeglin can't be reasoned with," I conceded. That much was evident from everything I had ever heard about him. I got the impression that Taeglin considered himself supreme and that the rest of the world was just there for his entertainment.

"He couldn't be bothered to meet with you anyways," said Fyorn. "He would just send you to Garond, the city master."

"But there is another I can meet with – the First King. If I can just convince him to listen—"

Fyorn cut me off. "That's a big 'IF.' There are procedures and rules for that sort of thing."

My uncle closed his eyes and let out a heavy sigh. He was deliberating. I believe he understood what it meant to be chosen by fate for a task specially suited to one and only one. It was about being in the right place at the right time, with the right means and the right plan. And the fact that Holly and I were in that place together, both with stones that tapped into the Hurlorn consciousness, was no small happenstance. I believe he knew what it meant to put his trust in fate. He had lived his entire life that way.

And so it was settled. Fyorn grinned and shook his head in a gentle "no" that meant "yes." Holly was coming with me.

"It's nearly an hour's hike, as the Hurlorn strides, just to get to the eastern shores of Dim Lake," the woodsman started. "It would be best to get there bright and early."

From there on, he explained how Holly and I could make our way past the docks, through the gate and the market square beyond, and then to the area that held the administrative buildings, the bethel named *Karna's Vessel*, and of course the Iron Tower.

"Don't mention the wrongful capture of Bobbin and Gariff to the tower guards," said Fyorn. "They confuse easily, and it might prompt them to incarcerate the two of you on orders long stale."

"If someone gives us trouble," said Holly, "I'll just say 'too late, the search is off 'cause they've already been found – ask anyone.' And that I'm a girl; they're not looking for a girl."

"You're not even a Stout," added Kabor.

Fyorn smiled and nodded, going on to insist that Janhurl

return and carry us to the edge of the woods. After that, Holly and I would be on our own, but not unwatched. In the mean time, Fyorn would see Kabor to Webfoot, as promised, check up on Paplov, wait for word from Janhurl, gather news and act accordingly when the time came.

The thing about plans is they never quite seem to work out, at least not when Hurlorns are involved.

Second thoughts

I had a few minutes to tidy myself up before departing. I would have to leave my cloak behind though, tattered and soiled as it was, and ask the Hurlorn to stop at a good swimming hole on the way. Holly was presentable enough to pass as my aide.

Janhurl arrived and the time had come to embark on our well-intentioned journey. Holly and I said our goodbyes and parted ways with our good friends. I was glad to see Kabor up and about, drinking tea and complaining that we didn't know what we were getting ourselves into. In the end, he thanked us. After all, Gariff was his good cousin. I wondered when we would see them again.

The morning sun had disappeared into dark grey clouds by the time we abandoned the cover of Deepweald. From our perch upon a high branch of Janhurl, leaves still dripping wet with the morning dew, we crested the first hill overlooking our destination. The vale that cradled Dim Lake opened up beneath us. Cobbled streets sloped down to the lakeshore on the outskirts of Harrow. Low and crowded stone-block buildings lined both sides. The Iron Tower loomed in the distance; one curtain wall outlined the city proper and a second, the royal grounds. Janhurl could go no farther. She fluted an incomprehensible farewell and gently set us to solid ground. We both thanked her and wished her well.

Down the hill were the piers that jutted out into Dim Lake, lined with floating workhouses. The shipyard was the closest building, where Men were already hard at work to beat the inevitable rain that would wash away the afternoon. Gulls waited impatiently on nearby pilings, crying incessantly for entitlements. Harrowians cut and hammered at planks in dry docks carved into the lakeshore. Occasionally, the usual talk of work, snippets of song, quick and clever rhymes, and bellows of frustration billowed up the hillside as we made our descent toward Harrow. Farther west near the city proper, scores of small fishing vessels were moored along the lakeshore, while a handful of oar-driven dories glided across the calm, grey-lit waters amidst sparse puffs of thin morning mist.

A large vessel sat dormant in its slip, next to three smaller, black schooners all moored in a row. Dim Lake was a fair size, but not big enough to justify the presence of a full war galley. The vessel could only be intended for travel to the south shore, where the lake's clear waters drained into the wide and deep Dim River. The Dim ran south to meet the Lower Malevuin, which hooked into Abandon Bay. The Malevuin's cool waters sourced from mountain springs to the north and west.

The east gate of the outer curtain wall marked the entrance to Harrow proper from the town's outskirts. On nearing it, the aroma of smoked fish filled the still air, and a lively fiddler sawed out a sailing and whaling tune that drew a small morning crowd to his wagon. The guards let us pass easily enough, once I showed them my colors.

"Here for the festival or for business?" one said. I nodded, nervously.

My stomach twisted in knots as I made my way through the entrance passageway and into the open square that defined the marketplace. Business was already picking up for the shopkeepers.

Open-air tents and colorful banners painted a festive atmosphere. Holly scanned this way and that, taking in the sights. She had never been to such a grand place. For once, she seemed at a loss for words. We strode casually towards the inner gate that barred passage to the protected royal grounds of the Iron Tower.

I could hardly believe that I was actually going through with the plan. The words I had said in the grove had taken on a life of their own, and were converging to consequence. I hadn't really imagined myself there at the gates, being scrutinized by intimidating tower guards and begging my way into the hall of a dead king. But that is where I was heading and by my own volition. I had said the words, and they came to be. I wondered exactly how I would call upon the laws of inter-state diplomacy, should the need arise.

CHAPTER XLVii

Interlude - Youth immortal

Time is pressing. Urgency is everything. Now that I am sheltered from the weather, I write with a pen fixed to every spare claw and to every spare branch. Masterful creatures Hurlorns are, slow and lumbering in the bulk, but quick-minded and coordinated in twig and bough. The paper strewn about me covers every flat surface beneath my leafy crown. Inkbottles sit upright and lie overturned about the chamber. I hear the wind howling above. If it ever reaches down this far there will be quite the mess to clean up… quite the mess indeed. I'll leave that to the young ranger. Words come in a flurry now.

You have to understand I was fifteen and girl stupid. More than that, I was naive about the dangers of the world – especially the familiar world, which I insisted I knew. Clearly, from everything I could put together at the time and the state I was in, the return mission to Harrow never should have happened. And Fyorn never should have allowed it. The political engines of the Trilands and Gan were far better equipped to handle such delicate negotiations than the two of us ever could be.

And I cannot say with certainty why Holly and I supported one another with such willful determination in the cause. Pheromones, testosterone and adrenalin, perhaps, bringing on some measure of uninhibited irrationality. Or perhaps it was something more. But what is risk to an immortal teenager? – not to say that I was really immortal; it's more like I did not fully appreciate the harm that could come my way or the harm that could be put on others as a result of my actions. As I said, Fyorn should never have allowed it – the notion of encouragement by his bark-skinned advisors must have clouded his good judgment. Who could expect a pair of Pips to divert the will of the Iron Tower? Harrow takes what Harrow wants.

Ahh… to be girl stupid, young and fearless again. Those were truly the glory days of youth immortal.

I feel nostalgia coming on. And as the end nears, I just want to enjoy everybody in being and in memory, and sip from the fine wine of life one last time.

CHAPTER XLViii

The Iron Tower of Harrow

The Iron Tower loomed over the displaced ocean-side town of Harrow, a pale reminder of more glorious days when the noble forefathers of the townsfolk thrived on the shores of former Fortune Bay. They thrived and conquered, lived and loved, died and were raised. Some say giants forged the iron blocks of the tower out of meteoric ore from Gabber's Bowl in the Western Tor. Others say the tower was raised by Karna herself to guard the entrance to another world that knows no death. None could argue the landmark's practical construction. Besides being a royal house and a hub of activity for the town, it also served as a lighthouse, built in the extravagant manner of old Akeda with a royal beacon that cut through the night fog and stormy weather like a scimitar of light.

As we approached, like typical out-of-towners we turned our eyes upwards to gawk at the Iron Tower's impressive height. At the top, six pillars supported an iron crow's nest over the lantern room, some four-hundred and fifty feet above the courtyard. Standing within was a statue of the First King himself, holding his staff to the sky. His stony gaze kept watch over town and lake.

The inner curtain wall was of black stone and it protected the courtyard surrounding the tower. Intricate depictions of leviathans graced the wall's corner towers: a white whale with smoke billowing out of its blowhole, a kraken, a giant mollusk, and a sea dragon that sparked fire from flared nostrils. Sentries carrying crossbows patrolled the wall walk.

One of the two guards in front of the iron-bar gate bellowed out to us on approach, nonchalantly: "Who goes there? What is your purpose? State your names and state your business with Taeglin, Rejuvenator of this Iron Tower and Protector of the Lake." He came off as abrupt and professional. The guard who spoke was the shorter of the two by near a foot.

Behind him, two tower shields served as wall mounts, and several more hung along the interior of the entrance passageway that tunneled through the wall. Each depicted the sigil of old Fortune Bay and now Harrow – a frothing wave gliding across ocean waters by night; one of the stars that shone in the backdrop was actually a lighthouse lamp, to guide wayward ships home again.

Using Paplov's most polite diplomatic voice, I cleared my throat, and answered loud and clear, doing my best to sound authoritative.

"I request an audience with Taradin, the Old King of Fortune Bay," I began. I halted in front of the two guards and fumbled through my pack. "Allow me to introduce myself," I said, checking the front pocket, "I am Nud Leatherleaf of Webfoot, here on official business… ah, there they are – my colors." I handed the shorter guard Paplov's rolled up leather. He unfurled it, gave it a quick glance, and then handed it back. I gestured to Holly. "And this is my aide—"

"Holly Hopkins of Webfoot," she interrupted, with as much of a curtsy as a girl wearing pants can pull off. The smaller guard nodded to her, and then addressed me.

"I haven't seen you two before. You must be new at this. You mean Taeglin, right? Everyone gets the two confused. Go see Garond, the city master across the way, he deals with the little

Triland folks." He pointed to a building diagonally across the square, built into the side of a flat hill. The buildings there had an administrative look to them.

"No, I actually do mean Taradin. The city master won't do." *Little folks? We're not just little people, you big oaf.*

"No one asks for Taradin."

"I am asking for Taradin, the former King of Fortune Bay," I said. He seemed taken aback. He just wasn't getting it.

The larger guard spoke. "What would Taradin want with a couple o'toads like yous? He doesn't see anyone. Go see Garond or git back to yer lily pads." He stood as tall as a man and a half, but was plainly stupid, that much was evident. Toads don't sit on lily pads, frogs do. Who doesn't know that?

I stepped forward and looked straight up at the burly guard, clearly showing my agitation – something Paplov would do when confronting big oafs. Both guards were veritable giants to my pippish eyes, but I took one to be a runner and the other a lumberer. The runner was younger, shorter, but narrow and long limbed. The lumberer was more seasoned, had girth and height above his comrade, and his legs stood as thick as tree trunks. *He won't take any criticism himself,* I thought, *but he won't mind me dishing it out to his subordinate either.*

I turned to the shorter guard instead, and pointed to the tower. Using the same stern voice that Paplov used when he felt he was being disrespected, I verbally blasted him.

"Get in there and tell him that I am wasting valuable time waiting here for you to do your job. Taradin himself requested this meeting." He took a step back.

"What's your name?" I demanded.

"Clandt, sir," was all he said.

"Now, if you can fit a second thought in that thick head of yours, tell him that I'm here to discuss artifacts from the bog lands – you might want to add the words *unique* and *valuable*, and how about *last chance.*" I raised my voice and enunciated the important parts: "U-NIQUE AND VAL-UABLE, LAST CHANCE… GOT IT?" The larger guard snickered at the scolding of his comrade.

I threw my arms up in the air. "And why not mention your belligerence towards his invited guests while you're at it… it will save me the trouble, Clandt."

Clandt looked to his giant companion, who, with a smirk, nodded his head and waved his hand to the guards inside.

"Just put the gates up for the day," the half-giant commanded to the gatehouse.

"Clandt," said the big oaf, with a sideways tilt motioning to the tower.

"Woe-woe-woe," said Clandt, shaking his head. "I'm not going down there."

Down? I wondered. *Why down?*

A loud clang initiated the rising of the two gates – one on either side of the wall – followed by a metallic grinding as they lifted off the ground. The larger guard raised his voice over the racket.

"What? 'Fraid of a little spooks, Clandt? Git goe'n."

"But—" With a slice of his hand through mid-air, the half-giant cut him off.

"GIT GOE'N!" he boomed, drawing the attention of a guard on the above walkway.

"Everything all right down there?" said the crossbowman.

"Just Clandt," replied the half-giant. "He's a'scared to see Taradin."

The guard laughed. "He won't bite," he said, then went on his way. After a few steps he called back. "Better you than me, though."

"I'm not afraid," said Clandt. He huffed a protest, but once the gate was fully raised, he quickly started off for the tower.

The half-giant took on a kind and apologetic demeanor towards Holly and me. "Terribly sorry, sir, ma'am," he said. "Clandt don't know better. Grew up in the Tor wrestlen' giants just for a bit'o rabbit 'n such. I think one'o'em picked'im up 'n dropped'im on his noggin. He was always the runt'o dem…"

Nothing the guard said made much sense to me, but I nodded in acknowledgement anyway and offered a gracious, yet pitying smile. I caught Holly smirking at me.

In the intervening time, the guard asked about what was in my pack. I told him only some rare wood: "Bog wood," I said, assuming he wouldn't know any better. He rummaged through and didn't make a fuss about the contents. "It don't look like much to me," was all he said. Indeed, only a few pieces of deepwood remained. I felt a little better knowing that *Shatters* was in there though. I never did recover *Sliver*.

Clandt certainly took his time executing his errand. While we waited, I could not help but to re-evaluate the rationale behind my decision to meet with the undying former King. Holly was on my side, at least. Back in Deepweald, her confrontational spirit had prodded me on, full of fire and fury about retrieving our friends and protecting the bog ecosystem. *Where is that fire now?* I wondered. Holly's behavior had become far more timid since entering Harrow, sticking close and not saying much at all when we strode through the town streets, and shying away from the tower guards. Maybe she was intimidated; maybe she was having second thoughts. *This is all new to her.*

My own doubts, I put aside. If the Hurlorns really did whisper to me, then I should treat the words as a benediction. They had their reasons and I needed to trust in them.

The guard finally returned with a reply in the affirmative. He looked a bit gaunt for the asking. With a slight shake in his voice, he also offered a polite apology from the First King himself, for neglecting to instruct his gatemen to be on the lookout for anyone offering something "unique and valuable, especially from a bog." It sounded like a slight, and his words lingered in my mind and imparted a sour feeling to the pit of my stomach.

Reluctance in his heavy footsteps, Clandt proceeded to escort us through the entrance passage. Midway, I noted a third portcullis, fully raised and easily overlooked. It could come crashing down at unawares.

Once through to the other side, Clandt led us along a slate path to the tower doors. Landscaped gardens, ornate statues, elaborate fountains, and private groves filled the yard, so visually pleasing and elegant that it put Proudfoot to shame. In stark contrast to the artful greenery, the black metal of the tower rose high above, bleak and imposing against the backdrop of overcast skies, not a single pit or streak of rust to mar its surface.

A wide, black hall lay beyond the oak doors. Although lacking in direct, natural sunlight, wall-mounted lanterns kept it bright. Our stroll through the hall was pleasantly hot and smelled of incense. The walls showed storm-driven ocean scenes on canvas. Wind swirled and water frothed as oared sailing vessels tossed about like toys on giant waves. The massiveness of the sea and the fierceness of the weather contrasted with the frailty of vessels on open water.

The arched ceiling hosted a nest of murder holes and a series of trap doors, cleverly worked in to the artful decor. At the far end of the corridor a gated archway, with the gate raised, led into another room.

"Are those originals?" I said to Clandt, gesturing to the paintings.

"Huh?" he replied, scanning the walls. He shrugged. "What else?"

Clandt took us through the arch and then swung to the left. The lighting beyond was far dimmer, and it smelled of torch smoke. I bumped into the wall once, before my eyes adjusted, and Holly stepped on my toes. We rounded another corner and came upon a long, red hall lined with torches and with a single red door at the end. Two female guards of the half-giant variety stood guard there, each holding a tall, black halberd and garbed entirely in a deep red suit of padded armor.

"Red Maidens," whispered Clandt, on approach. "The King's Guard. Don't be fooled by their good looks, they'll slice your heart out if you step out of line."

He raised his voice on approach. "I present Taradin's honored guests... a diplomat and his aide."

"Did you search them?" one asked.

"I did, m'lady," said Clandt.

"Did you inspect their passes," the same woman asked.

"I did, m'lady," said Clandt.

She called upon her comrade. "Khotahri," she said.

The one named Khotahri sprung into action. "Raise your arms," she told us.

Holly and I raised our arms as the Red Maiden patted us down. The other guardess picked through my backpack.

"Asthana," said the one named Khotahri, "They have nothing." She turned back to me. "May I see your colors?"

I handed Khotahri my documents. She looked them over carefully, and then handed them back. Satisfied, she nodded to Asthana.

"You may pass," said Asthana. She returned my pack.

Khotahri opened the door for us and Clandt ushered us down the shadowy stairwell that lay beyond. I felt a sudden chill.

It did not seem fitting that we should be entering the lower levels. *A former king should have a high chamber,* I thought. A single flight of stairs brought us down to a sloping corridor. *Into the belly of the beast,* I thought. Like the tower's exterior, the walls were of stone block construction, predominantly dull black with multicolored streaks and swirls, but mostly reds.

Torches lit the way, held in smooth, translucent sconces, each made to resemble a mask of sorts. Each mask presented its own unique facial expression and method for supporting the torch.

Some had long, drawn out faces of anguish and agony – a different kind of pain depending on the intrusion. As Holly and I struggled to keep up to the guard's long-legged pace, I noted the chiseled out face of one shining mask grinning at me from its roost, as though it knew some terrible secret. Another looked wickedly amused as it clenched a torch in its eye socket, and yet another seemed surprised that it had somehow swallowed one... whole. The latter's cheeks, nostrils and crystalline eyes glowed red with the light cast. A set of two opposing fixtures appeared to be enjoying some forbidden pleasure with their torches, not spoken of in polite company. Even with an abundance of fiery lights to guide our way, I could still smell dankness in the heavy air.

"The walls!" exclaimed Holly, pointing. She stopped, as did I.

"What is it?" I said, taken aback by the urgency in her voice.

"They're moving!"

Subtle but true, Holly was right – the pattern was not still. The walls were alive with a slow, sickly motion, fluid and churning like chaos. Shapeless forms danced and swayed amidst the mess of colors. Swirls of blood red, mustardy yellow, foul green and deep purple faded in and out, hypnotic and upheaving to the stomach if looked at too long.

"Just keep going," said Clandt, his voice firm and his eyes fixed straight ahead. "And try not to look." So Holly and I kept going in the same way you might if walking along a high fence and told not to look down.

"Unreal," whispered Holly, almost to herself. I had my own thoughts on the matter.

The down-sloped passageway curved around several turns before straightening, where it also widened. It never did level out though. Three stone doors lined one side of the sloping hallway. Mask sconces lit the way to the third door, but beyond that door, the corridor was lost in darkness.

Clandt brought us all the way to the third door. He used

the brass knocker three times and waited. The door and the wall shifted in color to a translucent aquamarine. Fiery light filtered through from the interior, giving a vague sense of what lay within the chamber. The swirling motion faded to the point of being barely visible, and two wavering splashes of red marked blazing fires on the other side.

I heard a click. The door swung inwards, half-open. Clandt alone stepped in, leaving us alone with the door firmly closed behind him. Silence filled the hallway.

I looked to Holly. She stood hunched, rubbing her arms to fend off the chill, and her face looked pale. She offered me a nervous smile. I took her nervous smile and sent back a reassuring one. It wasn't real though. I didn't know what undeath really meant, or what to expect of Taradin.

As we stood waiting for Clandt to return, the translucency in the wall turned dark and murky. Deranged notions darted through my mind about what we might find on the other side of the door: limp bodies hanging from the ceiling by nooses, or half-opened iron maidens propped up, with ghastly corpses staring out blankly. Or perhaps we would find a huge iron pot over a cooking fire, filled with stew and with an arm dangling out.

A minute later, Clandt emerged, only partially closing the door behind him. The red glow of the chamber radiated into the hallway.

"Taradin will see you soon," he said. The guard read our wan expressions and gave us both a pitying look. "Don't be afraid. He knows the Way. He can get you what you Want."

The words of the leviathan, I recalled. I knew exactly what I wanted. All I needed was the way.

CHAPTER XLIX

Hall of the undying

"Honorable guests of the Illustrious Bog," called a young girl from within the chamber. Proper, soothing and fully nasal, her voice carried the faultless accent of high society. "Vicegerent Taradin, the once and mighty King of Fortune Bay, will see you now. Enter and be seated at his table, if you would be so bold."

Bold? I wondered. *What is that supposed to mean?*

Clandt inclined his head to us, pushed the door open and held it firmly with one arm. I stepped through.

The reek of death was new to me then, but even so, I recognized its lingering presence in the air. What hit me first was a kind of sweet rot, interlaced with hints of a tangy aroma that swirled among the trails of smoky incense, disguising all but the slightest trace of cadaver.

The guard, holding his expression to the limits of composure, stepped back and stationed himself fully outside the chamber. He nodded to Holly, who was already struggling. She followed close behind me.

I pushed forward despite the smell, hiding my disgust as best I could. Holly entered and stood next to me. By her wan look and stooped posture, I could tell she wasn't doing so well. I patted her back and gave it a rub. She coughed and put one hand to her chest. Then she stuck her neck out with her mouth wide open and dry-heaved uncontrollably. It took a long minute for Holly to compose herself. When Clandt saw that she would be fine, he closed the door behind us.

I suddenly felt trapped – the air, the walls, the fire and the smoke, not to mention death lurking somewhere within. And two Red Maidens, standing tall and motionless on either side of the doorway, didn't help either. Their faces were placid, with eyes unblinking. They were near spitting images of the guardesses at the top of the stairs.

I need to breathe, I thought. *Breathe.* But I could only tolerate a few measured breaths at a time through the sleeve of my shirt. I scanned the chamber. The openness of it helped, and did much to alleviate my initial anxiety. We had stepped into a great hall with a high, domed ceiling supported by four intricate pillars of carved stone. I stepped in a little farther.

Central to the chamber, charcoal burned from a ring of large braziers suspended by thick chains. The fiery light cast long shadows on the stone floor, polished to a mirror-like smoothness with red veins streaking through it. The shadows also crept across the cured hide of a great, battle-scarred beast, hauled up from ocean depths unimaginable. The four pillars surrounding the braziers depicted marine life of intangible colors, bright and livid. Wrapped around them, life-like mermaids kept watch through dense kelp, glaring out at us with bright green eyes. Stalks of red seaweed clung to their sinuous forms.

Holly's eyes danced across the room as she took in the sights, and mine followed hers. Stunning in a freakish way, the scene was lush and captivating – an opulent suite abounding with priceless artwork, elegant decor, and lavish furnishings. The glow of metal was fluid and writhing in the wavering firelight, and the sheen of gold entered every quarter: woven into fabrics, inlaid to earthenware and spiraling up the mermaid columns in thin ribbons. Set on marble tables were gold vases, silver flagons and cups, candelabra, and intricate, aquatic-themed treasures. The heads of gem-encrusted corals served as bookends on shelves of dark wood where many old tomes had been laid to rest. Large shells of unusual shape and vivid colors mixed with the books.

Textures were plentiful and pleasing to the eye; a rich wash of blood red and velvety purple fabrics with gold accents covered chair frames and wall hangings. Elegant tapestries depicted seafaring scenes, with details barely discernible in the dimness. The walls themselves conveyed the active turbulence of grey weather on the rise. I could almost smell the salty air. In fact, the terrible odor subsided to some degree – that or I had just gotten used to it. I no longer wondered why the royal chamber was "stuck" below ground. Indeed, in all ways it seemed fit for a king.

Holly appeared to have gotten past the stench as well, and now bore a starry-eyed expression on her face. She whispered into my ear, "He really *is* a King. It's true isn't it?" Holly had every reason to be excited as we prepared to meet a celebrated character out of myth, and a hero at that.

I mouthed the words just loud enough for Holly to hear. "Red and gold for death and glory, purple is for royalty." She smiled. It was a line from *First King's Silver Thread*, spoken in the Great Hall of the story, where the Orbweaver is deceived.

Could this be the Great Hall? I wondered. I shook off the notion – even if the story were true, the events would have happened long before Akeda existed, nevermind Harrow.

There was no sign of our host, the so-called First King. The Red Maidens by the door had not broken their silence either – not even to greet us, although I appreciated not having to be searched again. Casually, we wandered about the chamber, admiring the display pieces. Holly commented on a prominent portrait of a stately noble, adorned in jewels and wearing the finest linens. Piercing blue eyes shone from under a silvery crown. Desiring to sit, she patted a pillow on the chair beneath the portrait. A cloud of dust flew up. A closer look at the fabric revealed its age: old and decayed.

Holly wandered back near the exit. After careful prodding, she discovered that the guardesses were actually statues, so lifelike they had passed for real at first glance.

I, on the other hand, approached one of the bookshelves. The leather bindings of its holdings were tattered and smelled of mildew. Much of the furniture was in poor condition as well – especially the chair cushions, split and frayed. Not all of it though. Near the far wall stood an intricate table with six plush chairs, all well kept. I moved closer for a better look. Cups for wine and a freshly filled decanter had been set upon it. The stone slab tabletop glimmered aquamarine in the dim firelight, supported from underneath by a single pedestal carved in the likeness of a sea serpent, finely sculptured. A shallow depression appeared in the centre of the table, rounded like a bowl. Holly joined me.

As we stood at the table, the image on the wall behind it began to shift. Still, overall, it showed the swirling dark grey of cloud cover in the night. Then, for a brief moment, a shrouded moon shone through. To our right, a patch of star-lit sky became visible in a parting of the clouds.

I heard a click to my left, followed by a voice. But the words spoken were gargled and incomprehensible.

We turned to see a statuesque figure, thinly veiled in a long purple robe. He stepped out of a dark corner against the backdrop of a storm passing. His robe was torn and the man was gaunt. By the crown he wore, he could only be Taradin. His slow and fluid approach seemed both elegant and yet unnatural for his critically ill appearance. The tattered remnants of what might have been considered fine apparel at one time hung ragged upon his imposing frame. As if the sight of the figure wasn't ghastly enough, an equally ghastly smell preceded him, increasingly vile as he drifted closer. His presence saturated the air with aromas of bile, urine, mildew, and some underlying flowery scent – perhaps to mask the others. It was more than enough to turn my nose. I looked to Holly and thought she might pass out by her pale demeanor. The man reached the corner of the table, cleared his throat and then addressed us again, rasping his words.

"Do you care for wine?" he said, before even introducing himself. "I hold all the best Proudfoot vintages. Fine little brewers, they are." His long teeth flashed when he grinned, like daggers of worn enamel. It was plain to see that only a scant bit of gummy flesh held them in.

"No thank you," I said, wanting to run. I fought hard against the instinct. It took every ounce of courage within to maintain a calm and steady tone. I tried not to think of the man that stood before me as decayed or deathly ill. I tried to think of him as a normal person with an unfortunate condition.

"We had our fill this morning," I lied. It may have been slightly rude to refuse an offered drink, but the thought of eating or drinking anything at that moment was repugnant.

"Yes, I'll have what you're having," said Holly, to my surprise.

"Spectacular," he said. "Please, join me little ones… my *great* guests of honor." His outstretched arm gestured to the ornate table. It hung in the air, frail and emaciated.

I took the opposite head table position to where he stood and carefully laid my pack at my feet, while our host grasped the flagon of wine. Holly paused, and then took a seat with her back to the door. I tried mouth breathing in shallow breaths to deal with the awful pungency in the air, and did my best to keep from showing the overwhelming disgust I felt.

Arm quivering, the grim figure poured a cup of red wine, raised it, and steadied himself with a quick swig. He paused for a long moment to ponder the flavor of the liquid as it swished and sloshed in his mouth. At the same time, he studied our expressions. Finally, he made a satisfied nod, swallowed, and poured a fresh cup. With a thin-lipped grin, made crooked by a patch of stiff flesh, he passed the cup to Holly and promptly refilled his own.

"It is quite good," he said. "You have to be careful with the Seawind Flats label; oft times it is vinegary."

Holly, by then, had taken to rubbing her arms. *Nerves*, I surmised, since the chamber was plenty warm. Taking note of her chill, the withered figure produced a metallic scepter from beneath the confines of his robe. He held it in front of him.

"I told the servants I wanted a strong fire in the braziers!" he complained. He looked to the wall behind him. "Good help is hard to find, these days." Seconds later, it was set ablaze with images of a leaping fire, except they were more than just images – I could feel the heat.

How is this possible? I wondered. But now was not the time to ask. Such things could be sorted through at a more appropriate time. Now was the time to get to the business of our visit.

Our host turned back to face us, the grotesqueness of his face in plain view. Remnants of dry and hardened flesh clung to his ghastly visage, and sunk-in eye sockets cupped exposed eyeballs with black irises – a slash of fiery light across each one. His whole left side appeared rough and ragged. Rusty orange and yellow patches of lichens, as cover rocks, old wood and tombstones, had taken hold to clothing and exposed skin and bone. Underneath the skin, the occasional glint of metal shone through. Revolting to behold, yet too remarkable to look away from, the First King appeared as though he belonged in a cemetery or the rubble of ancient ruins lost to the world. "Crypt King" was more like it, perhaps, given the jeweled rings of gold and platinum that decorated his boney fingers, and the matching platinum crown and necklace that completed the set.

With the grace of a bodiless spirit, our host took the expected seat across from me at the table and formally introduced himself. He addressed us in a hushed tone that adult's normally reserve for polite conversations with children.

"I am Taradin," began the gruesome spectacle, "former King of Fortune Bay and now Vicegerent of Harrow, an honor bequeathed to me by the rightful heir and ruler from the Iron Tower. I speak in his name and also in the name of Karna's Vessel – *He Who Finds the Way Beneath the Waves.*"

"I speak in his name" was exactly what I wanted to hear.

"I am Nud Leatherleaf, Councillor of Webfoot," I offered. "I speak in the name of the lord mayor in this dealing. My views and opinions also reflect those of the Triland Council."

"Reflect," repeated Taradin, who then nodded to Holly. The crown he wore caught the light in that moment, at the slight bow of his head. It sparkled with tiny diamonds encrusted in the froth of a wave as appears on the sigil of Harrow. Front and centre, beneath the frothing wave, it bore a large aquamarine gemstone, light blue and teardrop-shaped. Arcs of black pearls curved along each side.

Holly blurted out her introduction. "Hopkins," she said with a nervous tone, "Holly, of Webfoot also. I'm here to assist Nud… ah… Mr. Leatherleaf… Councillor Nud… Leatherleaf." She covered her mouth with her hand.

"Well cheers to you both, Councillor Nud and Hopkins Holly," he said, lifting his cup in salute.

Holly followed. "And cheers to you, Vicegerent Taradin," she replied.

Cupless, I offered a nod and an awkward smile.

After the salute, Taradin put his cup down and placed his palms flatly on the table. He then leaned his meager physique forward, and in so doing, his arms spread wide like wings. The First King stared at Holly. By all appearances, he seemed awfully concerned about her.

"Before we begin – Hopkins, do you require a quill and paper?" he said. "There is a writing desk near the archives." Holly and I looked to one another with raised brows and wide eyes. *He doesn't know.*

"That will not be necessary Your Highness," replied Hopkins, "Pips have perfect memory."

Taradin rubbed his boney chin. "Really?" he said. His eyes rolled up to one side, contemplatively. "All Pips?"

"Yep... I mean *yes Your Vicegerentship*, pretty much," she said.

Taradin nodded. "That explains a few things... yes... from what I've heard of... *Pips* as you say. Intriguing... very intriguing. Ah then, to what do I owe the pleasure of your company? A lesson in history, perhaps, connected to something you found in your bog?"

"I love history," said Holly.

"Shall I start from the beginning?" asked Taradin.

The prospect was tempting, but there was no sense beating around the bush. Holly finally appeared comfortable, at least, but I was not in line with her pleasant approach. She would try to put us on friendly terms with Harrow and win cooperation through kindness and reciprocation. No, that was not going to work. It would only serve to raise the ire of our Triland partners who are struggling to deal with Harrow's unreasonable demands. This negotiation required firm action.

"Perhaps another time," I interjected. "That would be wonderful, really, but it will have to wait."

I raised my fist and slammed it onto the tabletop. Not a hard slam; not one like Mayor Otis might have done, but forceful enough to make a strong impression. There was pause. All eyes looked my way. I raised my voice as well, and sharpened my tone.

"I am here because you have wrongfully incarcerated two citizens of the Trilands: a Pip by the name of Bobbin Numbit and a

Stout by the name of Gariff Ram. Further, I have been made aware of evidence to suggest that you are holding political prisoners."

"Do you represent the Trilands?" said Taradin, contention in his voice.

"I represent their views."

"Legally?" he enquired.

"No," I admitted, "Legally, just Webfoot." And even that was shaky.

"May I see your colors?"

Reluctantly, I reached down and pulled the bone tube from my pack, extracted the leather document, and handed it over. While he thoroughly read through it all, I began to make my demands.

"Webfoot respectfully requests that the two forenamed individuals and any political prisoners you might have in custody be released immediately, and that all charges and allegations against them be dropped. Secondly, we know about your plans to mine the bog, and we recognize that there is some legitimacy to your claim of mineral rights. I am also here to discuss possible alternatives to that course of action."

"You are well informed, aren't you?" The question was rhetorical. With a kind bow of his head again, he handed back the leather and continued to speak. "I am at your mercy then, and at your service."

The negotiations were going well. He could be a bit short at times, but all in all the First King seemed polite and cooperative enough, and, more importantly, legal-minded to the letter of the law. He had to be different from Taeglin; he came off as… honorable, although in a kind of twisted way. And how could he not be somehow twisted, being what he is?

"I hope to be at your service as well," I said, returning the bow, "but first, we must find resolution. Webfoot, the Bearded Hills and the whole of the Trilands will not stand for injustice – the Pip and the Stout must be released."

Taradin gestured to the scroll. "Remember, you speak only for Webfoot."

"Indeed," I said, and tucked the leather away. "But the Trilands will concur. Send a raven if you doubt it. Furthermore, the Stout is residing in Webfoot, currently. That puts him under my charge."

Taradin nodded in acknowledgement.

"With regard to the bog," I continued, "The entire Triland region has a vested interest in it. And I know my people – no amount of riches can replace our way of life or detach us from our forefathers. The bog waters course through our veins the same way seawater does through the blood of your people. Mining the bog will destroy our livelihood, our life-blood."

"And yet we survive, separated from that which we long for," he said. "In many ways, it has made us stronger."

Taradin grinned a secret thought. "Do not fret, little one, Harrow will restore the land back to its original condition after the extraction – as per the Treaty. And Webfoot promptly shall receive the agreed upon tax – a full tenth of the value after expenses. You will never know the operation was even there. It is only temporary."

"What do we do in the mean time?" I said. "You might be there for ten years… twenty even. During that time, the bog eco-system will collapse. There will be open pits, drainage, tailings, destruction of habitat…"

Holly interjected, "There are other solutions. We can section off one area at a time to excavate and build a solid road to it with-out ruining the town or the greater habitat."

She was out of place. Diplomatic aides were to remain quiet until spoken to, even when they thought that they had a good sug-gestion to offer. The only acceptable communication is a whisper into the ear of the one served.

Taradin gave her an annoyed look. I acted annoyed for show, before extending Holly's line of thinking.

"I apologize," I said, then looked to Holly. "It is not your place to interrupt." I turned back to Taradin. "She's new."

Taradin nodded with a forced smile, and repeated a phrase he had said earlier. "I gathered that," he said. "Indeed, good help is hard to find these days."

"She's quite good, actually," I said, "and what she says is true. Harrow could simply guarantee a higher duty for use of the land while excavating, sort of like the deal we have going with Stoutville. Webfoot would handle inspections, approvals and would also provide advice."

"Taeglin already has a plan in place, and your suggestions would just complicate it unnecessarily."

"Taeglin's plan dismisses Webfoot entirely. What I am suggesting is honest and forthright – and everyone benefits. You *must* convince him." My argument was passionate and sound. The only thing lacking was the fact that I was talking to a walking corpse.

"Must I now?" remarked Taradin snyly. If he had eyebrows, I'm sure one of them would have risen while he spoke. "Humph." A grim smile crept across his face. "To ease your strife, Taeglin is proposing to relocate your little bog people to more fertile grounds south of Harrow's Gate, between the two rivers. And at his own expense, for the entire duration of the operation."

I shook my head. And what of Bobbin and Gariff? He was avoiding the issue of my imprisoned friends, not to mention the political prisoners… my parents.

There was more to his proposal. "If you, Nud, act as our emissary and convince the Council to relocate without a fuss, lobbying the promise of a great reward for everyone personally involved in the decision, I am prepared to negotiate bonuses to make you all wealthy Pips, even beyond the dreams of your Everdeep clan, whom I have dealt with in the past."

Mrello. Internally, I cursed his name. *I knew it.*

"As a gesture of goodwill," he went on, "I will personally

arrange to send you home in a chariot loaded with precious art-work, jewelry, metal bars and other gifts to distribute as you see fit, along with your little friends who are currently... shall we say, enjoying our hospitality."

"What of the political prisoners," I said.

"Simple," he said. "There aren't any. Harrow put an end to that sort of thing years ago."

I did not fully believe him. It seemed to me that the words spoken were more Taeglin's than his own. From everything I had heard of the man, Taeglin was the type to take the easiest route to get what he wanted, and would tell us anything we wanted to hear. I imagined he would follow through only long enough to suit his purposes: fickle, capricious and plainly unreliable.

However, the thought of rolling into town in a chariot laden with expensive gifts gave me pause. And Bobbin and Gariff would be free. Holly gave me such a sharp look that I shook off the notion immediately. But there was more.

The First King had lapsed into an internal state, swaying back and forth ever so slightly – a pendulum corpse, it seemed, heavy with the weight of indecision. Taradin's jaw dropped slightly and his eyes looked up in thought. He stopped swaying, and then his gaze met mine. "There is one other thing I can offer you, Nud Leatherleaf; a great thing. In return for your loyal service, I am willing to put you on the path of rejuvenation. And your aide as well, if you fancy her." Taradin looked Holly up and down.

These words, too, were quite enticing. As I pondered how I should respond, the repetitive motion of his lichen-covered hand kept me distracted. I came to realize it was his habit. Repeatedly, he stroked the amulet around his neck and the chain holding it, as one might comfort a loved one or a favored pet. At first, I thought the worst part to be the weak yet nagging scraping sound he made while doing so, until I saw that the chain disappeared into the flesh where his fingers ran across it – a groove down to the very bone.

"What about Webfooters?" said Holly, speaking out of turn again. "They will have nothing."

"You must learn to control your aide," said Taradin. "She lacks the proper respect." He looked to me for action.

I had to nod to express my agreement. I sent Holly a scolding glance.

"Enough," I told her, "or it's back to the Red Rooms for you!"

Holly lowered her eyes and made a good show of being shamed into obedience.

"Without me, Harrow would be naught but a simple fishing village with a powerless fool at the ship's wheel," said Taradin. "But under my careful guidance, this humble country is on a most glorious path, and soon Harrow will become the hub of civilization as we know it, and the envy of all."

Evidently, "His Excellency" liked the sound of his own voice. *What about my proposal? What about Holly's idea? Had he even heard them?* Maybe not: I took notice that his ears presented little more than shredded scraps of flesh.

The lichen-covered king turned to face me. "Nud, you look a little pale. Are you well?"

By then, I realized that the fiend was only toying with me. My impulse was to bolt, and leave his empty promises behind. The fire in his eyes seemed to flicker and swirl, and there was a kind of inquisitiveness in his voice that made me believe he might be searching for something; something in between the words I might say, or written in the expression on my face, or hidden in my eyes. Behind him, on the wall, a foul weather scene materialized. It began to churn, grey and foreboding.

"I'm just fine," I said, "but thank you for asking. You look a little gaunt yourself."

There was just enough flesh on Taradin's lips to form a broken smile. Then a change came over him. He took on a more serious composure, cold and purposeful. The room darkened.

"As you said, you are here to get down to business. You are in a position to ease Harrow's exercising of agreed-upon rights under the Treaty to obtain something desperately needed by its good people, but you choose to put up barriers instead." Taradin leaned back in his chair. Elbows on the armrests, he folded his hands together upon his sunken chest.

"I fear we are at an impasse, for I agree with my son of sons. It is much easier to simply move the Pips out, bribes or otherwise, and drain the bog. And prisoners are wonderful for exchanges. I can tell you this much: those who would aid Harrow to achieve its goals will be richly rewarded." Taradin gripped one hand into a boney fist. "Any and all who stand in the way of the Iron Tower will be crushed."

The Vicegerent cleared his throat, coughed and sputtered. Raw muscles in his chest contracted as he heaved. He had worked himself up, it seemed, beyond what his bodily facilities could withstand. After a long moment, he regained his composure.

I looked to Holly. She raised her eyebrows and shrugged.

"I wish for you to be the one that helps us, Councillor Leatherleaf, I really do," he continued. "I am rather fond of your bluntness and adventurous spirit. The earth holds many secrets, young Pip, and each secret tells part of the story of a larger design, and each design is part of one higher, and derives from one lower, and joins many others across, and influences more that we haven't even dreamed of, and is driven by others we cannot even perceive or know to perceive..." He trailed off, introspectively.

"I will aid you in the negotiations and help find a viable solution," I responded. "Just send us on our way with the Pip and the Stout that you—" I was interrupted.

"You have to be my 'Man on Council,'" he said.

"Don't you have one?" I responded.

"He is a fool," said Taradin. "I want another."

"I'll do it."

"And inform me who my opponents are?"

I hesitated. "Agreed," I said.

Taradin sat back and stroked the chain around his neck yet again. "Too late," he said. "I retract the offer."

I felt like pelting him. The boasting about his great people and great kingdom continued, until the words grew faint to my ears. Instead, they penetrated my chest and gripped my beating heart. Then it hit me. This man was terribly cursed and terribly mad, with little more than curses and madness to offer. Fyorn had been right: he should have died a hero long ago.

"What is it you want?" I said. "What are you looking for?"

"I admire that you have come here to save your friends and preserve your village," he replied. "Noble causes, indeed they are... very noble causes and I commend you for taking them on. I did much the same once, long ago. But I made a decision to make good for my own line above all others. Family comes first. You plan to have a family one day, don't you?"

The lichen-covered king was rambling, and he wasn't answering my question.

"What is it that Harrow needs so much from the bog lands?" I said.

"Well, you will find out when the bog is drained," he continued. "There is new knowledge hidden beneath your mud flats – perhaps even directly beneath your village – and the way to begin excavating a bog is to drain it. Your precious wetland sits high compared to the lands south. All that needs be done is to dig a few channels and dam or divert the inflows."

I was desperate. "I know what you really seek," I said at last. "I have seen *IT*. I'm sure I can tell you exactly where *IT* lies. Release my... the persons you have wrongfully detained and I will prove it."

What exactly is IT? I was bluffing... sort of. My best guess was that the Iron Tower was searching for the Jhinyari battleground, of course, but perhaps there was something more: the "mother load" of sparkling stones similar to the one I found, or the "Spears of the Gods" cave for all I knew, or the Hanging City, or Dromeron Odoon, or Isotopia, or perhaps something special within the Hanging City – devices. Whatever it might be, I was treading into dangerous territory.

"You have professional informers then, don't you? Very well then. Prove what you say. Where is that which I seek most?"

"If I tell you, I have nothing to bargain with."

"Just tell me 'what' then."

I blurted it out. "The location of the Jhinyari battle—" He cut me off.

"Scoundrels, I say. Let them rot! You are getting warmer. So what of it?"

He had me cornered, for I could only speculate on the specifics of the Iron Tower's interest and intentions.

I fumbled my words. "I don't know... I mean, I can't explain because we were lost underground for so long," I said.

"Lost?"

Not knowing what else to do and fearing for my safety if the First King became more irate, I looked to Holly. She appeared tense. When she met my gaze, I shifted mine to where she kept her sparkling stone. She looked down, then her eyes met mine, and at that moment, Holly reached into her shirt pocket and pulled out her light-bearing crystal, gained from the hags. She unveiled the stone from its leather sheath and dangled it in front of her on the black iron chain.

Taradin stared at the piece without saying so much as a word. The light danced about and sparked in rapid bursts. Discreetly, I checked to make sure my own stone was still tucked well away, under my shirt. There was no doubting the vicegerent's sense of intrigue; he could not look away.

"Jhinyari... yes," he said, as though recalling a distant memory. "I remember now... this dancing light... the sword-stones... all of it." He closed his eyes and winced in pain, then shivered. "I will never forget the 'strikers' that cut us down from afar."

Good, I thought. *He's taken the bait. I have that lichen-covered corpse right where I want him.*

I continued with my plea. "And in my travels, I have beheld the Hanging City, and nearby, mammoth crystals I call the Spears of the Gods, and a Dancing Pool. I can lead you to all of these wondrous places. There are secret ways underground that can bring a crew to the bog without disturbing it or even revealing they are there. What you seek is underground, yes, but you don't need to dig out the bog to get to it. You can start somewhere below this very room… the entrance is literally beneath your feet!"

Taradin stroked his jeweled amulet and the chain holding it. The scraping of raw bone on metal sent a shiver through my spine. I tried not to flinch at the sound, nor at the sight of his fibrous neck muscles, exposed and contracting as he tensed.

"Compelling… and quite ironic, to say the least," he said finally. "I call for a game of Pirates' Dice to settle the matter. As you well know, it is within my rights to name the deciding game of chance. As I said already, we are at an impasse. Your trinket changes nothing."

There was no such "right" and I could tell he was bluffing. I could see it in his preoccupation with the stone, and I could see it written all over his rotting face.

CHAPTER L

Gambler's ruin

W hen the Lich King grinned, I wondered if his face might
split in half. He rose from his chair and sailed across
the floor to a narrow desk, set along the wall. There,
amidst the ornate paintings and statues, he gathered two sets of
dice and two shakers, one white set and one red set, then carried
them back to the table. Then he retrieved an ink well and a white
feather quill, and set them at my end of the table. He took his seat
and moved the game pieces in front of him, picked up the white
set of dice, and rattled them in their cup.

"The dice will reveal your integrity," he explained. "They always
do. If you roll true and wager well, you will be vindicated by the
will of Karna, as I once was. I have six rings to wager and a coin, all
quite valuable. You have your stone. The coin represents the bog,
so I own the bog for starters."

That hardly seems decent, I thought.

Taradin locked eyes with me: "My child, on top of your stone
you have your life and the lives of your sweet companions. That
only sums to three though – I'm counting all three friends as one.
Trust me; it's better for you that way. There are no political prisoners to add."

"I will start the game by fronting you two of my rings," he went on. "Now we are even at five a piece. The game goes on until one of us has lost all five wagers or we both agree to call it quits."

Holly overlooked the fact that she was talking to death incarnate. "That's not fair!" she snapped. "You would have us lay down our lives against your stupid rings? Forget it. Nud… we're leaving. Let's get out of here."

"I have no life to bargain with," said the lichen-covered one, "and if you abandon me now, neither will you, nor will your friends. So sit back and take in the game, and when your life hangs in the balance by little more than a silver thread, relish it! That is what it means to truly live… you must look Death in the eye, again and again, and dare it. You must do so until you can't bear it any longer, until you are sick to death of seeing Death. And then you must look Death in the eye one last time."

As his words faded into soft echoes, I peered into the eyes of the undying one. Staring Death down could not be much worse. I had seen Death already – in my dreams – and he was only a wraith.

If life did not sustain the thing that sat across from me, then what did? He counted himself not among the living, yet he was more than simply dead. Dead… alive… he seemed to be neither, or both. Perhaps he lay somewhere in between.

At least for the moment, I owned the lives of my friends. "I suppose you will not agree to end the game at this time?" I said.

Taradin's smirk disappeared and he gave me a vile look. He sighed and shook his head. I could almost hear the "tsk tsk" on his mind.

I agreed to his terms, in full realization of our dire circumstance. Holly nodded to signify her compliance as well. We had no real choice in the matter. We had to play, or die. We had to win, or die. We had to save our friends, and maybe save the bog. Or die.

The game was a simple two-player contest, and each must start with an equal number of tokens. One player acts as the "attacker" and the other the "defender." Each turn, the players agree on what to wager, then roll their dice in any order. Whoever rolls the highest die, or rolls a pair (the higher of both pairs if each rolled a pair) wins the toss, the tokens wagered, and defends next turn. In the event of a tie, the defender wins the toss. The game commences with a "roll-off" to determine who defends first. In the event of a tie in this case, the roll-off is repeated until a win occurs. The game ends when one of the players has nothing left to wager. There is no "honor" for a player in Pirates' Dice. The game is infamous for escalation during play – desperate players down to one token, with odds stacked against them, often plead with their opponent to add new and valuable tokens to the game, at the discretion of the opponent.

Taradin drew a deck of blank cards from his robe and passed two of them over. Holly took them. I picked up the feather quill, dipped it in ink, and passed it to Holly.

"You write," I said to her. "Mine is too messy."

Taradin watched as Holly wrote in neat cursive: "Nud" on one card and "Holly, Bobbin and Gariff" on the second. She had a particular way of writing "Holly," with a curvy "H" and an extra big loop under the "y" that underlined the entire name. When she was finished, the First King handed me two white dice together with the matching shaker, and kept the remaining red pair and shaker for himself. I took my seat and weighed the bringers of fate in my hands. The pieces appeared to be made of ivory, but heavier than expected.

"Ready to roll?" Taradin asked.

"Ready," I replied.

"Ready," said Holly.

We threw dice into the bowl carved into the middle of the slab tabletop. It was flat at the very bottom. A slightly curled lip at the top deflected any high rolling dice back down.

Taradin won the first toss for defender. I then rolled a "1" and a "2" on the attack. He rolled a "4" and a "5" as defender to win the toss. I gave Taradin a ring, of course. For the next turn, I gave the dice to Holly to role on our behalf. She rolled a "6" and a "1", and smiled confidently at her luck. The dice, unfortunately, were not kind to her either. Taradin rolled double sixes, winning the toss again. A wry smile crept across his face. I added another ring to his kitty. If we lost the next round, Holly would have to put in her light-giving stone. We gathered our dice to roll again.

I rolled "6" high and Taradin a "5" high. I was now the defender. He gave me back one ring. Then Holly rolled a "4" high and he a "6" high, winning the turn and making him the defender. The next turn was devastating. Holly rolled a "5" and a "4" – not bad, except for the fact that Taradin rolled double sixes – again! We had no choice but to hand over Holly's stone.

Holly leaned forward, palms rubbing her knees. "We would like to quit the game now," she said, pleading with her eyes as much as her voice. She looked to me.

I nodded. "This game has gone on long enough." I met Taradin's gaze. "You have the stone and the bog. Do you accept our offer to terminate?"

Taradin took a long moment to mull over the decision, or at least he pretended to do so for dramatic effect. While waiting for his response, I contemplated a passage from the legend of the First King: "He rigged the game so that no matter what the roll, the Orbweaver could devour everything *except* the First King and his followers…" Could Taradin have rigged this game too? *A game rigger is a game rigger*, I decided.

Finally, the lichen-covered fiend offered a way out. "You may quit now, if you like, for the price of one life."

Holly grabbed my wrist. "Quit," she whispered. "I will do it."

I shook my head and stared Taradin right in the eye.

"Next roll, winner takes all!" I said.

Holly and I were in this together. Together we would seal

our fates and the fates of our two good friends. The game had so quickly come down to our lives. My only hope lay in chance and the notion that his dice might be loaded.

There was no response from Taradin as he weighed his options. It was his way of torturing us. It would be courteous of him to accommodate my request, but nothing bound him to do so.

"Winner takes all," I repeated.

Repeatedly, Taradin ran his fingers down the chain around his neck. I could hear the bone scraping against the links. Slowly, he nodded his head. "Very well," he said.

"And we switch dice," I added. What little flesh that still clung to one of his eyebrows sprung upwards. He sneered when he spoke.

"What's wrong with your dice?" he asked.

"Can't you see? They're bad luck," I said.

Taradin leaned forward, resting his palms flat on the table. He had a serious look in his eyes. "You must know that I once rolled dice to save the whole of mankind, and won! Do you really think it is possible that I could lose to the likes of you?"

I didn't know what to say.

"Well... do you?"

Rather than nod or shake my head, I simply returned his stare, blankly.

"You're short," my ghastly opponent spat. Part of a tooth flew out of his mouth and clattered as it bounced along the tabletop and onto the floor. He had gotten himself all worked up again and was falling apart, it seemed. Taradin wiped his lip with the sleeve of his tattered robe.

"You only have two wagers remaining to my eight," he said, anger in his voice. "To keep the game balanced, you both have to offer something extra. A service perhaps... a small price to pay for all that might be gained, judging from your current predicament."

Holly tugged on my sleeve. I saw her head shaking "NO" out of the corner of my eye. But how much could it possibly matter?

Whatever Holly's reservations might be, we would have no choice but to accept once again.

"What are your terms?" I asked.

"In addition to providing me with the location of the stones—"

The First King tilted his head and paused to ponder the offer he was about to make. His jaw hung open.

"—you must seek out the leaders of your own community in the bog and convince them to join our league. Name it *The Rejuvenation League.* Webfoot will fall under the protection of Harrow and your village will share in our wealth and knowledge of longevity. A gracious and respectful associate of mine, who is attentive to the needs of Pips, will be assigned to your village council and will aid in all decision making henceforth. All your council need do is accept our generous offer, and a new and wondrous age will enlighten your people."

What possible influence could I have over the council? I was barely past pipsqueak in years and wholly new to my position; they would not pay heed to my words at all. My thoughts must have been written all over my face, for Taradin gave me the answer to my internal question.

"I will outfit you for the task as though you were a high lord. You will have our finest coach drawn by the noblest of steeds in all of Harrow, a most esteemed entourage, plentiful gifts of goodwill as I said earlier, and City Master Garond will accompany you to draw up the contracting arrangements. Your council will have to take you seriously. Tell them there is a great sage in Harrow who will guide them all to riches and immortality. And be sure to tell them this of Karna's Messenger, whom I speak for—"

By the way the next words rolled off his rotten tongue, you would think they were sacred.

"*He knows the Way. He can get you what you Want.*"

The words struck me. They were the words the guard had spoken, and they were the words of the leviathan.

"I will hold your lives to ensure that you do your utmost to fulfill the task agreed to. Holly, you would do well to help him. If you succeed, I will give you back your lives and the lives of those you seek to rescue."

"And if I am not successful?" I asked.

"Hmmm… then I would have to say that your life's work would become mine," responded Taradin, "to do with as I see fit… perhaps you would make a good serving boy, or maybe an acrobatic fool. You seem clever enough though, so the laboratory may serve you best – if you could learn to click with the Gropers. You are a good reader, I presume? The Gropers can do most anything BUT read. How are you at *story time?*"

I offered him a blank look. He turned to Holly. "As for you, my dear, I have other uses in mind for you. Perhaps Harrow could use a Red Room." He laughed a sinister laugh.

I did not like the idea of leading the council down this path, nor did I like the idea of becoming a slave. But it seemed better than bribes that would only benefit a precious few, and it would buy me time…

"If I did not succeed," I pleaded, "and if I knew of a stone like Holly's except brighter, could I trade that for one life back?"

"Have you seen such a stone?" he asked.

"I'm not sure, but I have an idea where one might be."

"Agreed," he said, all too quickly.

Taradin and I swapped dice. My knees went weak and I felt a sickness in the pit of my stomach. The next words to hit my ears sounded alien to me: "Then I agree to your terms as well," the voice said. The words were mine.

In a moment of clarity, I realized it was stupid of me to have listened to a forest of trees in the first place. And why Holly had insisted on accompanying me to pursue this folly, I could not fathom. She had her sense about her by then though, it seemed, signifying her disapproval with flared nostrils, pursed lips and a shaking head. She was scared too – really, really scared. I wondered if Holly truly realized that I had no real choice in the matter. I had to keep the game going at all costs… I had *to give luck a chance.*

Taradin handed me two more cards. On one of them I wrote: "Convince the council or be a slave – Nud."

Holly reached for the quill to write on her card. She spilled the inkbottle and knocked her wine cup off the table. The pewter clanged several times before rolling underneath a chair. Tardin rolled his eyes. His patience with her was up. Holly ducked down to retrieve the cup.

My hands trembled as I dropped the red dice into the shaker. I rattled them for a good long time, and then rolled my fate. Taradin threw his dice into the bowl as well. All four dice, red and white, bounced and jittered up and down the gentle slope. They clattered and they skidded. One die of his and one die of mine collided, stuck together, and began to slide down the arc of the bowl towards the bottom. My die was on "6" and his on "1". I gasped in anticipation. The other two dice were still in play.

The fact that I had not revealed that the stone was on my person gave me solace, as did the knowledge that the toss likely would be mine. *Win… WIN!*

But just as the final two were about to settle, I toppled. I did not even see the numbers, for my chair suddenly tipped over and I tumbled onto the floor. I heard dice clatter in the bowl one last time before they came to rest.

Two sixes for me, I bet.

I believed it whole-heartedly, but I will never know for sure. Only Taradin was privy to how the dice landed. A condition of diplomacy is that a witness must attest to the events that transpire during a negotiation and what is agreed upon, or it simply does not count. As far as I was concerned, the last roll had become null and void and the game forever spoiled.

CHAPTER LI

Into the gloom

I met the steady gaze of the sea serpent. Its painted eyes shone bright and yellow with the glaring constancy of a common house cat. The creature had small green legs that could pass for fins, and webbed feet tipped with black, hooked claws. A sinuous tail wound its way up and around the pedestal base of the table. It was so life-like; it could have passed for real.

My elbow had broken my fall. It stung like mad. I lay flat on my back, sprawled out on the floor and under the table, my chair overturned.

"Whoa… what the—"

Before I could finish, Holly pounced on top of me. She slapped her cold, clammy hand over my mouth and draped the wild elderkin cloak over the two of us. To the outside world, we suddenly disappeared.

There was a "tap tap tap" from above.

On its own, the cloak would not be enough to hide us for long. As quiet as I could, I sat up and slung my pack over my shoulders, then rose to crouch for a quick getaway. Holly moved with me, positioning herself on my right so we could both share in the cover.

The tapping stopped.

"What is going on down there?" said Taradin, sounding mildly frustrated.

"Ouch," I said, faking my pain. "Half a moment, if you will."

"He'll be fine in a second," said Holly. "Is your knee all right, Mr. Leatherleaf, Sir?"

We took the opportunity to creep away from the table.

"Come now!" he complained. His voice became grandiose. "Rise now, and behold your fate, Webfooters! Rise! Feast your eyes on the treachery and glory of Pirates' Dice!"

Taradin's patience soon wore thin. He slapped his hands on the table. "Come now, this is absurd!" he said. "You are taking too long. What are you two doing down there, anyway?" Then I heard his chair slide. "Get up here! No farewell kisses under the table… Whaaa?"

Surprise, surprise.

Holly and I actually did rise back when he bade us to, but wrapped in the cloak, careful not to budge a chair, knock the decor, or drag against the floor during our hushed escape. We snuck towards the door with small, quiet steps, practically invisible. There was no way for us to look back though, only forward, and only Holly could see enough to guide us by the slight gap in the hood.

The Flipside girl continued to usher me on and I followed her lead. Still, I could not see a thing. I kept my voice to a low whisper. "What are you doing?" My question was rhetorical.

"The door," was all she whispered back.

Taradin burst out at us, his voice suddenly hoarse and monstrous: "Get back here!" he growled. "Where are you hiding?" His anger was multiplied by our silence. "Come out!"

We were almost there, almost to freedom, when I bumped into one of the Red Maiden statues beside the door. It was a hard knock, a full check. The statue toppled over, smashing into the other on its way down. We jumped back as the two stone figures crashed to the floor. Bits of red stone exploded out from the impact and bit at my ankles. Holly let out a squeak. She leapt to the door, found the handle and pulled. But it opened only slightly – the bulk of the statues blocked the way. The cloak slid off me.

"STOP!" commanded the lichen King.

I shuddered and cringed.

"The game is not over until you behold your fate!"

To hell with that. I dropped to the floor, braced my back against the wall, and pushed with my legs at the broken statue blocking the way.

I saw Taradin coming for us, and redoubled my efforts as Holly yanked on the door handle with all her might. The piece gave way just enough for a Pip to squeeze by. Holly passed through the doorway. *Clandt, on the other side,* I thought, as I scrambled to my feet. I felt ready for him though. I thought maybe, in the initial confusion, we could slip past or even trip him up before he caught on to what was happening. I forced my way through the doorway, mentally prepared to meet the challenge that awaited.

But there was no initial confusion, at least not on his part. Although not the brightest conversationalist, Clandt proved to be quick-minded when it came to, well, being a guard. Before I even realized what was happening, he had pulled Holly up off her feet and with a kick sent me stumbling backwards. The back of my head smashed against the edge of the doorframe with a sickening thud. He grabbed hold of Holly's cloak and flung it down the hall. Knowing the Lich King himself would soon be upon us, in all his horrid gore and glory, I rolled away from the door and into the middle of the passage. I was just in time.

Taradin swiped at me, but he became stuck in the doorway while trying to force his way through. He was holding his scepter. The wall turned translucent again. "GUARDS!... GUARDS!" he called out.

I struggled to my feet and charged at Clandt to free Holly from his forceful grip. In one hand, he held her firm, and guarded his prize well. With the same fluid motion displayed earlier, Clandt extended one foot and effortlessly redirected my charge into the wall. I tripped and fell, hitting the wall face first and then the ground. There was a glint of steel, and his stance suddenly changed to that of a swordsman. He stood with a short sword drawn and upon me.

"That's enough," he said. There was no tolerance in his voice. Holly gave the guard a handful to mind, but he rough-handled her into submission.

Daring the sword, I slowly stood up and took a step towards him. The guard waved his weapon at me in warning. I don't think he wanted to hurt us, but I saw in his eyes it was not beyond him.

I unsheathed my stone and concentrated on the chain of thoughts needed to initiate it: my thirst for Holly's freedom, my hope for our escape from this horrible place. Then I imagined Taradin's lifeless body rotting away in the bog, back where it belonged. A dazzling flash issued from the stone. Clandt closed his eyes and looked away, but too late. Holly, unfortunately, also had her eyes on me at the exact wrong moment. *If only I could have warned her.*

In the aftermath of the blinding burst of light, I ran and grabbed Holly's hand. Neither of them could see, but Clandt would not let go. He and I immediately became embroiled in a desperate tug-of-war.

"Stay right where you are," commanded the guard, waving his sword dangerously.

At that moment, remarkably, the door to Taradin's chamber warped to let him pass. The solid stone slab bowed like a lithe young twig. I could hardly believe my eyes. Half a moment later, the corpse-like figure stood in front of the doorway.

"Honor your deal," he scolded, pointing an accusing finger at me. "You have lost everything… you are both mine, now."

"Never!" I said, and pulled harder. Clandt gave Holly a forceful tug back. Her hand slipped out of mine and I fell backwards.

Holly, in turn, fought harder to get free. "No," she grunted, clawing and kicking and twisting and biting. She was getting the better of him. "Let me go!" Holly elbowed Clandt in the groin and broke free. She was as blind as he was from the flash though, and the slope of the floor tripped her up. She stumbled and fell.

"Holly," I called out. "This way!"

She scrambled to her feet, as did I. She seemed confused though, waving her arms and stumbling.

"Nud?" she said.

At that moment, something changed. I noted Taradin manipulating his scepter. "Very well then, Leatherleaf," were his words.

The floor beneath my very feet completely changed. It became as slippery as oil, but still dry. Up the slope, where Holly and Clandt stood, the floor remained the same. I began to slide down the hall. I fell on my chest and scrambled on all fours to slow my descent, to no avail. I simply could not dig in or find any kind of hold on the smooth surface. In my frenzy, the discarded cloak became bunched up at my feet as I slid. Down I went into the unlit portions of the corridor. Clandt reached out and grabbed Holly before she could get away from him.

"Holly!" I called out. She grunted in frustration at her captor.

"Take the girl to the holding cells," I heard Taradin say to Clandt, "and send someone to retrieve the diplomat from the 'Catcher'… if he survives."

The Catcher?

Sliding faster and faster, I spun round to face in the direction of motion. I brightened my stone. A huge gaping maw was at the end of the hallway – the skull of some great beast. It was a trap and I was rushing straight for it. Directly to the right of the maw, I glimpsed an open hallway. In desperation, I pulled the cloak from around my legs. I pushed myself up into a crouched position and tossed the hood at an unlit wall sconce near the side tunnel. It caught. I heard an awful tear. Holding tight, my momentum swung me around, the hood acting as my pivot. The fullness of my inertia sent me crashing against the wall, just right of the huge skull. Battered and bruised, I scrambled into the connecting passage. It was level and not slippery.

"What… How?" I heard from above. It was Taradin's voice.

"He hooked into the tunnel." That was Clandt.

I glanced over to the gaping maw. As I suspected, it was a pit trap. Shining the light a little brighter, I saw deadly spikes at the bottom, long and razor sharp.

I turned to look up the sloped corridor, to Holly. Clandt had a strong hold on her and appeared to be tying her hands. I noted the two Red Maidens rushing towards the scene from their stations above ground, and more tower guards behind them.

"Run, Nud, RUN!" Holly screamed, still struggling to free herself. She had no hope of doing so, really, and I had no hope of reaching her – I could not climb a frictionless slope. She was right. Her words came in desperation, her advice the only way out of this mess.

"I'll come back for you," I promised. "The Trilands, Gan, even Fort Abandon… none of them will stand for this!"

"Go!" she yelled, just before being muffled.

A pang of guilt hit me as I unhooked Holly's cloak from the wall sconce. The face on the sconce bore a horrified look, with the unlit torch set like a spike through its skull. If anything unbearable were to happen to Holly… if harmed in any way whatsoever, I would never forgive myself. Kabor and I had been adequately provided for during our brief incarceration and were treated civilly. I could only hope that Harrow would extend the same level of decency to her, and for that matter, to Bobbin and Gariff as well… until I got help. *Real help.*

The walls morphed again. A thousand eyes stared out from them. They all focused on me.

A terrible, yet familiar voice arose. I sheathed the stone and peered back around the corner to confirm my suspicions. Clandt had hold of Holly. She was terrified. And yes, there were others. I jerked back quickly and flattened my palms against the wall.

Damn! Wraiths!... The slave master.

At least two, maybe four of the foul creatures were present.

The next words were faint, but audible. "He's long gone by now," said someone – it didn't sound like Clandt. "Pips are fast little creatures..."

I couldn't hear all of it.

"He won't get far," another seemed to say.

I looked to them again. The wall across from Taradin lit up.

"No, fools," he said. "Behold! Leatherleaf is still watching us!"

In the distance, I saw images of myself from many angles, projected onto the wall in front of them.

The eyes... of course!

I pulled back and wrapped Holly's cloak over me, torn and stretched out of shape as it was. I donned the hood and glanced back again, and saw that I had completely vanished from their view. I rekindled the bog stone and turned my attention to the passage ahead. When satisfied that I had it memorized the course as far as I could see, I sheathed the stone once more and, with a heavy chest, made my way along the corridor at a measured pace.

Bleary eyed, I mentally focused on my escape route. When I reached the limits of what I had seen and memorized, I flashed the stone again, briefly, to see what lay ahead. Every time I did, I noted the wall's searching eyes honing in on my position.

It was stupid to come here, came the first wave of self-loathing. *It was stupid to bring Holly,* came the next. *We should be safe right now, far away. We should be in Webfoot. Someone else – other than me – should be planning Bobbin and Gariff's rescue right now, and saving the bog for that matter.* I didn't want to think about the consequences. *Why can't he just die already? If anything happens...*

"You'll wish you'd stayed dead," I said aloud. That was the last thing I said in the dark, for fear the walls had ears as well as eyes.

Padding softly, I kept to the main tunnels and avoided the lesser ones where possible, navigating several divides in the hallways and passing many closed doors. Despite my maneuvering, every so often I could hear faint voices from behind, or footsteps, or clanging metal echoing down the hallway. *I'm being tracked.* The time had come to start exploring alternatives. The last flash had revealed something... something familiar. But I had to be sure.

I stopped and urged the light to a heightened brightness. A thousand eyes on the wall glared at me, instantly. I accepted the risk and carefully scanned the hallway. *Yes... yes... I remember this place*, I told myself. Taradin might know exactly where I was, but for the last time. I wrapped the stone in its leather sheath, took a long minute to focus my thoughts – on the verge of recall – and then continued on my way. In my mind's eye, I saw the tunnel as I had traversed it before, when led by the party of Glooms from the forbidden mine tunnels.

I walked a long way in silence and without any light to guide me. Every so often, I would stop to feel along a wall for a particular doorway, so as to recalibrate my position. I met not a soul wandering through the Catacombs as such. Eventually, I came upon an area that I remembered contained a particular room with Glooms working inside. I checked the door latch when I got to it. It was locked and no noises issued from within. I checked door after door. Half a dozen locked ones later I came upon a thick metal door, slightly ajar. Beyond, only darkness. A conversation of soft clicks and hushed trills filtered into the hallway, along with light sounds of metal clinking on metal. I opened the door just enough to squeeze through, quietly.

I uncovered the tiniest bit of the bog stone and directed a

beam of light into the room, hoping that none spilled out. Smooth blocks formed the walls and overall, the room had an infirmary's sterile air to it, as well as that same sense of operational efficiency. Six Glooms worked together at two long, metal tables, busy with small implements and chattering away to one another. They wore the same drab robes as those in the mine. The room was "eyeless," so to speak, both on the walls and otherwise. Softly, I shut the door behind me.

I recognized one of the Il'kinik from the group I had met near the "Spears of the Gods" cave. *The one with the spotted head.*

The space was cramped for all of the equipment present and activity within. Liquids and powders in glass containers with embossed markings occupied a short table near to the door, while a similar table held metallic cutting and hooking tools carefully laid out over a white cloth. On yet another stood a washbasin. Unhindered, the Glooms managed to work together flawlessly as one extended body, exchanging tools and coordinating tasks with the utmost grace. The long, metal tables occupied the centre of the room, bearing incised cadavers – the focus of the workers' attention. The Bound Ones appeared to be so pre-occupied with their work, I doubted they would even notice if I walked right up to them.

With all their chirrs and clicks, the Glooms paid no heed to the silent Pip in their midst. *I cannot wander these all-seeing halls forever*, I decided. *Eventually, someone will find me.* And so I set the bar lock down on the door without a sound, and then sized-up the room for hiding places. I couldn't imagine that Taradin's wraiths or guards would ever suspect that I was hiding among their own workers.

Compartments along the side walls appeared to hold the most promise for concealment, opening at about table height with doors hinged from above. Only two doors were up at the moment, held so by red, rusty chains fixed to iron rings in the ceiling. They opened into cavities conveniently sized to fit a man lying on his back – quarters for the deceased – and a little on the large side for a normal man, probably to accommodate the local half-giant sorts as well.

I treaded softly to the nearest compartment. Halfway there, one of the workers stopped what he was doing. He held his head up from the table he was working at, mouth clicking and ears twitching. He turned his head and honed in on my presence, then erupted in a chittering blast. They all turned to "look."

I immediately approached the familiar looking Gloom. "SHHH," I said. "Please help. Wraiths are coming. You know what they'll do to me."

A second worker exchanged a blast of rapid clicks with the first, flailing his arms and stomping his feet before sending a razor sharp trill my way. My Gloom friend, clearly defending me, raised his hand and pointed at me.

"I-so-to-pia?" he pronounced cautiously. He said it like a question. Others turned to one another to nod and click. The Gloom stood there gaping at me in anticipation. Stringy, grey hair fell in thin strands over his face; a thin veil to obscure the empty eye sockets and all but the tip of one ear. The other ear was either malformed or missing altogether. On top, he was bald and spotted with black dots, making the crown of his head appear much like an oversized raven's egg.

I nodded dumbly, eager to agree to any terms in exchange for safety. "Yes... Isotopia."

A hard knock to my head from behind sent me reeling. I looked up... from down on the floor. *How did I fall?* My head throbbed with pain. The room had erupted into chaos, ear-piercing screeches, forceful grunts, pushes, shoves, punches and kicks.

"Stop! They'll hear," I said. No one listened.

I reached behind to feel the back of my head. It was wet.

Slowly, I rolled over from my back to my front. I tried to get up. Gloom legs were everywhere pushing, kicking, bracing and struggling. I received a sharp kick to the ribs that sent me back down. Tables were knocked, metal implements clanged, glass fell and shattered.

Wraiths could be along any moment, I worried. I scrambled to my knees, head throbbing in pain. As I gathered the strength to stand, another glass container was knocked over in the scuffle. It landed beside me and broke, spewing its contents. Fumes rose. They had a familiar tang to them. *The slavers.* Everything went fuzzy, then dark…

*

I came to in utter darkness, lying on my side over cold stone and stuffed into a corner. The air was heavy and pungent, the smell of death all around. It was even worse than the smell of Taradin himself. I had no idea how much time had passed. In the haze of early wakefulness, I wondered where I might be and what possibly could smell so terrible.

The rise and fall of Il'kinik conversation drifted to my ears, muffled and hollow sounding. They were being civil to one another again, by the sounds of it, and going about their usual business. Cautiously with my palms, I felt out the area above me – bare stone. The smell was awful. I reached to my side… something soft on my fingertips… hair. I reached a little farther… supple… skin… someone's scalp! I retracted sharply. I was with company.

The Gloom chatter suddenly ceased, like crickets disturbed in the night. I pricked my ears. There was a pounding at the main door. A harsh voice followed. "Open up!" the voice commanded. A long pause followed, then some shuffling. The latch clicked. It could only be a wraith.

My body tensed. I was trapped.

Indeed, a wraith's voice, now from inside the room, lashed out rabidly at the Bound Ones.

"Where is the Outlander?" he said. "You are hiding that pitiful thing, aren't you? I'll tear out your tongues and trim the ears off of your ugly heads if you lie to me."

I'm sure the Glooms did not know they were ugly. They kept their silence.

The mess, I thought. *They'll be suspicious of the mess.*

"Search everything!" said the wraith. "If any of these retched Gropers tries to escape, feed him to the rats in thirty pieces!"

Guards with heavy footsteps and strong voices – male and female – stormed into the room. A table was overturned and the glass containers it held smashed to the floor. The contents of drawers spilled out with a clatter. Tools and implements clattered and clanged as they fell. One by one, the cavity doors creaked open and the holdings searched. I prepared the cloak, ducked behind the cadaver, and melded into the back corner as much as I could. I worried deeply about the cloak's integrity, given the abuse it had taken.

I barely heard the wraith's soft footsteps when he approached. I dared to peek through a slight opening in the hood, and saw the thing's black-robed arm. I hid my eyes, and did not stir or breathe. The wraith took his time at my compartment. A lone fingernail, claw-like, scraped along the stone surface of the opening. He grasped the cadaver and tugged at it. His breathing was quick and laborious, and he *sniffed* the air like a wild animal.

With an unsatisfied grunt, the wraith slammed the door shut, hooked it in, and moved on to the next compartment. After many long minutes, when the search had been completed, there was dissatisfaction and commotion in the air.

"Where are they?" asked one of the wraiths. "We saw him enter. He must be here! Search everything again!"

I was sure they would find something suspicious this time. Taradin's dark servants interrogated the Glooms. *Someone will break*, I thought. *How could they not?*

This time, the cadavers were pulled out and examined, and

the compartments thoroughly poked and prodded. When my turn came, a guard crawled in halfway, reached out and poked the sides and back of the compartment with his sword. For a moment, another guard interrupted, and while he was occupied I rolled into a space he had already tested. When he resumed, he poked where I had been and missed me entirely.

Unable to locate the small Pip tucked away with the dead, and after much cursing, searching and interrogating, the wraiths and the guards simply gave up.

"He must not have come in," said a tower guard.

"Perhaps the Gropers created the flash without knowing it," offered a Red Maiden. "They can't see a thing."

"That's probably it," said her cohort. "A false alarm. We see it happen from time to time when they work the burners."

Taradin's men stood waiting, silent, while the lead wraith made his final threats to the frightened Glooms. In a show of the utmost bravery and conviction, the Bound Ones held their tongues.

The wraiths left cursing; the guards left in silence.

Later that day, dogs barked in the distance. The door remained shut. No one else entered the room.

Heaven, to those underground dwellers who call themselves the Il'kinik, is purely metallic and situated somewhere beyond the reachable depths. In the beginning, there was only Hell – the surface world – and the protection of the rock ceiling was absent. Fire from above burned down through thin air.

It is said that, long ago, the fire in the sky became so hot that it burned off the eyes of the original Earth Born, and would have charred their bodies wholly had Kechekenibek not built chambers of rock for them to withdraw to, set with cool waters to quench the flames.

And so the Arch and the Pillar became the greatest holy symbols of Il'kinik theology, and spiritual deliverance is granted by a water-deity. The Arch, the Pillar and the Dim Sea are The Protectors, bestowed upon the eyeless people ages ago by the self-proclaimed god they worship, Kechekenibek, who is none other than the White Whale of many legends.

- The Diviner

CHAPTER LII

Raven

After at least a day spent mostly in hiding and no further visits from guards or wraiths, the compartment door creaked open. I sparked up the bog stone. A Gloom stood facing the opening in a watchful way, dried blood smeared from his cheek to the bristled eye socket above it. He hooked the chain dangling above his head to the door handle and let the metal slab relax, suspended. His voice was coarse and he seemed to struggle with every syllable.

"Out <click> Out now. Go <chirr>."

It was a welcome change from the words that had kept me huddled in darkness, my only companion a stuffy, stinking corpse. "Guards hall <click>. Stay," he had said many times.

I peeled off the hood of Holly's cloak and dispensed with the scrap of scented cloth that I had been given to breathe through; it was a thin disguise for the deathly odor in the confined space. I crawled past the fallen Harrowian and slid out of her compartment onto the floor. My head ached with the motion and my legs felt nearly as stiff as those of my bunkmate. I walked it off, giving each leg a shake to get the blood flowing. The room had been put to order again, fully restored since the ransacking.

While in hiding, I had heard the Il'kinik occupants squabbling over something unknown to me. Now that I was out of the cavity, they all bunched together, nearly nose to nose, muttering clicks and clacks punctuated with excitable chirrs and trills. No doubt, my presence had much to do with it. I stood aside to let them sort it out, whatever it was, and to stretch my tight muscles and make myself limber again. When the argument was over, they split up and got busy on a new task. The room, so neat and tidy, quickly began to come undone again, as each seemed bent on fouling the majority of the substances and implements in their stores.

"Are you sure you want to do this?" I asked the one who had set me free.

"Now <click> is time <chirr>," he said. I decided to help. It was liberating.

We scattered powders onto the floor, poured liquids down a central drain, and pulled up the floor grating to drop metal instruments down the hole it covered. The cadavers they left untouched.

A small collection of dusty old books lined a shelf built into the back wall – books none of them could ever hope to read. Even so, when an angry looking fellow began tearing out pages, another stayed his hand and delivered to him an earful of sharp and piercing ticks. Instead of destroying the volumes, the intervening Gloom loaded them into a carrying bag and slung them over his shoulder.

As the demolition continued, I was drawn to one of the bodies laid out on a table, the only one uncovered and ready to be worked on. She wasn't much beyond a girl by the shape of her face and the youth still showing in her skin. Her long dark hair contrasted the palest complexion. She did not look as dead as she did asleep. *A sleeping giantess*, I thought, for her length surpassed that of normal Men and Outlanders. She slept with her eyes open though. *And a noblewoman*, I gathered, by the refined features of her face and the gentleness in her hands. The native blood of the Dim Lake Tor

Lords once coursed through her veins, to be sure. Just to convince myself she was not alive, I reached out and touched her peaceful arm – it was not warm, but the skin was still soft and supple. I wondered what had brought her to such a place and what procedure had been in store for her.

By the end of the endeavor, the Bound Ones had smashed or otherwise rendered useless all of their holdings, and packed up those items deemed worthy and transportable – a serious act of defiance. If caught, the wraiths surely would slaughter them. Satisfied, one by one they exited into the hallway. Before leaving, I checked the spotter's cloak top to bottom, as carefully as I could in a hurry. The lasso maneuver had done a number on the garment, and several areas appeared to warp the background. *It will have to do though*, I decided. I donned my hood and adjusted the cloak as best I could. *It got me this far.*

On my way out, I gently closed the giantess' eyes, then left her behind. In the hallway outside the chamber, the wall sconces were lit and the walls had resumed their familiar pattern of ominous shapeshifting – no eyes. I checked both ways – all clear. Before departing, one of my companions spoke to me.

"Isotopia… go," said the Gloom. I believed this one to be a "she," but the conclusion was not obvious. The Gloom was a little taller and thinner than the others, or maybe just stood straighter, and was also fine featured. Thick white hair stuck up in tufts on the top of her head. She motioned with her hand for me to lead the way.

"Raven," I said, pointing at the first Il'kinik that I had spoken to earlier, the one with the spotted head. He stepped forward and "looked" me over – scanned is more like it.

"I don't know the way," I said. "But if you help me out of here, I will find your Isotopia. I promise. I just need to get to the surface."

Raven stepped back with a flurry of protesting chirrs, shaking his head and waving his arms at me. I stood there for a long moment, puzzled. But then I remembered the words of Nekenezitter. The Gloom with eyes had alluded to the answer; the source of Raven's unease. It had to do with the surface world: why would Isotopia – the "Land Promised" – have anything to do with his people's version of "Hell"? I tried to put him at ease.

"There might be clues about Isotopia in books, or in stories passed from one generation to the next, or in other records," I said.

Raven motioned to his companion's book bag. I nodded.

"Lots of things are in books," I explained, "and there are rooms full of books on the surface. Books are not bad, are they? Maybe that's why the answer is so hard to find – no one thought to look for Isotopia in a book."

Raven went still. "<click> Hidden <click> knowledge <click>," he said, "on Surface?"

"Yes," I said. "But it doesn't have to be hidden. And there are books you can read by feeling the words. Maybe one day…" I trailed off with the thought.

"<chirr> Bring <click> feelking books <pop> down to <Il'kinik> – Gropers?" he said, pointing to himself, and then motioning to the others.

"Yes," I said, "…for Il'kinik."

The Gloom raised his index finger to one side of his chin, snapped two rapid and sharp high-pitched clicks, and then followed with a low, popping sound. "I get it," was my guess. I started back the way I had come.

"Not <click> that way <chirr>," he said. Raven adjusted his pack and started down the hall in the opposite direction. I could not have asked for a better guide or friend in all of the Catacombs.

Marching on through the torch-lit passages, the company of Glooms proved to be less than gloomy company. Their spirits seemed high, this despite their trials with terrible wraiths, the dissention among them, and the danger looming over them by helping me. The Il'kinik clung to a kind of persevering hope – hope that their troubles might some day fade into the distant echoes of some long forgotten cave; hope that the future would give way to a sweet resonance of freedom and prosperity.

We met other groups of Il'kinik in the halls going about their business, and came upon two tower guards for a frightful minute. Without issue, we passed them all by.

As we made our way deeper into the heart of the tunnel system, the usual clicks and clacks of Gloom conversation matured into something more entertaining. The chatter took on a life of its own as streams of chirps and pops and other sharp sounds began to coalesce into a rhythm, picking up the pace of our march and bringing out the spring in our steps. Despite wanting to pass without notice, I could not help but to join in as best I could. My companions turned their heads to me one by one, quizzically. I supposed they were wondering what exactly to make of my nonsense. Slowly though, I deciphered bits and pieces of their language. Perfect memory is a great help in that regard.

After a drawn out stretch that lacked any features worth mention, the path began to slope downwards, eventually coming to a three-way branch. Raven led us through the left passage. Even I could tell it was older. The walls were still of stone block construction, but fragmented. There were no more doors, only open tunnels to lead us deeper and deeper underground. The floor became uneven and slick in places, with no shortage of fragmented rock to stumble over. The Glooms seemed better equipped to navigate the fallen debris than I did.

Without warning, the walls turned to eyes again. I kept with the middle of the group, silent, and carefully drew the cowl of my hood as tight as it would go. I did not even breathe. The Il'kinik simply carried on as usual, at unawares. The wall eyes searched for a long minute, and then faded away into the swirling backdrop.

At last, we came to an iron door, double locked by bar and key. Raven produced the key, wrestled the bar up and held the door open as the rest of us stepped through. On the other side, the stonework transitioned from well-ordered blocks to roughly hewn rock. The ceiling dropped about two feet. A full-sized man would have to stoop to make his way through.

"<click> Old workings," said Raven.

There were no torches within and the walls did not bear the swirling patterns of Taradin's Catacombs. *No more eyes*, I noted. I flipped off my hood and used the bog stone to light the way, but only sparingly, sparking it up in slow, regular pulses – just enough to catch a glimpse of the coming passage. It just so happened that my pattern of flashes closely matched the rhythm of clicks emitted by my companions.

Wispy strands of long abandoned spider webs matted the sides and ceiling in the passage ahead, and they spanned every nook and crevice. We pushed through, passing many grimy cave openings, small and infested. By the looks of the place, and by the scurrying sounds around us, the place was a nest of vermin – probably mice, rats, spiders, centipedes and other crawlers. We kept to a slightly worn path along the middle of the passage. The Glooms refrained from singing and returned to their usual clicks, except faster.

Eventually, we reached an area of the cave under construction. A work crew had partially widened the opening to a side tunnel, and then abandoned their work. Raven stopped and bit his upper lip, then shook his head in disappointment. Discarded chisels and hammers, open backpacks and personal items lay strewn about the area in front of the opening. There were enough tools for a good half dozen workers to chip away at the rock. It seemed they left in a rush. Raven made his way through the opening and beckoned the rest of us to follow. Hesitant at first and looking about nervously, the other Glooms gave in after a series of encouraging clicks from Raven.

The inside was less a cave and more the bottom of a tall and very narrow fissure in the rock. Sparse rays of natural light filtered in from far above. Dripping wet walls, unscalable, glistened red as Raven led us along the rubble-strewn path. We all struggled to keep our footing. At length, we arrived at a sharp divide in the passage – the meeting of two fissures. Before entering the new branch, Raven motioned with his hand and a single sharp tick for us to stop. Through it was a chamber, glowing red with torch light. I sheathed my stone. The Glooms went silent.

With slow and careful steps, Raven moved ahead, skillfully disguising his soft clicks in the plopping sounds of dripping water from above. Then he stopped, "peered" in with a short burst of clicks, and waited. A few moments later, he motioned us forward.

The coast clear, we followed him into a large, oval cavern with a high ceiling. Burning torches lit the way, supported by sconces of a familiar design – the same twisted faces of anguish witnessed in the hallway outside of Taradin's chamber. Jagged pinnacles of rock spiked out of the floor like the grey fangs of some great beast. The largest seven had flat tops and served as pedestals for statues. Again, ocean themes dominated. Each statue possessed a basin of some kind to catch the drips of the cave icicle hanging above it. Some held clam or cone shaped basins, filled with colorful stones and glistening coral skeletons. One statue featured a pool inside the gaping maw of a sharply inclined whale. It was the white whale again, carved with smooth, elegant curves, mathematically precise – a common feature of Harrowian artwork.

"<click> Nexus <trill> Chamber," said Raven.

Indeed, that is exactly what it was. Offshoot tunnels, seven in all including the one we entered from, fed into the cavern at varying angles, sizes and heights along the craggy wall. The Nexus Chamber's tunnels branched out in all directions: there were stairwells leading up, some smooth and some roughly hewn, together with a passage leading down, and many level to the polished floor.

On the far side of the chamber, a grand, gold-rimmed doorway stood at floor level as the main attraction. Runoff water flowed down hewn channels on either side into clamshell basins, each bearing in its waters the likeness of a shiny black pearl the size and shape of a man's heart. The doors themselves were plated with a golden whale motif and fastened shut with a short bar latch. Elegant script along the arch spelled out, in golden letters, four words of a phrase I had heard many times on my journey.

He knows the Way.

One of the seven passages – a main throughway by the size of it – stood out as being skillfully worked and lavishly decorated. A curved set of ornately carved stairs led up.

I turned to Raven and pointed to the stairs. "Is that the way out?"

"Up," he said. "<click> Surface <chirr>." He lowered his head.

I reassured him. "It's not that bad," I said. "You can come with me. You wouldn't be the first." I stopped myself from saying more, remembering the veil of secrecy under which Nekenezitter had traveled. He gave me a quizzical, head-tilting look.

"Go?" I said, pointing to the stairs.

"No. You go to Surface," he said, innocently, meaning "Go to Hell" in his parlance.

I grabbed the Gloom's wrist and tugged at him to join me. It was for his own good. But Raven would have none of it. He jerked free, threw his arms up and shot out an ear-piercing buzz with a razor-sharp edge to it. The sound struck me as an emphatic "No way! I'm not crazy! Go to Hell by yourself!" I was getting good at deciphering Gloom talk.

CHAPTER LIII

Song and trance

The Gloom stood still as stone. With his blank, grown over eye sockets, he could have been a grey statue. Had he been hunched over a little more, he might have passed for a gargoyle. I had one more thing to say to him.

"Raven," I said.

"Yes," he replied.

"I'll get you out of here."

He tilted his head, quizzically.

"Isotopia?" he replied.

"Of course," I said, "Isotopia." It was a bit of a white lie, but one I could live with. Isotopia seemed to be just about the only topic capable of releasing the Bound Ones' deep passions. It could just as easily sharpen their focus as cloud their judgment. Isotopia brought out the best and the worst in them.

I donned my hood and adjusted it so that it fit snug. Holly's scent lingered in the fabric, warm and reaching, woven in with the freshness of crushed pine needles early in spring and the slightest hint of a smoky seasoning underneath. As the soft material brushed over my face, I could almost taste her companionship.

"Can you keep an eye – I mean an ear – out for a special friend of mine while I'm gone?" I asked. "Her name is Holly. She is being imprisoned, unjustly."

"Bound <click>… like us <chirr>?" he said.

I nodded slowly, conscious of Raven's measured tempo of ticks. "Yes."

"She's about my height, with a sweet voice. Say my name to her, if you can. Please tell her I am coming for her and that I will not be long."

"Holky?" he said.

"That's right," I said, "Holly. Remember, my name is Nud. Tell her that Nud will not rest until she is free."

"<click> No go back <click>," he said. "Words… send <chirr>."

That would have to do. I nodded three times, slowly. Raven chirred again.

"The Council will act when they hear of these… atrocities against the Il'kinik. And the Bearded Hills will express outrage about what is happening here for sure – they're all Stouts, like Kabor. You've met Kabor. They get things done."

Given the two people's shared interest in mining and the mysteries of the underground world, I had in mind that Stouts would find it worthwhile to take the Bound Ones in as they would their own long lost kin. It wouldn't be Isotopia, but it would be progress. But even as the words came out, well-intended words, I knew a handful of smallfolk villages were powerless against the might of Harrow. The only true way to effect change would be to engage Gan or perhaps even Fort Abandon… if they were to sympathize, then maybe the Bound Ones would stand a chance – just maybe.

Raven nodded, slowly just as I had, and then tapped his head. "You know the way," he said, perfectly. I bade him farewell and began my climb. There were many, many stairs.

*

Softly, I crept up the helical stairwell, continually peering around the next bend as I went. Nearing the end of my climb where the stairway straightened, I first glimpsed a far wall of the next level and the very tip of what must have been the doorway leading out. From what I could see already, the room at the top of the stairs was grand and stately. The walls shone of polished stone and bore proud tapestries, the ceiling was high-arched and intricately carved, and the room itself was bright with natural light.

I peeked over the top stair for a more revealing look. The room was filled with casual loungers and lush furniture, guards in formal dress, and impressive statuettes. But that was not all. Two pairs of warning black eyes stared back, right at me. A throaty growl cut through the air. Twenty feet in, two black dogs with thick heads gawked at my position, ears perked. My heart raced and, for a moment, I doubted the cloak. Then one scanned a little to the left and a little to the right, licked its lips and sniffed the air.

"There's nothing there," said a man's voice, annoyed and authoritative. But the dogs were not convinced. Had a regular, casual person been coming up the stairs, the dogs might have yawned and let him or her pass without a fuss. But the discrepancy between that which was seen and that which was otherwise sensed disturbed them greatly.

In a sudden rush, one of the dogs bolted to the stairs, barking ferociously. His companion chased after. I gasped and scrambled back down as fast as I could. The two brutes skidded to a stop at the top of the staircase. I glanced back. They shuffled sideways on the smooth floor, crouched and barking, snarling and barring their teeth.

"What's gotten into them," said another voice from the room.

As I fled farther down the stairs, I heard choking yelps from the dogs as their master hauled them back by their collars.

There would be no getting around those beasts, I decided, not without a distraction or an entirely different way out. Defeated, I silently withdrew to the Nexus Chamber where I had said goodbye to Raven. I waited while a group of three men wearing robes and speaking in hushed tones passed by.

When their footsteps faded, I called out softly: "Raven." I should have asked him to wait for a bit, just in case things did not work out.

A little louder: "Raven!" The name echoed back through the offshoot tunnels. The walls gave no answer. Nothing stirred or sounded save drips from the ceiling and wavering shadows that swayed with the torchlight. I scanned the cave for some sign of where the Glooms might have gone. The bar latch on the heavy golden doors had been lifted. I stepped softly to the arch and pushed hard at one of the doors. It glided open.

I entered the empty hall and cast off my hood. A salty current of air swept over me. The throughway was elaborate, its floor blood red and polished granite. Hanging lanterns cast an orange glow over rich depictions of old Akeda, done in fresco along the walls. The ceiling was arched and richly gilded, end to end. I walked on through to the other side, passing two stairways leading up.

The other end of the hall opened up into a domed coliseum. It was massive, with seating for thousands, complete with its own cove and a half-circle centre-stage that bulged into its placid waters. Two small circular pools appeared a ways back from the waterline on the stage itself. I stepped in and felt the airiness of the structure's volume. Immensely open and lavish to the extreme, it had to be the most fantastic underground chamber ever known.

Pole-mounted torches and bright lanterns along the walls glazed the interior with a fiery glow. Bright red banners decorated the stands. Stretching over the inlet to the cove, a fantastic archway framed a watery view of twilit shores – the sunless sea of the leviathan. There, the waterway pinched to a narrow channel that met open water.

The emptiness and solitude of the place seemed altogether off. Even the water did not seem quite right, so clear and still and reflective of fire. Over the haunting silence, I could almost hear the roar of a thousand voices.

Once my eyes met the wall decor, there was no turning away. A kind of morbid curiosity set in. Violent scenes erupted out of the stonework, some large and lifelike, chiseled out of the natural rock of the cavern, others miniature and painted on flat surfaces of varying proportions. The scenes were arranged in panels, each separated from the next by a mast-like column, crows' nest and all. Above was the domed ceiling, intricately carved and decorated, with a squat, inverted rendering of the Iron Tower at its apex. Bright light shone through crystalline facets mounted on the miniature battlement.

"What is this place?" I called out. Unexpectedly, I received an answer – a familiar trill erupted from the stands. Raven popped up out of hiding, followed by his hesitant cohorts. "Back? <click><chirr>" he said.

"Guards, dogs, top of stairs," I said, mimicking his manner of speaking, then I made a barking sound.

"Oh," said the Bound One.

Before I could elaborate, he raised one hand and shook his head. He had something to say to the others, and consulted them with a flurry of quick beats. They chittered back and forth for some time while I waited. Finally, he turned my way again.

"No <click><click> problem," he said. "<chirr> Free Bound <click> Ones." He began nodding his head as he spoke. "<click> Bound Ones run everywhere <chirr>. Guards come; <clack> dogs chase; round up. Nud leave when guards gone <trill>." He stopped nodding and waited for my reaction.

"But the wraiths—" I began. Raven cut me off.

"<chirr> No wraiths. We say ground shake, <click> rocks crack <clack>." He nodded his head again, and actually smiled. "Happens. <click-click> Never come <tick> for that."

It was a great idea, and I was out of options. Raven seemed to know what he was doing, so I put my trust in his plan. I think that more than anything, he wanted me to fulfill my promise and find Isotopia. It is what they all wanted.

"Do I just wait here then?" I asked.

He lifted one hand to eye level, four fingers showing. "Four hours <click-click-click-click>. Highest cave <click> Nexus Chamber <clack>… be there," he said. "Guards, dogs <click> go down. <click> Nud <tick> go up <chirr>."

I reiterated his plan. "Yes. Nud waits high tunnel. Dogs, guards go down other tunnel. Nud leaves, up the stairs."

Raven nodded.

"No guards up there."

He nodded again.

"How will I know four hours have passed?" I said.

"You <click> not count? <clack>" he replied.

"No," I said.

"Eight <click> guard patrols. <trill> Leave by <clack> seventh to be sure. <tick>"

"OK," I said. "That makes sense."

"Soon go," said Raven. "First, <click> honor <click-click> Bound Ones. <click><clack> Lost." He pointed to the sea.

"Here?" I said. "The stadium?"

"Ritual," said Raven.

From what I could gather of his choppy explanation that followed, Dromeron Odoon entertains its own version of the same brutal practice. The Il'kinik rulers, it seems, are about as humble as those in Harrow: they honor the very best workers, slaves and scholars by sacrificing them. But they do not deem themselves or their kin worthy of such an honor, excepting a few isolated cases that had more to do with rivalry or politics than honor. Sadly, the Bound Ones must endure sacrifice both in Harrow and in Dromeron Odoon.

Raven and the others congregated at the central platform and stood facing the Dim Sea. As they exchanged hushed clicks at a slow tempo, I stepped past them along the water's edge and marveled at the massive columns supporting the arch, and then at the arch itself. A white whale, jutting out in high relief, formed its keystone. Something was off about the whale though. On closer examination, I could see that the creature had many sets of eyes, extending diagonally from just above the crease of the mouth halfway to the blowhole. Writhing tentacles lashed out in a flailing pattern from the forebody, clutching a woman who looked to be at peace.

I gasped. *The leviathan?*

Finally, it struck me. *But it can't be... why would Harrow offer up sacrifices to the White Whale?* The notion didn't make any sense. The leviathan that I met was helpful and wise, and would never lower himself to such a level – accepting sacrifices. Plus he's a he, and Karna – whom they worship – was always depicted as a she, a goddess. The beast I knew would much rather exchange news and stories with someone than witness that person sacrificed in his name, wasted, and the knowledge he or she possessed lost to the world, forever.

My mind raced. Kechekenibek was the name the Glooms gave to the White Whale. Karna was the Orbweaver in stories and the one Harrow took to be a goddess worthy of sacrificing their own citizens to. None of it made sense.

I looked through the arch to the waters of the leviathan. A few stretched fingers of ambient light reflected off the rippled surface to the greater blackness beyond. Rushing water sounded somewhere in the far-off distance. The soft noise seemed to filter in from all directions.

My chest heaved. I felt heavy.

And in that heavy moment, gently swelling over the rush of the far off falls and the rhythmic train of caressing wavelets, the most beautiful music filled my ears and prickled into my spine. It was nothing like anything I had ever heard before. Entranced, I turned to face my gloomy-no-more rescuers. They stood together on the central platform, united in voice and mind, blank eyes riveted on the open sea. Their voices, if indeed so plain a word as "voices" could describe the sounds they crafted, were purely ethereal. And as they wove crescendos, the uplifting joy of life and the brilliance of being awakened inside of me, like a fire rekindled. And as their tones deepened, my heart and soul fell through the hard stony earth, to touch loss unbearable and longing unfathomable... and the overwhelming desire to call back the dead from dark waves.

And there was no chorus. A chorus would bring you back, but this song marched ever forward, unrelenting. And when the song reached its climax, anyone listening would know it had to end that way, and that the only road to absolution was to complete the song right then and there, lest it linger and be diminished, never to rise again to such fantastic heights and such profound glory. In the final bar, the hymn released the living to life and sealed the dead in their watery tombs, forever subaqueous.

CHAPTER LIV

The sunless bay

E very half hour or thereabouts, two guards poked their heads into the stadium. Sometimes they walked the stage or the stands, sometimes not. Always, they would casually look about with firm expressions, any which way. And always, they would fail to notice the quiet Pip standing in plain view, and they would fail to notice how the laboring Bound Ones made passing glances to a particular blank space along the story wall. Blank, that is, but not unoccupied.

The stunted Gloom slaves hobbled in and out frequently, running errands for their masters. Some pushed sack barrows, others bore dishes and cups or carted maintenance gear for the stadium's many facilities. A Pip's form must have seemed child-like to their faculties, compared to the heavy-built Men of Dim Lake.

Besides the guards and the Il'kinik, the occasional townsperson or touring group would also show up to mull about, marveling at the wall art or tossing stones out to sea. All the while, I played the inquisitive ghost, quietly acquainting myself with the layout of the stadium and the artful decor, and secretly dropping in on private conversations whenever I could.

One area of the stands offered prime seating with private

booths and small, lavish rooms – luxury meant for the highborn, no doubt. The wall scene above that section was the most dreadful of all. One had to stand back a ways to fully appreciate it. *They must revel in gore*, I thought.

At first glance, the foreground was similar in style to most of the other flat story panels – an ocean scene with sailing vessels and wild water, painted in graduated hues of blue and grey. But something about it stood out: the presence of the color red, for one, streaking along the swirling contours of an all-consuming whirlpool that dominated the seascape. On the near edge of the whirlpool, the dark shade of a warship with tattered sails fought the draw to the centre. Blotches of faint yellow lantern light spilled out of the aft portholes into grey mist. Surrounding the vessel the water danced, alive with bubbling white foam and spray, and contrasting the dark blue-grey of an overcast sea that stretched out to meet a weather-bearing horizon.

The shock of what I saw bobbing within the whirlpool's dark waters caused me to examine the details ever so closely. I confirmed that the image of swirling horror that bled through to the eyes was not a mistake or some trick of light – that it was meant to be seen *that way*.

The eyes could not resist but to follow the circular trail of panicked swimmers and severed body parts, set adrift in a messy red wash that rippled as it twisted downward. In the violent waters near the rotating rim, a fountain of pink spray shot up laced with white frothing. Blood and guts drew towards the depths of the maelstrom, red water gradually darkening to a central black hole. There were no sharks, as one might expect of such a dark scene. Instead, the White Whale swam amongst the carnage, torn flesh streaming from its teeth. In the background, grey ships with black sails kept a safe distance. The true-to-life detail extended to the innermost confines of the whirlpool, down to the minute figure of half a woman rapidly descending into the tightest swirls of perspective distance. No more than a thumbnail in size, as far as the eye could tell the workmanship was complete in every feature, even the dazed stare and misplaced grin etched onto her terrified face.

The hush inside the stadium was broken when a fish flopped on the surface of the cove's waters below. I turned to look. As the ripples spread out, my eyes wandered to a narrow walkway that I hadn't seen before. It began just past the arch and curved right, hugging the shoreline out of sight.

Another way out? I thought back to the daylight holes in the leviathan's vault.

With renewed hope and having had my fill of artful slaughter, I abandoned the ocean scene and descended to the stage, crossed over to the boardwalk and passed under the arch. Ambient light from the stadium revealed a small island not far off shore, little more than sheer cliffs set against a backdrop of gloomy, honeycombed rock walls, thin and frail and shadowy.

Around the first bend and after a short walk, the path led me to a small bay, complete with a wharf and jutting piers. The yellow blaze of post lanterns and the glowing windows of small, wooden shacks lit up the shoreline. The shabby shacks seemed to have sprung up out of the rock, anywhere and everywhere, without regard for order or planning. A thin trail of smoke streamed out of the pipe chimney of one shack. Teams of men and half-giants worked on the lit up piers and wharf, tending to vessels, ropes, and cargo. Small rowing watercrafts – dories – heaved and swayed gently alongside their berths.

Two larger vessels were also present, everything about them sleek and dark. Longboats, I would call them, but one much longer than the other, each with a sail and oars. They sat lonely and unoccupied. The three slips beside them were empty.

I continued to slink along the bay shore, unseen and unheard, and drew near to the shorter longboat's pier. As a ghost, I treaded softly, keeping to the edge of the walkway where the boards never creaked. Pacing alongside the longship, I saw she had a high gunwale. End-to-end she must have spanned nearly sixty feet, close to fifteen in breadth. I ran my fingers along the overlapping hull strakes. The wood was dark and dull. Scribed across her hull in elegantly scripted, dull gold letters were the words "Karna's Whim." The second longship was nearly of the same construction, but twice as long and almost as narrow, with the name "Black Sliver" on her bow in the same gold lettering.

The pier offered a better view of the shoreline than the boardwalk had. From my new position, it was hard to miss the wide cave opening on the other side of the small bay and the steady stream of traffic through it. Voices carried loudly from the throat of the passage. The wayfarers were all mariner-types, carrying ropes, packs, tackle and other such gear. Echoes revealed their talk of fish and winds and supplies and shoals. One even mentioned leviathans in the water. I watched as he led a fully loaded mule down to the wharf.

Unseen and unheard, I closed the gap to the entrance. Burning braziers stood at either side and lanterns lined the passage walls. As another group passed by, heading into the bay, I quietly stepped into the cave. I glided along one wall for several minutes, making my way in complete silence and dodging the odd passerby, until I came to a three-way split. I decided on the rightmost branch. As suspected, it wound its way back to the Nexus Chamber with the golden door. *So much for that idea,* I thought, *no new exits here.* Just as well – by my reckoning, six or seven guard patrols must have passed since Raven left, and he would be creating the diversion soon. It was time to get into position.

Activity had picked up in the Nexus. Harrowians sauntered down the stairs from the surface, casually making small talk with one another while passing through the chamber and then through the golden doors to the stadium. To keep out of the way, I flattened myself against a part of the wall where the shadows pooled, behind one of the naturally formed ground spikes.

This will complicate things, I realized. I might have to make my escape against the flow of the show-goers.

People from all walks of life had come for some special event, it seemed, all sporting their best attire. Anticipation reveled in the air. *A play*, I surmised, from the snippets of conversation that I overheard, *something about mariners battling sea monsters.*

"…never seen a leviathan before…" said one lady in a fine dress as she passed. That comment disturbed me. The woman was small for her kind and slim, probably from the coast.

At the next lull in traffic, I stepped briskly to the foot of the passage Raven had chosen and climbed a narrow flight of hewn stairs to the opening. Inside, I found a convenient cranny masked in shadows. I backed into it. As the highest cave, it made for an ideal vantage point overlooking the Nexus.

Once settled, I took the opportunity to sift through my backpack. I sipped from my waterskin and had a quick bite to eat. Half a loaf of bread and heavily salted fish tightly wrapped in paper set my head straight, compliments of Fyorn.

Without warning, the blast of a loud horn echoed out of one of the downsloping tunnels. *The alarm,* I thought. I kept watch for the guards and their dogs.

At that moment, as though the horn were his cue, a diminutive doorman entered the Nexus Chamber. He was an older man with white, wispy hair sticking out sideways from beneath his cap. He scanned the room as the blast sounded again.

He took off his hat and waved it high. "Carry on," he called out to the passersby. "Nothing to be concerned about. Carry on to witness the Miracle of Rejuvenation! Come one, come all!" The man wore a navy blue suit of fine cloth. The cap in his hand was also blue, with a gold rim. His face was oddly long – mostly in the chin area – a dwarf of sorts. By dwarf, I do not mean that he was a

Pip, a Stout, or some variety of halfling. No, he was a small man. His proportions gave him away – the larger head and stubby limbs. He might, with some effort, pass for a smaller Stout, but never a long-limbed Pip.

Mayor Otis Dagger's man? I wondered. *His informant in Harrow?*

The dwarf held the door open for the next arriving show-goers and flashed them a courteous smile, extending warm greetings as they strolled on by. As others followed, he graciously accepted the occasional gratuity dropped into his outstretched cap.

Just like Raven had promised, the commotion started with the guards. I heard the dogs barking from up the stairwell. "Clear the way, coming through," a voice boomed from the same direction.

The crowd divided, and through the open path rushed four guards and their two leashed dogs. The dwarf gave them an animated look of surprise and backed against the wall as they shot past, dogs bounding with their masters in tow. They took the down-tunnel, just as Raven had expected.

Now is my chance.

I took a deep breath, adjusted the fit of my cloak, and prepared to cross the chamber. The flow of people continued to thicken, but I would not be deterred by the crowded stairwell.

I can do this, I convinced myself. *I just have to keep quiet and weave through them.* They were not really paying attention anyway, walking and chatting away, some snacking on fruit or sipping from cups. About to leave, I thought I heard something, half a whisper maybe.

"Nud, are ya'in there?"

I didn't answer. My instincts told me to go.

"Nud," the voice whispered again, closer, louder. "I can smell the fish," it said. "Bobbin cooked'em up the other night." I looked behind me, down the passage. Rounding the corner was a Stout carrying a pick. Raven followed. They both stopped.

"Nud, are you there?" He turned to Raven. "What if he's already gone?"

I threw back my hood. "Gariff! What are you doing here?" I said.

"Nud," he came over and patted me on the back. "Glad to see yer OK." He gestured to Raven. "I met this feller here who thought I was Kabor."

"Shshsh," said Raven, holding a finger to his lips. "<click> Too loud <chirr>."

I kept my voice low. "C'mon, we can get out of here," I said to Gariff. "Now's our chance." I stood on the tips of my toes to peer behind them. "Wait a minute... where's Bobbin?"

Gariff shook his head. He spoke quietly. "Hear me out," he said.

I looked to the stairs, and back to Gariff. "There isn't much t—" He cut me off.

"Your friend here told me all about you... and what you said about Holly, so I asks him if he can bring me to ya. Then there's this big fuss and a loud horn – Did ya hear the horn? – with these little fellas running all over the place like blind mice. We have to talk."

"Who's up there?" called the dwarf by the door. Were it not for a well-timed gratuity and the accompanying obligatory acknowledgement, our presence might have been discovered. We scuttled further back into the passage, out of sight and out of earshot.

"Kabor's OK," I assured him.

"I know," he said. "Off to Webfoot."

"How d—" I started.

"I'll git to it," he said, "but first, listen."

Anxiety was building. "Tell me later," I said. "I can't wait. This whole crisis is a fake – it's just a distraction to get me out – us out... NOW. But we have to get moving. I'm coming back for Holly... Bobbin too. I can't get them out without help from the

Council and help from Gan. Fyorn will know what to do… and whom to raise the issue with."

"Whom to raise the issue with?" Gariff gave me a look as though I didn't know what the heck I was talking about. He shook his head again and folded his arms. He wasn't going to budge.

I bit my lip and looked to the stairs. They were empty for the first time in a long time.

"Gariff!" I complained.

"First off," the Stout began, as if he had all day, "Bobbin and I went lookin' fer ya's in town here and gots into a bit a trouble. It's Bobbin – he'll strike up a conversation with just about anyone. I blame everything on his flapping lips. He just doesn't know when to shut up sometimes. Anyways, he see's this humongous off-duty guard sittin' on a pile of logs set there to make repairs, just outside the Harrow Inn. Well, Bobbin drags me over and starts yappin' in his ear."

"Can't we sort this out later? We can both hide in Holly's cloak. The stairs…"

"There isn't gonna be a *later*," he said. "If we don't fix this *now*. You need to hear this."

Finally, what he was trying to say hit me. It hit me like a heavy weight sunk deep into my stomach. I had an awful feeling… very awful… about what he was going to say next. I didn't want to even think about that feeling, let alone have it. But it wouldn't leave. The worried expression on Gariff's face only amplified my fears. I lowered my head and nodded. His words were changing everything. There would be no quick escape up the grand stairwell leading out.

Gariff went on with his recount of all that had happened.

"So the big lug asks him, 'Is you a Pip?' And so Bobbin says, 'Yep, pippy as they git.' Then Bobbin sneaks me a smirk, and this guy stands up and blocks out the sky – not just the sun, the 'whole' sky, clouds and all. Then the guard says to 'im, point'n his giant finger at me, 'Is this oaf a Stout?' I didn't fancy being called an oaf."

"'Yep', says Bobbin, 'as stoutly as they git.'"

"Well, Bigfoot cracked a big'ol half-toothless grin from up there in the clouds. 'Well, it's me lucky day,' he says like he's some kind o'half-ass pirate. 'Looks like yer comin' with me, maties, you's them two the tower guard's been after.'"

"Unbelievable," I said, recalling the moment Fyorn heard the whisper. I shook my head.

"Well, we protested that we was not 'them two,' whatever two he was talking about. Turns out half the city was looking for you and Kabor, and it just so happens we fit the description perfectly – a froggy Pip and… er… a stumpy Stout."

"I know all about it," I said. "Fyorn warned me. That's why I'm here – to get you out."

"Well, fine job at that yer doin'," he said.

"You're free to go, aren't you?" I said, gesturing to the stairs.

He gave me a scornful look, and then continued with his story. He started by shaking his head, in genuine disbelief.

"That there hairy mountain giant just picked us up one at a time – Bobbin no less than by the scruff of his neck – and slung us over his wide shoulders like sacks of potatoes. Then he brought us to a room in the tower. The guard in there just sits around guarding keys, by the looks of it."

A group of young girls on their way to the stadium giggled loudly as they raced through the chamber below. A few seconds later, an older man laughed and commented to a middle-aged woman about their exuberance.

Gariff kept talking. "That giant got a reward for us too, the lousy lug – the guard flipped him a few coppers. And he smelled awful too. Bobbin said right to'im on the way over that he smelled like old beer and farts and sweaty shorts. Now *that* earned him a solid thump on the giant's shoulder. Knocked the wind clear out of the poor hopper!"

"How did you get here then, if you were jailed?" I said.

"Before we even get thrown in the slammer, this pompous sort strolls in with a glass of red wine in his hand, acting like he's King Prissy. He says to the keys guard, 'These are not the thieves we are looking for – one is too round and the other is too stocky. But thank you for your excellent service.' Then he flips him a silver. Imagine that! Just fer sitting there look'n at keys!"

"Gariff, that probably was the king," I said, "King Taeglin."

"Well, he didn't *seem* much like a king. Whatever… 'Let us go then!' I says, but the bugger just waves his hand like we don't matter and then leaves."

"And how did you get here?" I said.

"Oh ya," he said. "It gets really bad, Nud, really bad." Gariff shook his head again, pursed his lips and stomped one foot hard to the ground. "It's like Bobbin joked, but worse – oh ya, you weren't there."

"Where is Bobbin?" I said.

"I'm gettin to it," he replied. "We weren't in the clink long before some crazy bag'o bones comes to visit."

"You mean Taradin," I interjected. "The first King."

"Whatever," said Gariff. "Anyhow, first Bag'o Bones looks at me and says 'This one won't do.' Then he takes one look at my pipes…" Gariff patted his biceps. I have to admit, they were impressive. "…and he sends me down to the mining level with a pick and a bunch of eyeless freaks that just never shut up." Gariff looked over to Raven, "No offence intended."

Raven just stood there, blank.

"But before I go, Bag'o Bones looks at Bobbin and says to the guard, 'Find out more about this one.'"

Gariff had more to add. "After he sent me away, I pick'n hammered all day and slept back at my cell at night. Bobbin was right across from me. One night I came back and Holly was there right next to'im. At least we got to talk some when the guard dozed off. Bobbin said a tall, thin man visited him three times and asked him all sorts of questions about himself, and then wrote it all down. Holly too."

Gariff drew in a deep breath and let it out slowly. He put his pick down against the wall.

"But that's not the worst of it, Nud," he continued, shaking his head, "That's not the worst of it."

"So, Raven freed you with the other slaves?" I said.

"Raven? Oh… this fella? Yep, but there's something you gotta know." Gariff steadied his gaze, his eyes on mine. Then he looked down, shoulders slumped, deflated.

"Nud," he said, staring at his boots.

The strange feeling worsened in the pit of my stomach. The Stout looked up, eyes begging.

"'Bag'o Bones' has Holly pegged for some kind of wicked ceremony; Bobbin too. It don't sound good, Nud. It don't sound good at all."

I felt sick.

"We have to do something," I said. Gariff nodded.

And then I remembered my deal with Raven. I felt even more sick. I looked to him. His hopes hung on my shoulders – all their hopes, the Il'kinik. We had a deal.

"I'm sorry," I said to him, "Isotopia has to wait."

Raven shrugged. "Plans change," was all he said.

It put me off guard, how easily he accepted the collapse of our grand scheme. I thanked him profusely for his patience.

"Time <click> short," he went on <click>. "Burning arch <chirr>. Kechekenibek take <click> knowledge <chirr>."

"What does that mean?" said Gariff.

I already knew the answer and it was not pleasant. It came from all the legends. He meant *devour* and *archive*. It finally occurred to me that the central platform in the stadium was not just for show. It was an altar, with stairs descending into the waters of the leviathan. And through the act of devouring, knowledge lost by one would be gained by another.

CHAPTER LV

Clear as mud, Nud

No, *it just won't work.*
Fleeing from Harrow just to organize a long-winded political response through official channels would be a death sentence for my good friends. How could I ever face Mr. and Mrs. Numbit again, after losing two at once? How could I live with myself?

No, circumstances called for a new plan. The lives of Holly and Bobbin depended on it. They depended on me. And all I had to work with was my bog stone, an obstinate Stout, and a blind but friendly Gloom with underworld connections.

Gariff was fidgety. His hands seemed to have minds of their own, acting as though they could do something about the situation just by pulling at one another or waving about. He kept staring at his boots as he shuffled back and forth.

"Nud," he said, "can't you just call a meeting or something right here and now, and spring them with fancy talk? Yer diplomatic mumbo jumbo? That's what yer good at, isn't it?"

I shook my head. "I thought I was good... until now. I can't reason with the leadership here. They just do what they want to do. And I have nothing to hold over them to make them listen."

Gariff shook his head. He looked pale.

"Dealing with Taradin is out of the question," I continued. "He's just mad. Maybe Taeglin, if I could meet with him. But I really doubt it from everything Paplov told me. Even if he agreed to see me, what do I have to offer that might compel him to go against his own flesh and blood?"

"There's barely any flesh and blood on him," said Gariff. "There has to be something you can do, Nud... Anything."

My mind was still numb with all the bad news.

Gariff kept talking. "Maybe we can just rush in, grab'em, and rush out."

"No," I said. "That won't work." I turned to the Gloom. He seemed very interested in everything that was happening.

"Raven," I said. "I need to speak with Gariff alone for a bit... we need to make an important decision."

"Arone?" he replied.

"Yes, alone," I said.

Raven nodded politely and disappeared down the passage and out of earshot. If he was offended, he didn't show it. The Stout leaned against the wall of the tunnel and put his hands in his pockets. I gathered my resolve.

"Gariff," I said, "I need you to go with Raven."

Looking down at his boots again, he bit his lip and shook his head.

"What am I gonna do with the likes of him?" he said. "No, no Nud. I'm stick'n with you."

I chose my next words carefully. "I need you to go with Raven. You need to convince him that if he can get help to rescue Holly and Bobbin, we will show them the way to Isotopia."

"Isotopia?" he said.

"Yes. It's like 'Heaven' to them. They'll do anything to get there – the slaves will, not the slave masters. They will need to be convinced though... and fast."

"What makes you think they'll believe we can bring 'em there?" said Gariff.

"They have a prophecy, that someone with 'The Fifth' – who can see – will lead them to Isotopia."

"That could be just about anyone, 'cept them."

"But they've only ever known wicked Harrowians here in the Catacombs. That's why they keep asking about Isotopia. We're the first they've met that don't treat them that way, and I'm sure the fact we are more their size doesn't hurt either."

"So, ya think they really believe it?"

"Yes, I do. And we can deliver. You know the Bearded Hills will make a place for them."

Gariff nodded. "It won't be Isotopia."

"They can call it that, if they want to. Tell them about the mines you admire the most. Tell them about the vein of gold that runs like a river. They'll like that."

"I sort of made that one up."

"Tell them anyway."

"Why me? Why not just send Raven?"

"You have to find the one named 'Clickety-clack' or something or other – Kabor got to know him. He flies… giant beasts – Kabor calls them stone ghosts."

"Stone ghosts are real?" he said.

"Sure as I'm standing here," I said. "And tell him you're Kabor's brother."

"But he's my cuz—"

"You two are practically brothers."

I gave Gariff some time to sort through the proposition. In the minute that followed, the Stout measured his worth. I could nearly see the indecision churning in his head, weights balancing on a scale. In the end, and without another word to the contrary, he nodded.

"I'll do it," he said.

I smiled at his nervousness. "It's the only way," was all I could say. Gariff grabbed his newly acquired pick and we caught up with Raven.

I tried to repeat the pilot Gloom's name to Raven, as Kabor had said it to me, but "Clickity-clack" did not ring any bells with him.

"<click> I will ask <clack>," he said.

My plan was for Clickity-clack – or whatever his real name was – to swoop in from the open water on his flying mount, drop out of the dark heights and whisk Holly and Bobbin away the moment they appeared on stage, just as Kabor had rescued me. Unprepared, I wagered that few, if any, of even the half-giant variety would dare mess with such a frightful beast as a full-grown cloaker. And it would happen fast – a quick "grab and go." I explained every-thing to Gariff and Raven. When I was done, I turned to my Gloom friend.

"Watch out for the guards," I said to Raven.

"<click> I will," he chirred.

I didn't realize until later that I had used the word "watch."

"Catch ya at the Flipside after this one," said Gariff.

"I owe you a barkwood," I replied.

With those parting words, the two unlikely companions went on their way.

*

Until their return, my role was to do the only thing I could think to do: keep tabs on events in the stadium and be prepared to act when the time came, with or without help from the stone ghost riders. I had no idea exactly what I might try to do, especially if things did not go as planned. Something would be done though, no matter what. I had to, for Holly's sake, and Bobbin's... and for Mr. and Mrs. Numbit.

CHAPTER LVI

Diversion

I'd like to say I had a plan. And I'd like to say that plan included a clever diversion, a coordinated break out, and a daring escape, all orchestrated by yours truly. But there was no *real* plan. A *real* plan does not hinge on an off chance, in this case, an uprising of disgruntled stone ghost riders. That might be called "hope" or "desperation." Most certainly, it does not constitute a well-defined course of action. That is what I needed – a well-defined course of action. No, the odds did not look good, but there was still time. And a little time can reveal its own mysterious value in equally mysterious ways.

Certain undeniables about the situation kept gnawing at me. No matter how I played the scene out in my mind, any rescue ended seaward. By the time the ritual started, the guards and their dogs would be back at their posts, so a quick escape up the stairs was out of the question. If we fled to the back tunnels, the wraiths surely would hunt us down, and even if they didn't, we would be faced with the difficult problem of finding another way out. No... the trick would be to break out and make our getaway across the open water, before a pursuit could be organized, and then disappear amidst the maze of honeycombed rock walls. With the stone ghost riders on hand, that task could be trivial. Without them, a breakout seemed impossible. We could still head for the waters, but the leviathan would be waiting. *Maybe I could convince him to let us pass.* I quickly dismissed the notion.

I knew what I had to do. Padding softly and wrapped in Holly's elderkin cloak, I retraced my steps back through the tunnel to the sunless bay and the boats. The wide passage made it easy to avoid bumping into anyone and those traversing it were far too caught up in conversations about the sacrificial ritual to notice my passing. "Who will it be this time?" they asked one another. An elderly woman commented: "My favorite part is the thrashing, with the body still in its mouth." I wondered what these same people might be talking about after it was all over: "Did you see that crazy Pip run in and try to save the girl, and then get eaten?"... perhaps.

When I reached the divide in the tunnel, hints of smoked fish on a steady breeze beckoned me towards the wharf. I only met a handful of mariners along the stretch of tunnel that led there, and they were easily avoided. At the bay, I first made my way to an old, abandoned-looking shack that leaned heavily to one side. Its crooked and splintered door hung open, supported by little more than a sliver. Set atop a high rocky outcrop, the shack provided a wide view of the wharf. On the other side of the bay, smoke billowed out of the pipe chimney of a slightly less dilapidated shack – the source of the fishy smell.

Activity in the bay had dropped to only a few scattered hands. I slipped into the shack and rummaged about. The place was a wreck, but I did manage to find a tinderbox, a rusty old fisherman's knife, and some lamp oil in a collapsed cupboard. By the time I snuck a peek out through a broken window, the remaining dockworkers were all heading for the other side of the bay. They disappeared inside the smoking shack.

I snuck down to the waterline, unhitched the smallest dory on the pier, climbed in and quietly began rowing out of the bay. A dog barked at me from in front of the smoking shack, but no one took notice except to shush him.

With quiet strokes, I paddled along the coast to the mouth of the great stadium's inlet. No one seemed to notice. Even as I rowed to shore, nearing the arch, I did not have a plan beyond creating options for myself. My head started racing. If the Bound Ones did not show up, I would have to create a distraction to draw people's attention away from Holly and Bobbin. *Then,* I imagined, *using the cloak, I just might be able to slip past the onlookers and the guards, cut my friends loose and make them disappear with me. Holly and Bobbin would vanish right out from under their noses.* That was a Kabor move, so bold and unthinkable it just might work. I only hoped that we could all squeeze together tight enough to fit under the cloak.

The only real distraction I could think of was to set the rowboat on fire and launch it across the mouth of the cove with a firm push. With all eyes on the burning boat, I could attempt my disappearing act. That was it. That was my plan. Nothing else sensible even came to mind. Sure, I tried to come up with a legal argument that would hold water, something I could just blurt out that would bring official process down to bear on the heinous ritual. In thinking it through though, it became evident that Harrow regarded their own laws and customs as the only ones worthy of consideration. Harrow would find some way to justify the sacrifice of two harmless Pips to a hungry whale. The reasons did not matter. All that ever matters is that Harrow gets what Harrow wants.

To hide the boat from prying eyes, I brought it ashore and dragged it under a raised part of the walkway. I gently placed the oars inside and then doused the boat's interior with the lamp oil I had taken.

There was nothing left to do but wait and watch as the masses poured into the stadium to claim their seats. The event was shaping up to be standing room only. It would not be long before the stadium filled to capacity. Indeed, as I sat and watched, the golden doors soon slammed shut with a loud clang.

Serving men and women, showing exceptional poise and grace, kept everyone of status comfortable. Beer, wine, and steaming appetizers were made available to all of the affluent. The masses, on the other hand, formed long lines around small serving booths that suddenly sprung into existence throughout the common stands.

When the ceiling torches finally dimmed and the last of the highborn took to their seats, the drone of casual conversations escalated to a dull cheer. Musicians were the first to spill out onto the stage, dressed in sharp black and bright white, attended to by an entourage of chair and instrument bearing Glooms to help them set up.

As the musicians took their seats and warmed their instruments, the crowd murmured on. I crept a little closer to get a better view, and found good cover just back of the arch. Finally, the conductor stood in front of his band. He raised his hand high; a hush came over the crowd. And when he lowered his hand, the air resonated with the beginnings of a lively mariner tune.

The crowd "oohed" and "awed" later on when acrobatic dancers tumbled onto the scene, rolling and throwing themselves about the stage. They topped off their performance with a series of springing dives into the cove. All in all, they were nearly as talented as the Flipside performers.

Next, the crowd marveled at twin, scantily clad contortionist sisters. While balancing upside-down on one hand, each held a bow with one foot and drew a bowstring with the toes of the other, legs impossibly bent backwards. They released their arrows at one another. The crowd gasped. The blunted shots collided in mid-air and stuck together, then dropped to the floor as one. The audience went wild with applause.

Songs, dances and more feats were offered up to the crowd in the plenty before the music subsided and an intermission was announced. The aroma of steamed shellfish filled the air as a new wave of vendors fought their way through the common stands to pawn beverages and niblets, no doubt for exorbitant prices. During that time, Bound Ones cleared the staging area.

It was time for the main attraction.

CHAPTER LVii

Ritual of the brilliant

A slim, well-poised man stepped out onto the stage. He stopped, and turned only his head to smirk at the crowd. A buzz of expectation electrified the air, building to a dull cheer. They knew him well. With his back to the audience, the man strolled casually to the central platform. He was not overly tall for these parts – the height of a normal man, well groomed and finely dressed, all in light blue save for his white, frilly shirt.

"Lord Marlin!" cried members of the crowd, sporadically.

"Lord Rhyale!" cried one vocal woman, high and clear above the rest. At that prompting, one of the more handsome noblemen in the stands stood up and waved to the crowd. A Tor Lord, no doubt, by the looks of him, so tall and proud, puffing out his chest. More wooing women cried out his name in chorus. Lord Rhyale waved to them all before reclaiming his seat.

All eyes soon returned to Lord Marlin, who displayed a talent for showmanship. The crowd adored him, which might strike one as odd at first because he, in turn, was quite dismissive of his audience. It was his game and they knew it. They had to be louder to get his attention.

"Marlin… Marlin… MARLIN… MARLIN!" they chanted,

and continued chanting. There were no more "Lord Rhyale's" to be heard. "Ogres!" bellowed over the chant, and many smiled or chuckled at that.

When it seemed the cavern roof would collapse from the sheer volume of noise, sudden flames sprung up from the edge of the stage and the central platform. Swaying, colored light filtered up from the bottom of the two small pools. Marlin, facing the sea, threw his arms up into the air as though reaching to the sky beyond the stone. The chanting turned roar, and the longer he stood there soaking in the fame, the more deafening the roar of the crowd became. He turned to face them, and was met with wild screams. A faction began to chant his name again. It grew louder and more rhythmic as it spread from end to end. At last, they were his. All eyes on him; all minds bent to his will.

Marlin raised one hand and waved it slowly around the room. His loyal subjects gave him silence.

"Thank you," he said at last, tossing them one small morsel of the recognition hungered for. The lord's voice was strong and carried with it an air of refinement. "I want to thank you all for coming out tonight," he began. "Twice a year, Harrow comes here to pay tribute to the glorious Karna and her messenger, and to honor our best and our brightest. Twice a year, you bear witness to the abandonment of flesh as the mind ascends to become one with the divine. For this, I thank you all."

The crowd cheered high praise, and then dampened to a hush again.

"We have a spectacular evening planned for you," and then he paused, "...and an absolutely *brilliant* line-up!"

The audience applauded, and Marlin went on to introduce himself – as "Lord Marlin of Ogres" no less – and followed with eloquent words for his noble kin. Among them sat Taeglin and Taradin, dressed in rich purple robes. They were next on his list, followed by the many Tor Lords, their Ladies and even their mistresses.

"Taeglin, Keeper of the Iron Tower and the Crown," started Marlin. Taeglin sipped red wine from a rich goblet and raised it in toast, to himself no doubt.

"And his father of old, the founder of this brave city of Harrow, I give you Taradin, Vicegerent of Harrow, and the First King of Fortune Bay!" Taradin lifted a boney hand in acknowledgement of the lord's introduction, but remained mostly out of sight. Tall, slender serving girls attending to him competed for his attention, and a step back stood two Red Maidens, on guard and holding firm their pole arms. The crowd was less than enthusiastic at the calling of Taradin's name and that of his son of sons. Nonetheless, the Lich King drew many a stare.

Then there was Lady Gilirain of Limbo, Ambassador Crulerion – a Gloom, and of course handsome Lord Rhyale of the Western Tor. Then there were Ladies Barra and Ganadra, and Grenna. After Marlin said Grenna's name, he paused for a brief moment; just long enough to mouth the words of her less than flattering, non-official title. I had heard of her. "Grenna the Sea Bitch," many said. She was as haggard in appearance as her name implied, with long, knotted hair and greenish, wrinkled skin – reminiscent of a bog queen. The empty air seemed to resonate with her unspoken title. And lastly, even visitors of note from Gan made attendance: "Lady Elise Faelin accompanied by Lord Sevaleyr the Crystal Grey." There were others among the nobles, ladies and gentlemen of various sorts, the likes of which he brushed over with a single statement of introduction: "...and the other fine Ladies and Gentlemen in attendance."

Some of the highborn afforded a weak wave to the crowd as though it were a chore; others raised a hand dismissively. Only Lord Rhyale stood high and mighty among them, one strong arm raised high and mighty in-and-of itself. His eyes scanned the audience for attractive young women, and he basked in the splendor of their suggestive remarks, exaggerated poses and crazed admiration. One overly excited girl flashed him some skin when he looked her way. Those beside him smirked, or shook their heads, or whispered to one another. Rhyale raised an eyebrow, smiled and nodded to the girl.

Taradin remained subdued among his noble kin, withdrawn in the shadows of his private booth, away from prying eyes. He wore a dark purple hood atop his long robe. Back when he had entered, many eyes followed him until he was seated and out of sight.

Marlin called back the crowd's attention.

"Let us begin with a glorious memory from the past," he said. The charismatic lord strolled this way and that way as he spoke, pointing to individuals in the crowd and nodding his head.

"Some of you, yes you, and you, you too, may recall a small group of brilliant little Outlanders who graced our hall some years ago. They came upon us from a little-heard-of village in the marshes. You may also recall that Karna's Messenger was especially pleased with that year's harvest of fine minds. Although barely a morsel to the physical being of Karna's great vessel, the sweet nectar of their intellects was fit for the divine!"

The crowd cheered, and many chanted: "WE LIVE FOR GLORY!"

My stomach dropped. A terrible thought crossed my mind, watching the events unfold from behind the arch. I mouthed the words. "Who? When?... Mother? Father?"

Marlin continued to inform his townsfolk. "Today we have a special treat to refresh that knowledge and close the festival. Giants of the Tor, Men of Harrow, Gropers of Dromeron Odoon,... Grenna," the crowd laughed, "lend me your hands for the one and only." He looked down to a card, carried in his hand. "Bobbin Numbit!"

From the back hall, a giant, muscular man pushed Bobbin out

onto the walkway. The man wore only a white loincloth with black and gold trim, together with a wide bead necklace – deep blue and white. The Pip was bound, gagged and frightened. He looked like a scared rabbit, and a well-fed one at that.

"Have you ever wondered what it would be like to be young again?" Marlin asked the crowd.

"FOREVER YOUNG!" came the reply.

Lord Marlin pulled another card out of his vest pocket and read from it. "Bobbin Numbit is an innkeep's son. He is twelve years old. He knows every rumor this side of the Outlands and every story that ever passed through the most popular inn on the bog! Karna has a sudden interest in those quaggy waters. Let's hear it for Bobbin!"

The crowd applauded. Some blew whistles at that point and others rang bells or banged sticks together. Bobbin was "led" to centre stage.

Nervously, I scanned seaward for Gariff and Raven. It had been hours. I looked to the sky-ceiling of the Dim Sea and to the openings in the rock walls, hoping to catch a glimpse of a gliding cloaker. But there was nothing. I needed to act soon, but not before seeing Holly, not unless absolutely necessary.

"Before we move on to deliver our first gift, I'd like everyone to think back to the message that Karna's Messenger blessed us with at the Opening Ceremonies a few days ago. You all heard it, loud and clear."

The crowd did not respond. "Oh, come on now!" cried Marlin.

Taeglin stood up from his chair amidst the nobles, swishing his goblet of wine and slurring his words. "I will help them, Lord Marlin of Ogres," he said. Taeglin beckoned the audience with open arms, and bellowed out. "Seek the stones with fire inside, the spark that never dies!" he cried.

"HE KNOWS THE WAY!" answered the crowd.

"Take what is ours!" cried Taeglin.

"IT'S WHAT WE WANT!" answered the crowd.

Taeglin raised his goblet again to the audience in approval, drank deep, and nearly missed his seat when he sat down. In return the audience, suddenly warm to the rightful heir and already under the spell of consumed spirits, cheered Taeglin on.

I began to piece together the role that I had played in the events unfolding in front of my eyes and the role of the leviathan as well. Karna's Messenger – the leviathan – had gone so far as to command Karna's subjects to dig up the bog for stones that *I* had told him about. And that isn't all I told the leviathan – I told him *everything*. The chain of disasters seemed to lead straight back to me, to the conversation I had with the White Whale. *Did I do this?*

The announcer took over where Taeglin left off. "Harrowians, what do we want?" he said.

"SPARKS!" cried the crowd.

"Why do we want them?" he cried back. A long pause followed. "IT IS…" He led the audience on, rolling his hand at them in tight circles.

"KARNA'S WHIM!" answered the crowd. Lord Marlin nodded in satisfaction.

"Thank you," he said.

Apparently, that was enough. *Unbelievable,* I thought. *"Karna" tells them what they want, commands them to get it, and then calls it his "gift" to them. How wonderfully convenient.*

Lord Marlin reached into his pocket again. This time he pulled out a plain iron chain and held it up for all to see. The audience gasped in amazement.

"Behold! The first reward of Karna's Whim!" On the chain, Holly's SPARX stone dangled for all to see, sparking green fire.

"Who leads the path to rejuvenation!" he cried.

"WE DO!" rang out a great many voices. The crowd roared, clapping their hands, ringing their bells, blowing their whistles and beating on their small drums.

Next, Marlin pointed to Bobbin. "That one is big on knowledge, but he makes a small, rather round morsel." Bobbin shook his head frantically. The crowd laughed.

"So, we are going to double it up for you tonight, folks! Lend me your hands once again, this time for the lovely, wonderful, street smart and full-of-spunk, Holly Hopkins!"

My heart sank. A sickening feeling swelled inside me. Holly was shoved and dragged out to the central platform in the same manner as Bobbin. They had her dressed in elegant, white, ridiculous evening wear. I crept in closer for a better look – nearer to the arch.

Marlin took out another card to read from, then put his arm around Holly's shoulder. He dangled her stone in front of her eyes. "Recognize this, my dear?" he said.

Holly's angry response was muffled and restrained. She had been bound and gagged just like Bobbin.

The host continued on. "Holly here works at the same inn as Bobbin and has the same perfect memory. That's right my countrymen. A perfect memory! Apparently, she's a *real* know-it-all."

"And… she knows everybody's secrets – including where to find the sparking stones." Marlin shook his head slowly, and shook one raised finger at her as well. "But she won't share her secrets with us, folks." The crowd booed.

"But guess what?" Marlin continued. "She'll share them with Karna! Not only that, citizens of Harrow, Giants of Tor." Marlin paused to press his index finger to his lips. He let go of Holly and rushed to one side of the stadium, then whispered loudly to those nearby. "She's never known a man." He rushed to the middle crowd, "Never once," then to the other side, "She doesn't know *everything* after all, does she?"

Marlin returned to centre stage, gestured to Holly, and proclaimed loudly: "A perfectly pure sacrifice, fit for the divine! Let's hear it for Holly Hopkins!"

The crowd was ecstatic. They roared, and initiated a fateful chant.

"KAR-NA... KAR-NA... KAR-NA..."

The arch flared up. I jumped back and only barely avoided being set on fire. All eyes turned to the open water. I could not resist the temptation to do the same. And that's when I saw the leviathan for the second time, gliding in alone from the edge of darkness: slow, steady and purposeful. I looked back to the two helpless Pips. Each struggled against a guard's hold at the top of the stairs on the platform. Bobbin's toes dipped in and out of seawater. With a smirk on his face, the guard holding the terrified soul lowered and then lifted him, again and again. The Pip's eyes were as wide as the moon.

Bobbin and Holly also marked the advance of Karna's Messenger. And they knew what it meant. One shove and a splash was all that separated them from certain death.

No one was coming to save them. *It's now or never.*

The time for my distraction had come. I felt my pocket for the tinderbox. It was still there. I stepped back towards the dory, and bumped right into something big.

I turned around and saw only boots, and then I looked up. A giant stood there. He was of the mariner type, by his salt and pepper grizzled beard, his thick wool sweater, and the cap he wore.

He could not have seen me properly, but he hauled me up just the same before I could say "boo" and stripped the cloak right off my back. I yelped. I don't know how I didn't notice him. I got my distraction all right, but not the one intended.

"What've we got here?" he growled.

The giant's actions did not go unnoticed by the audience. People pointed my way at the commotion as I struggled to free myself. They exchanged puzzled looks and a chorus of whispers quickly rose out of the stands.

The mariner had probably come over to investigate and became caught up in the fanfare as I had, standing in the same place I had chosen by virtue of its combination of superior view and superior cover so as not to attract attention. He stepped out into the open and held me up in front of him with one huge arm for all to see, like the catch o'the day. The giant looked to Lord Marlin.

"I caught yee another," he boomed, "spying, he was." Marlin was not even looking his way.

Yes, I had failed to keep a proper watch to cover that possibility; but how an ogre of a man snuck up behind me unintentionally, breathing hard, stepping heavily and smelling of fish as they often do, I will never know. Yet, there it stands as a true record of events that evening.

Marlin caught the draw of the crowd and followed their eyes to meet mine. "Well now, what do we have here?" he asked.

The crowd hushed. Karna's Messenger sensed something was afoot, and slowed his advance.

"Two's not enough," explained the mariner, "but three morsels make a nice bite for this lot, I'd say. Found this one spying, and look!" The mariner held up the cloak, invisible side out, then spun it around and around in his hand so all could see the effect of the camouflage.

"Gan is spying on us!" yelled Taradin from the stands. His voice was weak and coarse compared to the other speakers. Then he coughed desperately. The two Elderkin looked to one another, nervously.

There were catcalls from the audience, accusations of all kinds, and derogatory remarks about Pips, the Elderkin, and Stouts; even Glooms were not spared. A cantankerous old man yelled out, "Gan has broken the *Non-aggression Treaty*, so why shouldn't we?"

Lord Marlin raised his hand at the crowd. They hushed.

"What's going on?" I asked, stupidly. I knew full well what was happening. Perhaps a part of me wanted to hear him say it, or perhaps I was buying time. It was just one of those things you say, and regret afterwards.

Marlin faced the audience, gesturing back to me. He addressed his people with the most sincere look on his face and concerning inflection in his voice.

"'What's going on?' said the curious halfling. The sight before him seems to be baffling."

The crowd laughed and jeered.

"Let's help him figure it out," grumbled the mariner.

"Indeed," said Marlin, looking to the crowd for their approval. He got it.

"I'm not a halfling," I started to say, but it mattered not. The remark was drowned out as the volume of cheering in the stadium soared to new heights; and higher still when the mariner hauled me to the platform, kicking and screaming, to join my companions. A new guard rushed on stage to keep me from going anywhere, as big and burly as the rest.

A small minority cried out in pity, including the doorman – I could see the empathy on his face. But most mocked me, and they mocked my friends. They went on to mock all Pips and their ilk. I got to hear how good it was that we possessed perfect memories, because otherwise we would be perfectly useless, and we were reminded of just how small and weak and scrawny we were compared to them. Someone thought we should have remembered how *not* to get caught.

Holly shook her head in disbelief at this final turn of events, at how badly things had gone. Tears were in her eyes. Bobbin quivered beside her, the pudgy rabbit in him lying low, hoping to be overlooked. The bravery he had shown against the bog queens had departed him that day. I could not fault him for it, under the circumstances. He was so very young.

For a long moment, the banter between Marlin and the crowd faded to something far-off and hollow, and my eyes locked with Holly's. Nothing had worked out for her – ever. Once again, high hopes drowned in tears.

As the White Whale drew near, an expectant hush came over the audience. He was a wondrous creature to behold, really. Majestic. When his graceful bulk loomed at the narrows of the inlet, I thought it doubtful that a creature such as this, so worldly and inquisitive, could take part in the barbarism that was to follow. I entertained the notion that, perhaps, the entire production was just for show and we would all leave unscathed, laughing at such a ridiculous prank played on unsuspecting Pips. He once showed me kindness and I had thought him an ally. After all, he went out of his way to expedite my return to the surface world.

But now he's hungry, I thought. *Hungry for knowledge. And this is no joke.*

I struggled against my captor, scheming to trip him up and topple him into the water. It was to no avail. He was too solid and the attempt was stifled by little more than a strengthening of his already strong grip. In retribution, the guard went so far as to dangle me outward above the water, feigning twice to let go. Again, I felt like the "catch'o the day." If only I could slip out of his grip, flip into the water and swim away, like so many pickerel had done to me on the shores of Blackmuk Creek. If only we could all do that. But the leviathan waited.

Marlin very publicly commented to the guard. "We should let him go, don't you think? Look at him, he wants to be free. Do you want to be set free, baffling?"

I did. And I tried. In my unrelenting struggle with the guard, the SPARX stone unsheathed and all Hell broke loose. It began with little more than a feeling of utter helplessness – helplessness against the man's strong grip on me. I did not fight the cascade of emotions that followed, for I knew them to be true. Maybe I could have shaken it off, but not easily, and to what end? It was over. There was nothing left to draw upon, so I just let the emotions swell within, run their course, and break through to whatever lay beyond. Beyond was some kind of strength, an inner tap.

The sea was the first to hand over her will. She knew the lesson of the Dancing Pool. The cove water began to swirl. It swirled and rose to the level of the stage. A wide and shallow whirlpool thus formed. The leviathan arched his thick body and held his place at the narrows leading in, as though hesitant to enter. Water began to spill onto the stage. The guard holding me seemed bewildered. He put me down and stepped back.

There were calls from the stands that it was a miracle of Karna. There were stares of disbelief. Lord Marlin was optimistic. He took a step back as well, and made a grand gesture at the phenomenon.

"Behold the glory of Karna!" he said.

Marlin spun around to face the crowd. He walked hurriedly about the stage, addressing different sections as he spoke. "What do you think it means?" he said to one section. They did not answer. He went to another. "It means she is here, with us today," he said to another. He looked to the high stands and gave them exaggerated, reassuring nods. "Right?" he said. The high stands were in agreement. Lastly, he approached the V.I.P. section. "She has come to deliver her message to you, personally."

All the while Lord Marlin spoke, the whirlpool strengthened. All the while he went on and on about Karna, I pushed the limits and found new ones.

Violently, a great swell of water heaved up in front of the stage and thrust out to sea. Then came another, and another, mimicking a pattern I discretely traced into thin air with my hand.

Members of the crowd gasped. Some praised Karna. Others were scared, and called out "No, no." Concerned mothers hurried out of the stadium, children in tow.

The high waves smashed hard against the forebody of the beast. The White Whale, wise in the ways of water, submerged as much as he could and made headway straight into the waves, rolling like a well-captained ship in a storm.

But the dance was soon over. Having run its course, the

whirlpool ceased. The leviathan saw his chance. He pushed through the inlet and into the cove.

Lord Marlin had the crowd chanting. "KAR-NA's WHIM… KAR-NA's WHIM." With an air of victory about him, he thrust his fist high above his head as he urged the crowd on. The charismatic lord relished in the excitement and soaked in the escalating feedback. He and the crowd were of a single mind, rejoicing in the anticipation of just how dramatically helpless Pips could be devoured.

Fury overcame me. *Blood for blood,* I promised myself. I glared at the vile fiends responsible – the nobles, Lord Marlin, the guards – and then I glared at their mob of followers. *Just as guilty,* I decided.

Angered over all they had done and what they were about to do, and in a mental state such as I had never known before, I cast aside my thirst for water and replaced it with a thirst to be quenched by blood alone – their blood. I hoped a dark hope, far beyond wishing for the simple freedom of my friends. And I imagined the gratification, as though I had a wolf's jaw. In willful coherence, the SPARX stone opened up to me and offered something more than the mere guiding light provided thus far. She offered me poetic vengeance, and I accepted.

A flash of scorching rays burst forth from the stone, striking down our captors. The guards let loose their grips, and instead grabbed at their own smoldering eye sockets. Marlin's own eyes went wide and his mouth dropped open. The crystal pulsed as waves of energy passed between us, blackening his shielding arms until they smoldered. He fell to his knees in agony, convulsing. When the stone finally went dark, Marlin's charred body dropped. His blackened head dunked into the cold seawater.

Screams of horror erupted from the audience. Many shielded their eyes or looked away in fright. Some ducked behind the stands. Blank faces stared in disbelief, unable to fully comprehend what just happened. Holly and Bobbin were spared the touch of the intense light. The strike had been as precise as it was crippling. Only the guards and Lord Marlin had been affected.

Free at last, Bobbin pulled the gag out of his mouth, wriggled a hand loose, and undid the bonds on his feet – just in time. He leapt at another guard charging at us from the back passage. The portly Pip barreled into him straight on. His pudgy little hands gripped the guard by the neck. The two toppled into one of the pools and disappeared into its scintillating depths.

I undid the bonds on Holly's hands. She pulled the gag out of her mouth and squatted next to Marlin's remains to untie the rope binding her feet. "Lookout!" she said. "More guards!"

"And we're out of Bobbins to hurl at them," I replied. In all seriousness, the young Pip had bought us a few precious moments at a critical time.

Without the cloak, a clean escape was impossible. I had only my wits and the stone. I searched for dark thoughts – they came easy. I allowed them to coalesce. The chamber began to flicker. I allowed them to consume me. It went completely black.

Gasps arose from the audience and wild speculations circulated among the commotion. "She's come for us all," some said, and "A demon is among us," said others. I reached for Holly. She was crouched over Marlin.

"Come with me," I said, and took her by the hand. Together we fled to the boardwalk, relying on our keen memories when we got there to navigate along it. We made it as far as the arch, then slammed square into someone blocking our way. I immediately thought of the giant that had discovered me in the first place. The impact knocked us flat on our backs.

I lost concentration. The darkness lifted. The fire of the arch burned up bright in front of us, casting an eerie, orange glow over the depictions of horror and gore painted on the stadium walls. They seemed to come alive in all the mayhem, as if they had found their place. I felt as though the eyes of History kept watch as the events unfolded.

My own eyes met those of the fiends that blocked our way. Terror gripped me by the throat and squeezed the air right out of my lungs.

Wraiths loomed over us like black, crooked towers. I saw in their eyes and hateful expressions the utter emptiness of heart and foulness of soul that can only come by forsaking all that is good. I do not know where they came from or how they got there, but there they were. We scrambled backwards and then to our feet. But before we could retreat to the main stage, yet another wraith moved to block passage that way – the slave master himself. The only way out was the inlet, where the White Whale lurked.

Over the mayhem, Bobbin's voice called out. He had popped his head out of the pool. "Hey 'Bones,'" he said to the wraith leader. The wraith turned his head to look. Bobbin waved his hands hysterically. "Over here! Sorry I missed your funeral." The Pip hadn't seen what the wraiths were capable of. He didn't know what he was dealing with.

Holly and I used the distraction to edge our way along the boardwalk, back towards the main stage. When the two closest wraiths came for us, Holly stopped them dead in their tracks. Her voice rang out, defiant.

"Dare me," she said.

Holly had reacquired her SPARX stone from Lord Marlin's burnt corpse. She dangled the pendant above her head and stared down the advancing wraiths. The stone was at its brightest. She put on a convincing act.

It was a stand-off.

"Get them!" said the slave master, no longer concerned about Bobbin. I heard a splash as the Pip dove underwater.

"We have them now," he continued, mocking us with his wicked grin.

Death hung in a droplet of time.

Without warning, a buzzing sound filtered into the stadium. Whether it startled the wraiths, or whether they thought it was a message from the White Whale, I will never know. But all of them stopped what they were doing and fixed their eyes seaward.

Seizing the opportunity, I grabbed Holly by the hand. Our eyes met, and a kind of dare passed between us. Together, we ran and took a wild leap over open water from the boardwalk to the stage, bypassing the slave master blocking our way. It was a long jump, even by Pip standards. He glanced back at us over his shoulder. Pure bewilderment washed over his cadaverous face.

The buzzing grew louder and louder into a deep, resonating drone that echoed throughout the chamber. Something was coming. Screams arose from the remaining show-goers as they scrambled for the doors with a renewed sense of urgency, pushing and shoving and trampling over one another as they fought for position. The dwarf tried to calm people down, but was overwhelmed. The leviathan, well into the cove, stopped to raise his ghostly horns. He oriented them out to sea.

From across dim waters, a dark cloud raced for the shore. Its swirling mass arced up at the mouth of the cove and poured through the arch – chaos on black wings.

Young cloakers – the face suckers – swarmed the stadium like bats, so thick they blocked much of the light. Those still trying to get out were sent into full hysteria, and even the wraiths were swarmed. A large cloaker swooped down out of the dark heights directly at the wraith commander. To his credit, the slave master did not yield, but snarled and stood his ground, batting the smaller cloakers aside as he prepared for the larger assault and readied an impaling swing. But the swooping cloaker contorted his body around the weapon's blow and knocked the wraith into the cove. The wraith commander flailed and thrashed about furiously in the water.

With barely a passing thought, I willed the water in the cove to swirl again, whisking the wraith away.

A dozen cloak riders dropped out of the swarm. Mounted by Bound Ones, they swooped down this way and that, causing more and more panic and mayhem. The cloak riders showed no mercy for nobles and guards alike. Even the bystanders were not spared – a cloud of smaller face suckers broke off and flew through the stands, latching on where they might.

The larger beasts clutched guards in their claws and carried them up, screaming, then dropped them to smash upon the stone floor of the stadium. Lord Rhyale drew his fine rapier to fend them off – more suitable for ornamentation than real battle – and stabbed at his darting enemies. The Red Maidens and a handful of nobles mounted a coordinated defense, clustering into a tight group high in the stands, poking at the cloakers with polearms and spears as they drew near. But most of the high-born ducked down where they could, or massed against the clogged exits with the Harrowian commoners. Some escaped past the arch, only to find themselves blanketed by face suckers.

The acrobatic archers, held up in a high booth, felled young cloakers with their deadly arrows as easily as swatting flies. Together, they brought a larger beast crashing down onto the stage.

Holly and I darted across the main stage, sidestepping the felled beast. I looked for Bobbin on the way. He was nowhere to be seen. As we sped past centre stage, I shoved the blinded guards into the churning water, still moaning and holding their burned out eye sockets. We fled past the stands of the fighting nobles, towards the sea. Just before reaching the arch, I waved to the swooping cloakers, sorting through the confusion for Gariff or Clickety-clack.

I spotted the two of them circling about together. Gariff spotted us as well, tagged the pilot, and the giant cloaker abruptly changed course and rushed our way.

I thought we were safe. I thought we were in the clear. But

the game was not up yet: The wraiths were gaining traction and Karna's Messenger was not revered as divine without reason. Again, he stayed his course against the force of the whirlpool. The waves pummeled his massive bulk, but he did not budge. I applied more focus. The cycles grew larger and wilder.

The White Whale struggled against the current. He began to glow, just like he had done after our long conversation on the shores of the Dim Sea. His horns unfurled like reptilian fans. They pivoted and angled this way and that way, and as they did so, cloakers plummeted to the ground. The juveniles fell in thick masses. A scant few evaded the assault, either they were able to resist it or somehow it "missed" them. Gariff and Clickety-clack were among the less fortunate. Their cloaker splashed down into the cove. The tortured mount writhed and twisted in agony. Show-goers still in the higher stands put their hands over their ears, shrieking.

Gariff and Clickety-clack had dropped near the stage. They clambered out of the water while others splashed about the cove frantically, struggling to reach the shore against the rotating current. The White Whale joined the foray. He swam in a circle against the flow and snapped at them all, even the cloakers, thrashing his head when he trapped one in his great jaws. The swirling water ran red.

In their gliding way, the two remaining wraiths closed in on Holly and me. I drew *Shatters* from my pack and brandished it boldly. With the loss of their leader, they seemed less confident, less aggressive. But deterred fully they were not. Slowly, the wraiths advanced, scythes readied. The whirlpool ceased as I recalibrated the splitting of my focus.

In my head, came a voice – *the voice* – in a low and regretful rumble. "HUUM ha… Goodbye young Pip," it said. "I call you my friend. I am sorry it ends this way. It is as it was meant to be."

I looked to the cove and saw that we had drawn the attention of the White Whale. Debris bobbed in the water around the great beast.

"Fear not," the voice continued. "Huum ha… all that you have ever known will be preserved… forever."

The leviathan closed in to support Taradin's undying servants; in his wake a brutal, bloody mess of flesh and blood and guts.

"Yes… get them!" Taradin cried out to his men. He was still held up in his booth. Taradin then called out to the beast. "Thank you, great vessel of the sea, for this superb intervention."

At the water's edge, the White Whale raised himself high above the surface until he loomed over Holly and me. The Flipside girl fell back into my arms as the beast's many eyes danced with pleasure at the promise of more flesh and secret knowledge. And from beneath his massive forebody, tentacles writhed out of the water. Holly and I were within his grasp. We both just stood there, paralyzed.

I closed my eyes and shook my head, and in the process shook off the fear and wonderment. *I had been misled.* The hard edge of betrayal cut through me. I had thought the leviathan wise – an advisor. I had believed in his Dim Sea lair, and that it would be a safe haven in the otherwise harsh world of darkness underground. *He devoured my parents, and now he wants us.*

The betrayal then burned like acid through my veins, and brought the phantoms of fury and darkness within to convergence, and then to resonance. A strange vibration fed back into me from the stone and from *Shatters*. I felt the tingling presence of Holly's stone too. Something was happening, something different. Something *big*. The power of shaping flowed through me, and of building, organizing, but most of all, undoing.

A pulse of energy injected into my forebrain. *Betrayal is a command*, I realized. I looked to Holly. Her SPARX stone shone strong and bright, and as green as mine was red. They pulsed in unison like two chambers of a single heart. The wraiths held back, uncertain, as the brightness shot up and the pulse quickened. Even the leviathan paused. *I need more power.*

"Holly, hold tight," I said. Then I told her what she needed to hear. I told her what I needed her to hear. "It's over, I'm sorry. These simple lights will not do. Fyorn sent you here to your death. He sold you out to feed this hungry beast information. He sold us all out to get what he wants. I never should have introduced you to him."

"Whaa?" was all she said.

"It's true," I reaffirmed. "The Elderkin betrayed you."

I saw in her eyes that she denied it. Slowly, I nodded. Then Holly's green eyes widened and her lips pursed. She shook her head. I could literally see the realization spread through her mind like a fast virus. She was mine.

Kechekenibek exposed his gaping jaws. The wraiths stepped back to give him the room he needed.

I raised *Shatters* defiantly, but I did not attempt to strike the beast. In full rage and desperate anger, I struck the platform at our feet. A new command of matter issued forth, the strongest yet – a wave like those in water, except to make the stone dance. But cold stone is brittle. A pulsing surge of energy coursed through my body from the ground up, then into my arm, and through the deepwood club before closing the circuit back into the stone. Like with the Dancing Pool and the whirlpool, I had set something in motion. A vibration. I could feel it. But I had no conscious control of what followed.

The stone platform shattered like a thin sheet of ice, and all who stood on it were scattered as it exploded outwards. I was thrown back against the stands, ears ringing. The leviathan was knocked off-balance. He crashed down on jagged rubble. The room flickered again, in and out of darkness. The force of the hit had knocked Holly down. We were both scraped and bloodied, but otherwise unharmed.

The wraiths came at us, scythes raised. Then three arrows whirred past and felled one. I recognized the fletching – orange feathers. Suddenly, the air seemed to fill with arrows. And before the other wraith could attack, he was felled as well. *Fyorn.* I stumbled to Holly, grabbed her hand, and looked her in the eyes. She nodded as I raised *Shatters* a second time. I bashed the stands.

We leapt out of the way and ran towards the seashore, past the arch. Behind us, the stands crumbled to the ground. I turned and watched as Taradin himself came tumbling down, riding on huge blocks of stone. One Red Maiden quickly disappeared from his side, swallowed by the rubble. The other struggled to protect him from it. The Vicegerent crashed at the base of the flaming arch. Dust was everywhere, the tunnel exits impassable. Shell-shocked, the last remaining crowd members stumbled around stupidly. Others soon returned to their senses and tried to clamber out of the stadium to the shore.

I caught a glimpse of Gariff and Clickity-clack. They had made it to the other side of the inlet with many of the onlookers. With an ear-piercing stream of chirrups, the Glooms broke off their attack. A single wraith lay impaled in the water, twitching, and the leviathan struggled with a long sliver of stone wedged in his lower jaw. Those nobles who had remained to fight in the stands now lay buried somewhere in rubble. Taeglin had run off.

One wounded cloaker, of the small variety I had first encountered, dragged itself along the rock floor by only one claw. The other had been severed, and a wing was crushed.

"There there," I said, as I quickly scooped up the poor thing by the tail and stuffed it in my pack.

The leviathan, jagged sliver and all, turned full about and headed for the mouth of the cove, impeded by his impaled jaw. Gariff's booming voice cut across the inlet. "NUD, THE ARCH!"

The instant before the last cloaker was to retreat and moments before the White Whale could make for open water, I abandoned the shoreline and bounded back into the stadium, just inside the arch.

Taradin lay there, trapped under rubble, a Red Maiden crumpled beside him. His hood had come off and his body was broken, but no blood spilled forth. The First King beheld me standing next to him. He looked up. I met his gaze. *Death Incarnate.* He spoke.

"I once rolled dice to save mankind," he said, "and won." Then he coughed dust, and spat.

I delivered to him the words of my uncle. "Yes, Taradin," I said. "You died a great hero long ago." I raised *Shatters* for one last time that day. "You should have stayed that way."

Taradin closed his eyes and nodded. At last, the First King laid his crowned head to rest on the stony surface. I think he realized Fyorn was right. I think he was tired of what his life had become.

I took his crown – his heir didn't deserve it – and then I looked away – it was madness. I smote the arch of the grand cavern. The act had been mine alone, without Holly. It was a dark moment. Looking back, it was the darkest ever, in all my flesh-bearing years.

The rock ceiling of the stadium came crashing down with a thundering CLAP! As I exited the stadium, debris piled into the cove and a great wave spilled forth from it. Everyone on the shoreline took cover amidst jagged rocks to shield themselves from the water and the splintering fragments that rained down. Dust billowed up and around, and strong waves rolled in and out. When the air finally cleared and the waves dissipated, a heavy silence fell over the Dim Sea. Only our breaths and the rush of distant falls dared disturb it.

CHAPTER LVIII

Karna's Whim

Black Sliver was far too large a vessel for us to handle, even with two of the giant kind at our sides. So we commandeered a smaller vessel at dock that went by the prophetic name of *Karna's Whim*. Fyorn took the helm, the giants had the oars, and the rest of us did what we could to get her out to sea. Lord Sevalyr gave the orders – he had seafaring experience, while Lady Elise watched the shoreline disappear. Harrow would blame the Lord and the Lady for the catastrophe.

Holly knew then that I had lied to her about the woodsman, and she knew why. Fyorn quickly explained that the Hurlorns had lied to me. I had a pretty good idea why. I hoped the Glooms would understand why I lied to them.

When we passed the rock wall, the faerie sky beyond luminesced a pale green and the calm waters glimmered in the twilight. A thin veil of folding sunlight broke through the darkness in the far-off distance. *Karna's Whim* caught a fair wind to carry us there. The rush of falls grew nearer.

CHAPTER LIX

Hollow

I would like to say that, glad to be done with the trying ordeal once and for all, I lifted the latch on the front gate to our yard, casually strode along the garden path to our front door, opened it and walked right back into my life as though nothing unpleasant had ever happened. But that is not how it went. It wasn't even *our* yard or *our* front door any more – they were just *mine*, and I had no sure way of keeping them.

So instead, when I reached for the gate, I found I could not open it. Welling up right then and there, I nearly lost composure. A lady and child walked by at that exact wrong moment, expectant looks of greeting on their faces. I managed a polite nod without giving myself away completely, and then froze just to stare at the rusty metal latch and the gentle arc of the once lithe branch that formed the top of the gate frame. I could have walked away, but I would only have to come back again, eventually. There was nowhere else to go.

The neighbors were grilling fish for dinner. A gusty breeze cast about the sweet aroma of the catch, mingling it with the flavorful scent of strong oak butter and herbs. The next neighbor down had her clothes hanging out back. She would smell like fish tomorrow.

Paplov should have been grilling too, right about then. He made the best barkwood batter...

The meticulous old Pip painstakingly had woven the gate and fence out of piles and piles of twigs that he had collected years ago and spaced out neatly on the front lawn, sorted by size and length; plus a few larger branches for extra support where needed. Posts made of solid bog oak, dragged from who knows where, lay scattered about. I had been quite young when he built the fence. It was during the first summer I spent just with Paplov. I had "helped" in full belief that I was indispensable, and received much praise for my hampering efforts.

Besides bringing him the proper sized twig from a pile, or more twine, or his hammer that had somehow disappeared, Paplov engaged me in the interlacing. He patiently demonstrated exactly how it was done so that I, in turn, after casually trying one or two weaves on my own, could dismiss it and turn my attention to becoming as troublesome, noisy and annoying as possible. I got away with such behavior, despite the disapproving looks Paplov received from neighbors and passersby. "Discipline that child," they might as well have said.

Disciplining was not Paplov's way and patience was a meek substitute. He simply did not know how to be unkind. Not in any way.

Paplov probably built the fence out of some instinct to be protective. Well, it didn't keep snakes out or pipsqueaks in, so in the end the effort amounted to little more than decoration.

Now Fyorn is a drillmaster and had forced a mean pace back to the bog lands, marching south along the banks of the Upper Malevuin and then across Whisperwood, straight through to the crossing at Proudfoot. My feet and legs ached from the grueling hike and I longed to sit down in a cozy chair and put my feet up. Inside, I walked past such a chair and into the next room. As is usual in muggy weather, the heavy, midday heat had already crept into the study. An odd odor lingered about the room as well – the entire hut, really – a staleness that arises when a dwelling sits too long unattended. A home needs to breathe and be lived in. It needs people stirring things up, traipsing in and out of doors, burning scented candles, cooking, and opening windows when it is too hot. Paplov had often sat in the study sipping tea and going over agreements or running numbers, comfortably laid back in his favorite chair.

Evidence that neighbors had come by to tidy up was everywhere. Books lay stacked neatly out of place, Paplov's blanket hung nicely folded over the end table instead of the back of his chair, and the wrong pillow had been placed there. I would have to go over and thank them later. One thick book lay atop the end table next to Paplov's favorite chair. It was in the right place for one actively being read. I opened it on the table. A black feather neatly marked the very last page – he had finished the book, at least. On his writing desk were less than neat stacks of the usual assortment of agreements and legal documents, arranged by type and locale. I would have to sort through them all and determine whether or not any contained urgent matters.

Standing in the study, staring blankly at Paplov's desk and the jumble of his unfinished business, suddenly I felt more than just physically empty from a lack of regular meals. Hollow. Some part of me was missing; so much as some part of that room had been vanquished forever. I needed some air and so did the hut. I went out through the back and headed for the workshop, leaving the door ajar behind me.

The workshop appeared exactly as it had always appeared. It was the only area that Paplov had ever permitted to get out of sorts. By the looks of it, he had been busily attending to a dozen or more projects, none of which were finished. Arrows in various states of completion lay scattered about tables, and unfinished animal carvings sat here and there on tables or shelves. All manner of boards and logs and sticks were stacked on the floor, including some interesting pieces of bogwood that were not quite interesting enough to be put on display in the garden.

I removed my backpack, unloaded the remaining deepwood, and then left the way I had come. A walk would clear my head.

On my way to the road, I thought back to something the woodsman had told me on the path home, shortly after handing over the last of the odd tablets I had taken from the Hanging City, the same as those I had seen in the Catacombs. Once through the gate, I decided to head towards Everdeep.

We had just put the Ghost Pines behind us, and Fyorn had asked if I ever thought about the whisper received in the sacred grove, the one informing us that Paplov was much improved. I needed no reminder of that whisper – it had been instrumental in my decision to return to Harrow. It had initiated all that followed, both wondrous and tragic. In an almost apologetic tone, he had commented that such blunders were unheard of and that the Hurlorns had never before been so far off the mark in any of their tellings.

"They have a higher purpose in mind," the woodsman had said. He seemed to let himself explore the thought a little further rather than defend it, all the while examining the small tablet from the Hanging City. I fixated on my footsteps over the soft pine needles as I wove my way around jagged rocks and over jutting roots. "If this is what I think it is, Gan should be able to pressure Harrow to cease and desist any activities planned for the bog. I'll just say that a 'source' acquired it from the Catacombs. Got it?"

"Close enough," I replied.

It was a good idea, but unnecessary. I did not know it at the time, but by then Harrow's excursion into the bog had already been delayed – mining hands and equipment had been diverted to the task of clearing out the collapsed stadium and putting the dead to proper rest.

To this day, I wonder if I had been misled purposely by the Hurlorns. It must be said that I never questioned Fyorn's motives. He was forthright at the grove and was not opposed to me turning my back on Harrow and instead heading home to see Paplov immediately. If only I had done just that, I would have made it back in time to say goodbye, and maybe a few other important things.

CHAPTER LX

Interlude - Velut arbor aevo
As a tree with the passage of time

"So... what brought a Hurlorn such as yourself here, now, to tell of this tale?" you might wonder. My role in these important events ended and began anew on a day much fairer than today, some significant decades ago as measured by you, but only a handful of slumberous days by my waking. One can never fully prepare for such things.

On that fateful day, I stood in the sacred grove, as stunned and amazed as might be expected from one so recently returned from the dead. And although I had lived enough adventure for a hundred lifetimes, and a hundred lifetimes of adventure was plenty enough to live, the saga of the SPARX stones had only just begun.

For the precious stone that I had possessed all that time, the light that guided me through the Everdim and the Catacombs, was a light like no other in my life, save Holly... for a time.

I had learned through Fyorn's whispers that the site where I made my most fortunate discovery had been disturbed not long after by none other than Mer Andulus, the talented and persistent Stout prospector whose uncanny ability to make great finds was unsurpassed in his time. Using the map we had left for him at the

Handlers' Post on the Mire Trail, Mer had reasoned out the location of my discovery and ultimately noted a boulder that seemed out of place in the geological context of the setting. It was the very same boulder that had caused the light of my stone to intensify and dance with vigor when I went near, just prior to encountering the bog queens. Mer Andulus cracked it open with a mighty swing of his pick, and found at its core three colored crystals.

Now Mer had heard talk of Fyorn and his reputation for knowing the area like the back of his hand. So, in time, the prospector brought the stones to him, who in turn made Mer a proposition he couldn't refuse: realizing their potential, Fyorn offered to bring the stones to Gan where he believed they would fetch a handsome price. Mer agreed, and held many of Fyorn's own treasures as collateral while the woodsman alone made the voyage.

And so it happened that my uncle passed into the Hidden City on the very day that Princess Xara of the High Elderkin was born, her mother the lovely Queen Eleonara and her father Xarfor, King of Jhinxar and Protector of the Third Eternal Race. Immortal births were rare, those of the noblest family rarer still, and the city was rejoicing in a great celebration on the very day that Fyorn arrived.

The ranger brought the crystals of Mer to the Tower of Wills to display before the King and Queen of the Hidden City. He called for the curtains to be drawn and the torches to be snuffed out in the throne room. The courtiers thought him mad, but the Queen in her state of mind entertained his request, while the babe suckled. Only then did Fyorn unveil the spark of the stones. The crystals shone bright red, blue and green. Magnificent motifs of multicolored light and dark bands danced on the smooth stone walls, the tapestries, and the drawn curtains. The courtiers of Gan marveled at their beauty. "Pretty lights," said the new mother to her babe. The babe's eyes were full of wonder. The diminutive oracle of the court, Nekenezitter, pushed giant spectacles up the bridge of his nose and declared the find a great sign of things to come.

"Great deeds will be done and undone by the light of these stones," he proclaimed. Powerfully wise words they were, coming from one representing the blind. In honor of the newborn heir to the throne, the crystals were dubbed "SPARX stones," where the trailing "X" was inserted to honor the new babe, Princess Xara.

Mer Andulus, the determined Stout prospector, received his just reward, and kept his promise to me and my companions. We all became rich beyond the wildest dreams of common folk, and Mer himself founded a city under a far away mountain in the wild east where, as he put it, "the gold flows like a river with tributaries of sparkling gems and white metal." He rose to become a wealthy and influential lord mayor in his own right.

The remainder of the tale is not recorded here, for it is unwieldy, to say the least. So forgive me for skipping past many fateful years. The full account resides in a series of books bearing the heading *SPARX* – a collection of writings that I assembled over decades of travel and through careful study of the monumental events that took place during the *Age of Rejuvenation*. During that time, Harrow never let up, and I was forever a thorn in its political side.

It suffices to say that life went on. I attended the university in Gan and had many grand adventures near and far, only to return home eventually and settle less than one league east of where I had grown up. At the university, I learned of matter and energy, living things, non-living things, and how difficult it can be to tell the difference between the latter two, nevermind the former two. I even learned the mechanics of how to create a universe and slide between them – in theory, but not in practice. In Webfoot and during my travels serving the Trilands, I learned of healing the natural way, diplomacy, the balance and optimality of negotiation, and the completeness of chance. Each of these great things played a role in what was to come. But of all these things, none played more grand roles in the great deeds of the time than these three: folly, young love (for they go together like peas in a pod) and, yes... well, not surprisingly, as you have seen... an odd sort of way of manipulating what was termed "tainted matter." There were many theories floating around the university at that time about how it all worked and why it existed, and how I was merely a vessel to it. Only one explanation ever held water. According to some, the implications about what it all meant screamed absolute insanity and impending doom for all humankind in the years to come. But isn't that always the case? I tend to look forward less despairingly.

Optimism has its rewards. I eventually ran for lord mayor and won on the strength of my status as a mildly famous adventurer. I had children and grandchildren. All the while, as Fyorn had revealed to me, the SPARX stone pushed me ever forward, gently prodding me on with just that extra little bit of grit and resolve when it was most needed. As mayor, I expanded bog-friendly industries and brought in new business through traders and prospectors, and imposed stiff penalties for logging in Deepweald.

It might be noticed, by someone attentive, that the above list of events exhibits a certain one-sidedness: there are no failures mentioned. Failures are messy and difficult to explain and handle. I would much rather forget that failures played an integral part in just about everything... if forgetting were only possible. If anything, those memories are etched in my mind even more deeply.

All in all though, I lived well. And when my time had finally come, and in that final breath, I left behind the pain of a broken body and was released into the greatest of unknowns, the Mark on my arm a distant memory of childhood. And then it should all have been over, the sweet passing of a long and full life. But if it had been over, this tale would have already ended. Indeed, it never would have been put to ink! Yet oddly, the story continues, for the strangest of reasons...

CHAPTER LXI

Hurlorn

Unrolling the scroll turned out to be quite the complex task in my new form, but patience and persistence eventually prevailed. The artful words on that water and earth stained parchment were scribed in thin, elegant arcs of black ink, and the stamp of Gan filled the bottom margin – a Gryphon perched on the branch of a large tree, poised for takeoff. Despite my many seasons, I never really believed the day would ever come. Nevertheless, there I was, undeniably, although it seemed out of a dream. I decided to take a moment to read the scroll through first, before speaking it aloud and committing my new life:

With the vows of my former life fulfilled or pardoned by my untimely departure, I am now released of them, and make one and only one vow anew. By sun, wind, rain and earth I take this final oath, to protect the woodlands and the meadows, the lowlands and the marshes, the stands of tall pines and the fields of grass. I hereby declare my acceptance of the earthen form granted to me – Hurlorn of Deepweald – and accept all duties and responsibilities commensurate with that great honor.

The words sank beneath my newfound scales of bark, searching for the pit of my stomach, no longer there. It was all happening too fast. *Couldn't I have just a moment to think this through?* – a fleeting thought, but I knew in my heartwood that delay was not an option. I read the words aloud while the offer was still good.

And when the final syllables rolled off my gnarled tongue, there seemed a momentary hush in all the wild, the land at attention all around. While pondering my fate, the sounds of rustling leaves rose up in the ancient grove as a gust of cool wind relayed an answer to that hollow voice of mine. I stood there somewhat overwhelmed, in the midst of my gargantuan tree brothers and sisters, their branches reaching up and out of the grove to the very stars in the cool night sky. A sudden rush came over me, a realization. *As the years pass, I will grow tall too. And if I live to be a thousand, I might reach four hundred feet* – a mighty tall state for one that began as a mere pipsqueak!

A hooded figure, slightly hunched over and with head bowed, stood next to a large stone slab in the pale light. It was Fyorn, and I was glad to see his weathered face, and glad to have been born once again. I had sidestepped death-inevitable in the Wild Elderkin way – the Mark of the Hurlorn. I glanced over at my primary left bough, where my wrist might have been. The Mark once there had faded, or vanished, or perhaps had never been part of this hard and ligneous exoskeleton. All of my equipment was also gone. Only the SPARX stone remained, clutched by stemmed toes like roots about a rock in the earth. They would not open; the stone had become a part of me – the seed of my new being. The familiar flicker of red light within it persisted, as it always had… entrancing and soothing, yet urging me on, to keep moving, stay sharp and stay active, change the world. I felt as though the stone was hinting that I was not quite done yet, or rather, that *it* was not quite done with me yet. From whence such a will might arise, I could not even begin to fathom. Perhaps it was naught but a delusion of mine.

Fyorn beckoned that I follow. I lifted a heavy foot, tearing roots from earth, and then another, and then another, and then another – four in all. Behind me, swinging this way and that way of its own accord, came a long and woody whip of a tail. The Kith ranger led me away from the glyphic stone slab and out of the grove, past the palisade of sharpened branches that surrounded the sacred meeting place, and into the deeper woods. "I am taking you to the lowlands," he explained, "the soil there is rich beyond compare, and you are sure to get a good start. I know of a clearing with plenty of sunshine, next to a quiet pond. The water table is high there too, but not overly high. You will draw water easily when you thirst, and your roots need not dig too deep."

I'm a glorified tree, I thought to myself, *Green Dragon of Deepweald – Bah! This is ridiculous and I'm a tree. I'll soon have birds nesting in my armpits – I don't even have armpits; spider webs over my limbs to look forward to, and a woodpecker pecking out my eyes! I'm a tree!*

After having waited a few polite moments for a response that never came, old Fyorn continued, "You'd best arm yourself first chance you get. A good sized club is best – camouflaged in your branches y'know." Mid-stride, he passed me a familiar looking piece of deepwood.

Shatters.

"I've heard of all kinds of crazy things happening to Hurlorns while they slumber, and even worse to those that have grown lethargic. Arm yourself, I say. Heed my words, *Tree King.*" He smiled warmly and that was that. Without further words, we trekked through the night on mystical dark paths that give way only to the druids and their ranger kin. Together, in early morning, we came upon the clearing that Fyorn had spoken of, and straightaway I found a comfortable spot. I was sore all over and ever so tired – VERY tired – and after digging in a ways, I drank deeply from the earth and began to drift off to sleep.

Fyorn gently stroked my new protective shell, as rough now as his hands ever were. "There now," he said softly, "…there ye'go… there ye'go." Those were the last words I heard on that extraordinary day, and for some time thereafter, and they were the last words I ever heard from my uncle.

CHAPTER LXII

The Sapling

I slept a long stretch. In fact, by my reckoning it was decades. And while I slept, I dreamt of my former life, all the time soaking in dissolved minerals from the earth. Over time, the sun gave me sustenance and the wind strengthened my limbs – at least, those limbs that were not blown off by excessive gusts. My branches and leaves angled to match the sun's incidence and my roots followed the water vein. But never did I move from that perfect spot. I was comfortable, content and… settled, slipping in and out of consciousness as the years passed by.

One morning, I noted visitors about. Occasionally, I had seen or heard Fyorn nearby (or so I thought), but never any other. That day was different. That day, I awoke in my lowland sanctuary to the sounds of children laughing and playing. One young girl and two younger boys ran full tilt around my trunks, the youngest boy intent on tagging the others while the older ones taunted him. Fyorn, appearing as tough and gnarly as always, but fresh looking, stood alongside an older Pip bearing likeness to Paplov, but it could not be Paplov since he had passed on many years prior. Fyorn and the Pip scanned the ground in the vicinity of my roots, eventually picking up a branch that had cracked and fallen off in a windstorm.

"This one's a good size… as big as you'll ever see," said Fyorn, "a fine enchanted carving it will make. By the shape of it, I'd say a fantastic bear."

"I see what you mean, Uncle Amot," replied one of the young pipsqueaks through an awfully wide grin.

The older Pip spoke next, his voice steady and sure. "You'll hear it growling by next visit," he said. "You never know what's in the wood, waiting to show itself." He paused to examine the find, and then looked to the old Hurlorn looming over him. "Why don't you just take a whole tree, Amot?" asked the Pip – obviously his question was directed to the one who I had thought was Fyorn, but who was called Amot. "You and I could make a grand fortune."

I became angered at the mere suggestion and, with a lithe branch, instinctively raised my club, still hanging high in my topmost branches. I could see that this Amot character was angry too, but he handled his passion well. "It would not be long before there were none, don't y'know," he said, "if you cut them all down."

"I know… you're right," replied the Pip, "I don't know what I was thinking. Sometimes I just think stupid things out loud."

With that comment, I relaxed my grip on the club. I was once that way.

"Time to go," the older Pip said to the young ones. The boys ran to him first, faces sticky with taffy, then the girl.

Amot squatted and looked squarely at the three children. "You must never tell anyone where your Papa gets the deepwood – it must remain, to outsiders, a secret and a trick of your own design. If everyone knew they'd farm it all out in no time."

The young girl looked up through my branches with big orange eyes. "Goodbye!" she said as she patted my trunk. And when her palm touched my bark I felt the life inside of her like a rush, a surge of days gone by and those to come filled my being. The fire of my SPARX stone flared up. *That one has it,* I thought. *We need more like her,* a voice whispered inside of me. Suddenly, something occurred to me. It was something that had eluded me all this time.

You old fool, I thought, *that elderly Pip with Amot is the son I never knew, and this girl must be his granddaughter.* With that sudden realization and in that very instant, my branch lashed out and I bestowed upon her the gift. She drew back and looked me in the eye, crossly, instantly branded as I once was, so long ago. One day, she too would receive a Spirit Hurlorn seed – a SPARX stone. I would see to it. She would be given the same choice I had been given. It really was that simple.

My great granddaughter examined the sting, wincing.

"Sweet Gale, come!" said the old Pip. Without a second thought, the girl kicked my root collar, dismissed the lashing altogether and bounded away jovially to catch up with the others. She did not seem to care much about the Mark it left, but I knew she would before long. My granddaughter would have to endure the choice that I had been given. And Amot, son of Fyorn, would have to explain to her what it meant and how it all worked… some day. Until then, she would feel bound to the natural world as I had, her mind ever bent on healing and protecting the land and others, and she would work, in her own ways, to preserve *the woodlands and the meadows, the lowlands and the marshes, the stands of tall pines and the fields of grass.* And here they would persist. Finally, I understood. This was how the oath worked… it was not through me alone that the forest would stand protected, but rather, it was through the gift passed along to the saplings.

CHAPTER LXiii

Shadow and lightning

The time for action has finally arrived and my last inkbottle is nearly dry. I must bring this daunting task to a close. I have done my part, and I have an important... person – I suppose person is still the right word, even now – to meet. I will make this short, for she arrives soon. It always strikes me when two unlikely events coincide. This time, I am the focal point, the centre, the attractor. The greatest light in my life will shine upon me in my greatest hour of darkness, once again. The light may flicker, but over time it will prevail – it must, it has too.

What caused all of this? As it turns out, the light of the SPARX stones was no match for the Heart of Darkness, and the destructive will of Karna – the Orbweaver – continues to be the greatest of all wills to counter. The Elderkin have nothing to rival Her raw power over life and death – nothing save a small hope, a subtle force, a hidden flicker; hidden but all-permeating and reliant solely on the goodwill of Men. That is an entirely different tale though, and no more of it will be written here, except to repeat that which Queen Xara said best, not so long ago, in her address to the leaders of the Nations of Fortune against our one common enemy:

"Think not of the needs of Gan, or Jhinxar. Think not of the troubles of the Scarsands, Akeda or Harrow. Instead, imagine all eternity undone. It is not the Jhinyari we need worry about, it is all the things that are, were, and ever shall be."

The Iron Tower chose to ignore the obvious truth and thereby put all living things at great risk. They believed Karna would deliver them, but Karna was worse than any devil that could be conjured. It suffices to say that Harrow must now fall or all will be ruined. A pity for the goodly, hard-working folks that dwell there – they have been misled; their city will be destroyed, but I assure you they will not be harmed by the invading armies and they will eventually learn to govern themselves from their own ranks, if all goes as planned. The assault comes as a long overdue deliverance of justice to the sharks who run the place.

Ahh, there she is. A little dazed but she makes a lean and beautiful elm. Such smooth, shiny bark and fine, elegant arcs about her branches. Amot is her escort and a fine escort at that – tall and fierce and kind like his good father. I will charge him with the care and safe transport of this book, my account of the beginning and the near-end, so that philosophers, historians and future leaders might come to understand the bare facts about our plight. Maybe, just maybe, one who reads this manual can solve the greatest dilemma for all life in all the worlds in all the universes. Hail to Gan! Rage against Karna!

Now, Mrs. Holly Numbit and I must take cover before the lightning arrives – trees in a storm and all. The bolts will streak down in crooked forks and wide sheets to blast the city to bits. The docks and the shipyards will be blown to oblivion, and ball lightning will gently drift into the halls of the Iron Tower itself and decimate its caged interior until nothing remains but an empty shell. The Temple of Karna will fall, crumbling to the ground from which it was raised. The Tor Lords are out of my reach though, held up in the rocky hills, tucked away in great underground halls and mining tunnels. They will persist and are like to rise again some day, although substantially weakened by the coming fury. I know all of this because I personally called the Shadow. I called the lightning and I set the propagators, although I can no more control it now than one who pushes a boulder off a mountaintop can control the avalanche that follows. That light is beyond me. This path was the only way and it was necessary. I see that now.

"Ah yes… dear Holly, together at last. You must be shaken. Here, take my limb." The mere decades behind us, comprising our former lives, are but a droplet in the pool of time compared to the millennia ahead. Love is truly a patient and everlasting thing. The wait has been long and the weight a heavy burden.

This part of the story, this first record of events as I saw them unfold, is now complete. As I stated earlier, it was the beginning of my story, the middle of others and, most importantly, the beginning of the end for some great thing. It was that which set things in motion. The Hurlorns set things in motion.

There is one final matter to make closure on, a simple question posed at the very beginning of this tale. Now that you have experienced the wonder and the terror of *the things that are,* and through my eyes, I ask that you reconsider: "Is there such a thing as magic?"

To that, I now say, "There are enough things in this world so powerful or so little understood, there might as well be!"

It is time. I must bid you farewell. The ink runs dry.

It was the Orbweaver who created the universes for Her own consumption, but only after they produced Knowledge. So She infused a strand into every single thing and wove them all together, like a great web, to track the production of Knowledge. One man learned the secret of the Orbweaver. One man realized when it was time for the Orbweaver to reap what She had sown. And when She came for him, he rolled dice for all humankind, and won.

And this man devised a way to make peace with the Orbweaver, or so he thought. His people had to be disciplined though, and obedient, giving, and most importantly, forever creators of new Knowledge.

But the man was wrong. The only way to beat Her was to out-learn Her.

And the only way to out-learn Her was to become Her.

- The Diviner